CARIBBEAN CONTRACT WITH HER BOSS

NINA SINGH

CINDERELLA'S FORBIDDEN PRINCE

RUBY BASU

MILLS & BOON

First published in Great Britain 2023
by Mills & Boon, an imprint of HarperCollins*Publishers* Ltd,
1 London Bridge Street, London, SE1 9GF

www.harpercollins.co.uk

HarperCollins*Publishers*
Macken House, 39/40 Mayor Street Upper,
Dublin 1, D01 C9W8, Ireland

Caribbean Contract with Her Boss © 2023 Nilay Nina Singh

Cinderella's Forbidden Prince © 2023 Ruby Basu

ISBN: 978-0-263-30637-8

01/23

MIX
Paper | Supporting
responsible forestry
FSC™ C007454

This book is produced from independently certified FSC™ paper
to ensure responsible forest management.
For more information visit: www.harpercollins.co.uk/green.

Printed and Bound in Spain using 100% Renewable Electricity
at CPI Black Print, Barcelona

Nina Singh lives just outside Boston, USA, with her husband, children, and a very rumbunctious Yorkie. After several years in the corporate world she finally followed the advice of family and friends to 'give the writing a go, already'. She's oh-so-happy she did. When not at her keyboard she likes to spend time on the tennis court or golf course. Or immersed in a good read.

Ruby Basu lives in the beautiful Chilterns with her husband, two children, and the cutest dog in the world. She worked for many years as a lawyer and policy lead in the Civil Service. As the second of four children, Ruby connected strongly with *Little Women*'s Jo March and was scribbling down stories from a young age. She loves creating new characters and worlds.

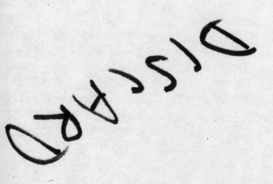

Also by Nina Singh

From Wedding Fling to Baby Surprise
Around the World with the Millionaire
Whisked into the Billionaire's World
Wearing His Ring till Christmas

Also by Ruby Basu

Baby Surprise for the Millionaire

Discover more at millsandboon.co.uk.

CARIBBEAN CONTRACT WITH HER BOSS

NINA SINGH

MILLS & BOON

To Becks, for being more loving and loyal
than I could have ever imagined.

CHAPTER ONE

RAFAEL MALTA SIGNED off on the final document and closed the file on his laptop. That was it. Everything was settled, all the *i*'s dotted and all the *t*'s crossed. He'd left no detail unattended. His life here in Seattle was essentially over.

Good riddance.

And not a moment too soon. He wouldn't miss it in the least. And he certainly had no plans to look back.

His last brief relationship had gone sour. Really sour. Rafe blew out an ironic laugh. That was one way to put it. Trina had said all the right things when everything had begun, but in the end, she'd walked. She hadn't been able to stand by him through the turmoil.

No, there was nothing left for him here. He'd never really had many friends in the city to begin with. Nothing remained but painful memories, sharp anger and hurtful loss. It was beyond time to make a clean break.

And make a clean break he would.

By this time tomorrow he'd be deplaning on Puerto Rican soil in San Juan. His titles of developer and investor would be wiped off his profile. Now those monikers would have the disclaimer *former* in front of them. His new official title, as of about 9:00 a.m. this morning, in-

cluded the words "Owner/Operator, Gato Rum Distillery." And if he was a novice at this next endeavor he was
embarking on, well, so be it. There had to be a reason
this opportunity had randomly fallen in his lap. Besides,
he considered himself a fast learner, especially when he
was highly motivated to achieve a particular goal. And
this goal had him really, really motivated. He couldn't
fail. There was no plan B at this stage in his life. He'd
used up all his second chance cards.

This next stage of his life would be much more than
a business venture. It was an adventure—a whole new
way of life. His goal was to become a completely different person. He'd shed the ghosts of his previous life.

A brief knock on the door pulled him out of his
thoughts. A moment later, his administrative assistant
walked in. He'd employed Patty since he'd started his
businesses many years ago. She was the only person
who had stuck by him throughout the scandals and ac-
cusations.

She held up a yellow folder full of paperwork. "Look
what you've done."

Rafe had no idea what she might be referring to. He
knew for a fact he hadn't overlooked anything as far as
her severance and retirement package were concerned.

"Are you sure you won't want to come with me after
all?" he asked rhetorically. They'd been over this before.
"The offer still stands, you know."

Patty walked farther into the room and held the folder
to her chest. "My dear Rafe, if only I was a couple of
decades younger and hadn't become a devoted grandmother of four yet. I would take you up on your generous offer in a heartbeat. But alas, I'm old and I'm tired."

"You're not that old, Patty. And you have more energy than most of the newly graduated college students I've employed over the years."

She sighed with a small smile. "I'm old and tired enough, Rafe. With this project, I'm afraid you're on your own."

Rafe had to scoff at that. Nothing new there. He'd been on his own for quite some time now, even while he'd still had a living parent.

Now there was no one. And that suited him just fine.

Patty continued, "But I might take you up on the offer to come visit at some point. I've never been to Puerto Rico. It sounds like paradise."

He was counting on it. "Anytime. On me. I'll arrange for your flight and you can stay at the hacienda that houses the distillery. Just say when."

"You have yourself a deal, Mr. Malta."

"That includes Frank and the grandkids, by the way."

Her smile widened. "You're too generous." A mist appeared over her eyes. "I'm going to miss you, Rafe."

Rafe could only nod. He appreciated the words—he really did. But in the end, they were just words. Patty was one of the most loyal and genuine people he'd ever met. In fact, she'd grown close to serving as a mother figure in Rafe's life. No doubt she meant what she said. But he wasn't naive—she'd eventually stop thinking about Rafe altogether. Her employment at Malta Enterprises would just be a fond memory. She may visit once or twice but in due time, the visits would stop, too. Everyone eventually moved on. It was just the way of the world.

"Promise you'll take care of yourself." Patty's voice hitched.

Dear heavens, was she about to cry? Despite himself, a lump of emotion settled at the base of his throat. Patty had been the only person who had genuinely expressed concern for him during the hell on earth that was the past year. She had been the only one to listen to his side of things, ignoring the salacious gossip about the physical altercation he'd been involved in at a swanky nightclub that fateful night—a night that had turned his entire life upside down.

Apparently, she'd been more worried about him than he'd realized or acknowledged.

Rafe stood up from his desk and moved to where the woman stood. He couldn't recall the last time he'd so much as touched her, but the moment appeared to call for a hug of some sort.

"I'll miss you too, Patty," he said past the unfamiliar lump in his throat and limply looped his arms around her shoulders. Her response was to wrap her arms tight around his midsection and hiccup against his chest.

Rafe felt disoriented. Of course, he'd had women cry in his arms before. But those occurrences had been the result of broken relationships, the aftermath of romantic entanglements having run their course. What was happening now, this true display of emotion, was unfamiliar to say the least. This felt raw and exposed. As much as he appreciated Patty's affection for him, he didn't know quite what to say or do.

So he did all he could think of. He just returned her hug.

The new boss needs to see you.

Eva bit back the curse on her tongue at the text from her brother that greeted her first thing in the morning. The man he referred to was not her boss. He was the reason her whole life had just been upturned.

Well, not the sole reason. She bore plenty of responsibility for that turn of events herself. Now everyone she loved would have to pay for her mistakes. Eva squeezed her eyes shut against the pain. She'd make it up to them all if it was the last thing she did.

Her phone pinged again.

Get down here, already. He's waiting for you.

Eva couldn't help the bristle that ran through her body at that thought.

Who was she kidding? Technically he *was* her boss—for the next forty-eight hours at least. The purchase agreement said she had to stick around that long to show him around the operation and answer any questions he may have. Eva fervently wished Papá hadn't signed off on that part.

Not that she could blame her father one bit for any of this. Eva was the reason all this was happening. The loss of their family distillery. Their very home.

As far as she knew, this Rafael Malta was a technology entrepreneur who'd developed an application used around the world. The man didn't know a thing about distilling rum. How forty-eight hours was going to be enough time to get him situated was beyond her.

Well, it wasn't her problem any longer.

She scoffed. As if she really believed that.

What happened here would always concern her, even if she couldn't do anything about it anymore. Eva had to bite back the ever-ready sob that sat consistently at the back of her throat these days.

Gato Rums would always be a part of her. The place was in her genes, her very bones. Her ancestors had cultivated this land and distilled high quality product for close to a century. The hacienda and distillery… It was all part of her genetic makeup. And she'd destroyed that legacy.

The stinging behind her eyes grew to fully shed tears. Whatever it took, she would make this all up to her family somehow. She had to. Or she wouldn't be able to live with herself.

It was past time for any kind of despair or wallowing. She had a goal and she'd do whatever it took to achieve it. Regardless of the obstacles, she'd rectify this mistake.

Not that she had any clue as to *how* at the moment.

Aside from the lack of resources, one inconvenient variable in the form of a tech billionaire immediately stood in her way. Rafe Malta didn't seem the type who would budge easily. So be it. Eva would simply have to move around him. In the meantime, she had to make do with the cards dealt to her. And for the next forty-eight hours, she had to play Rafe Malta's helpful assistant.

She could do this. She just had to stay strong and focus on the future, when she could finally try and fix her mess.

It really didn't help that the man was so good-looking: Tall with bronze, tanned skin and dark green eyes that could make a woman wallow in their depths. Dark hair that fell in waves over his forehead. Not that she had any way of knowing, but she got the impression he didn't wear his hair so casually all that often. Eva made a mental note to look him up online later. She'd done a cursory search, but her psyche hadn't been able to endure dwelling too much on the various personal details of the new owner of Gato Rums. She'd been much too focused on how to rectify the calamities that had led to Rafe Malta becoming owner in the first place.

Now, dressed in khakis and a crisp white silk shirt, he seemed out of place on the dirt road leading to the main house.

He was talking to Teo and seemed to be taking notes on a tablet. Eva couldn't help her audible scoff at that notion. Rum distilling and distribution wasn't a process one learned by taking notes.

She must have been louder than she'd intended as both men immediately looked up and Rafe's gaze landed squarely on her face. Teo gave a small nod in greeting. Her brother seemed visibly relieved to see her. She couldn't really blame him. Teo had never been terribly invested in the family business. His interests ran more along the lines of fast cars and the international racing circuit. Eva and her father were the real backbone of Gato Rum. Another stab of guilt lanced her chest. Her brother's return to the distillery was supposed to have been short-lived. But then everything had gone to Hades.

All because Eva had trusted the wrong man. She'd been foolish enough to fall in love with him, even. She'd never believe in love again.

So it annoyed her that there was a tingle of awareness traveling over her skin as Rafe Malta's gaze held steady on her.

Shut it all down.

After her disastrous sham of a marriage, she was done with men—especially the tall, dark and handsome types—for the foreseeable future. Maybe forever, in fact. Giving Victor any control over her family's estate and business had been the biggest mistake of her life. Her ex-husband had literally gambled it all away.

Her brother gave her a wave as she started making her way over the gravel path to where they stood. "Hey, sis, we've been waiting for you."

"Here I am."

Rafe extended his hand to her as she approached them. "Pleased to finally meet you, Ms. Gato."

Teo clapped him on the back of the shoulder in a familiar gesture, as if they'd been friends for decades. That was just Teo's nature, she knew. But she couldn't help the hint of irritation the action caused within her.

"No need to be so formal, my man," her brother said. "That's just Ev."

Whoa, just because Teo was already growing friendly with the man didn't mean *she* was anywhere near ready for that kind of cordiality.

She thrust her hand out to shake the one Rafe offered. "Evalyn."

Teo quirked an eyebrow at her with a hint of a smile on his lips. True, she never used her full name in any context. But it seemed appropriate to do so under the current circumstances.

"Nice to meet you," Rafe said again, still holding on to her hand. He had strong fingers, warm and roughened. Surprising, given that he was supposed to be a straitlaced, businessman who probably even had people to do his grocery shopping.

But as she studied him, Eva realized her mistake. This man wasn't soft in any way, shape or form. She'd be a fool to underestimate him. The awareness traveling over her skin intensified.

She tugged her hand out of his grasp.

Teo cleared his throat and made an exaggerated show of glancing at his watch. "I'll leave you two to it, then."

He was leaving? What the…?

"Where are you going?" she demanded to her brother's retreating back.

"I told Sam I'd cover the shop for him while he goes to an appointment. I think you can handle this on your own."

Ha! She wasn't as sure about that as Teo seemed to be. *Traitor.* So tempting to yell the word out loud, but Eva bit her tongue and watched silently as Teo jogged to his classic Mustang parked on the other side of the driveway.

She was on her own, then.

An awkward silence ensued, one Eva had no idea how to end. And Rafe didn't seem inclined to. He just stood there, smiling at her. Waiting for her to make the next move.

Which made sense, she supposed. She was the one in charge of getting the new owner accustomed to the estate, after all.

"Teo mentioned you had already begun a tour?" It was as good a start as any.

Rafe nodded. "A very general one. I was told you'd be the one to get me into all the finer details."

Eva toed one of the small pebbles at her feet. "Lucky me," she muttered in a barely audible tone.

"I beg your pardon?" Apparently the man had bat-sensitive hearing.

"Nothing. Never mind. Forget it."

He crossed his arms in front of his chest, his gaze fixed squarely on her face. "I'd rather not forget it. You clearly don't want to be here."

Wow. Straight to the point. No shirking the issue with this guy. Eva wasn't sure she liked that.

Besides, it wasn't the location that was the issue. Under normal circumstances, Eva loved being here. She loved every inch of this property. This was her home. Well, it used to be.

"How perceptive of you." She couldn't help the mild taunt. If she was making him uncomfortable, well, that made two of them.

His only reaction was a slight quirk of an eyebrow. "Anything you'd like to get off your chest, Ms. Gato?"

Did she ever. But where would she even start?

"I'm not sure you'd understand, Mr. Malta."

He sighed and rubbed his forehead with a weariness that surprised her. What exactly was his story?

Not that she cared one way or another.

"Look," he began. "Why don't we at least start by dropping the formalities? Please call me Rafe. May I call you Evalyn?"

She nodded in silence and he continued.

"I haven't been here long enough to offend you. So why the animosity?"

Eva narrowed her eyes on his face as she tried to summon an appropriate answer. One thing she could say for him—he was pretty direct.

Maybe she needed to be as well.

The greenish-hazel eyes staring back at Rafe held an intensity that unnerved him, more so than any high-stakes negotiation or high-pressure client meeting he could recall. Something about this woman was throwing him off, making him second-guess himself and the words he chose.

How very uncharacteristic for him.

But there was more behind her eyes. A clear wound.

Whoever had put that hurt there must have been very important to her…at some point in time, anyway. Was he still?

Rafe gave his head a small shake. The answer to that question was none of his concern. He was here for one reason only: to begin his new life in his new field—that of rum distillery proprietor and operator. He couldn't be thinking of anything personal when it came to this woman.

In fact, he shouldn't have even asked her what he had. It really was none of his business why she seemed to have taken such a keen dislike to him. Something about his personality seemed to rub some folks the wrong way, as he'd found out at a young age. Even his mother had barely tolerated him.

He was used to it, after all. Just another person all too ready to think the worst of him, without so much as getting to know him in any way. He supposed at least this time said person had good reason. Somehow, that made it less personal. Less cutting.

Not that it mattered one way or another.

He watched as she chewed the inside of her cheek and examined him. He got the distinct impression he found him lacking based on what she saw. Just when he thought she was going to ignore his question, she finally spoke. "I have nothing against you personally."

That was something, at least. But she didn't give him a chance for any kind of victory celebration as she continued. "But your presence here does indeed offend me."

That was harsh. "Ouch. That sounds rather personal indeed."

She lifted an eyebrow. "It isn't. Just an observation. I don't think you're here for the right reasons. And I don't think you'll last here long."

She had no idea just how wrongly she'd pegged him. For all his faults, Rafe had never been a quitter. There hadn't been anyone there for him offering support or guidance throughout most of his life. So he'd made sure to find the drive within himself. And he'd succeeded.

Clearly, the woman before him was no quitter either. No doubt that was part of her resentment. Whereas Rafe had chosen to give up the life and career he'd built for himself, Eva was being forced to relinquish something she clearly still wanted and she obviously resented it. Apparently, she was set on taking that resentment out on him.

Not exactly the way he'd hoped to start this venture. But so be it. A challenge was simply an obstacle to overcome. He'd certainly had his share of those.

Eva was hardly the first to resent his presence. He hadn't been wanted as a child and he hadn't been wanted at the fancy, expensive boarding school he'd attended on a scholarship. No one had exactly befriended him at university either.

"What if you are underestimating me?" he asked Eva now, pulling his mind away from the useless memories.

She shrugged one elegant shoulder. "I don't think I am."

He would have to prove it to her. For some reason, despite having just met her mere moments ago, Eva Gato's impression of him mattered. In fact, he couldn't recall the last time he'd placed such importance on the opinion of another individual. Surprising, indeed.

"You sound like you don't give me much credit as a businessman."

She immediately shook her head. "No. You've clearly reached pinnacles of professional success. That's not the issue."

"What is?"

"Isn't it obvious? I have no faith in your ability to run a rum operation. You have no experience, no knowledge. This was clearly an impulse buy for you, the way someone might grab a pack of gum in the grocery store as they check out."

Rafe couldn't help but chuckle. She really didn't think much of him, did she?

"I put a bit more thought into it than that. A lot of research was gathered and analyzed."

"Sounds like you did some reading, huh?"

"You really think I'm going to fall flat on my face here, don't you? That I'm going to fail."

She remained silent, but the answer to his question was clear in her eyes. Suddenly, nothing in the world mattered as much to him as proving her wrong. And there was something else. Rafe realized he was actually enjoying himself. Verbally sparring with her was the most pleasure he'd experienced in weeks, if not months. "What if I told you I'll be able to turn this place around and have it earning a higher profit by next season?"

"I believe that's what you think."

He should be insulted, but instead he felt a hint of excitement at the challenge in her tone. "We could place a bet on it, even."

Eva's reaction was swift and wholly unexpected. Her jaw clenched, her eyebrows pulled together, her lips snapped tight. "I don't care much for gambling,

Mr. Malta. Especially not about matters that involve the property and distillery that have been in my family for two generations."

She was back to calling him Mr. Malta and he could have sworn the temperature had just plummeted several degrees. Or maybe that was just the iciness in her tone.

What had he said? He couldn't seem to stop his missteps around this woman. "Of course. I only meant to suggest a simple, friendly wager."

She remained silent, her eyes still cold. Finally, she turned on her heel without so much as a preamble or any kind of acknowledgement of his apology. "Let's get started," she stated without sparing him another glance.

Rafe did the only thing he could. He silently followed her.

CHAPTER TWO

WHAT WAS IT about her that pulled such men into her orbit? Men who were so eager to recklessly gamble on things that meant nothing to them but meant the whole world to others. Men like her ex-husband. Not that Rafe would be around her for long. Thank heavens for that. There was something about the man that was unsettling her, rattling her nerves.

Even now, despite her irritation with him, his presence behind her had her off-balance. An awareness seemed to be sizzling between them.

She had to get a grip on it already. After the calamity that was her former marriage, she knew better than to feel any kind of pull toward any man, let alone this particular one.

As it was, this handoff process was tantamount to emotional torture. The sooner she got it over with, the better for her psyche.

"We'll start with the fermentation room." She threw the words over her shoulder as she led him around the pathway to the gray brick building behind it. "It's where we start the process. We begin with only four ingredients—raw sugarcane, fresh mountain water, unrefined yeast and unrefined molasses."

She led him through the large wooden doors and pointed to the large vat in the center of the room. "It's all fermented in here for about six days or so."

Rafe appeared to be studying his surroundings with interest and total focus. That was something, at least. "Got it," he said.

"After fermentation, we take the resulting wash and transfer it into sills."

He nodded once. "I recall reading about that."

Again with the reading.

"I beg your pardon?" he asked.

She hadn't meant to say it out loud, hadn't even realized she'd spoken the thought.

"Never mind," she answered.

But Rafe remained still where he stood. "No, please. Go ahead and speak your mind. I get the feeling you typically do. What is it that you're thinking at the moment?"

Fine. If that's what he wanted, she would oblige. "Simply that this isn't the kind of business you can learn from the pages of a book. It takes years of trial and error."

The corner of his mouth lifted. Was he smirking at her? Ire spiked in her chest.

"Luckily, you and your family have already taken care of that part," he said without an ounce of irony.

Eva's ire turned to flat-out fury. Did he think he was making some kind of valid point?

"Yes. We did. All so a billionaire could swoop in and take the reins because he became bored with his life."

The smirked widened. "You think I'm swooping, huh?"

Eva rubbed her forehead. This was useless. She was getting all worked up while he acted like this was just a big joke. Rafe was the type who clearly didn't understand that book smarts could only get a person so far in this business. Something told her he was going to find that out the hard way.

"Why don't we move on?" She turned on her heel and continued forward without waiting for a response. "Then the wash is heated until the alcohol separates. Then it's just a matter of aging it."

He paused before finally falling in step with her once more. "How long does that take?"

"We're very particular about our aging process so we take a bit longer than most other family-owned distilleries. At least two years. The aging is done in a different warehouse. We can head there next."

The rest of the morning went by in a blur. Eva did her best to relay information about the process as clearly and precisely as possible, and Rafe's expression toward the end told her he was beginning to finally realize what a massive project he'd taken on. Throughout the tour, she introduced him to the foreman and various other employees.

The resignation in her foreman's eyes had nearly broken her. The man had been with them since she was a teen. Now he'd found himself employed by a stranger from the States.

All thanks to her.

With a shake of her head, Eva forced herself to focus on the task at hand—getting through this tour.

She'd saved the best for last. "We can head to the tasting room to finish up," she told Rafe, leading him up the steel steps to the second floor, which housed the small kitchen and bar area. "It's run by an amazing chef,

Francesca Riberi." There was no need to tell him that she and Francesca had been friends since college in Boston. Or that her family had hired Fran right after they'd both graduated, Fran with a hospitality degree and Eva with one in business management.

"Fran is a genius at creating bite-size crudités to accompany our rum tastings," Eva told Rafe. "Her mini appetizers are works of art. We're lucky to have her."

That was the absolute truth. With Fran's talent and drive, Eva knew she wouldn't be here much longer—especially now that Eva's family didn't even own the establishment any longer.

Unless, of course, Rafe made Fran an offer she couldn't refuse. Why that thought had her gut clenching, Eva didn't want to examine. The truth was hard to ignore, however. The distillery and everyone involved in the operating of it would move forward.

All without her.

The operation was much smaller than he'd envisioned. That bothered him. Rafe made his way up the main staircase and to the master bedroom after a stop in the tasting room, where he'd met the chef.

His new residence was going to take some getting used to. He'd never lived in an actual house before. All his previous addresses had been apartments or penthouses. Or dorm rooms.

He squelched the memories before they could fully surface.

He needed a moment to gather his thoughts. Eva's tour had given him a lot to process. For the first time since he'd made the decision to purchase the distillery and move out here, Rafe found himself questioning if perhaps this time he had indeed been too impulsive.

Sure, small was a good way to start. But he had much bigger aspirations for this next venture in his life. Only he had no clue how to go about it. One thing was certain: Eva had been right. He didn't know nearly enough at this stage about running a rum distillery. One thing had stood out to him from their tour around the property: he was going to have to be much more hands-on than he had counted on. For that, Rafe was going to need help. The foreman seemed knowledgeable enough, as did all the other staffers he'd met today. But they were each one of many cogs in a well-oiled machine. If he was going to get to where he wanted to be, Rafe needed the assistance of the machinist herself.

One Evalyn Gato.

Damn it. She'd been right. Though her delivery left a lot to be desired, her point had been a valid one. Learning this business was going to take much more than search engine queries on his tablet.

As much as he hated to admit it, he was going to need Evalyn's help to get situated here. And it was going to take a lot more than two days of instruction from the previous owner.

She was the only solution he could think of. Despite the clear competence of the workers he'd been introduced to so far, the thought of trying to run this place without Eva around filled him with trepidation. Rafe groaned out loud and plopped himself down on the bed. What a lousy, unexpected predicament. Convincing Eva to stick around was not going to be easy. They'd gotten off on the wrong foot and she'd made no effort to hide her disdain for him.

He rubbed a palm down his face. There was absolutely no doubt that if he asked her to stick around, she would question his every decision and probably argue his every move. But what choice did he have? It wouldn't be prudent to try and recruit someone new. That would take time and effort that could be better put to use elsewhere…like an expansion of the business.

Rafe was running out of time to figure it out, one way or the other. Eva was due to stop by tomorrow morning to finalize some paperwork and round out the remaining details. Then she'd be on her way.

Rafe swore silently and sat up. The dirt and grime from walking around the property still clung to his skin. He needed a shower, and it might help to clear his head.

The master bathroom had clearly been recently renovated. A marble tub and closet-size shower stall glittered in the soft yellow light, while black-and-white floor tiles sparkled with a fresh sheen and a three-panel mirror hung above the dual sink counter.

He stripped off his clothes and jumped into the shower, turning the water to a punishing level of heat. Not too long after he'd begun showering, he heard the digital tone of an incoming call ring on his cell.

Rafe ignored it. He was no longer the harried executive who jumped out of the shower to answer a call—or worse, who had even brought his cell phone in the stall with him on occasion. Rafe had left that part of him behind. He had no interest in reviving it anytime soon. His sanity depended on it.

But he wasn't made of stone either. As soon as he stepped out of the shower, barely dried off with the thick Turkish towel, he reached for his phone and checked the received calls. He didn't recognize the number, but the caller had left a voice mail.

Rafe was surprised at the voice that greeted him when he clicked on the voice mail app. Teo Gato, Eva's brother.

"Hey, Rafe. Just thought I'd check to see how your tour went. Hit me back if you get a chance."

Rafe hit the redial button. The other man answered on the second ring. "Hey, man. Thanks for getting back to me."

"No problem. You wanted to ask about my tour this morning?"

"More or less."

What did that mean? "Okay."

"Look, this is going to sound like a strange ask, and she'd kill me if I she knew I was doing this, but I think you should ask my sister to stick around for a while longer."

Rafe sat down at the edge of the bed. What a strange coincidence. "Funny you should suggest that, Teo. I was thinking of doing exactly that."

"Yes! I knew I liked you!" Teo replied after a chuckle. "Feel like we could become good friends if you decide to stay long-term."

Rafe decided to ignore that last part. Why were Eva and her brother so intent on believing he would bail? The first part of Teo's statement rang strangely true, however. Rafe had felt a fondness for the man immediately upon meeting him, almost as if they'd been old friends who were reacquainting. "I'd like to think so."

"She's not going to make it easy for you, bro. She'll say no at first and may stick to that answer."

Rafe had absolutely no doubt about it, from what little he already knew of her. Eva Gato was stubborn and headstrong. And full of pride.

"I'm asking you to try," Teo added.

"I could definitely use her help. She clearly knows her stuff when it comes to producing rum."

"Sure does. She was responsible for the whole operation. Our old man is getting up there in years and I never played much of a part in the family business." Teo paused briefly before continuing. "I thought twice about calling you. Wasn't sure if I should. Glad I did. She may think she is, but she's not ready to walk away from this place just yet. I know it."

"Thank you for the information." Teo's input would come in handy. Rafe clicked off the call, a complicated swirl of emotions flooding his system. He couldn't help but feel touched at Teo's concern for his sister. The man had clearly been uncomfortable making the call but he'd done it for his sibling's sake. Rafe had never had someone in his life do likewise for him.

His mother came the closest, but she'd always been too busy battling her own demons. And the last time he'd seen his father had been through a toddler's eyes. He wouldn't recognize the man if he ran into him in the street.

He cursed silently again. When was the last time he'd felt sorry for himself? These lines of thought were coming perilously close to just that. He knew all too well how futile such thoughts were and had no time for them.

Pulling a T-shirt over his head and putting on a fresh pair of khaki pants, he replayed Teo's words in his head. *She may think she's ready to walk away, but she isn't just yet. I know it.*

Rafe definitely hadn't seen any of that coming. But it

was always nice to have verification from the universe about his decision.

Teo had mentioned that Eva usually stopped at the tasting room before leaving work for the day to visit with her friend, the chef. Hopefully, he still had time to catch her before she left.

"You should have warned me," Fran declared, placing a tray of freshly baked popovers in front of her on the counter. They smelled heavenly. "About the way that man looks in person. Those online photos of him do not do him justice."

Eva gingerly took hold of one of the pastries, her fingertips burning. "It hardly matters what he looks like. All that matters is he now owns this place. The distillery, the house, the land. All of it."

"True. But it certainly helps that he's easy on the eyes."

Despite the steam wafting off the popover Eva could wait no longer. Her tastebuds were screaming in temptation and the topic at hand was further fraying her nerves. Utter failure certainly gave a girl an appetite. She tore off the top crust and popped it in her mouth. "Well, you'll be the only one laying eyes on him after tomorrow," she said between chews. "The less I see of the man, the better."

Fran's shoulders slumped. "Does that mean you won't be coming by often?"

She could only shake her head at the question.

"Eva, you can't mean that. I can't imagine this place without you."

She would never have imagined it either. But about twenty-two months ago, she'd made the mistake of falling for the wrong man. And now she was paying for it with everything she held dear.

Fran's gaze locked on hers. "Hasn't that man taken enough from you?" her friend asked. "Are you going to let his memory keep you from where you belong? This is your home."

Fran was wrong on that score. "It was. Past tense. The man I fell in love with took loans out on it after I gave him permission. And then he gambled all those loans away."

Victor had done it right under her nose. All the while, she'd been blinded by what she thought was love.

Eva reached for her popover again to distract herself from the depressing and guilty thoughts, but an unexpected noise behind her had her dropping it back onto the plate. Someone behind her was clearing his throat.

She didn't need to turn around to know who it would be. Why was Rafe here now? They'd said their goodbyes about twenty minutes ago and she'd watched him go up the front steps into the house he now owned. Why was he here in the tasting room?

Then it occurred to her. Of course he'd run back down here at the first chance to see if he could chat up the pretty, young chef. And here Eva was, being the third wheel.

"Sorry to interrupt," he began, his glance traveling from Eva to Fran, then back to her. He'd changed into a soft cotton T-shirt and khaki pants. The hair neatly combed off his face appeared thoroughly wet. It made zero sense, but somehow the casual, freshly scrubbed look gave him a hint of ruggedness that served to somehow up his attractiveness only further. The pulse at the base of her throat jumped as she took in the chiseled chest, which led to her imagination running away with thoughts of that aforementioned shower.

Eva gave herself a mental thwack. What was she thinking?

Rafe was no doubt thrilled to find Fran still here and he was probably trying to figure out a polite way to tell Eva to scram.

Fran was what one would describe as classically beautiful: thick blond hair, sparkling blue eyes and a head-turning figure. Eva wouldn't be surprised if Rafe was already intrigued by her. Most men were.

"I was hoping I'd catch up to you before you left."

Eva was about to hop off the stool to leave when she gave pause. Rafe's words had been directed at her, not Fran. She was certain. Her friend must have thought so, too, as she excused herself with a vague explanation about having to clean the oven before disappearing behind the swinging door back to the kitchen.

"You were?"

His lips formed an amused smile. "You sound surprised. Why is that?"

"Never mind. It's not important. What can I do for you?" *That couldn't wait until tomorrow morning*, she added silently.

He rammed a hand through his hair, as if uncertain how to proceed.

"I had a bunch of questions pop into my head in the shower. About the exact process. How you get the flavor just right every time."

All of that could have waited till the morning. But Eva let him continue. "Then I realized I was hungry."

What did that have to do with her? "You were hungry?"

He nodded once. "Famished. And there's hardly any

food in the house, aside from a few staples that someone was kind enough to stock up the pantries with."

"That would have been my grandmother. Nana takes care of people. Makes sure they're fed."

"Please thank her for me."

"I will. But that can't be why you wanted to find me."

"Well, I noticed on the drive from the airport that the hacienda is near a quaint little coastal town. I thought maybe you could accompany me there. We could grab a bite to eat while I pick your brain some more."

Maybe she was being petty, but she couldn't help but goad him. "Questions you couldn't find answers to by reading up on it some more?"

Rafe rubbed his jaw, his eyes appearing to size her up. "My questions are very specific to Gato Rums in particular. I can hardly deny that you're the expert here between the two of us."

Well, at least he was giving her that much in the way of acknowledgment.

"Go ahead and gloat," Rafe added. "May as well get it over with."

Eva bit back a sardonic laugh. How could she gloat about any of this, given the part she'd played in how it all came to be?

Still, Eva's first impulse was to say no, to turn him down then and there. But a sneaky voice crept into her brain before she could come up with some excuse. What would be the harm? The man simply wanted some company while he ate dinner his first night in town. And she was the only person besides Teo he knew on this island, as far as she was aware.

Purely platonic.

As much as she wanted to deny it, even to herself, Eva

did care about the distillery and how well Rafe would take to running it. The least she could do was answer a few questions to ensure the place continued to run smoothly without any glitches in the transfer.

She nodded once. "Sure. I have no plans this evening."

The smile he returned at her answer sent awareness surging down her spine. "Great. Take all the time you need. I'll meet you outside when you're ready."

Eva watched him walk away and tried to ignore the urge to study his physique from this angle. Maybe going to dinner with him wasn't such a great idea.

Well, too late to back out now. And besides, this was barely more than a work outing. Rafe only wanted to pick her brain further about the business and the rum distilling process. It wasn't as if he was asking her out on some sort of date.

And if a small, ridiculous piece of her felt a hint of disappointment at that thought, well, that was just silly on her part, wasn't it?

They arrived in the center of town in less than fifteen minutes. Eva wasn't surprised to find it full of people and noise. This time of day, particularly on a Thursday night, always brought out crowds of people looking to shop, dine or just hang out. She noticed with no small amount of gratification that plenty of tourists were included in the number. A lot of them would be visiting the distillery at some point. That was always good for business. Then she had to check herself. It really was no longer her concern, was it?

Rafe found an empty spot on the street to park his car. Teo had told her it was a Lamborghini, a car that screamed money and privilege—nothing like the used cars Teo bought for a bargain, then meticulously rebuilt.

"What was that sigh for?" he asked, turning off the ignition.

She hadn't realized it had been loud enough for him to hear.

"I was just thinking about how packed the tasting room will be tomorrow. There appear to be a lot of tourists in town."

If Rafe noticed that wasn't any kind of a real answer to his question, he didn't press her on it. "I guess I better figure out my way around that process as well. Greeting visitors to the distillery."

He hopped out of the car and appeared by her door to open it for her before she could so much as reach for her pocketbook by her feet. She had to say one thing about him—he certainly appeared eager to learn about his new role.

"Charming town," he remarked as he helped her out of the car.

"Us locals think so," she replied. "There are plenty of shops and restaurants, most of them housed in historic buildings built in the eighteenth century."

"I'm looking forward to exploring. I need to do a little shopping, as well."

That made sense. He probably had loved ones back in Seattle to buy souvenirs for. He might even want to stop at the jewelry shop for a lady he might have left behind there.

None of her business. Eva forced a smile on her face as they made their way down the cobblestone pathway. "What would you like to do first?"

Rafe patted his stomach. "Definitely dinner. I'm starving."

Eva had been thinking it through on the drive over, and she knew the best place to take Rafe for his first outing. There really was only one answer, as only one restaurant in town would keep her safe from the curious stares and whispered gossip. People were still talking about the poor Gato girl who'd been duped into losing her family's estate by the swindler she'd married. Being around any of that was the last thing she needed right now. It might just take her right over the edge. Worse, she didn't need Rafe to hear any hint of it either.

"I know just the place," she said, motioning for Rafe to follow.

He fell in step with her, no questions asked. Another mark in his favor. Not that she was counting.

It was a pleasant evening to be out. A gentle breeze afforded just enough of a counter to the tropical heat. The sun, slowly beginning its descent, still hung round and bright in the sky. The waves of the ocean crashed softly against the beach several yards away. To her surprise, Eva found herself happy to be out and about. If she hadn't agreed to Rafe's request, she'd be wallowing in her rented flat right about now, elbow-deep in a bowl of papaya sorbet. Or she'd be at her grandmother's cottage just off the Gato estate, letting Nana soothe her with empanadas and coconut cream pie.

The thought of all that food had her stomach grumbling. Rafe chuckled, having clearly heard. "Good thing we decided to go with the dinner first option."

Eva ducked her chin as they reached the door of the Escondido café and restaurant. The place was fully packed as usual—no surprise there—but Eva wasn't concerned. Rosa would make sure they had a table, even if it meant sitting at the server's corner. Rosa and Nana had been friends going back to their girlhood days. She was almost as protective of Eva as Nana herself was. It was one of many reasons Eva was assured none of the diners would dare risk getting caught whispering about her. Rosa would give them an earful if she heard.

The older woman caught sight of them as soon as they entered. She sauntered across the restaurant and was beside them in moments, depositing two full plates on a couple's table along the way. For someone her age, Rosa got around efficiently and swiftly, something she had in common with Eva's grandmother. Eva could only hope to be as sprightly at their age. Rosa still ran this place mostly by herself, with help from her two sons.

"Eva!" Rosa took her in a big bear hug. "Hola, *bebé*. We weren't expecting you this evening." She turned her attention to Rafe, who flashed her a brilliant smile. Wow, of course the man had a smile that could melt icebergs. "And you have company," Rosa added. Eva watched as Rosa's bright expression faded. She was putting together who Rafe might be.

"Rosa," she began through the rock that seemed to have formed at the base of her throat. This was the first time she'd acknowledge to anyone other than family that there was a new proprietor of Gato Rums.

After Eva made the introductions, Rosa led them to a table at the edge of the dining room. They were as close to being outside as possible while still having the roof above their heads.

When they were seated and Rosa had left, Eva slid over to Rafe one of the plastic-coated menus on the table.

She certainly didn't need to look at one. This restaurant was one of her many "homes" on the island.

"Seems like you've known her for a long time," Rafe remarked.

"Mmm-hmm," she answered him. "She's like a grandmother to me. Just like my own nana."

Rafe pulled the menu toward him, eyeing it with curiosity. "I haven't had a chance to meet your grandmother. I hope to do so soon."

"You'll definitely be able to meet Nana soon," Eva told him. "She practically lives on the estate. Her cottage is just off the cane field." They'd made sure not to include that parcel of land in the purchase agreement.

Once again, a rush of sadness swept through her. At least that was one thing to be grateful for. For all of Eva's mistakes, at least she'd managed not to displace her own grandmother.

CHAPTER THREE

IF HE DIDN'T know any better, Rafe might think Eva was on the verge of crying. It had come about rather suddenly, sometime between handing him a menu and answering a question about her grandmother. Granted, it had been quite a while since he'd last been out with a woman, but surely he was better company than causing the onset of tears. Perhaps he had brought up a tender subject without meaning to. Was her grandmother ill? Not that it was any of his business, but he found himself genuinely intrigued by Eva.

He was trying to come up with a way to ask her about her grandmother's well-being when Rosa reappeared at the table to take their order. She inadvertently answered the question to his relief.

"Tell that nana of yours not to be late this Saturday for our Briscas game. We nearly had to start without her last time."

Eva gave a shrug of her shoulders. "You know Nana's always been on her own schedule, Rosa. But I'll try my best to convince her to be prompt."

So this nana of hers clearly wasn't ill, or this conversation between the two women wouldn't sound quite so lighthearted. But Rafe knew he hadn't imagined it: the topic of her grandmother had brought tears to Eva's eyes.

Rosa quickly took their food requests without bothering to write it down. Eva took care of ordering for the both of them, asking for two servings of black beans and yellow rice, rotisserie style pollo and two bottles of local cervezas to go with it all.

"What? No rum drinks?" Rafe asked after the older woman walked away.

Eva took a small drink of her ice water. "I figured you'll be sipping on rum all day tomorrow. You don't want to lose your taste for the stuff before you've even begun."

He saluted her with his own glass. "Smart."

She shrugged. "Just common sense."

The woman was so very quick to downplay herself. He had to wonder if there was something specific that may have caused that. Eva had accomplished a lot in her life so far. "Still, I would have ordered the rum punch. It didn't occur to me that I'd be rummed out by tomorrow."

She gave a small shrug of one shoulder. "I've been doing this for a while."

Which led him to the reason he'd asked her here. She'd just given him a perfect segue, but before he could figure out a tactful way to broach the subject, a young server appeared with two sweating bottles of beer and tall frosty glasses.

"Hey, Eva," the young woman greeted her after a polite smile in his direction. Then she proceeded in Spanish with what sounded like a question. Eva visibly stiffened in her seat and her lips tightened into a thin line. Whatever she'd just been asked, Eva clearly did not want to talk about it.

"Just fine, Elena," she finally answered in a brittle voice. "But this is a business dinner." No question, the words were meant to dismiss the other woman. If Elena was offended, she hid it well. With another polite smile, she deposited the contents of the tray on their table and turned on her heel.

"Business dinner, huh?"

She lifted an eyebrow. "That's what this is. Isn't it?"

"I guess technically."

"Technically and in every other sense, Rafe. I hope you understand that. This isn't some kind of social outing. You said you had questions about the rum. I agreed to have dinner with you so that I could answer those questions."

Looked like it was his turn to try and not be offended. "And here I thought you just enjoyed my company," he said with as much drollness as he could muster, then took a swig from his beer.

The corner of her lip lifted ever so slightly in the semblance of a smile.

"Why don't we get started with your questions? They sounded rather pressing."

He only had one ask that was rather pressing. But this wasn't the moment to bring that up. The exchange with the server earlier made it clear there were things she hadn't shared with him. Rafe hadn't come this far as a tech mogul turned investor by jumping into things blind. He had to figure out exactly what was going on before he made Eva any kind of offer.

He was going to stall. For now. "Can we eat first? I can't think too well on an empty stomach. And the smells in here are completely ruining my focus. Rosa must be one heck of a cook."

She leaned back in her chair, the smile growing wider and no longer hidden in any way. The realization sent a surge of pleasure clear to his toes.

"I'm guessing Briscas is some sort of card game?" Rafe said to further lighten the mood.

Eva nodded. "It's fun, but it takes a lot of concentration. There are cafés around the country that have pop-up tables. You should try it sometime."

"I'll have to learn the game first." Asking her to teach it to him would probably be pushing his luck at the moment.

By the time their food arrived, Eva's shoulders had dropped about an inch. She was finally starting to relax around him.

Rafe could only hope it would last.

She did enjoy his company. That was the whole problem.

So much so that Eva had almost been able to brush away the pity she'd seen in Elena's eyes as she'd served them their beer. She'd asked how Eva was holding up given all the changes her family was dealing with. The whole town wanted to know.

Of course, she appreciated everyone's concern. But what could she possibly say to answer their questions? Had Elena honestly expected Eva to launch into a dissertation about her current emotional state? Right there in front of Rafe?

How would Eva ever be able to explain that she was racked with guilt from the moment she awoke in the morning right up until she was faced with the prospect of another sleepless night? Or the way she could barely bring herself to look her brother in the eye, let alone her father?

Yet right now, somehow, despite all of the above, she found she was actually enjoying herself for the first time since her nightmare had begun.

She watched as Rafe dove into his food with all the gusto of a man trying authentic Puerto Rican food for the first time. Her initial treatment of him embarrassed her now. Of course she'd been unfairly placing the blame for her misfortune on Rafe, when all he'd done was take advantage of a sound business deal.

But she couldn't lose sight of reality. She'd be fooling herself if she didn't acknowledge the current running between her and Rafe, or how drawn she was to him despite having just met the man. Nor could she ignore the warmth in his eyes when she caught him looking at her.

But she needed to be laser-focused right now about where she was in her life at the moment and where she wanted to go. This magnetism between her and Rafe was inconvenient and ill-timed. And how could she even trust her judgment anymore as far as men were concerned?

Betrayal sure did do a number on a girl. Especially if that betrayal came at the hands of the man she'd loved enough to marry. Victor had charmed her from the day she'd laid eyes on him. Somehow, he'd duped her into thinking that he cared for her, but all he'd really cared about was getting his hands on some money he could gamble away. But Eva had fallen for all the lies he'd fed her until it was too late and the hard truth was staring her in the face.

She couldn't even be certain now if the attraction she felt was genuine. What if it was merely being flattered that a man might be interested in her, even though she could offer him nothing? No, she couldn't risk examining such feelings. Tomorrow Eva would be leaving the only home she'd ever known, saying goodbye to her childhood memories. She'd leave both them and her old life behind. Then she had to figure out her future. The days ahead of her were a completely blank slate. It was terrifying.

Rafe cleared his throat and she snapped her head up to find him studying her. Surprisingly, his plate had been cleared.

She blinked. "Sorry, guess I drifted off."

He braced his elbows on the table. "I'll say. You hardly touched your food after the first few bites."

Eva glanced down at her own meal—food that had now grown cold. "Guess I wasn't as hungry as I thought."

"Can I ask where you were just now?"

For just an insane moment, Eva wanted to spill all of it, to confide in Rafe the way she couldn't bring herself to with anyone else, not even Nana. But she squelched the temptation. There was no use. "It's not important."

He nodded once. "You know, I listen better than most if you change your mind."

Whoa, they were approaching dangerous territory. She'd only just met him this afternoon. They'd shared one meal together, and already he was reassuring her that he could be counted on as a confidant.

It was much too fast.

Wasn't this how she'd gotten burned the last time? Victor had swept her off her feet from day one. She'd dove headfirst, following her emotions rather than her good sense.

Eva refused to risk making the same mistake twice.

"Thanks," she answered simply, crumpling the napkin on her lap and dropping it onto her plate. "You said you wanted to do some shopping? We should get to it before the shops close." Not that many would anytime soon, but she needed an out right now from this conversation. She searched the dining floor for Rosa or Elena, or whoever else could hand them their check so that they could be on their way.

Not the most subtle of avoidance tactics, but it was the only play she had at the moment. Elena finally noticed her plight and scurried over with the check. Rafe handed her a credit card that he seemed to have pulled out of thin air. He didn't bother to look at the amount.

Moments later, they stepped back onto the sidewalk. The evening had grown colder and a slight breeze blew from the direction of the ocean, carrying with it the scent of the salty sea. A street band played bouncy Latin music on the corner.

"Plenty of souvenir shops along this street," she informed Rafe as they began to walk. "There's also Roja's Jewelry. They have a stunning collection of pearls and other baubles. How many people are you looking to buy for?"

Rafe shoved his hands into his pockets. "I'm not shopping for souvenirs. Not for anyone."

Her steps faltered at the way he'd said the last three words. His voice had been flat, resigned. "I thought you said you wanted to shop?"

"Not for souvenirs."

"Then what?"

He shrugged. "I wanted to grab some items for the house. Maybe wall art. Some things for the kitchen. I noticed there's a press for coffee. I prefer it brewed."

He stopped suddenly, then rammed his hand through

his hair. "Of course. You must have lived there your-self. And Teo."

She shook her head. "Not so much Teo for a while now. He doesn't stay in any one place for long."

"I'm sorry, Eva. I should have been more sensitive that moving into my new home meant you had to move out of yours."

Just like that, the tension crawled back into her shoulders, then stiffened along her spine.

She didn't need his sympathy or for him to feel sorry for her. "No need to apologize. It was part of the deal. You paid the asking price. All fair and square."

Great. Now Rafe pitied her as well. As if seeing it so starkly in Elena's eyes earlier wasn't enough.

He had no idea what he'd said, but Rafe had clearly stuck his foot in his mouth somewhere along the way. He seemed to be pretty good at doing that. Darned if he could figure out why. Had he picked at a painful scab when he'd mentioned owning her old house? He really did feel bad about that, regardless of the reason for the sale.

All he knew was that one minute they were chatting amicably, strolling along the sidewalk, and the next they were shooting awkward glances in each other's direction without a word between them. After they'd gone about a block farther, he couldn't stand it anymore.

Merely to fill the void, he turned to ask if she knew what might be on the tasting menu tomorrow, just as Eva turned with her own question. They both ended up speaking in unison, which just led to yet another awkward moment.

"Please, go ahead," he insisted.

"You mentioned you're not really looking to shop for souvenirs."

He simply nodded.

How pathetic that must have seemed to her. Because it was. Rafe had no one in his life to buy anything for. His mom was gone. He hadn't seen his father since the ripe old age of four. The man just hadn't come home after one of his benders, as his mom had explained during one of her own many drunken episodes. Sure, he had employees and he'd make sure Patty remained on the yearly holiday bonus and gift lists, but other than those superficial connections, there was no one.

"You said you wanted to find things to decorate the house."

"That's right."

"I was going to suggest a local artist. She has a small shop just past the town square."

He gestured in front of him. "That sounds great. Lead the way."

Within minutes they were walking through the doors of a quaint little store sandwiched between a café and a shoe shop. Rafe had no trouble picking two canvas paintings as soon as he laid eyes on them. One, a landscape, could have been a window to the scene outside the shop—the sun setting on the horizon over the ocean, framed by the beach. It would remind him every time he looked at it of his first night in his new home, his new life.

The other was just as powerful an image to his eye: a colorful phoenix rising out of the ashes, aiming for a bright blue sky.

"Interesting choices," Eva remarked as a clerk completed the purchase and took his number so that they could be in touch about the delivery date.

"You don't like them?"

She followed him out of the store. "On the contrary. I think you've shown taste with the two pieces you picked out."

He had to chuckle at her tone. "Uh, thanks, I guess. Though you sound surprised that I demonstrated I might have taste."

She shook her head, a smile dangling at the corners of her mouth. "Let's just say you've managed to surprise me more than once since you arrived on the island."

"Let me guess. You thought I'd look nerdier?"

She laughed in response.

"I get that a lot," he added.

"I must admit, you weren't what I pictured when I heard that a tech mogul had made a bid on the business."

It was curious that she hadn't seen any of the news reports or looked into him enough to get wind of all the happenings this past year. Then again, Puerto Rico was half a world removed from Seattle, Washington. It was one of the reasons he had chosen this place, after all.

And what a place it was. Rafe took in the view of the ocean in the distance, the bright oranges and reds of the sky as the sun sank lower and lower and the golden sand of the beach where it met the water. When was the last time he'd had his feet in the sand? For the life of him, he couldn't remember. So many of the past few years had been spent working, with little time for anything else.

He hadn't realized he'd stopped walking to stare at the view. Eva stood waiting patiently for him.

"Beautiful, isn't it?" she asked.

"Breathtaking. If you don't have to head back home just yet, can I interest you in a walk along the beach?"

She bit her lower lip, clearly hesitant. "It's getting late."

He glanced at his watch. "Not that late. Come on, it'll be like walking through the painting I now own."

She eyed him speculatively. "What a charming thought."

He gave her a mock bow. "Honored to have gone from nerdy to charming in your estimation." He gestured behind him toward the water. "Does that mean you'll walk with me?"

"I suppose I have a few minutes."

Rafe tried to tell himself the pleasure and relief he felt at her answer was insignificant, nothing to overanalyze. But there was more to it than that. Rafe didn't want the evening to end just yet. He'd fully expected to be elbow deep in spreadsheets and distribution maps his first night in Puerto Rico. This was so much better than being immersed in figures and locked up behind a study door. That had everything to do with the company.

They walked across the street and down the stone steps to the beach area. Eva secured her windblown hair in a small bun at the top of her head but several wayward strands refused to be contained and fell out of the band, cascading down the delicate curve of her neck.

She kicked off her sandals and Rafe followed suit with his sneakers.

"Is the water as warm as it looks?" he asked. But Eva was way past him now, dashing toward the waves. He watched as she jumped in with both feet. Her laughter echoed over the crashing water.

"Only one way to find out," she answered.

"We don't have any towels."

"Don't need any. You're not afraid of having muddy feet, are you?"

There were worse things, he supposed. Without another thought, he joined her just as a rather large wave crashed against the shore and soaked the bottom of his pant cuffs. Make that muddy feet and slacks. Eva was wearing capris that reached just below her knees so she wasn't affected.

An older couple walked past them, waving and chuckling. What a picture the two of them must have made, splashing around the water like a couple of children. Not that he'd ever done anything like this as a child, even. There'd never been trips to the beach, no outings to have fun. Just the daily fight to survive.

That thought was perilously close to self-pity so he pushed it aside. Why couldn't he simply enjoy the moment? The way Eva clearly was. They began walking, feet still immersed in the warm sandy water.

"Can I ask you something?" she began, leveling a steady gaze on him. The brilliant colors of the sunset brought out the golden specks in her eyes. They seemed to change color depending on the lighting of the environment. It was downright beguiling.

Here it was. Time to come clean about his past. He could guess what she was about to ask him—the real reason he'd sought out a different career. A different life. How much of it did he want to reveal? The real story, not the salacious one the tabloids kept recycling.

But she surprised him with her question. "Why did you really ask me to come out tonight?"

He was about to reply when she cut him off. "And

please don't try to tell me you had questions to go over. So far, none of those questions seem to have come up."

"You're right," he answered, pausing to face her. "There's really only one question I had in mind. I want to ask you to work for me."

CHAPTER FOUR

It MADE SENSE. Total sense. In fact, she should have seen it coming. Rafe was smart enough to figure out early that he was in over his head. But there was no way she could say yes.

Could she?

Rafe stared at her, gauging her reaction. But it was hard to come up with any words. It didn't help that he looked so handsome with the sun setting behind him, the wind blowing his hair over his forehead.

"I'd like you to stay on long-term, a year or so, and then we can evaluate the next steps."

"A year, huh?"

"Six months at the least."

"I see."

"If it's a matter of another job, we can talk about which is in your best interest. Do you have something lined up?" he asked.

"There've been some prospects."

That was something of a fib. The only opportunities she'd interviewed for involved moving to a new town. Some would even relocate her to a different island. But Eva loved this town and the thought of leaving had her on the verge of tears every time it surfaced. It had been one of the major reasons she hadn't gone after any of those jobs as zealously as she might have otherwise.

"I'll match or exceed any salary," Rafe said. "But how about this as a starting point to negotiations?" He threw out a figure that had her eyes growing wide.

"That's your starting point? That high, I can't see how there'd be any room to negotiate."

He winked at her playfully and she had to remind herself to breathe. "There's always room to negotiate. And I really want you on my team."

Her steps faltered. "I'm not sure we'd work well together."

"Because you think I'm a dilettante who's only here because I was getting bored back in Seattle."

She bit her bottom lip. "Something like that."

He shrugged. "I don't take it personally. I've been called worse than inexperienced."

Eva had to wonder what that could mean. Probably that he was a demanding and harsh professional who expected the same of those around him. Those traits would no doubt rub some people the wrong way.

"Look," Rafe began. "I may be a novice to the business, but I'm a really fast learner. And I won't deny that I do need a teacher. Only makes sense that you be that teacher."

He sounded far from happy about that, simply resigned.

She didn't get a chance to respond before he pressed on. "Can you set aside your doubts about me and my abilities until I get more up to speed?"

She released a breath. "To be honest, I'm not sure that I can. I get the feeling we'll clash quite often."

"Given the way this morning went, I have no doubt.

But I think we can both be professional enough to work through it."

So he was proposing a truce of sorts. But this was her life and livelihood they were talking about. Eva didn't know how she'd garner the strength to face the prospect of having to walk away from Gato Rums yet again in the future.

"What if you wake up one morning and realize you've learned all there is to know? What happens to my role then?"

He rubbed his palm down his chin, over the slight hint of dark stubble. "Fair questions. Beyond all you have to teach me, I think we'd make a strong partnership combining my novel ideas with your firsthand knowledge and experience."

She'd spent the last several weeks, day after day, coming to terms with her new reality. She'd forced herself to accept that she'd have to walk away from the hacienda and Gato Rums and figure out the next path she would chart for herself. To have the option of staying on threw in a whole other variable that vastly complicated the equation. He'd thrown her such a curve ball.

There was one more consideration as well. She was used to running the show at the distillery. Her father's word was the final one, but he rarely disagreed with her. Would she be able to handle having to answer to someone else when it came to Gato Rums?

"It could be a win-win for us both," Rafe pressed.

She rubbed her fingers over her forehead, trying to figure out what to say in response. One thing was certain—she couldn't give him an answer right now.

"I'll have to think about it."

He nodded. "Of course. You can have all night. But I

need an answer tomorrow morning. After that, I'll have to look into other possible solutions." There it was, the side of Rafe that made him such a shrewd business-man. Yes, his offer and proposed salary were beyond generous, but he was also making it clear he had set boundaries.

Given all that was at stake, one night to decide hardly seemed enough time.

Her nana's house had always served as a place of com-fort. Even as a child, when she'd needed to get away from her father's strict rules or the demands of all the chores in the hacienda, Eva would run there to clear her mind. And right now, she could use a bit of mind clearing.

She wasn't surprised when she walked through the door to see Teo on the couch with a cold soda, his feet propped on an ottoman.

"Hey, sis," he greeted her with a salute of his soda bottle. "Wasn't expecting to see you."

"Hey, Teo. Where's Nana?"

He tilted his head toward the small hallway that led to the kitchen. "In her usual environment. Insisted on fixing me a snack even though she fed me dinner less than an hour ago."

"I need to talk to her for some advice. It's a good thing you're here, too."

"Everything all right?"

No. Nothing had been all right since she'd said her *I dos* all those months ago.

She nudged him slightly to move over and sat next to him on the two-seater sofa he was taking up so much of. Nana's furniture had changed over the years, but never the sense of coziness and welcome it afforded. Home-made curtains, a soft throw rug over the mahogany hard-wood floor, cheery figurines scattered throughout the room... The house could be something out of a fairy-tale picture book—as could the woman who inhabited it.

Before Eva could answer her brother's question, Nana appeared from the hallway carrying a tray laden with plantains and other fresh fruit. Her eyes lit up when they landed on Eva. In an instant, the tray had been deposited on the coffee table and Eva found herself in Nana's tight embrace. It was just the way her grandmother said hello. "Eva! Hola. I'm so glad you decided to stop by."

It never got old, the way Nana always behaved as if she hadn't seen her in forever. Eva had just been here for a light afternoon siesta the other day. She squeezed into the small space left on the couch, and Teo took the hint and moved over to the upholstered chair across the throw rug.

"How was your day? Weren't you supposed to be showing that new American around?"

"That man happens to own the place now, Nana."

Her grandmother waved a hand dismissively. "Who-ever he is. How did it go with him?"

"Well, that's kind of what I'm here to talk about."

Nana patted her cheek gently, her palm soft and warm. And so familiar. "You look so concerned, *mi bambina*. Tell me."

"Yeah," Teo declared. "Tell us."

A gentle knock on the door interrupted her answer.

"Come in," her grandmother called.

To Eva's surprise, Fran walked through the door. "Oh, hi," she addressed her friend. "Wouldn't expect to see you here this time of day."

"Sometimes I like to stop by to visit with Nana before heading home," Fran explained.

Was it her imagination, or did Fran's eyes linger on Teo just a little too long before turning in Nana's direction? And why did her hair look different than it had this afternoon? Like she'd taken the time to adjust it just so in a tortoise hairpin.

Fran scanned the room. "What's going on?"

"Eva was just about to tell us," Teo supplied.

Looked like the gang was all here. Just as well. The more opinions she trusted, the better. For that matter, the three people in this tiny room and Papá were the only people Eva would ever feel comfortable trusting again for as long as she lived.

She took a breath, then stood to address the room in general. "Well, the short of it is, I got an unexpected job offer this evening."

Her words were met with a round of excited gasps. *"Muy bien!"* Nana clasped her hands together.

"The offer came from the American," she explained. "Rafe Malta wants me to continue working at Gato Rums—as his operations manager. He says he has a lot to learn, and I'm the best person to teach him."

"That's fantastic, sis!" Teo exclaimed with a fist pump in the air. "I knew that man was a smart *hombre.*"

Eva had to give her head a shake. "Wait. So you think this is a good idea?"

Teo's eyes narrowed on her, as if she'd grown a whole other head. "Of course I do. How do you not?"

She lifted her hands, palms up. "For one thing, it's no longer our business."

Teo lifted his head to aim his gaze at her. "That's

just a technicality. You'd likely be the one making all the decisions."

She'd considered that. It might be very true—at least for the short term.

"Come on, sis," Teo continued. "You need this—" He cut off abruptly, cleared his throat. "I mean, this place needs you. So does the American."

Both Nana and Fran were glancing from one of them to the other.

"What do you two think?" Eva asked the women.

"I think you should say yes," Nana immediately answered. "For purely selfish reasons. So I can continue to still see you every day." No surprise there.

"Why don't you ask your *papá*?"

Eva immediately shook her head to shoot that idea down. "I don't want to bother him." The truth was, she still had trouble so much as speaking to her dad without the overwhelming guilt of what she'd cost him nearly crushing her. "He has enough on his mind right now."

"Well, I'm sure he'd tell you the same thing," Teo offered.

She looked over at her friend, who seemed to have drifted off somewhere, her head tilted in Teo's direction. Was Fran even paying attention?

"Fran?" The other woman immediately snapped her head to where Eva stood. "What do you think? You haven't said anything."

Fran cleared her throat. "Like your nana, I have my own selfish reasons for wanting you to stick around. You're my best taste tester."

So, all three thought she should take Rafe's offer. And that was before she'd even mentioned the generous salary.

"You were just saying the other day that a sign from the universe would be nice about where you should go and what you should do next," Fran added.

"Why are you even hesitating?" Teo wanted to know.

Eva rubbed her forehead and dropped back down next to Nana on the couch. "I'd be lying if I said the money he offered wasn't tempting. It would go a long way toward…" Her words trailed off. She hadn't meant to go there.

"Toward what?" Teo asked.

"Never mind. It's silly, really."

"Tell us," he insisted.

All three of them were looking at her with anticipation. "It's just—there are days I fantasize about maybe being able to purchase what we lost, that I can somehow figure out how to afford buying the place back. Maybe with the right investments, a lucky break or two…" She squeezed her eyes shut, hearing how unrealistic the words sounded when spoken out loud. "Forget it. Like I said, it's silly."

Teo stood and walked to where she sat. "I didn't know you were thinking along those lines, sis." He ruffled the hair atop her head as if she were a small child. They were only two years apart, but Teo had always behaved as if those two years meant he somehow held rank. "If that's what you want, I'll do what I can to help. I have some money saved—"

She immediately held her hands up to stop him from going any further with that line of thought. "No. No way. I will not have you paying any more than you already have for a mistake that I made."

"That would be my decision."

Eva thought she heard Fran sigh across the room. She didn't have time to ponder what that might be about.

First things first. She took her brother's hand. "Look, it's a moot point, and not worth arguing about because it's highly unlikely to happen. For now, I just need to decide what I'm going to tell Rafe in the morning."

She was running out of time to figure it out.

Rafe pulled out a wicker chair on the back deck patio and took in the view as he sat down. He was looking at miles and miles of rolling green hills and could hear the soft sound of the ocean in the distance. The air was crisp and fresh. Not a bad way to start the morning.

Coming here, moving to Puerto Rico, had been the right decision. If he played his cards right, and things went according to plan, he could get used to feeling at home here. That would be a first for him—a place where he belonged. He hadn't found that sense of belonging with his mother, or at school or anywhere else for that matter.

But being here finally felt right.

Three days ago, he would have done anything to prevent the sequence of events that had caused that fateful night in the city. He would have given anything to keep from throwing that first punch, as much as the receiver had deserved it. But it had all led Rafe right here. So maybe it had all happened for a reason.

He took a sip from the mug of steaming hot coffee he held and grimaced as several coffee grounds landed on his tongue. Apparently, using a French press wasn't as straightforward as one might think. Too bad. He sorely needed the caffeine. Sleep had been elusive last night. Usually, when insomnia hit, he could attribute it to pressing business matters that needed his attention. Not so last night. Instead, he'd been flooded with images of a dark-haired, hazel-eyed beauty walking on a sandy beach with him. Those thoughts had led to other, more heated ones, where the two of them were doing much more on the sand than walking.

He hadn't bothered with any warm water in the shower this morning.

It was all so wrong in so many ways. If he had his way, the woman would be his employee, for heaven's sake.

"Hello?" A soft melodic voice sounded from just by the screen door that he'd left open. Eva appeared, as if he'd willed her there with his thoughts. She was dressed in a flowy yellow sundress, and the color reminded him of part of the sky last night on the beach. Her hair was done up in a neat bun and she held two paper cups with lids.

"Good morning. Is one of those for me?" he asked, resisting the urge to come right out and ask about her decision to work for him. Another reason he'd tossed and turned all night was wondering if she would turn him down, and what he might do if that was the case.

"I remembered we never got around to getting you that coffee machine." She handed him one of the cups.

"Thanks," he said, taking her offering with gratitude. "It's like you're an angel sent from heaven. Part of your duties this morning might be a tutorial on using the French press."

She pulled out the other chair at the small table and sat down. "I already ordered a machine for you. Should be here within a day or two. State-of-the-art, makes single serve or a pot. Options for espresso, cappuccino or even cold brew."

Impressive. "Wow. Thank you."

"We can send it back if you don't like it."

"Based on what you said, I'm guessing I'm going to like it."

Rafe went to take a sip and realized the cup was completely sealed.

"You have to take the lid all the way off," Eva informed him. "In Puerto Rico, people don't actually expect you to be on the go when you have a cup," she explained. "They figure you'll sit down to have it somewhere else. Unlike the mainland, where everyone is usually on the run, we like to take time to enjoy our beverages and meals."

"Huh." He lifted the lid as told, then took a sip. A burst of sweet, savory flavor exploded on his tongue. Was that a touch of coconut he tasted?

"It's usually served black," Eva said, sipping from her own drink. "That's how I got it for you. Hope that's okay."

He let the flavors linger on his tongue before answering. "More than okay. This is great stuff. I'll have to get bags of it to brew in that machine you've gotten for me." He set his cup down. "How much do I owe you for that anyway?"

"I'll submit an expense form," she answered. "I figure it could be my first official act as your operations manager."

CHAPTER FIVE

RAFE PAUSED IN the act of lifting his coffee to his lips. "Does that mean what I think it means?"

"Yes," she replied simply, turning to look into the distance. "I've decided to accept your offer." She didn't seem terribly happy about it. Rafe decided he'd worry about that later. Right now, he was beyond relieved—elated, in fact, that she'd be joining him as he found his way around this place. Somehow, someway, within the past day, Eva Gato had become essential to him.

Go figure.

As far as the role she'd played in his restless dreams last night, he'd make sure that never happened again, now that she was officially an employee of Malta Enterprises, of which Gato Rums was now a part.

Their relationship had to stay completely professional. Both his professional and personal reputation had taken quite the hit over the past several months. He didn't need gossip about his transgressions with employees added to the mix.

Speaking of which, it would behoove him to come clean about what had happened back in Seattle, given that what she might hear secondhand, if she ever came upon it, would undoubtedly be the less truthful, more salacious version.

"Look," he began, not exactly sure where to start. He'd never bothered to explain himself before. There'd been no need. Everyone back in the States had made up their own minds depending on how well they knew him. And not too many people knew him all that well. "There are some things that happened last year that I think we should talk about. None of it will impact your duties in any way. But we should probably talk about it."

She tilted her head and waited for him to continue.

"Seattle is half a world from here." That must have sounded like such a random way to start. But Eva still seemed wholly focused, so he pressed on. "I know for most of the buyout process, I was something of a silent investor. You probably didn't even hear my name until much later in the sale process."

She nodded once in agreement. "These deals are usually handled by slews of lawyers through trusts and second or even third parties. I know this case was no different."

"That's right. So you probably didn't hear much about an incident that drew some attention about a year ago, mostly on the tech sites. It had to do with an altercation I was involved in. With someone from my past."

She nodded. "I would have been distracted with some…issues of my own around that time."

Rafe steepled his fingers on the table. Talking about all this was making him much more uncomfortable than he would have anticipated. He'd thought he'd left all the emotions of it behind when he'd moved here. "The whole thing was blown way out of proportion," he said.

She studied him. "You're right, I don't recall hearing your name back then. Not that I would have recognized it at the time."

That made sense…but not what she said right after. "But I've learned about the events you're referring to."

"You have?"

She settled deeper into her chair. "Yes. Just last night. Figured I'd do some research on the man I'd be working for."

How had he not seen that coming? "Yet you still decided to take me up on the offer to work for me."

She shrugged one sun-kissed shoulder. "We all make mistakes," she answered simply. "You got into a fight at a nightclub. Hardly the end of the world considering no one was seriously hurt."

He swallowed, both apprehensive about the topic at hand yet relieved at her reaction. "I want you to know that was the first time I had ever so much as thrown a punch. I'm not a violent man by any means." He hadn't been, until that night when he'd been pushed too far one time too many.

Her gaze narrowed on him. "I believe you. Like I said, I don't like to judge people for their mistakes," she repeated.

Something told him that probably held true. Except when it came to herself.

She stood suddenly, then tossed her now-empty cup into the nearby receptacle and smoothed down her skirt. "Now, shall we get started?"

The rest of the morning went by in a flurry of activity. Eva went over spreadsheets, sales figures and marketing plans. There was a slew of paperwork he needed to sign.

Next stop was the bottling center. Different labels

ran through a belt with various flavorings marked on them: dark, spiced, even fruity selections like peach, mango and berry.

Rafe made a mental note to ask later about how the flavor was added. Right now, his brain was so overloaded with information he doubted he would even absorb the answer.

Plus, he was famished.

As if he'd cued her to do so, Eva glanced at her watch. "It's approaching noon. Most of the distillery shuts down at this hour. An informal siesta."

Rafe shoved his hands in his front pockets. Sorely tempted to ask her what she was doing for lunch, he resisted the urge. He was no stranger to solitary meals. A sandwich on the patio was more than adequate. "Well, I won't impose on your personal time. Go get some rest."

"Okay. See you in the tasting room in about an hour."

"It's a date," he replied, then immediately cringed. Why in the world had he phrased it that way?

Eva had only walked a few steps when she suddenly pivoted on her heel and turned back to face him.

Great. After that disastrous response, now he'd been caught staring at her retreating back.

"Do you have plans for lunch?" she asked, surprising him. Had he looked that pathetic at being left to his own devices? He had to learn to hide his reactions better.

"None whatsoever."

"Come with me."

Rafe knew he shouldn't have been so thrilled at her words. But he couldn't deny the surge of pleasure he'd felt at the invitation. "Is there another authentic restaurant you're about to introduce me to?"

She shook her head. "Even better. There's someone who would like to meet you."

That was unexpected. "I thought I'd already met all the employees over the course of the past day and a half."

She cast him a winsome smile. "Not an employee. Follow me," she ordered, turning back and walking again. "It's just a short walk. And you're bound to get a delicious meal out of it."

Curious and intrigued, Rafe caught up to her and fell in step with her stride.

Within minutes, they were approaching the door of a small redbrick cottage. The beach sat practically in its backyard, just a stone's throw away.

It might have been the most inviting little house he'd ever seen.

"I take it I'm about to meet Nana," he guessed.

"You are indeed," Eva answered. "Prepare to be charmed."

"She liked you," Eva informed Rafe as they made their way back toward the hacienda over an hour later.

Rafe's reply was a genuine, wide smile.

Nana didn't always warm up to strangers, but she'd taken an immediate liking to Rafe. So far, he'd been able to charm her brother, most definitely Fran and all the distillery employees—basically, everyone he'd met since arriving on the island.

She had to admit that he'd even charmed her. To make matters worse, Eva hadn't even seen it coming. It had probably happened last night at dinner, then some more when they'd walked along the beach together. She studied him now as they reached the stone pathway leading to the portico that held the tasting room.

A warning cry of danger sounded in her head. She remembered all too well what had happened last time she'd followed her heart and let the allure of a man lead her down a path with no return. Victor had charmed her as well…only to use her in the end, in a way that had completely upturned her life.

"Penny for your thoughts?" Rafe asked, pulling her out of the painful memories.

"Oh, just wondering what delightful morsels Fran might have come up with for this afternoon." Never mind that it wasn't what she'd been dwelling on at all, and that she'd only had that question occur to her that very second when the smell of smoked bacon traveled to her nose from the direction of the portico.

When they reached the sliding screen door of the tasting room, Fran greeted them with a warm smile. "There you two are. A tour group is due to arrive in a few minutes."

"What heavenly concoctions have you come up with today?" Eva asked, inhaling deeply the wonderful aroma.

"Kept it simple today. Scallops wrapped in turkey bacon and crisped eggplant."

Rafe chuckled. "That's simple, huh?"

Fran had six seating services set up on the bar with small plates and several shot glasses in front of each place mat.

"What can we do to help?" Rafe asked.

Fran cast him an appreciative smile. "As a matter of fact, I seem to be low on the spiced. Someone needs to run down to the cellar to grab a fresh bottle."

Eva grabbed one of the kitchen towels off the bar. "Come with me, Rafe. I'll take you down to the cellar stockroom and show you around." It was as good a time as any to get him familiar with where they kept the freshly bottled spirits.

Eva led him through the kitchen, past the appliances and to the service steps that led down to the basement. Motion sensors switched on the ceiling lights as they made their descent. "After labeling, the bottles head to two different locations," she explained. "The vast majority of cases are taken to the warehouse to be shipped. A few cases come down here for use in the tasting room."

She'd never noticed just how small this staircase was. Though they were taking the steps with Rafe behind her, she could still feel the warmth of his body behind her. The lemony mint smell of his aftershave tickled her nose.

Her nerves came alive with awareness. In her haste to place some distance between them, she took the next step a little too carelessly. Her heel caught and she found herself tipping forward. Eva cried out in a panic, bracing herself for what was sure to be a punishing fall. Suddenly, a strong set of arms gripped her about the waist and pulled her back before she stumbled. The realization that she'd been caught brought tears of relief to her eyes, until she put it together—she was standing in a dark stairwell being held tight in Rafe Malta's arms. Heat rushed through her body, her skin tingling where he was touching her.

"Whoa, steady there," he said, so close behind her.

Eva took several breaths to pull herself together. Her heart pounded in her chest. She couldn't even be certain what was causing it—the way Rafe was holding her, or the fact that he'd just saved her from a painful spill. Most likely, it was both.

"Uh, thanks," she managed to stammer when she found her voice. "That was close."

"Sure was," he said behind her, his breath hot on her cheek.

"I guess I should slow down." *In every sense*, she added silently.

For several moments, they both stood as they were, neither making any kind of move or shift. Eva knew she should pull away, but something about being held by Rafe felt so right, so familiar. It made no sense, she knew. They'd just met under the most vexing of circumstances. For his part, Rafe didn't seem to be making any kind of effort to let her go, either.

Finally, she forced herself to grasp for some sanity. "I think I'm steady now. Thanks." His arms loosened around her waist, though he still hadn't fully let go of her, not until she shifted out of his grasp.

Fran was finishing setting up when they returned to the tasting room. She efficiently twisted open the new bottle and set it with the others on the counter. Slowly, their tasting guests started strolling in.

When everyone had arrived and was seated, Eva began her spiel.

"Gato Rums has been in my family for two generations," she began, then cringed. She hadn't gotten around to updating that part of the speech. She forced herself to continue.

After completing the brief intro about the distillery's history and the rum-making process, she began pouring. The tasting always started with the basic light rum and it took about half an hour to go through the different bottles.

Fran reached her side as soon as she was done.

"I'm glad you're still here for these," she exclaimed, throwing her arms around Eva's shoulders. "I wasn't looking forward to doing the first tasting by myself."

Eva returned her hug, fighting not to show the surge of emotion rushing through her. She was glad to be here, too, she realized. "You would have been absolutely fine on your own."

Fran let go of her and stepped away. "Maybe. But it wouldn't have been the same without you."

Eva smiled in response. Fran was as close to her as a sister. She didn't know how she would have gotten through the despair of the past several months without her dear friend by her side. Fran sniffled before turning away to tend to their customers.

Only time would tell if she'd made the right decision. But for right now, it certainly felt right.

How could she have even imagined leaving this place?

Rafe watched with no small amount of curiosity as the two friends embraced. That led to images of the way he'd caught Eva on the stairway. In fact, he'd thought of little else during the tasting, though he really should have been paying attention.

She hadn't pulled away when he'd caught her and he hadn't imagined the way she'd reacted—her breath quickening, her pulse jumping along her throat. Eva was attracted to him as well.

Nothing could come of it, though. He was too damaged for her.

Eva had so many people in her life who appeared to be wholly devoted to her—not a reality he'd ever experienced, not even with his own mother. Justine Malta had cared for her son, the way one might care for a... Well, a child who was simply a responsibility.

But there was never any warmth or affection. The two of them were simply in survival mode most days. Rafe couldn't really blame his mother for not having anything else left over for her dependent child.

How different Eva's life must have been in contrast. Her relationships with her grandmother, her brother and Fran clearly held mutual adoration. He wondered if she had any idea how lucky she was.

He hadn't been here long, but he couldn't imagine this place without her. The business, the haciend—any of it. She may as well have been one of the physical fixtures.

She turned to him now, motioned for him to join them. He strode over to her side. "After the tastings, we like to mingle a bit with clients so they associate a personal connection with our product. They're more likely to become repeat customers that way."

"That sounds very smart," Rafe said, though he wasn't much for small talk—especially not with strangers. "I'll follow your lead."

Fran split off in a different direction while Rafe and Eva approached an older couple stocking up on several classic, unflavored bottles. Their name tags said they were Paula and Stan.

"Thanks so much for coming to visit us today," Eva addressed them both. "You can't go wrong with the simple classic," she added, pointing to their haul.

"Really?" Paula responded. "I'm planning on throwing a Fourth of July party and want to serve rum punch."

"That will work perfectly," Eva answered her.

"She's been into those punch drinks since our vacation last year," Stan offered. "The resort had self-serve vats of it scattered all around. We've been doing a lot of traveling after retiring a couple years ago."

"Oh, how fun," Eva said with an indulgent smile.

Rafe reached out his hand to them both to shake and thank them for coming. But his mind had traveled elsewhere during the exchange. The couple had mentioned visiting a resort where the rum was apparently flowing freely. It was giving him a germ of an idea.

The couple offered their thanks and walked away.

"You might want to work on your conversational game, fella," she teased him. "You'll have to be more talkative than that at these tastings."

"Sorry, I was a little distracted."

He wasn't going to tell her why just yet. Not until he thought it through some more and weighed the pros, cons and possibilities. But he thought he might be on to something.

"Here, let's try again," he added, leading her back toward the bar where another couple, younger this time, were still taking sips of their shot glasses. By their conversation, it sounded like they were trying to decide which flavor to go with.

"I say you get them both," he said by way of initiating a chat. Then he introduced himself, adding, "This is Eva. She's in charge of running the place."

Eva cast him a brilliant smile, evidently pleased with the way he'd presented her. Rafe had to remind himself to focus.

"I'm trying to convince him to do just that," the young woman exclaimed. "I'd like to buy both."

Rafe eyed their name tags—Kayla and Kyle. He resisted the urge to comment on that. It wasn't easy. This would take some getting used to, the social piece. Being a tech pro, he'd never had to actually interact with those who used his products. This was a whole new world.

"Two bottles seems a bit much," Kyle offered.

If he had to guess, Rafe would say they were on their honeymoon. Too bad they already seemed annoyed with each other, in a disagreement about a minor purchase.

Kayla glared at her husband. "But the bartender on the cruise we were just on said he used the spiced rum for that drink he served. And I'd like to buy the flavored one because I really like peach."

Rafe made another mental note. Both sets of guests so far recalled drinks they'd been served while on vacation—a luxe resort and a cruise ship respectively. Interesting.

Eva stepped in then, perfectly smoothing over the tension with her suggestion. "I would go with the spiced then, if you're trying to recreate a cocktail you enjoyed in the past. Though I'd be remiss if I didn't mention that our flavored rums are award winning and they only get finer with age. You'll be enjoying them a long time."

Kyle eyed the bottles on the bar, reconsidering. "All right. I guess we'll go ahead and invest in both." His use of the word *invest* was an interesting choice, as if the man was justifying the cost to himself. Eva had known exactly what to say to convince him.

Rafe couldn't help but be impressed. Eva really was good at this. She clearly knew how to make a sale.

But if the idea that had struck him during these conversations were to come to fruition, it would take Gato Rums to a whole new level.

CHAPTER SIX

THE NEXT MORNING Eva stepped through the large mahogany doors of the main house and immediately sensed there was something different about the place. It took her a minute, but she finally placed it. One of the paintings Rafe had purchased his first night in town was hanging on the opposite wall—the phoenix rising out of the ashes. That evening seemed so long ago that it was hard to believe it was just the other night. A lot had happened since.

The art looked good there, really added to the aesthetic of the room combined with the dark wood panel walls and the colorful, handcrafted throw rug in the center of the floor. The effect was so striking, Eva had to wonder why Papá hadn't thought to hang something there himself. She glanced around the room but saw no sign of the other painting. She would have to ask Rafe where he'd hung that one.

A low, humming mechanical noise diverted her attention. What in the world? The sound was coming from the direction of the kitchen. She headed that way to investigate. Her breath caught when she reached her destination. Rafe stood in front of a tall, complicated contraption, his back to her.

He was shirtless, his skin glistening with sweat. She debated turning right back around, composing herself and making her presence known before entering. But before she could decide, it was too late and he turned to face her. Eva had to remind herself to breathe. Heavens. The man looked like something out of a fitness magazine. Chiseled chest, sculpted arms, washboard abs.

"Hey there," he greeted her, speaking over the noise. The coffee machine she'd ordered for him appeared to be the culprit of the humming noise.

"Just back from a run on the beach," Rafe told her. "Trying to figure out how to work this thing to make a cup of strong, black iced coffee."

Stop gawking at the man and say something.

But for the life of her, she couldn't get her mouth to function.

"I don't suppose you know how it works?" Rafe asked.

Somehow her brain finally kicked in. "It sounds like it's grinding the coffee beans. Did you read the directions?"

The smile he sent her way nearly had her focus crumbling already. She made sure to lock eyes with him to avoid staring at his sculpted, bare chest.

"Men don't read directions," he informed her. "We like to try and figure things out on our own."

"Right," she responded, with as much nonchalance as she could muster. "And how has that been working out so far?"

He answered her with a mischievous wink she chose to ignore.

With a few clicks of her phone, Eva called up the site she'd ordered from and pulled up the instructions online. Then she walked over to his side to show him the screen. Big mistake. They were a hair's width apart now, the scent of him playing havoc with her senses. A curl of heat formed at the base of her stomach and moved lower.

She had to step away, and in her haste to do so she handed him the phone with such speed that it almost fell to the tile. It didn't help that her hands were so unsteady.

Get a grip, already.

Rafe was just a man, for heaven's sake. No need to be so flustered around him. Just a handsome, successful, disarmingly sexy man. One who smelled like sun and sand and salty sea and was standing shirtless in what used to be her kitchen.

He also happened to be her boss now. As if she didn't have enough reason already to not be interested or attracted to him.

He looked down at her phone screen, then back up at her.

"Something wrong?"

The corner of his mouth lifted. "Uh, this is in Spanish."

Eva swore under her breath and took her phone back. Honestly, she was acting downright silly, like a schoolgirl talking to her high school crush by the lockers. "Right. Sorry."

Rafe chuckled. "I mean, I've been doing some studying to learn the language, but I'm afraid the owner's manual to a complicated mechanical barista is a bit beyond my abilities at the moment."

"Yes, of course," she stammered. "Here, let me."

Rafe stepped around her to give her full access. She could only hope that he planned to put on a shirt while she tinkered with the contraption. Fortunately, she had the thing running and dispensing two tall glasses of *fresca* café in no time. Not so fortunately, when she turned to hand one of them to Rafe, he was still bare chested.

Eva cleared her throat, pulled out a chair and sat down at the round center table, scrambling for something to say by way of conversation. She recalled the painting newly hanging in the foyer.

"I noticed you've hung the painting," she began.

He nodded. "They both arrived yesterday. Around the same time that thing showed up." He pointed with his thumb to the coffee maker behind him.

"It looks good there. Suits the room."

He saluted her with his cup and leaned back against the counter, his legs crossed at the ankles. "Thank you for saying so. I thought long and hard about where each should go."

"Where'd you end up hanging the other one?" Eva asked, making sure to keep her gaze focused on his face and not any lower.

"In my room upstairs," he answered, a heavy tinge in his tone. "Right across from my bed. It reminds me of the two of us walking along that very beach whenever I look at it."

The atmosphere suddenly grew thick and heated. Eva's pulse quickened as a flush crept up her cheeks. What exactly was Rafe saying? That he lay awake in his bed, remembering the two of them frolicking in the water? Heaven help her—the images she was assaulted with nearly had her rushing out of her chair to see if he might take her in his embrace the way he had yesterday on that stairwell. It had taken all the will she had then not to try and kiss him. It was taking even more now to stay still where she sat.

How much longer could they ignore what was clearly present between them? Eva knew the attraction wasn't one-sided. She could see it in the heat that swam in Rafe's eyes even now as he looked at her across the kitchen. She wasn't imagining it. Rafe wanted to kiss her, too.

The break for sanity came from a voice calling her name from the other end of the house. Fran.

Eva couldn't decide if she was relieved or frustrated at the interruption. Either way, the moment broken, she answered her friend. "In here."

Fran appeared in the doorway seconds later. Her gaze travelled from Eva's flushed face to Rafe's bare chest. Her jaw fell slightly open.

"Um, I was just wondering if you'd come taste the hors d'oeuvres I just made. It can definitely wait, though." She started backtracking before Rafe stopped her.

"It's okay. I have something I need to discuss with Eva, but it can wait. I'll just grab a shower in the meantime."

If that meant he'd come back down fully dressed, Eva was all for it.

One Week Later

"I'm still not sure how you convinced me to go along with this idea," Eva said, as they approached the car waiting for them at the hacienda gate.

Rafe greeted the driver and helped Eva into the back seat of the late-model SUV before joining her.

"What have we got to lose?" he asked her as they settled in. "Worst case scenario we spend a lovely, sunny day in beautiful San Juan, Puerto Rico. I've been meaning to visit since I got here anyway."

Barring any traffic or road delays, they should arrive in the city within an hour or so and Rafe took it as a good sign that the weather was cooperating. It would give him and Eva a chance to explore the grounds and amenities of the resort before meeting with the hotel manager for dinner later tonight.

"Tell me again," Eva said, buckling her seat belt. "This all came to you that day in the tasting room after talking to those couples. Do I have that right?"

Rafe pinched the bridge of his nose. For some reason, Eva thought if she had him repeat his reasoning enough times, he might discover some fault in his thought process. The reality was quite the opposite. A lot of his business success came from following his gut instincts, and he knew what said gut was telling him about this.

Her attitude regarding the endeavor was hardly surprising. Eva wasn't thrilled about the idea of Gato changing in any way, and as far as she was concerned, Rafe was the catalyst for any attempt at change.

Still, he'd indulge her for now. "Those couples mentioned enjoying cocktails that they still remembered months if not years afterward. Resorts like the ones they visited serve countless cocktails. They need a steady supplier of specialty spirits. We could be one of those suppliers."

Right on cue, she began her counter argument. "Establishments like resorts and hotels get their supply from the industrial-size producers. It's a mass market."

He had to agree there. "Correct. Our selling point is if we become their supplier, they can boast that their cocktail recipes use a specialty Puerto Rican rum made exclusively in one distillery. The artisan factor."

"I have reservations that they won't see it that way."

"We just need one resort to make an offer. Others are certain to follow if that happens. I figured we'd start locally on the island, then test the waters in the rest of the Caribbean, so to speak."

"We're too small for such exclusivity," she argued.

"It will only take one large investment to start growing the distillery. Leave that part up to me. I have the means and ways to finance the growth."

Her lips thinned. "I thought you got your start as a tech mogul. You developed an app that boosted office productivity for administrative offices."

"Yes. That's right."

"And you grew the profit from that success via investments?"

Something tightened in Rafe's midsection. Despite his professional success, this wouldn't be the first time he'd been questioned about his qualifications as a businessman. Hell, he was used to not having anyone believe in him, for it rarely happened.

Yet somehow, this instance felt deeply bruising given the source of the doubt.

"Look," he began, "if I'd followed the advice of every so-called expert who told me to stick to coding—"

She cut him off. "That's not what I was implying."

"It certainly sounded that way."

She leaned back in her seat. "Then I apologize. That wasn't my intention."

He was taken aback by her words—so simple and direct, offered without any pretense or prompt. He tried to recall when anyone had apologized to him for anything and couldn't recall a single time, though plenty of people had had good cause to do so. "Thank you for that."

"You're welcome." She leaned back against her seat. "But I'm not sorry for speaking my mind. I think we're trying to bite off more than we can chew."

"Your reservations have been noted." *Several times over*, he added silently.

Eva nodded an acknowledgment and turned her head to look out the window. The ocean sparkled crystal turquoise in the distance on her side. Rafe indulged himself by studying her profile. She really was quite beautiful. Soft chin, delicate features. So far, he'd been doing a fairly good job of ignoring his inconvenient attraction to her. He didn't have any other choice. He made himself look away before risking getting caught staring at her.

Several moments passed by as they drove in silence. Surprisingly, she'd dropped the argument. Why did he get the feeling it would only be temporary?

Finally, the car pulled up the circular driveway of the beachfront La Ola hotel and casino in the heart of San Juan.

A large front patio, set up with several tables around a wraparound bar, was bustling with patrons despite the early hour. Most diners seemed to be enjoying a cocktail with their meals.

Yet another good sign.

This was a colossal undertaking.

Wasn't growth supposed to be gradual? Her grandfather had started Gato Rums with one vat and a decrepit building on a small plot of family land. They'd grown exponentially since then, but it had taken time. Rafe had only been on board a matter of days and already he was trying to take them to the next stratosphere. She had to wonder if he was being too ambitious for their own good. One thing she could say for him: the man was certainly driven. What was behind such an intense level of drive, she couldn't guess. Maybe he'd see fit to tell her one day.

For now, they were in San Juan, about to enter the first resort Rafe wanted them to pitch to. He'd somehow secured a formal dinner tonight with the resort manager.

Eva took in her surroundings as the driver hauled out their bags and handed them to the waiting bellhop. La Ola hotel and casino certainly seemed to be a popular spot, though the thought of being anywhere near a casino and its gamblers gave her an uncomfortable bristle down her spine. She had Victor to thank for that. Her ex-husband had had a strong addiction to games of chance. And he'd used her to feed his last binge—at much too high a cost.

In fact, it had cost her everything: her pride, her peace of mind, her very home.

So she couldn't explain or understand the sense of longing she felt when they walked through the outdoor lobby and she saw several couples clearly there about to begin their honeymoon. One young woman still had a costume bridal veil on, to go with her bright neon green bikini. Her husband couldn't seem to stop touching her—a brush of his hand against her cheek, his other arm draped around her shoulders. They wanted the world to know how in love they were.

Eva thought she'd had that. Victor had been affectionate and attentive. How utterly wrong and naive she'd been to believe all that had meant he'd loved her. He'd merely been using her.

Rafe's voice pulled her out of the unwelcome memories. "Eva, you coming? We're all checked in."

She gave her head a shake and followed him to the glass elevator at the side of the building. The view outside was breathtaking as they rode up several levels to their floor. A heart-shaped infinity pool was spread out below them, the turquoise blue ocean in the distance and fluffy clouds above.

She noted that the pool had a swim-up bar, which was packed with people just like the one by the entrance.

Rafe was right about one thing: they certainly seemed to be serving a lot of cocktails. Even from up here, she could see almost every adult held a beverage, whether they were in the pool or not.

The bellhop awaited them outside the door when they stepped out of the elevator. He looked barely out of his teens. Rafe thanked him and handed him what Eva figured had to be a tip. Whatever the amount was, it had the other man grasping Rafe's hand and shaking it with gusto.

She waited to be shown to her own room but the bellhop turned back toward the elevator instead. How curious. Looked like she would have to find it for herself.

"You're here, too," Rafe informed her.

Wait. What?

"I am?"

He nodded. "I meant to mention. They told me downstairs it's a suite with adjoining rooms and a shared salon. I had an admin assistant back in Seattle book it and something must have been lost in translation."

"I see."

"I did ask for it to be changed just now downstairs, but they're completely booked."

"Huh." Not ideal, but she could hardly complain. They had different rooms, after all, just a shared parlor area in between. Still, close proximity wasn't exactly conducive to her mental well-being, given how drawn she was to the man. Especially given that they'd be staying at a resort so clearly targeted to newlyweds and lovers in general.

"If it's uncomfortable for you, we can see about finding a different hotel," Rafe was saying.

That would just delay their schedule and make her look unreasonable. Besides, they'd be a whole room apart. It wasn't as if she'd have to share a bed with Rafe. She almost groaned out loud as soon as she had the thought. Why did her brain have to go there?

Eva shook her head. "No. That's okay. This should be fine."

With a nod, Rafe motioned her into the room and pulled their bags in.

Eva took in her surroundings, marveling at the luxury. Soft beige walls lent a relaxing, spa-like feel. A plush L-shaped couch laden with cushions faced a decorative fireplace.

"Why don't you look at both rooms and pick which one you'd like for yourself?" Rafe offered.

That was a no-brainer. She didn't even have to look. "I'll take the one with the ocean view," she answered, pointing to the door behind her that led to the room facing the beachfront.

"It's all yours."

Just then, the silliest and most useless thought crept into her head.

Rather than two business colleagues who were here to explore a deal, what if she and Rafe really were here as a couple? What if they were just like those newlyweds downstairs, swimming and dining by day, then enjoying each other at night—in every sense? Heat rose to her face and she felt her cheeks flush as wanton, unbidden images flooded her mind. Images of the two of them, right there in front of the fireplace on the thick throw rug. Her mouth went dry and she sucked in a rapid inhale.

"Eva?"

Rafe's voice brought her back to reality. He was looking at her expectantly. Had he asked her something?

"I asked if you wanted to freshen up before we head back downstairs," he said.

"Yes, I'd like that. Thanks."

He had no idea how badly she needed to do just that, starting with a cold splash of water on her heated skin.

CHAPTER SEVEN

RAFE STEPPED OUT onto the balcony, greeted by the sound of the waves in the distance and boisterous conversations from the crowds below. A mariachi band near the bar area played a bouncy, happy tune.

The cheerful music did little to assuage his concern. He had to be careful; he was already so tempted whenever Eva was near him and now he'd have to maneuver around sharing a suite with her.

His mind should be completely focused on trying to secure a deal here. Instead, all he could focus on was how to navigate being in such close quarters with a woman who called to him in every possible way—a woman he had no business desiring.

He felt her presence behind him, and a moment later Eva stood next to him, draping her forearms over the railing to stare at the view below.

"Wow. What a stunning picture," she said on a breathless sigh.

He couldn't agree more. But he wasn't looking where her gaze was directed. Eva had changed into a spaghetti strap scarlet red dress and the vibrant color brought out the subtle highlights in her dark hair. Her skin glowed in the sunlight.

There was that temptation again. He had to wonder if she felt it, too. There were times when he was certain of it, like that afternoon in the stairwell. Rafe knew he could have kissed her then. Everything about that moment was seared into his memory—the way her breath had hitched, the heat swimming in her eyes. She must have wanted him, too.

But other times, he couldn't be sure. She was so good at keeping her distance. Perhaps he should have kissed her that day. At least he would have found out one way or another if whatever was developing between them was in any way mutual.

"There appear to be a lot of couples here," Eva remarked after several moments.

Rafe had noticed that, too. "Nothing in the write-ups online indicated the resort was targeted or marketed toward that particular niche. Guess it must be a romantic season."

"Ah, a season for lovers," Eva said with a wistful smile. "How lucky for them."

Rafe wasn't sure what to say to that so he simply remained silent, taking in all the sounds and the scene. He knew they should stop lingering out here, should head downstairs and get a cursory look at the place—all the better to sound knowledgeable and well acquainted with the property when they met with the manager later. But he couldn't bring himself to suggest leaving just yet. He didn't want the moment to end. It felt peaceful up here, tranquil, as if they were far removed from the happenings below and life in general.

Or maybe he just wanted Eva to himself a little while longer. Eva started swaying to the music and humming low under her breath.

"You like this song, I take it?"

She smiled wide. "It's one of my favorites."

"What's it about?" he asked. "What are they singing?"

She became animated at the question and turned to face him fully. "It's about making sure not to let life pass you by. Enjoying every moment."

"Sounds like a pretty solid message."

"The major verse is all about how the best way to do that is to go on living, no matter what happens."

"To keep the past in the past, in other words."

She laughed, but there was no merriment in it. "Easier said than done, right?"

If she only knew. "I'd say so. The only reason I find myself here in Puerto Rico is to do just that—push the past back to where it belongs."

She braced her elbows on the railing and leaned forward, her gaze focused on the horizon. "Quite a life change. Must have taken a lot of thought."

"Not really. My old life held nothing positive for me anymore. Only pain." And no small amount of anger. Anger that ate him alive from the inside out. He'd had no choice but to get himself out of the toxic spiral.

"Want to talk about it?"

He chuckled at the question. "That would hardly be keeping the past in the past now, would it?"

She shrugged her shoulders. "All right. You have a point. I won't push. But my ear is there if you decided you'd like to bend it."

"I wouldn't know where to even start."

"Start with the good. Tell me how you got the idea for your app."

He tilted his head, remembering how the concept

had all come about. "It wasn't one particular moment. The idea came in bits and pieces over the span of about three years."

"And you were able to bring it to fruition. No easy task."

He nodded. "You're right. Getting the idea was the easiest piece. Bringing it to life was the blood and sweat."

She *hmph*ed a small laugh. "Sounds like most goals worth pursuing."

He'd thought so. And he'd been right—at first, anyway. The app had brought him wealth and success beyond his wildest dreams…until it had all come crashing down around him.

"What about you?"

"How do you mean?"

"What good would you start with?"

"That's easy. I'd start with the time I was about sixteen or so. That's when my father really began to involve me in the happenings at the distillery. He explained the latest sales figures. Marketing plans. More detail about how the various processes worked."

"You really love what you do," he said unnecessarily. "I'm guessing you weren't happy when your father decided to sell."

"He didn't. Make the decision, I mean. It was made for him."

Her response confused him. Eva was clearly not happy about the distillery changing hands so she wouldn't have prompted the sale, and he would have known if there was any kind of silent partner. "I don't understand. Surely, it wasn't your idea."

Pain flooded her features. "No. Not my decision either. But definitely my fault. I was the reason my father had to sell his ancestral home and his family's business."

Rafe directed the same question at her that she'd asked him a minute earlier. "Want to talk about it?"

Eva blew out a sharp breath. "The short story is that I trusted the wrong man. And I wasn't the only one who paid for my mistake." Eva paused, gauging herself to see how much she wanted to reveal. She wasn't even sure why she was contemplating it. When she'd stepped out onto this balcony a few minutes ago, she wouldn't have thought she'd end up deep in conversation with Rafe about such consequential topics.

"Quid pro quo," Rafe stated. "Same goes for me. I'm here to listen if you want to get into the longer version."

To Eva's surprise, she was thinking about doing so. Maybe it was due to being up here, under a clear, bright sky. The air felt light and fresh. Breathing it in was helping to clear her mind. Or maybe it was being up here alone with Rafe, as if they were the only two people in the world and they were standing on top of it.

Whatever the reason, Eva found herself taking him up on his offer. "I mentioned that first night at dinner that you had arrived at Gato Rums just as I found myself at a life crossroad."

He nodded once. "I remember."

"I said that because my divorce had just been finalized."

Rafe betrayed no reaction at her words. "You were married."

"That's right."

A muscle skipped along his jaw. "How long?"

"About a year. Not quite."

"I'm sorry to hear it didn't work out. How does your broken marriage relate to selling the hacienda? Did he sue you for alimony?"

She tilted her head back, a sardonic smile on her face. "If only it were that mundane. He swindled me. The marriage was a farce. For him, anyway."

Rafe turned to fully face her, then crammed his hands into his pants pockets. "What did he do, Eva?"

"He used me. What I thought was love and commitment was nothing but a ploy on his part—a way for him to get his hands on some money so that he could gamble it away." The words poured out of her. She felt part relief, part anxiousness. Would Rafe be judging her now? Would he think less of her as a business professional— or as a woman, for that matter?

"We met at one of Teo's car shows," Eva continued, her muscles quivering with tension as she spoke of her biggest regret. "My brother said Victor frequented a lot of the races and such events—a regular on the racing car scene. Teo had even seen him put money down on a classic sports car at a recent auction. My former husband gave off every impression that he was well off. Turns out, he'd never had money of his own."

Rafe let out a low whistle. "Wow. The guy sounds like quite a piece of work. How'd he pull it off?"

"By charming me enough that I was blind to what was happening."

Saying the words aloud made her sound so gullible, so lovesick that it made her naive…which of course was the sad truth.

"He convinced me to use the property and business as collateral for a major loan. He swore we needed it to invest in a major real estate venture he was pursuing, and sounded so excited about the opportunity. I loved him so much that I did it."

"What happened?"

"When the bills came due, he was nowhere to be found. And all the money was gone. I still have no idea where he is." Pain lanced through her core. "Our divorce was handled through attorneys. Teo managed to track his whereabouts at one point just long enough for him to be served."

"Can Teo locate him again?"

The thought of so much as laying eyes on Victor had her feeling nauseous. "For what? I don't ever want to see his face again. The money is most likely all gone or close to it." She shook her head. "No, Victor can stay lost forever."

"You can hardly be blamed for feeling that way."

"I even talked my father into going along," she added with a disgusted huff. "Convinced him it was a once-in-a-lifetime investment opportunity from my loving husband. It's a wonder Papá still acknowledges me as his daughter."

"You thought he would disown you?"

"He would have had every right. My father is too decent a man." So decent he still remained on cordial terms with her mother, the woman who had left them years ago to gallivant around the globe. Eva only heard from the woman on her birthday or various holidays when she deemed it within her abilities to mail a card. That's why her closeness with her father and brother was so important to her.

Enrique Gato had not once belittled Eva for her folly, not so much as a chiding. But things between them hadn't been the same since the ordeal.

"I'd be lying if I said the whole experience hadn't caused a strain on our relationship," she found herself confiding. "There's a tension between us that wasn't ever there before."

She had her ex-husband to thank for marring her relationship with her very own family. For that, she would never forgive the man.

That's why she could absolutely not let herself fall for someone again. How could she trust her judgment when it came to love and attraction? Her one real relationship had been a colossally disastrous error. Not to mention, look at how her parent's marriage had turned out.

No, she couldn't risk being tempted by love ever again…despite the feelings she was rapidly developing for the man standing next to her on a small balcony atop the world.

Rafe shrugged on his suit jacket and straightened his tie in the mirror. He was still reeling from all Eva had told him on the balcony earlier. Her ex had certainly done a number on her.

Yet another example that confirmed a truth he'd concluded long ago: some people simply were not good. In fact, people could be downright heinous. He'd had more than his share of run-ins with such types. They had rotten souls and only served to make life miserable for those around them—even those who loved them the most.

Not that he himself had ever actually been in love. All of his relationships with the opposite sex had been brief, convenient and rather superficial. He just wasn't built for commitment.

By contrast, Eva must have been head over heels for

the man she'd married. Look how much he'd been able to blind her with that affection.

Why that thought had his gut tightening, he didn't want to examine. Nor did he really want to visit the way his stomach had plummeted at her first mention of an ex-husband. She'd been so in love with this man that she'd allowed him to con her. The notion ran counter to everything he'd learned about Eva Gato. Her ex must have swept her off her feet.

Only to kick her down. A surge of anger shot through him. The man had cost Eva the security and comfort she'd enjoyed her whole life. Her family, her very home.

The more Rafe thought about it, the more his ire grew for a man he hadn't even set eyes on—anger he had to control and tamp down. His temper would not get the best of him ever again. He'd sworn an oath to himself.

Not like the night when he'd let it take over and ruin his life with one impulsive act. Rafe took a deep breath and pushed the painful memories aside.

Eva was already out in the shared center room when he stepped out of his door. Rafe tried hard not to react when he saw her. It wasn't easy. Dressed in a silky red dress in midnight navy with strappy black sandals on her feet, her hair done up in some complicated style that accented the heart shape of her face, she looked like a stunning vision out of every man's fantasy.

He made himself look away, feigned intense focus on the gold cuff links at his sleeves. "Ready then?" He was surprised his mouth even worked.

"Yes. All set," she answered.

They left the room and approached the elevator.

"I think you should move back into the house when we get back to the distillery."

She visibly bristled, her shoulders growing rigid. "I don't need your pity, Rafe. Don't make me regret confiding in you."

Leave it to Eva to have that be her first thought at the suggestion. He couldn't really blame her for being defensive, though, not given what she'd been through. He stepped closer to her. "That isn't why I suggested it." Pity had nothing to do with it. He was simply doing what was right. The hacienda was Eva's home. He hated that he'd played any part in her having to leave it. "It's a large house. Too large for one person. Corporations provide housing for employees all the time. In this case, it's purely logical."

She eyed him with skepticism. "That's the only reason you're suggesting this?"

He nodded once. "Absolutely the only reason. I can't believe I didn't think to ask you before."

Her facial features softened ever so slightly. "I suppose it would be nice to be back in my own room."

"It's all yours," he told her. Eva didn't answer but she wasn't protesting either. Rafe would take that as a positive.

When they reached the first-floor lobby, a uniformed server awaited them and instructed that they follow him. They were led through the lobby, down a back hallway and outside to a quaint brick patio surrounded by rich vegetation. Statues of angels dotted the four corners of the square space. Rafe felt as if he might have walked into a Spanish noble's garden.

The resort manager greeted them. "Señor Malta… Señora Gato. Hola, buenas noches."

The two of them answered in turn.

"Hope you don't mind. I prefer dining out here in the evenings to enjoy the fresh air."

"I think it's lovely," Eva answered, following him to the center of the patio, where a large, round table was set for three.

They were seated at the table and a different server appeared to serve them their salads.

The next course was a mouthwatering sea bass served with lemon butter and roasted vegetables. Eventually, the discussion turned to business and the reason they were all here.

Rafe started the pitch, Eva jumping in with her expert details as needed. The manager listened intently and tried the rum Eva and Rafe had left with the beverage service earlier, first drinking it straight with one ice cube, then in a premade juice cocktail that sat in a pitcher at the table. Rafe couldn't believe the level of anticipation in his gut as he watched the other man. He'd closed his eyes after the last swallow, a look of intense concentration on his face.

To Rafe's surprise and delight, by the time the dessert plates were cleared, they'd been offered a verbal agreement to supply the next shipment.

He didn't allow himself a sigh of relief until they were back in the hallway. "That went brilliantly," he said, beyond pleased at how the meeting had ended.

"Congratulations," Eva told him with a genuine smile.

"Thanks. You, too. I feel almost elated."

She laughed. "You should. You just got your first exclusive deal."

"We both did, Eva," he countered. "I've never been in charge of a tangible product before. It's a whole different ball game."

"I have to say, you played this inning very well."

He winked at her. "I did, didn't I? Had an answer for all of his questions."

She chuckled. "Yes, indeed. Noble of you to be so humble about it."

Rafe pumped the air with his fist, perhaps childishly. But he couldn't seem to contain himself. "That couldn't have gone any better!" In his excitement, without thinking of the ramifications, Rafe leaned over to give her a quick peck on the cheek.

What happened next was wholly unexpected. Eva turned her head to speak just as Rafe's lips reached her and the result was his mouth landing square on top of hers. Rather than pull back, for a moment Rafe could only stand there in stunned silence. He waited to see if Eva would react in horror and step away. She didn't. She stood firm. Then his mind went blank. He couldn't even place who'd initiated it, but somehow he was kissing Eva and she was kissing him back.

His arms moved of their own accord and wrapped around her back. He pulled her closer, tasting her, absorbing her warmth. She tasted like berries and honey and the most tempting wine. Fire shot through his chest and he could feel her heartbeat against his. A low rumble of a groan escaped her lips and he thought his knees might buckle in response. This was madness—a wanton assault on sanity.

He didn't ever want it to stop.

CHAPTER EIGHT

EVA AWOKE WITH a start the next morning, disoriented and groggy. She'd spent the night tossing and turning, restless with an uneasiness she couldn't place. Her dreams hadn't helped—dreams of where she and Rafe may have ended up if she hadn't come to her senses and broken off their kiss. If she hadn't put a stop to their passionate encounter, would they both be here now, in this very bed?

Eva took a steadying breath, shoving the thought away before it could go any further.

Then there was the reason for this trip. Worries about the business had only added to her bout of insomnia last night. If Rafe got his way, Gato Rums would be rapidly expanding. All her life, it had been a small family operation, catering to small stores around the island and the tour groups who visited. What Rafe had in mind was a completely different goal. She didn't know the first thing about running a massive distillery. And Rafe was so new to the entire field. It would be like the blind leading the blind.

The two of them would have to work closely together if they had any hope of success. Side by side, day after day. She'd agreed to move back into the house! Eva groaned out loud. How could she trust herself to be near the man, given what had happened between them last night?

Not that she had a choice. This was her job now.

Slivers of sunlight escaped through the heavy curtains she'd drawn tightly closed the night before. The bedside digital clock read 8:00 a.m. She'd overslept. The driver would be back to pick them up at nine o'clock sharp. That gave her barely enough time to shower and dress. For the life of her, though, she couldn't seem to make herself rise off this mattress.

What was Rafe doing now? Was he still in bed? Or was he up and showered already, wondering what was taking her so long to come out of the room?

The long drive from home yesterday and all the activity must have taken more out of her than she'd thought.

Who was she kidding?

The reason she was lingering in bed was because she was delaying the inevitable. At some point she was going to have to face Rafe and the awkwardness that was sure to hover between them.

He'd kissed her! And she'd kissed him back. She rubbed the back of her hand against her lips, recalling the way he'd tasted. The scent of him still seemed to linger in the air around her. Heat shot through her as she remembered every tantalizing detail.

Ugh. She had to try and get it out of her mind. Right now, she needed to get dressed and get out there to face the man…finally.

They couldn't just ignore what had happened.

With no small amount of reluctance, Eva made herself stand and pull the curtains open. Then she went about the motions until she was showered, dressed and had her bag packed—all done in under twenty minutes.

But when she stepped out into the common area, Rafe sat on the couch wearing a cotton undershirt and loose-fitting athletic shorts. His feet were bare. He hadn't even gotten dressed yet.

Eva glanced at her wristwatch. Had she made a mistake with the time?

The smell of fresh coffee hung temptingly in the air... along with a doughy, sugary scent.

"There you are," Rafe stated, looking up from the laptop he had on the coffee table in front of him. "I'm just catching up on some work emails." He pointed to a serving cart behind him. The source of the scrumptious aromas tickled her nose. "Have some breakfast. I took the liberty of ordering room service. Coffee, toast and eggs. And some pastries."

She stepped farther into the room. "I thought we were leaving soon. Isn't the driver due to arrive in minutes?"

Rafe shrugged, his eyes lingering on her just a moment longer than they needed to, and Eva felt her pulse quicken. He looked away, back to his screen. "I called and asked him for a delay. Figured you were still asleep when I didn't see you up and about. Didn't want to wake you."

Eva blinked. He'd thought to order breakfast after letting her sleep in because she might have been tired. She couldn't recall a single time Victor had made any kind of similar gesture. His needs had always come first.

Eva gave her head a shake. Comparing the two men could lead to very dangerous pathways, especially considering that kiss last night—the kiss Eva didn't want to bring up and hoped fervently that Rafe wouldn't either.

Thankfully, he seemed pretty preoccupied with whatever he was working on.

"Thank you," she uttered, walking over to serve herself the much-needed jolt of caffeine. She couldn't deny the surge of relief that ran through her. The ride back into town would have been straining enough, but without coffee and breakfast first it might have been downright torturous.

"You're welcome."

She lifted one of the silver covers off a plate to reveal a mound of scrambled eggs with fried potatoes and roasted vegetables at the side. Her mouth watered in response. Exactly what she would have ordered for herself. Her gaze traveled to where Rafe sat engrossed in whatever was on his laptop screen.

He had no idea how much he'd just lifted her spirits by delaying the travel back to the hacienda, nor how much she appreciated his thoughtfulness.

For the first time in what felt like years, Eva felt taken care of.

An hour later, Eva settled into the seat in the back of the SUV feeling much more ready to take on the rest of the day. She would just have to get through a ninety minute ride with Rafe a mere two feet away in a cramped space. Was he still thinking about it, too? Their embrace and mind-blowing kiss in the hallway after the dinner meeting?

He gave no indication any of it was on his mind at all. In fact, Eva wondered if it had even registered for him, while she couldn't get it out of her head. It was happening just like it had before. The first few days after she'd met Victor she'd been enthralled, couldn't stop thinking about him. But look how that had turned out.

For her own self-preservation, she'd make sure to forget about the kiss the same way Rafe seemed to have.

Rafe interrupted her thoughts. "The hotel manager last night mentioned that we'd be driving by El Yunque National Forest on the way back."

She nodded, not sure where he was headed with this. Rafe didn't seem the sightseeing sort. "That's right. I haven't been there since I was a little girl."

"I've never been to a rain forest at all. This might be a perfect time to rectify that. Any interest in stopping?"

Guess she'd pegged him wrong about the sightseeing part. "We have quite a lot of work ahead of us," she responded, adding silently, *thanks to your aspirations for Gato Rums*.

"All the more reason. Who knows when I'll get a chance to visit again?" At her hesitation, he prodded. "Come on, I'm sure the foreman and rest of the crew have a handle on the distillery. He can manage being in charge for another few hours. With Fran's help."

True enough, but something about experiencing yet another adventure with Rafe had her feeling unsettled. Strolling through the lush rain forest, surrounded by all that vegetation and wildlife… Those were the types of activities that led to lasting memories. She didn't need too many of those that featured the man sitting next to her.

She turned to find Rafe staring at her expectedly, still awaiting her answer. As leery as she was, Eva was going to agree to go. After all, if there was even the possibility that Victor was the reason she was hesitating to do something, she couldn't let that stand. The man had taken enough from her. Besides, it was hardly a romantic and intimate outing. They'd be visiting a national park, for heaven's sake.

She shrugged one shoulder. "Sure. Why not. Let's go."

Rafe grabbed her hand and gave it a gentle squeeze, appearing thrilled at her answer. That sent a shiver of pleasure down her spine. He leaned over to communicate the change in plans to their driver.

Less than half an hour later, they turned into the road that led to the national park. She hadn't exactly planned for a day hiking through slippery trails. Thank the saints she'd worn comfortable flats.

The driver dropped them off at the entrance with the understanding that he'd be back to get them in a couple of hours.

A chorus of sounds rang in the air as they walked through the park: several different bird songs, the hum of running water over the falls and simply Mother Nature in general.

Flats or not, the pathway was wet and slippery; Eva stepped gingerly and walked slowly. To his credit, Rafe didn't seem to mind her speed, as he was taking in his surroundings and appeared totally engrossed. For that matter, so was she. Why hadn't she made her way back here over the years? The forest was magical, as if they'd stepped onto an entirely different planet.

He cupped a hand to his ear. "Is that—"

She chuckled, cutting him off. "Yes, what you're hearing is the native coqui frog. This is their natural habitat."

He returned her laugh with one of his own. "Go figure. It really sounds like that's what they're saying."

"If we're lucky, we might even catch a sighting of one, though they're very shy creatures."

"I'll keep my fingers crossed."

"If we're really lucky, we might lay eyes on a parrot."

He chuckled. "Why would seeing a talking bird make us lucky?"

"Because this would be the rare Puerto Rican Parrot. The only place they call home is here on the island."

"Huh. All right then, I'll keep my eyes open for bright green birds who might be chatty."

She laughed at his description. "Bad news is, they're endangered. Only a few hundred left."

Rafe rubbed his chin. "That's too bad. Then the odds of seeing one are probably low."

Eva resumed walking down the path. "There have been sightings. Legend says seeing one will lead to good luck and fortune. That's what Nana told me, anyway."

As if on cue, a flock of colorful birds flew overhead, gliding majestically through the sky. None of them were the coveted parrots, however.

Rafe pointed up. "I don't suppose...?"

"Afraid not. Keep looking. Like Nana always says—keep your eyes open and your heart full of hope."

She'd have done well to heed that first part before getting married. The thought of Victor dulled her mood, so she pushed it—and him—aside. It was too beautiful out here to dwell on regrets.

When they got to a waterfall, they watched the more adventurous types who were rock jumping into the lake below.

"I might have to try that someday," Rafe said next to her. An unbidden image flashed into her mind before she could stop it—Rafe holding her hand as they leaped off the edge of a cliff into the warm pool of water below. The two of them holding on to each other while swimming... Eva blinked the picture away before it could go any further. What was wrong with her? So much for seeing the rain forest as less than romantic. Then again, Rafe seemed to elicit such thoughts from her no matter where they were.

Before long they'd reached the opening that led to the Torre Britton, an observation tower that afforded panoramic views of the park and the neighboring mountains. The structure was surrounded by visitors. Tourists flocked to this location as one of the top attractions on the island, though Eva figured just as many of them could be locals, given the amount of Spanish she could hear.

She turned to Rafe. "Do you want to go up?" It was a pointless question. Eva knew with one-hundred-percent certainty what his answer would be.

"You have to ask?" he said, his smile widening. He tugged on her hand, then sprinted to the tower, keeping her hand in his as they climbed the stairway. In his haste, he probably just wanted to make sure she kept pace with him—nothing to read into. Still, it was a challenge to ignore the electric current that sparked where their skin touched.

When they reached the top, Rafe was barely out of breath, while Eva had to pause to catch hers...only to have her breath taken away again when she caught sight of the view. It was beyond magnificent: miles and miles of lush greenery, colorful birds dotting the bright blue sky, the majestic mountain in the distance. The air was clear and crisp, so fresh she could almost taste it with every breath.

"Wow," she heard herself utter.

"I can't think of anything better to say," Rafe answered quietly next to her.

"I guess I didn't appreciate all those years ago what a rare sight I was looking at. This is amazing." She might have never thought to visit this part of Puerto Rico if it hadn't been for Rafe.

"Aren't you glad I suggested coming?" he asked, as if reading her thoughts.

She was, truly. "I am. Thank you. I'll admit that you were right. About this, anyway," she couldn't help but add.

Rafe's eyes held merriment and curiosity when he turned away from the view to look back to her. "All right, I'll bite. What is it that you think I'm incorrect about? Though I'm fairly certain I know the answer."

"I think the expansion might be more difficult that you think."

He dropped his head. "Ah, I was right. That would have been my first guess."

"We're just not there yet, Rafe. Gato isn't big enough to become such a major supplier. I don't know that we ever will be."

Rafe returned his gaze to the view of the horizon before answering her. "If I didn't know any better, I might think you're doubting your abilities to adapt to a more demanding role."

Eva was taken aback by his suggestion. "My trepidation does not come from lack of confidence, Rafe."

"Are you certain?"

"Yes," she answered, perhaps a little too quickly, though a hint of doubt had slithered into her mind. Darn Rafe for putting it there.

"I think your self-confidence took a big hit because you made one bad decision. Granted, it resulted in dire consequences, but you're letting that cast a shadow over your entire future."

Was that what she was doing? Living in a shadow? She immediately tossed the notion aside. No, Rafe couldn't be right. Her betrayal at Victor's hands had nothing to do with her apprehension about this expansion. That was just common sense on her part. She was certain they'd be biting off more than they could chew.

Rafe just didn't know any better.

Rafe feigned interest in his cell phone screen as they drove in silence back to the hacienda.

He never should have kissed her. And he certainly shouldn't have tried to scrutinize her mentality the way he had up at the viewing tower.

Eva was still hurt and bruised from the calamity that had been her marriage. It was one thing to nudge the woman out of her comfort zone when it came to business. But Rafe had absolutely no right to share his opinions about her personal life.

Given that he was much too damaged to risk any kind of relationship himself, he had no business toying with her emotions by losing control enough to kiss her. So why couldn't he stop thinking about the way she'd tasted? The way she'd felt in his arms? Rafe let out an ironic laugh and turned to stare out the window.

He was so good at doling out advice. If only he could take some of it to heart himself.

His new home and environment were definitely helping. He'd be a fool to risk having it go south in any way because he couldn't resist the temptation that was Eva Gato.

The day had grown cloudy by the time they turned in to the gravel driveway of the Gato hacienda. Eva hadn't done much talking during the ride, and for the life of him he couldn't think of much to say either. If only he'd kept his mouth closed when it had mattered, back at the tower. But he'd wanted so badly to tell her what was so obvious to him: that she was a talented, smart, accomplished woman. A beautiful one, at that. The only reason Eva doubted herself or her abilities in any way was because of what that scoundrel had done to her.

What was wrong with him? Regardless of his attraction to her, Eva was his employee. He had zero right to speculate about anything beyond her duties as his operations manager. If she had doubts about his business plan, they could sit down and discuss her reservations and come up with ways to address each one.

So that's what they would do. First thing tomorrow morning, he and Eva would sit down and develop a project plan based on all the concerns she had regarding Gato Rums becoming a supplier to an exclusive San Juan resort, with many more resorts to follow if Rafe got his wish.

He needed Eva's help if he wanted to be successful with this venture and Rafe knew without a shred of doubt that Eva would meet any challenge the expansion might bring.

Eva just had to believe it, too.

CHAPTER NINE

Nassau, the Bahamas, Two Weeks Later

DESPITE BEING A native daughter of Puerto Rico, Eva still shivered when stepping out of the hot sun and into a highly air-conditioned building. The sudden drop in temperature never ceased to shock her momentarily, though one would think she'd be used to it having lived on a tropical island for most of her life. It was no different now as she stepped into the lobby of the New Paradise Hotel and Resort, the next establishment on their list to try and recruit as a buyer. Rafe had been right: once the manager in Puerto Rico had signed on, other establishments had indicated interest in hearing their pitch.

The lobby was decorated to look like an underwater city and the entire wall behind the reception desk was a functioning aquarium full of colorful fish.

Eva took it all in as Rafe went to check them in.

"I'm afraid it's another suite," he told her when he returned to her side.

Pretty standard setup at these resorts, apparently. She would be sure to handle it better this time, though. For one, Eva would make sure to spend as little time in the suite as possible. Less chance of running into Rafe as he exited the shower or returned sweaty and breathless from a morning run. And less chance of another unplanned kiss.

They were only here for three days. How hard could it be? The resort manager had insisted they stay on after their meeting as his personal guests, regardless of which way the negotiations went. Eva suspected the man's generous invitation had less to do with rum purchases and more with finding out who Rafe was and learning about the app he'd created.

Since their trip to San Juan, she and Rafe had developed something of a solid working relationship. Though she wasn't entirely convinced about his plan to take Gato Rums to a higher stratosphere, he'd made her feel less anxious by taking the time to chart out his exact goals for the expansion and the way he intended to finance those goals. One thing was certain: if the distillery was to exclusively supply several resorts with their rum, there would be some major investments that needed to be made, everything from purchasing more equipment to hiring new staff.

He'd certainly made it sound doable. So she would reserve judgment. For now.

A bellhop relieved them of their bags and they made their way down a concrete path to their accommodations. The golden sand of the beach glittered in the distance and a gentle wind alleviated a small amount of the heat. A sideways-walking land crab moved by her toe into the nearby bushes. This place had an apt name, as it really was something of a paradise.

Much like the hotel in San Juan, there appeared to be a lot of newlyweds. Just a cursory glance around showed her several couples holding hands, feeding each other at the outdoor tables or frolicking in the pool together.

"I guess resorts are popular places for honeymooners," Rafe commented, clearly thinking along the same lines.

"Not surprising," Eva answered, hating how wistful her voice sounded. Her own honeymoon had left her tired and frazzled by the time it was over. "Considering what a romantic and relaxing time these resorts offer."

"Is this the kind of place you flew off to after getting married?" he asked. His eyes were hidden behind shiny aviator sunglasses with a gold rim.

Eva laughed with a bitter tone. "No. Victor insisted we go to Las Vegas. That should have been my big clue about how he liked to spend his time." She'd been blind to so much—foolishly so.

The layout of the suite was quite similar to the one they'd shared in San Juan. A wet bar stood in the back corner of the room, while a flat-screen TV hung above the mantel. A sliding glass door led to a balcony overlooking the beachfront. The bedrooms were set up to look like the cabin of a boat, complete with fake portholes in the wall.

After freshening up, Eva left her room to find Rafe had already changed. He stood staring at a promotional video about all the attractions the resort had to offer.

"So I was thinking," he began when he saw her. "We don't meet with the bar manager until morning. I say we take the time to check out the property and take advantage of some time in the sunshine while we're here."

Eva couldn't think of a possible reason to say no to that, so moments later, they were standing at a tall table in the bar being served the resort's signature cocktail. The menu said it was called New Paradise tropical iced tea. It tasted divine, a burst of fruity flavor on her tongue.

Rafe seemed to be enjoying it also, as his tall glass was already halfway empty. She studied him, trying not to be discovered doing so. The lines of tension along his lips seemed to have softened; his breath was steady and slow, and he appeared much more at east than he had those first few days after he'd arrived. In fact, she'd noticed him becoming more and more relaxed with every passing day back in Puerto Rico.

"What made you do it?" she asked, surprising herself. She wasn't aware that she'd even intended to ask the question. Maybe it was the tropical iced tea. "What made you leave your life behind to move to an island and into an entirely different career? Did it have anything to do with the incident you referred to that first morning after you arrived?"

Rafe leaned his elbows on the small table. The action brought them practically nose to nose. She could smell the citrus scent of his aftershave, the mint on his breath.

"Let's just say it was the proverbial straw that broke the camel's back."

"Must have been a very heavy straw." Why was she pushing this line of conversation? Rafe hadn't been very forthcoming about what had happened back in Seattle that had him replacing his whole life with a new one. The articles reported that he'd been involved in a late-night brawl, Eva didn't know how much might be mere gossip.

"I guess you could say that," he responded.

"There must be people back in Seattle who miss you," she prompted.

His eyes clouded over as he shook his head. "Nope. Afraid not. Not a single person."

He'd implied as much that first night when they'd gone shopping in town. Eva set her glass down. "How can that be?"

"It was just me and my mom growing up. She's gone now. And coding is a very solitary career. I didn't make a lot of acquaintances."

"What about girlfriends?" She cringed as soon as the words left her mouth. Such a personal question, but she was genuinely curious. How could someone like Rafe Malta not be attached to a woman at all times? He was successful, devilishly handsome and wealthy.

"I was seeing someone rather casually for a few months. She didn't like the unwanted attention of a scandal while she was auditioning to replace the lead in an Australian soap."

An actress, then. She must have been exceptionally beautiful. Not surprising, considering what a catch Rafe would be considered by most women. A twinge-like sensation ruffled in her middle, but she refused to acknowledge it as any kind of jealousy.

Rafe held his glass up in a mock salute to her before taking a large swig. "So, no one. That would be the correct answer to your question about who might be missing me."

Maybe she was pushing, but Eva couldn't seem to stop herself. "Would you have invited her to come with you to Puerto Rico otherwise?" The thought of Rafe showing up that day with a woman by his side made her shoulders tighten, and Eva shivered at that thought. How out of place she would have felt as a third wheel, how awkward and uncomfortable.

Why was she punishing herself by pursuing these questions?

Rafe's reaction was immediate. "Absolutely not. No. The relationship wasn't that serious, for one." He answered her question with a clear shudder. "Our split was just another step on the way to making my decision. There was nothing and no one left for me to stay in Seattle for."

The words *I'm sorry* hovered on the tip of her tongue, but they seemed oddly inappropriate for the moment. Before she could think of anything else to say instead, Rafe ordered another round for them.

Eva made a mental note to go slowly with her second. The bartender had been rather generous with the spirits and she needed her wits about her being alone with Rafe—especially considering they'd be returning to the same suite yet again at the end of the evening.

They didn't need a replay of what had happened in San Juan.

Rafe couldn't recall the last time he'd felt this relaxed, this carefree. A man could get used to this vacationing-on-a-tropical-resort thing. Though something told him his present company might have something to do with how much he was enjoying himself.

He studied Eva now over the rim of his glass. Dressed in a spaghetti strap cropped tank that showed just enough of her tan midriff and a colorful sarong, she was turning more than a few heads in their direction. Rafe couldn't seem to take his eyes off her himself, for that matter. The woman was downright striking. Did she even know it? He suspected not.

Steady there, fella. She's your most important employee.

How many times did he have to remind himself to avoid such thoughts about her? But that was becoming more and more difficult to do with each passing day in her company. Especially when he remembered the way her lips had tasted against his, and the way she'd felt in his arms. Three days didn't seem like a long time on a calendar, but it could be an eternity when one was faced with constant temptation.

More than once, he'd caught himself wondering how things might have been different between them if they'd met under any other circumstances. Rafe suspected he would have fought harder for Eva if she'd been the woman he was dating back in Seattle.

The train of thought led to other questions that unnerved him. How might Eva have reacted if she'd been the woman with him that night? If she'd seen the way he'd behaved after losing his temper?

The relaxation he'd been enjoying only moments ago flushed away like a dam had been demolished. Unwanted images snapped through his mind before he could stop them: The flashing lights of patrol cars. Cuffs snapping onto his wrists. Black ink on his fingertips. Pain and regret surged through his core. Eva's voice interrupted his thoughts in the nick of time, before he could spiral further down the hole of dark memories.

"And where did you just drift off to?" she asked, concern and curiosity clouding her eyes.

"Trust me, you do not want to know."

She lifted one eyebrow. "You sure? Because wherever it was, it had you cursing quite bitterly."

He hadn't realized he'd said the explicit words out loud. "Sorry."

Her lips curved into a small smile. "What are you apologizing for? Zoning out just now? Or for cursing?"

Rafe couldn't even be sure. "Take your pick. I'll let you decide."

Eva's smile turned to a chuckle. "Well, if it's the latter, I'll have to remind you that I grew up with an older brother who's fairly active in the very male dominant world of sports car racing. Plus, I also grew up around field and factory workers who often let go of any polite pretenses at the end of a long and laborious day. My ears are accustomed to naughty words. Not to mention, I did my own fair share of cursing when I realized what a charlatan I'd married."

He tapped two fingers to his forehead in a salute. "Got it. No apologies necessary for colorful language."

What a pair they made—Rafe still licking his wounds from the ramifications of his own actions, and Eva still recovering from her sham of a marriage. Maybe that was why he felt such a strong connection to this woman he'd only met a few short weeks ago. None of it should have made any sense. All he knew was that he felt right talking to her, sharing things about his past he wouldn't dream of speaking of to anyone else. And he didn't want to leave her side just yet.

They'd both gone silent, but no awkwardness hung in the air between them. It was as if no more words needed to be spoken in the moment. The afternoon had grown darker, evening settling in around them. He was about to polish off his drink when a loud cheer erupted behind them, followed by the loud roar of applause.

Eva's head perked up in the direction of the noise. "Sounds like some kind of show."

A chorus of oohs and aahs echoed in the air.

"An impressive one from the sound of it," he replied. "Let's go check it out." He could use some kind of distraction.

Eva followed Rafe down a sandy, wooden pathway toward the beach. The raucous noise grew louder as they approached a pavilion stage near the water and a drumroll began to play just as they reached the crowd.

She gasped when she saw what all the commotion was about. The performer on stage held a torch alight with fire. Astonished, she watched as he put the entire flame in his mouth.

When he was done, he turned to the audience. "Want to see that again?" he asked, smiling and seemingly unscathed. "How about bigger this time?"

She joined the others in enthusiastic applause as the fires he lit grew larger and larger. Effortlessly, he swallowed each one.

"How does he do that?" she asked Rafe, incredulous at what she was watching. How exactly did one train to become a fire-eater?

"The man must have a steel pipe where his throat ought to be."

By the fourth flame, Eva didn't think she could handle watching much more. The fire was the size of a traffic cone at that point and she could have sworn she felt the heat of it even at their distance from the stage. Mercifully, the man finally took a bow and waved to the audience. Everyone responded with a much-deserved standing ovation.

"Oh, thank heavens," Eva muttered, hand to her chest.

A tuxedoed MC appeared on stage with a microphone to announce a reggae band would follow as the next performance.

"A fire-eater is going to be a tough act to follow," Rafe announced as they watched the four musicians set up.

Within moments, they were listening to the upbeat sounds of island pop music. Several people hopped onto the makeshift dance floor in front of the stage.

To her surprise and, admittedly, to her delight, Rafe straightened and offered her his hand. "How about it?" he asked, his smile sending a shiver along her skin. "Dance with me?"

Despite having nursed it, Eva figured the drink back at the bar had to have gone straight to her head. Why else would she be taking Rafe up on his suggestion? She took the hand he offered and followed him down near the other dancing couples.

Dancing with Rafe was so not a good idea, and hardly a professional activity covered in her job description, but it was hard to contain her enthusiasm.

In her defense, it had been so long since she'd danced with a man. Victor had declined most opportunities to do so during their brief time together, protesting that he had no rhythm and possessed two left feet. Now that he was gone and out of her life, Eva could see his many refusals for what they were: signs of a narcissist who refused to step out of his comfort zone for anyone else's benefit.

Eva began swaying to the bouncy tune. To her surprise, Rafe was impressively coordinated and completely in step with the beat. A man of many talents. She wouldn't have pegged him as the dancing type.

"You've been holding out on me," she yelled over the music. "You never mentioned what a good dancer you are."

He winked at her and it sent a wave of pleasure through her center. "In my late teens I worked as a busboy at a grunge club in Seattle," he told her, his voice raised above the noise. "Sometimes the bands booked at the venue stayed on and kept playing after closing. The rest of the staff and I took advantage of the free private shows."

"Grunge, huh? Not a lot of that playing in Puerto Rico or the Bahamas."

"The music may be different, but some dance moves are universal," he told her. To demonstrate, he took her by the wrist, then twirled her. Laughter bubbled up from Eva's throat as he proceeded to spin her around in a slow circle, then dipped her low. The gentle breeze felt like a caress on her cheeks and the salty scent of the ocean tickled her nostrils.

Eva soaked it all in: the joyful noises around them, the pulsing tempo of the music, the pure glee of dancing on the beach.

Heaven help her, she was having fun! For the first time in about two years, she was actually allowing herself to just enjoy the moment. Reality would come soon enough.

A low voice in her mind nagged that she had no right. How could she be out here enjoying herself as if she hadn't a care in the world?

After what she'd done to her family.

Her step faltered and she felt herself tipping. Rafe reached out and grabbed for her before she could stumble. Suddenly, Eva was sprawled against him, held tight in his arms, her cheek resting on his shoulder just as the song ended.

The band wasn't silent for long. Before Eva could make any kind of move to step away, it started up a reggae version of a traditional tango song.

Rafe straightened. His arm went around her upper back, and he held her other hand in the air in the classic beginning position.

"You'll have to help me out with this one," he said, his eyes darkening on her. "I can't say I've ever done the tango before. I'm guessing you might have, though."

Without thinking, Eva led him through the first few steps. He got the hang of it in no time. Then they were dancing like two familiar lovers, matching each other move for move.

The thought brought a rush of heat to her cheeks and her heart hammered against her chest. They could have been the only two people on the beach in that moment. Moving with him this way, so intimately, felt right and real…even as alarm bells rung in her head that she had to stop whatever was happening between them.

But right now, she felt powerless to do so.

Finally, the song ended and they were surrounded by silence for several beats. Then a chorus of voices erupted around them and Eva became remotely aware that they'd somehow garnered attention from their fellow dancers who were applauding and cheering them. The noise hardly registered in her ears, though, the pounding in her head drowning out all else. Her vision had narrowed to a tunnel. Only Rafe remained in her focus. Heaven help her, if he tried to kiss her now, she would let him. Despite the slew of people around them, she would lean into his kiss and return it.

Stop it.

On shaky legs, she finally forced herself to pull away. Rafe cleared his throat, then crammed his hands into his pockets. "That was, uh…" He trailed off, then looked off to the side and the gentle crashing waves.

She'd be hard-pressed to find the appropriate words herself. There was no point in even trying.

"I think I've had enough dancing for tonight," she stammered out. There was no way they could continue. The next song playing was a soft ballad that had everyone around them slow dancing in each other's embrace. "I'm suddenly very tired." They both knew it was a lame excuse, but it was all her scrambled mind could come up with.

Something shifted behind Rafe's eyes. He motioned for her to lead them off the makeshift dance floor.

When they reached their suite, she didn't bother to linger in the common area.

"I think I'll order room service," she said, making her way hastily to her door. "If it's all the same to you. All that spontaneous dancing has left me rather beat."

"Of course," he replied, his voice gravel rough. "Whatever you prefer."

She nodded, certain that he wasn't buying the excuse but grateful he wasn't asking any questions about her sudden bout of fatigue. "Then I'll see you in the morning. Good night, Rafe."

She stepped into her room and shut the door before he could so much as return the pleasantry. It took several moments to regain her shaky breath.

Rafe was up earlier than he would have liked the next morning. He had no idea what he might say to Eva when he saw her. Lines had been blurred yesterday in a way that had confused and rattled him. Their kiss in San Juan had been easy to dismiss. It had been a spontaneous moment, coming about by accident.

Dancing together yesterday couldn't be so easily downplayed. He'd lain awake half the night trying to process exactly how to address the proverbial elephant in the room. There was an electricity of attraction between him and Eva that was becoming more and more difficult to ignore.

If he was confused, Eva had acted downright skittish.

They still had to get through this meeting with the resort's food and beverage director.

Rafe poured his second cup of coffee and had just started rehearsing his pitch mentally when Eva stepped out of her room, greeting him with a hesitant smile.

Damn it. This was exactly what they didn't need— this tension and sense of awkwardness between them. He thought of all the reasons he should have kept his hands off of her last night. As soon as the music had changed to that tango tune, a dance that required intimate contact, he should have simply declared the dancing over and stepped away.

"Good morning," he offered.

"Morning." She pointed to the serving tray. "Thanks for ordering coffee already."

"Sure thing."

Dressed in an emerald green button-down shirtdress, cinched at the waist, and strappy leather sandals, she looked freshly scrubbed and ready to tackle the day ahead. He had to hand it to her. The outfit she wore was the perfect balance, professional enough for a business meeting yet casual enough so that she didn't stick out at an island resort.

Then again, the woman would look good wearing a canvas sack. Or wearing nothing.

He swore silently. *Don't go there.*

Fifteen minutes later, they were seated at an outdoor picnic table by a crystal blue infinity pool. Paolo Bertrand had been the New Paradise beverage and food director for over ten years. A heavyset man with thinning hair and a thick mustache, he had a warm smile that immediately made them feel welcome. Like in San Juan, Rafe started with the numbers part of their spiel. Then Eva took over with her detailed knowledge of the rum and all the distinctive taste patterns Gato Rums could provide for the resort's cocktails.

The meeting went well enough, but unlike the last one, they weren't able to secure any kind of agreement, though Paolo assured them he would get back to them within a week or so. Rafe had been in business long enough to know that not every decision maker would have an answer immediately, but he would have much preferred to walk away with an understanding and signed paperwork.

"What do you two have planned for the rest of the day?" Paolo asked, escorting them back to the resort lobby.

"Hadn't really thought about it past this meeting," Rafe answered.

The other man clasped a hand to his chest with no small amount of exaggeration. "Oh, but you cannot waste this beautiful day in paradise." He turned to Eva and shot an imploring look to her as well.

"What do you suggest?" Eva asked him.

"There's so much to do," Paolo declared. "Snorkeling, parasailing. Or the excursion we're known for here—Calypso Island."

Rafe recalled reading briefly about the small island a few miles off the beach. It had been established as both a tourist attraction and a habitat for several flora and fauna species. The resort offered daily boat rides there for small groups of tourists. Beyond that, Rafe didn't know much else about it.

"What's Calypso Island?" Eva asked.

"An exotic wonderland," Paolo answered, "home to several species of wildlife and fauna indigenous to the Bahamian islands. Exotic birds, rare wildflowers and the endangered cyclura lizard. You can't come here and not visit."

Eva returned the man's wide smile, clearly charmed by his enthusiasm. "I'm definitely intrigued," she told him, glancing at Rafe with question.

They had a whole day ahead of them. At the very least, such an outing would distract them from the awkwardness that was sure to appear once the two of them were alone again.

"I'm game if you are," he answered.

Paolo clapped his hands together. "Fantastic. My nephew is captaining the boat this afternoon. I'll call him to let the crew know to expect two last-minute guests."

The three of them shook hands and Paolo bid them goodbye, leaving them by the check-in desk.

"That's the afternoon sorted, then," Eva offered as they stepped out into the brilliant sunshine. The day had grown considerably hotter, with little to no breeze. The ocean in the distance was waveless, dotted with swimmers trying to cool off.

"Not a bad way to spend an afternoon like this one," Rafe said, rolling up his sleeves and unbuttoning the top two buttons of his shirt. So far, the island temperatures since they'd arrived had been fairly comparable to the Puerto Rican clime.

"And I've never seen a Bahamian cyclura lizard before."

"Neither have I," he offered rather lamely.

Good thing they had found something to do, Rafe thought. Their small-talk game was swiftly becoming pretty dry.

Now they just had to get through the rest of the morning.

CHAPTER TEN

THE BOAT RIDE from the resort to the mini refuge island took less than ten minutes.

"Enjoy your explorations," a smiling crew member yelled after them and the other tourists as they disembarked. They'd been given detailed instructions about what was acceptable with regard to interacting with the animals.

After spending most of the day lying in a lounge chair and struggling with a paperback that wasn't holding her interest, Eva was happy to finally be up and about. The idea had been to avoid awkward time alone with Rafe. Not that she'd had any kind of success with that goal— she hadn't been able to stop thinking about him.

The way he'd moved to the music last night, how he'd held her in his arms… The intensity of his darkened, heated gaze on hers as they'd danced the tango.

The whole day had felt like scenes from some kind of dream or a romantic movie. Quite a fanciful thought— one she couldn't entertain right now. Her head wasn't in the right place, and she could hardly process her emotions.

She wasn't naive enough to think they could avoid addressing what was happening between them much longer, but it made more sense to do it back home. Playing tourist at a romantic, tropical resort full of adoring couples who couldn't seem to keep their hands off each other was an all-too-tempting environment. They were even sharing the same suite, for heaven's sake.

She'd have a much clearer head back in Puerto Rico. Or maybe she was just procrastinating because she had no idea how to even start such a conversation. What would she even say?

Hey, boss. So I think maybe we should try and cool it a bit and not act like hormonal teenagers who have a crush on each other.

"The sign says we're likely to see some iguanas that way," Rafe said, pulling her out of her thoughts. She'd been absentmindedly following him down a sandy path toward the center of the island. The other tourists seemed to have dispersed in myriad other directions.

"Or we could head the other way, where there's supposed to be some large African violet bush that houses several species of exotic birds."

"I say we start with lizards," she answered. Not a phrase she'd have anticipated saying before today. In fact, there were a lot of things happening to her she wouldn't have anticipated.

Rafe nodded, then stepped the other way. "Lizards it is."

They'd ventured a couple of yards or so when a black-and-white ball of fur darted in front of them and under a bush a few feet away. Startled, Eva clasped a hand to her chest. "What was that?"

"Not a lizard," Rafe answered. "Unless the Bahamian ones have fur."

A low mewing noise sounded from the bush the furball had run under. "Do you hear that?" Eva asked, straining her ears. "It sounds like a cat."

Rafe rubbed his chin. "What would a cat be doing here? I doubt felines are one of the rare indigenous creatures inhabiting this island."

"I don't know. I suppose it must have stowed away on one of the boats and then gotten stuck here."

The mewing seemed to grow louder. "We can't just leave it here, can we?" Rafe asked.

She wouldn't even entertain the thought. A kitten didn't belong alone on an isolated island full of wild creatures who may hurt it. Or worse. "Absolutely not."

"Huh. Let's go tell the crew, then. Maybe they can send someone out to fetch it and take it back to an animal shelter on the main island."

That sounded like as good a plan as any. Before they turned to do just that, the little creature darted out once more and ran farther away, deeper into the rough. Despite moving rather fast, Eva could tell it was limping drastically on one side, which would explain the mewing cries. "I think it's hurt," she said, following the little paw prints in the sand. "The poor thing."

"I wonder how long it's been here."

Eva felt a rush of tears to her eyes. "She must be in pain. And so scared."

"I'll bet it's starving, too."

They followed the sound of mews until they reached yet another bush. A large insect jumped across Eva's foot and she bit back a startled yelp. "We can't just keep chasing it. We might be making its injury worse."

"I don't suppose you have anything that might lure her out?"

Eva reached into her dress pocket. "You're a genius!"

Rafe tossed her a pleased smile. "I am?"

"Yes!" she declared, pulling out what she'd been carrying next to her cell phone. "Because you reminded me of this. As luck would have it, I grabbed a granola bar from one of the breakfast buffets because I wasn't sure how long this tour would be." She flashed him the granola bar.

"I'd say the genius is the person who happens to have food in her pocket."

Or maybe they just made a good team, Eva thought—though she would keep that thought to herself.

It took some coaxing, and a trail of granola bits thrown its way, but the cat slowly made its way to them. Eva deftly managed to pick the animal up without spooking it while it was distracted by the food. She stood with it cradled in her arms.

She immediately saw what had the poor animal in such distress. Several sharp burrs had dug into its two hind legs.

"Help me hold her steady?" she said to Rafe. He immediately complied and she cautiously removed each offending burr. For her efforts, she was gifted with a few swipes of needle-sharp claws. But the poor thing was too weak to do more than scratch the surface of Eva's skin.

Finally, when Eva had removed the last sharp prick, the cat mewed softly, then set its head down on her forearm.

"How ironic that someone named Gato would be rescuing a cat," Rafe commented.

That was rather amusing. "Perhaps it's fate, predestined," Eva speculated. "I've never rescued one before, or anything else for that matter."

"Let's see if we can get this little one on the boat and then back to civilization."

Gingerly, she stepped out of the shrubbery and started heading toward the beach. Rafe stopped her with a hand on her shoulder. "That's not the right way."

"Are you sure?"

He glanced over his shoulder. Then past hers. "I guess not entirely."

It appeared they were lost. After several false starts, they finally determined the right path and started walking back to the shore.

But when they got to the dock where the boat had been, it was completely empty.

Rafe swore. "I don't believe this. Looks like they all left. We must have been gone longer than we thought."

Eva maneuvered around the animal in her arms to click on her cell phone. Her heart sank when she saw the screen. "I have no signal."

Rafe quickly scanned his own phone. "Neither do I."

Her heart pounded in her chest. This couldn't be happening. "So now what?"

Rafe rubbed a hand down his face. "Maybe we can catch a cell tower signal farther into the water."

Rafe kicked his shoes off and ventured several feet into the ocean. Even from this distance, Eva could tell from his expression that he was having no luck. When he came back to her side, he was soaked up to his waist.

"Any thoughts of a plan B?" she asked, the trepidation now cresting into a full peak in her chest.

Rafe shoved his phone into his now wet pocket. "Well, Paolo said the tours come daily. Worst case scenario, we're here until the next one arrives tomorrow."

Blood rushed out of her face at the thought of being stranded. "That's a pretty bad scenario."

"Maybe there are other resorts who send guests here." Although Rafe didn't sound convinced, Eva decided she would latch on to that possibility—and fervently hoped it was a feasible one.

She was stranded on an island with a man she'd been trying to avoid being alone with. If the scenario weren't so dire, it would have made her laugh.

This couldn't really be happening. How had he ended up in what could be a scene out of an adventure movie? Rafe powered off his phone and reset it for what had to be the dozenth time.

"Anything?" Eva asked, studying the device. The cat still slept, curled up in her arms. As happy as Rafe was that they'd rescued the poor thing, the silly castaway was the reason they were in this mess.

Stranded on an island. It was almost comical. If it weren't so dire.

"Not a single bar," he answered Eva, slamming the phone back into his pants pocket.

"I don't understand how they could have just left us here."

"Paolo said he was going to call to add us to the manifest. I'm guessing it was so last minute no one informed the crew member in charge of head count."

"Maybe they'll figure it out and come back for us," Eva stated. The words sounded like a plea to the universe.

"Maybe," he agreed, though he didn't believe it for a second. Most likely, everyone was off the boat and on to thinking about their dinner plans by now.

He and Eva needed some kind of plan. They couldn't just stand here lamenting their luck. Plus, Eva was clearly agitated, her breath coming in gasps, her voice sounding pitchy and strained. She was panicking. They had to expend some of her nervous energy.

"Let's walk around the perimeter of the beach," he suggested. "Maybe we'll see a sailboat or someone out deep-sea fishing."

She nodded. "Good idea."

He sure hoped so, though it was a risky one. Being so far from the dock meant they might miss the boat if it did happen to come back for them. But he really didn't want to split up. The idea of leaving Eva alone on the beach didn't sit right, not in her agitated state.

They strode in silence for several minutes right on the edge of the water, the cat still cradled in Eva's arms, but nothing appeared on the horizon, not so much as a sailboat.

They'd been walking for close to ninety minutes when Rafe finally decided he had to admit the inevitable. The sky was growing darker, the possibility of any other boats arriving growing dimmer.

"How can the waters be so empty?" Eva asked, as if reading his thoughts.

"Maybe it's just our luck."

As if he'd tempted fate with his words, a massive storm cloud seemed to appear out of nowhere above them in the sky. Strong gusts of wind blew from every direction. Eva's dress skirt whipped around her legs. The kitten in her arms stirred at the disturbance.

That settled it. Some deity above was most definitely toying with them.

"You've got to be kidding me." Eva groaned. "This cannot possibly get worse."

A fat raindrop landed on her nose before she got the last word out. It was followed by several more. The cat let out an outraged meow as a few landed on her dark fur.

"We have to find shelter," he told her. "Follow me."

They'd seen a small cave during their quest for the kitten earlier. Not ideal, but at least it would provide a roof over their heads. Otherwise, they were about to be drenched and left dodging flying sand and other debris.

He could only hope a pack of lizards didn't have the same idea to take shelter there.

Eva fell in step behind him and within moments he'd located the dark opening. He sensed Eva's steps faltering behind him before they'd reached the mouth of the cave.

"What's the matter?" He turned to ask over his shoulder.

"Uh, is it safe in there?"

"Safe?"

"Like…is it empty?"

Rafe pinched the bridge of his nose. The cave was safer than being out here. Still, he couldn't exactly blame her for being apprehensive. The opening looked ebony dark. "I'll go check it out first."

She nodded, her eyes filling with gratitude. "Thank you."

A cursory investigation a few feet in told him the cave was empty enough, sparing a few earthworms that moved out of the way when he stepped in. He motioned for Eva to come in after him.

She gingerly stepped inside, still cradling the cat, who seemed all too comfortable in Eva's arms.

"Well, it's not the Ritz," he said, striving for a light tone. "But it's a hole with a roof."

"A very dark hole," Eva said, eyes glistening in the darkness.

He fished his phone out of his pocket, called up the flashlight feature and clicked on it. A circular ray of light illuminated a small area around them. "No service but it's good for this, at least."

"Do you think there are bats in here?" she asked, her voice tight with apprehension.

Most certainly, Rafe thought. Eva had to know it, too. She was aiming for denial. "I don't know," he lied. "If there are, I'm sure they're much deeper into the depths. We're barely inside."

The tension in her face muscles seemed to relax just a bit. "I'm good with most animals. Just not bats. They give me the heebie-jeebies."

He had to smile at that. "The heebie-jeebies, huh?" Speaking of animals, she had to be tired of holding the one currently glued to her middle. "Here, let me take the cat for a bit."

She gently handed the animal over. The cat lifted a small paw in protest at the change, but then seemed to give in and settled against his chest. With one hand, he helped Eva lower herself to a seated position against the wall.

"Nothing to do but wait it out, I guess." She leaned her head back, then closed her eyes. The soft white light cast shadows over her features: regal jawline, soft nose, long, dark lashes. She had a dark smudge of dirt on her right cheek, and her hair had come loose out of its bun and fallen wildly over her face and shoulders. She was utterly stunning.

"I hope it stops soon," Eva said in a weary whisper, her eyes remaining closed. She looked utterly exhausted. Rafe's heart tugged in his chest. How had he let them fall into such a ridiculous predicament? He should have told Eva they needed to get back to the boat to have a crew member find the feral cat. If he'd only done that one simple thing, they'd be nice and warm and dry right now back at their suite. Hindsight and all that.

Rafe settled in next to Eva against the wall. "I'm guessing it's a flash storm that came out of nowhere and will probably be gone just as fast." Another lie. The commotion outside showed no sign of letting up.

Not anytime soon.

CHAPTER ELEVEN

How in the world had she ended up here? Eva shifted her weight in an effort to get more comfortable against the hard rock wall. To no avail. There was no way to make any of this more comfortable.

Her world had somehow turned to utter chaos when she hadn't been paying attention. It had only taken a few short years. She'd once been so proud of herself and all that the future held for her. School had come almost too easily. She'd gotten stellar grades and been a star with her professors. The only career she'd ever wanted was there waiting for her upon graduation. She'd had so much that she'd taken for granted: a beautiful home, a doting father, a loving sibling and a devoted friend in Fran. It had been almost perfect.

Aside from the trauma of her mother leaving, she'd led a picture-perfect life. And somehow it had all come crumbling down and she'd ended up here—shivering and wet in a dark cave with no clear idea as to when she'd be able to get out and back to civilization.

Eva felt tears of frustration and sadness sting her eyes and she fought them back. Crying wouldn't do her any good. It hadn't so far.

She had no idea how long she and Rafe had been in

the cave. They simply sat in the quiet, neither one speaking a word. Finally, Rafe broke the silence.

Rafe leaned over the cat in his lap to pick up the phone on the ground next to his leg. "I hate to do this, but we should really turn the flashlight off. We might need it later and can't risk it running out of battery."

"All right."

The world went completely dark when he shut it off. Only the sound of the pounding rain and harsh wind outside filled the air, along with a gentle, soft purring that somehow served to soothe her nerves a little. How could the kitten be sleeping through all this? Probably due to the relief of finally being free of the painful burrs. She didn't regret helping the poor creature. Of course she didn't. Eva just wished she'd thought of a different way to do so.

A bolt of lightning flashed outside, lighting up the sky and her view out of the cave. The scene outside the opening looked like something out of a gothic movie, right before it all went pitch-black again a split second later. The ocean had appeared like ebony ink in the distance. The shrubbery just outside looked dark and eerie. A shiver ran down her spine.

"Are you cold?" Rafe asked, mistaking her shudder. Without waiting for an answer, he shifted closer to her and wrapped an arm around her shoulders.

Though she hadn't felt chilled, the warmth of his body sent a wave of soothing comfort through her skin. Reflexively, she nestled in closer to his length.

"I'm so sorry, Rafe," she said with a deep sigh.

"What are you apologizing for?"

He had to ask?

"Isn't it obvious? I'm the one who chased after a cat,

getting us lost in the process, then sat with her until our ride back to civilization left us behind. This is all my fault." The laugh out of her that followed sounded nearly maniacal to her own ears. How many times had she uttered that phrase lately?

"I'd like you to try and get those words out of your vernacular, Eva. Just try."

"How can you deny that my actions led to us being here?" she demanded. Her voice sounded harsh, though she realized how unreasonable that was. Rafe was simply being kind.

Rafe gave her shoulder a squeeze. "We're equally culpable."

She grunted a chuckle. "How do you figure that?"

He shrugged against her. "I was just thinking how all I had to do was suggest we go back to the boat to notify someone that there was a domestic animal on the island that clearly didn't belong here. I followed our little pal just the same way you did."

"As if I gave you a chance to do anything else."

"Last I checked I had free will. I was perfectly capable back then of telling you no."

"That seems to be my problem. No one ever seems to tell me no. Or that I've messed up." Something about sitting in the dark must have loosened her tongue. She'd had no idea she was going to utter those words until they were out of her mouth.

"You think that's a problem?"

"I'm saying it's a double-edged sword."

"I think you've gotten too used to swallowing blame. Guilt is almost second nature to you now, isn't it? Because of one bad move you made."

"It was a disastrous move, Rafe. A calamity that led to other calamities."

"I agree."

His answer surprised her for its bluntness. "You do?"

"Yep. You experienced the type of betrayal most people would never recover from. They might become bitter and angry for years after. Maybe forever."

Ah, so that was his angle. A dose of reverse psychology. She wasn't going to fall for it. "I'd say they'd have every right." As would she.

He rested his head back against the wall, Eva sensing and hearing the motion more than she could make out anything in the dark. "Maybe. But it would be a terrible way to live. A waste of life."

She supposed he had a point. But she was in no mood to entertain it at the moment—or to tell him that he might be right.

Rafe spoke again. "You mentioned no one told you no, that your father and brother were forgiving and understanding through it all."

"That's right." The same way Rafe was being now, about the fact they were stranded on an island as a direct result of her impromptu decisions.

"Have you ever thought of forgiving yourself?" he asked, his voiced drifting to her in the dark.

The question rattled her.

"The way your father and brother have?" Rafe added.

Of course, she'd thought about it—wished there was some way that she might. The effort had been futile, beyond reach.

"I don't think I can."

"Why?" He sounded utterly exasperated.

"Not until I've made some kind of restitution or figured out a way to undo the damage my actions caused."

"Like what?"

She honestly didn't know. Not that she hadn't racked her brain trying to come up with a solution. "That's the question, isn't it?" The obvious answer was to get the distillery back somehow. But it belonged to Rafe now. There was no way she could afford a repurchase. Not without a miracle.

"Look," Rafe began. He sounded like he was about to try a different tactic, as the last one had clearly fallen flat. "As someone who's never been given any kind of grace throughout any part of his life, my suggestion is that you do your best to try and move on and appreciate the way your father and brother love you. Trust me."

His words gave her pause—not so much his advice, but the first part of what he'd said. *Never been given any kind of grace.*

Eva had been sitting here, doing what she so often did—focusing on herself and what she'd been going through. What exactly was Rafe's story?

She'd been telling herself she didn't want to push. But it occurred to her that maybe she should have.

"Tell me." She reached for his arm, took his hand in hers. "I want to hear it, Rafe."

Rafe felt his muscles tighten up at Eva's prompt. The poor animal in his lap must have sensed the tension in his muscles as it stirred with a stretch, then moved over to settle on top of Eva's thighs.

"I want to hear whatever you're ready to tell me," she repeated. The words nudged him toward a trip down memory lane he wasn't sure he was ready to take—a trip he'd been avoiding for as long as he could.

"What happened that night in Seattle?" Eva's voice was barely more than a whisper.

His heart hammered in his chest. Sitting here in the dark, with her delicate yet strong hand holding tight to his, a part of him wanted nothing more than to vent all of it. Just let it go once and for all.

An equally strong part of him wanted it buried deep and well in the past where it belonged. Except it wasn't really fully submerged there, was it? Not judging by the way a layer of sweat had formed on his forehead.

He took a deep breath, trying to figure out how to begin in such a way that he might shut the conversation down if it became too much. The pitch-black of the darkness helped.

He released a deep sigh. "The same thing that had been happening for years. Only this time I reacted."

Eva gave his hand a reassuring squeeze, silent encouragement to continue.

"The one time I didn't walk away."

"How so?"

The answer to that question was where his thoughts got all jumbled up. What had gone down that day had started years earlier—scab after scab that had been repeatedly picked at, leaving countless scars.

"I ran into someone from my past that night. It didn't go well."

"Your past?"

Maybe it was the complete darkness, or maybe it was simply the way Eva was holding his hand, but his mind didn't immediately shut down at the thought of getting into the telling of that night the way it usually did.

"I didn't have a lot growing up," he began, grasping for the right words. "It was just me and my mom. She resented me. I sensed it before I was old enough to form coherent thoughts."

He heard her suck in a breath. Though his mouth had gone dry, he made himself continue. "My mom stuck around, but we both might have been better off if she hadn't. The older I got, the colder she became. For her, a preteen son meant nothing but responsibility and another mouth to feed."

"Oh, Rafe." Eva's voice held no trace of pity, just understanding and sympathy. She had no idea how much that meant.

"So I did my best to stay out of her way," he continued. "Studied a lot. Stayed after school to use the computer lab. Went to the library on the weekends to use the computers there."

"You must have been so lonely."

He hadn't realized it then, hadn't felt alone. And compared to what had come next in his life, the solitude had been a blessing.

"The hard work paid off." In one sense, anyway. "A teacher noticed I had a gift, as he called it. He helped me to reach out to a prestigious boarding school outside of Seattle. I got in with a full scholarship."

"That sounds like quite an accomplishment."

"It was the beginning of a nightmare. I tried to leave more than once. But whenever I asked to come back home, my mom immediately shut it down. She finally had her freedom and didn't want me around. For months, I couldn't even reach her." He drew a breath deep into his lungs. "She didn't return my calls."

"Oh, no," Eva said on a soft whisper.

"I didn't fit in at Brimford Boarding School for Young Men. The other boys made sure to remind me in frequent and often humiliating ways just how much I did not belong there with them."

Thoughts rushed through his mind of the frequent beatings he'd taken, the humiliating shoves for simply walking down the hallway to class. The laptop he'd had to learn to fix after it had been pulled out of his hands and thrown into a nearby bush. The sneers and taunts that made fun of his clothes, his hair, his very self.

"What did they do?"

"I wasn't a terribly bulky teenager. In fact, I was downright scrawny by comparison. I hadn't reached a growth spurt yet."

He heard her sniffle and hoped she wasn't crying for him, because he couldn't bear that.

"I survived it, obviously, graduated and got into Berkeley, again with a full scholarship. Then I developed the productivity app that was successful beyond my wildest dreams. So I did my best to put it all behind me. Until about a decade later, when I ran into one of my old classmates. And then it was as if nothing had changed."

Eva's heart was slowly splintering in her chest for the boy Rafe had been, and all the obstacles he'd had to overcome to become the highly successful man he was now. How different their childhoods had been. Eva had always enjoyed the bastion of love so freely lavished on her by her family—Nana's maternal comfort, Papá's quiet yet fierce affection, Teo's brotherly protectiveness.

Rafe hadn't enjoyed anything remotely similar.

He'd been silent for several moments now, only the sound of his breathing echoing through the darkness.

She waited patiently, willing him to continue for both their sakes. She'd bet her next breath that he needed to get some of this out and off his chest. For her, she desperately wanted to understand him better, to learn more about what he'd endured to get to where he was as the accomplished tech tycoon who'd come so far from his origins.

Just as she considered how to give him a little nudge, Rafe slowly began speaking again.

"Trina convinced me to go out that night. Wanted to be seen at the newest dance club that was opening to VIPs only that evening. Clubbing is one of my least favorite things to do."

Eva hadn't missed the "to be seen" part of his statement. An interesting side note.

Rafe continued. "But that night I decided I liked arguing with her even less than going out. So I agreed." He sucked in a breath before going on. "A few minutes after we got there, I heard a loud, familiar voice call my name from behind, just as a heavy hand fell on my shoulder."

A knot of apprehension twisted in Eva's middle.

"I recognized him immediately despite the years since I'd seen him last: someone I'd gone to school with. A senior who'd been particularly cruel."

Eva could guess what had happened next.

"He acted like we were long-lost buddies or something. Talked about how he'd been reading about my successes over the years."

Bingo. She'd been right.

"I tried to brush him off, wanted nothing to do with his fake memories. He'd made my life a daily hell and now he wanted to pretend we were simply old school chums."

"What happened next?"

"He became hostile immediately. He made derogatory comments about how I might have fooled everyone but he knew who I really was. I tried to walk away. I really did." She heard him take a shaky breath. "But as soon as I turned I felt a forceful shove that nearly sent me to the floor. Just like back at school."

"Oh, Rafe."

"And then something I can't even describe just came over me. I couldn't take it one more second, not one more thing. I turned back around and threw the first punch—hard enough that I heard his jaw crack. I knew I'd broken it."

The brute had had it coming, more than deserved a punch and worse. But Eva kept the thought to herself and let Rafe continue.

"He had others with him who quickly became involved. Someone decided they were on my side and jumped. Before I knew it, the altercation had grown. Several more club goers became involved until it was some kind of crowd riot. By the time the authorities showed up, the place was a mess."

"Oh, my," Eva whispered. She'd read various reports but hadn't looked into the details. Those gossip sites weren't ones she visited; she hardly considered them credible.

Rafe went on. "I awoke the next morning with a cut lip and a bruised face and a heart full of remorse. Then there were all the tabloid headlines online. They all read something to the effect that it was no wonder given my background and where I came from. Such behavior was hardly surprising given my upbringing. Someone started a rumor that I might have stolen the app idea, that a man like me couldn't have come up with it and developed it myself. It all became too much. I had no place in my own life."

Eva supplied the rest. "So you walked away from it all to become a rum distiller in Puerto Rico."

She felt him nod next to her. "That's right. I paid the establishment for damages, covered the cost of medical bills for anyone who was injured and completed a short probationary penalty. Then I began to pack. You know the rest."

Eva took a moment to process all that she'd just been told. It was a wonder the man hadn't rebuffed all of humanity and gone off to become a hermit somewhere. She was about to tell him how much his resilience and strength impressed her when Rafe surprised her with his next words.

"I'm just sorry my newfound life came at such a personal cost to you, Eva."

Eva sucked in a breath. "I did that to myself, Rafe. If you hadn't bought Gato Rums, someone else would have." That was the absolute truth.

She felt him squeeze her hand before he let it go. "I will say that I'm not sorry I made the purchase. Because otherwise, I would have never met you."

Eva couldn't help the small chuckle that escaped her. "Yeah? Well, you also wouldn't be stranded on an island in the middle of a violent tropical storm stuck in a cave."

Rafe didn't laugh in response. "Small price to pay."

CHAPTER TWELVE

A PAIR OF reptilian eyes were staring into his.

Rafe awoke with a start and tried hard to focus on his surroundings. It took a moment to recollect where he was. He and Eva had spent the night in the cave, and a large iguana had decided to share their space at some point.

A glance outside told him it was light out. Shockingly, they must have fallen asleep and stayed that way till morning. He had no clue what time it might be.

He used his foot to gently shoo the creature away. It swiveled its head in disgust but slowly started to saunter out of the opening. It appeared their rescue feline wasn't any kind of guard cat.

What he discovered next was almost as alarming as waking up to a lizard—Eva sat cradled in his lap. A vague recollection of her yelping in discomfort in the middle of the night surfaced in his mind. He remembered lifting her onto his thighs in an effort to make her more comfortable. Luckily, she was still asleep now as he pondered what to do about the predicament.

He was trying to figure out a gentle way to shift her from his lap when her eyes fluttered open. "Rafe?" Her voice sounded gravelly, full of sleep.

"Good morning, sweetheart."

Her gaze traveled to the opening, then filled with surprise. "I can't believe we were here all night."

Rafe watched her eyes widen as she registered exactly where and how she was sitting. But she made no effort to move. And he made no effort to let go of her. In fact, his hands seemed to move of their own volition and he grasped her tighter around the waist. And then the world seemed to stop, for Eva had moved to straddle him, her eyes clouded with desire. A searing need shot through him at the intimate contact.

"Rafe?" she repeated. His name on her lips only served to spike his desire. She was asking an entirely different question this time, and he was all too eager to answer it.

He thrust his hands into her hair, then pulled her head closer. But then he waited; the next move had to be hers. Her lips found his a moment later and he was mindless with need. He wanted her, so badly he ached with need.

She devoured his mouth with her own, sending heat and longing through his core. He would never get enough of her—her taste, her scent, the soft feel of her curves in his palms.

A warning cry shouted in his mind that this was madness. Neither one of them was thinking straight…or thinking at all. But he couldn't bring himself to heed it.

Yearnings he'd fought since he'd first laid eyes on her refused to be contained any longer, though he knew it was so wrong.

Eva moaned into his mouth and it was the sweetest sound he'd ever heard. But another noise reached his ears just then—a sound that had him slowly spinning back to reality.

With great effort, he made himself pull away. "We have to stop, sweetheart."

She blinked at him in confusion and he swore silently at how strong his urge was to take her mouth once more. The sound echoed from the distance outside again. If Eva heard it, she made no indication.

Rafe swallowed, fighting to catch his breath. "We have to stop," he repeated. "I think I hear a boat."

That seemed to finally catch her attention. Eva's eyes widened and she scrambled off him, holding her lips with her fingers. She hesitated for just a moment before reality seemed to dawn in her eyes.

"We have to get out there," she announced, her voice full of panic. With haste, she reached down to cradle the sleeping cat. Rafe stood with no small amount of effort, his stiff legs crying out in pain. He reached a hand to help Eva up. She groaned as she stood on wobbly legs.

When they stepped outside, a small speedboat could be seen in the water fast approaching the beach. It appeared to be carrying two men. Rafe recognized them as Paolo and his nephew, the captain who had brought them here yesterday. Even from here he could tell the former looked furious.

"Let's go." He took Eva by the elbow, helping her through the shrubbery and then the sand.

They reached the water just as the boat reached the shore.

Paolo jumped out, his hand clasped to his chest, offering a flurry of apologies. He pointed with his thumb behind him at the other man. "My nephew is a fool who should have been more competent than to leave two guests stranded on an island."

Rafe couldn't argue with that.

"I was looking for you this morning to discuss our deal and the two of you were nowhere to be found," Paolo explained. "I realized what must have happened after speaking with the crew."

It was just as they'd suspected; they hadn't been added on to the manifest list in time and had been forgotten as a result.

"I'm just glad you're here now," Eva said behind him. She lifted the load she held to show him. "We found a stray cat and chased him to make sure he wasn't left behind again. So it's partly our doing that we missed the boat."

Rafe bit back a retort at her statement. This wasn't the time to point it out, but the woman was practically apologizing for having been deserted, for heaven's sake.

The captain ducked his head, mumbling an apology of his own.

"How can we ever make this up to you?" Paolo asked, his tone full of remorse.

"Just get us back to the island," Rafe answered, taking Eva by the hand and helping her onboard.

The engine roared to life and they circled around. Eva sat next to him staring out at the horizon. The cat stretched and yawned in her arms, apparently not bothered by the motion of the boat.

Rafe swore under his breath. There was no way to deny any longer what was clearly happening between them—though now that they were headed back to the main island and back to reality, the folly of losing control the way he had back at the cave became undeniably clear. There was no question that he would have made love to her if the boat hadn't arrived when it did. He'd lost control both then and the night before when he'd overshared, telling her so much about Seattle and his life before.

And there was no way he could take any of it back.

It was hard to wrap her head around what had happened over the past twelve hours. Eva watched from her perch starboard as the main island came into view. Fran wasn't going to believe any of this when she told her.

Her phone immediately started buzzing as soon as they got within range. Eva was too tired and too emotionally drained to even check the screen. Whatever it was it could wait. She could still taste Rafe on her lips, and her body still felt heated where his hands had touched her skin.

A flush crept into her cheeks and she uttered a silent prayer of gratitude that it was too windy to notice—not that Rafe was so much as looking in her direction. He seemed just as wrapped up in his thoughts as she was.

When they disembarked on the dock moments later, her phone vibrated in her pocket once more.

She handed Paolo the cat. He assured them he'd bring it to a local veterinarian to be checked out and then to a shelter. A pang of loss swept through her as she handed the animal over. But she hardly had the mental nor physical room in her life right now for a pet.

Finally pulling the gadget out, she frowned at the screen.

"Everything all right?" Rafe asked as they made their way down the pathway leading to their suite.

"I'm not sure. Looks like everyone but Teo has left me messages. There's some from Nana, Fran and my father."

"That's curious," Rafe offered, though he sounded distracted. Eva could hardly blame him for not being hyper-focused on her at the moment. They'd been through quite an ordeal.

"I'll call them as soon as I can think straight," she told him. "Which isn't remotely likely to happen until I can take a shower and find some caffeine."

The rest of the walk followed in awkward silence. Eva released a sigh of relief when they finally reached the suite. She shut her room's door, then leaned against it to catch her breath.

Her phone vibrated again.

The screen popped up with the contact photo of her father. With a resigned sigh, Eva unlocked it and clicked on the icon. After what she'd done to the man, the least she could do was answer his phone call.

"Hola, Papá," she began. "I'm sorry I missed your calls. You wouldn't believe—"

But he cut her off before she could explain. What he told her turned her blood to ice.

Did she think less of him now? Rafe braced his palms against the tile wall of the shower and let the hot spray wash over him. The water felt welcome and soothing on his sore muscles but inside he still felt raw and bruised. He never talked to anyone about his past. For some reason, he'd poured out his soul to a woman who worked for him.

A mocking voice sounded in his head. That was a ridiculous way to describe Eva. She was so much more to him now than any employee. Even before the heated moment of passion, he'd grown to feel emotions and longings for her he'd never felt before. Too bad the timing and circumstances were so wrong. Rafe had no clear idea of who he was and what he wanted. He had no one in his life he was close to, no one he could so much as call a friend, other than his former secretary. What could a man like that offer a woman like Eva? Not much. She needed so much more in life than a loner who hadn't been able to establish even one close in every environment he'd ever found himself in. She'd been burned too badly before by her ex-husband. He didn't need to add any more turmoil to her life.

So what was he going to do about it?

With no easy or clear answers, he shut off the water in disgust and stepped out. He'd just toweled off and thrown a pair of shorts on when the sudden noise of loud knocking sounded at the door. He bit out a curse, not ready to deal with anyone or anything right now. All he wanted was a strong cup of coffee and to put his feet up until he regained some more blood circulation through his legs.

The knock sounded again.

Sighing, he walked over to the door and pulled it open. Eva stood on the other side. She was ghostly pale and visibly shaking. The urge to pull her into his arms was immediate and strong, whatever her anguish. He fisted his hands at his side instead.

"Eva? What's wrong? Has something happened?"

She nodded, tears flooding her eyes. "Yes. It's Teo. He's been in an accident."

Rafe felt his jaw fall open in shock and concern.

"I don't have the details," Eva continued, her voice shaky. "But I have to get back home right away. I have to get back to Puerto Rico as soon as possible."

Rafe did take hold of her then, embracing her tightly until the trembling slightly lessened, as if he could somehow absorb all her dismay. "Leave it to me," he said against her ear. "I'll take care of everything and get us back right away. Go pack your things."

She hiccupped a thank-you, then fled back to her room. Rafe absentmindedly found a shirt and threw it on. Then he started making phone calls.

They were on the runway about to take off in a private jet an hour after Eva had first knocked on Rafe's door. She had so much to thank him for. He'd arranged for a flight and even helped her with her packing. Right now, he sat in the seat next to her, holding tightly to her hand, simply offering the emotional crutch she so badly needed.

"You said Teo was in an accident," Rafe said as they taxied. "What happened?"

Eva closed her eyes, a shudder racking through her whole body. "A car accident. He's shattered his leg and hasn't woken since they took him in."

"Oh, my God, Eva. I'm so sorry, sweetheart."

She wanted so badly to shut down, to just switch off her emotions until they reached Puerto Rico, where she would have no choice but to confront all her fears. But she didn't deserve that luxury. She had to get this out, had to tell someone what she suspected. "My father said he was in Cordaro. There's an international raceway there. Papá said Teo was racing one of his cars."

Rafe lifted an eyebrow. "I thought he just collected and worked on cars. I didn't realize he raced them himself."

Guilt washed over her before she could answer. "He didn't. Not until now."

"What made him start?"

She groaned aloud as the tears flooded her eyes. "I think it was because of me."

Rafe turned to face her fully. "I don't understand."

Eva gripped his hand tighter, trying to absorb some of his strength and comfort. "Teo said something to me back at the hacienda, that first night after you arrived. He said that if I really wanted to buy the distillery back, that he would find a way to help me. I think that's what he was doing."

"How?"

"Apparently, it was a private event held by some hotshot businessman who offered a large cash prize. Teo must have entered. Then he crashed." The horror of her words threatened to overwhelm her, but she made herself continue. "And he did it because he wanted me to have the money."

"Eva, you can't believe that."

She did, because it was the only explanation that made sense. "I wish I'd never laid eyes on that man," she said, full of anguish and misery. Rafe could have no doubt who she was referring to.

Rafe released a deep sigh. "You couldn't help who you fell in love with, Eva."

Eva sucked in a breath, gathering her thoughts. "That's just it. What Victor and I had wasn't love. Deep in my soul I knew it. Real love wouldn't have asked so much of me until there was hardly anything left."

"What do you mean?"

Eva sucked in a much-needed breath, gathering the words she wanted to say. He had shared so much with her last night. Would it be so bad for her to share a little bit herself now?

She pushed ahead. "I was convinced there was something missing in my life when I met Victor," she confided. "I didn't even know what. But as much as I loved the hacienda and living on the island, I was yearning for some kind of excitement. Something different."

"Enter your ex," Rafe supplied.

She could only nod. "He seemed perfect, appearing at the perfect time." She paused until she could pull herself together a bit more. "People warned me about him. Everybody did. Fran, being such a close friend, was the most vocal."

"You had to find out for yourself. You know you did."

She immediately shook her head in protest. Rafe was just being kind, saying the things he thought would make her feel better. But she knew the truth: her brother was in a coma with a damaged limb and Eva was the one who'd indirectly put him there. "I refused to see what was right in front of me."

"What was that? At first, I mean."

"He made me feel so special. Like I was the only person that mattered. He told me I was beautiful and smart and accomplished. All the while he was plotting. In the meantime, he grew manipulative."

Rafe remained quiet, giving her all the time she needed to get this out in her own way.

Eva inhaled a shaky breath, the memories searing so painfully through her she thought she might burst. "The compliments eventually grew few and far between, until eventually I seemed to be able to do nothing right in his eyes."

Rafe still didn't speak, just let out a low whistle of a breath.

"It was almost habitual, then. My daily mission became trying to ensure he was happy with me, that I'd pleased him."

The stinging behind her eyes had grown into a burning sensation now. She wiped away a tear before it could fall. "If I didn't agree to something he'd suggested right away, even something as simple as what to have for dinner, his entire demeanor became hostile and vindictive."

Eva saw Rafe's other hand curl into a tight fist. "Did he…?"

She immediately shook her head before he could ask the question. "No, he never became physical." Though she had no confidence whatsoever that he wouldn't have—given enough time. Thank God she would never have to find out.

She went on. "Eventually, it became so hard just to get through the day. Every thought I had was consumed with what I could do to make my husband happy with me. Then I would just try harder when things inevitably went sour again. It was a vicious cycle that kept repeating."

"He tormented you," Rafe bit out.

"I let it happen. I wasn't strong enough to see it or stop it."

Rafe leaned toward her, then cupped her chin with his hand. "Men like him are good at what they do, Eva. Tell me the rest," he prompted.

"I'm not sure how or when it happened. But one day I woke up and decided I just wasn't going to do it anymore. I pushed back when he insulted me. Countered with my own opinion when I didn't agree with something he'd said or done. I think that's when he decided he would leave. His reign of influence was coming to an end, and he must have sensed it." She puffed out a breath. "But by then it was too late. So much damage had been done."

"But not to your soul, Eva. He never managed to crush it."

"How can you say that?" She forced out the question, her voice shaking.

"The fact that he manipulated you has nothing to do with how strong you are. You were taken advantage of. And you didn't let it continue. You pushed back, eventually."

Eva tried to grasp at his words, to take them to heart. But the effort was futile. Maybe someday she'd see reason behind all that Rafe was trying to tell her...but not today.

So she did the only other thing she could think of. She leaned into him, letting the tears fall freely now. He simply held her without saying a word.

Offering her so much more than she deserved.

CHAPTER THIRTEEN

RAFE STUDIED EVA as they rode the elevator to the fourth floor of the San Paolo Clinicia in Cordaro, Puerto Rico. She was spent. Dark circles framed her swollen, red eyes and her lips were drawn tight, her skin a faint shade of her normal color.

Anger still beat like a jackhammer in his chest. It had started on the jet as she'd been speaking of her ex.

Maybe all the tabloids were right. Maybe he was a brute with a violent past from the wrong side of the Seattle streets. Because he didn't think he could restrain himself if he ever came across the man who had caused Eva so much pain, when all she'd done was fall in love with him.

How could anyone be fool enough not to realize how fortunate that made them?

He wished there was a way to wipe his entire existence from Eva's memory, to replace it with peace and tranquility. He'd give anything to free her of the pain and anguish she was in right now.

The elevator dinged when they reached their floor and Eva stepped to the doors before they'd even slid open. She rushed out in a flash, jogging down the hallway until she reached the room they'd been told housed her brother. Rafe was a step behind her, and he entered to find her in a tight embrace with her grandmother. A man he recognized as her father stood by his son's bedside. Teo looked bruised and battered; Rafe hardly recognized him against the sterile white sheets of the hospital bed.

Eva rushed to her father next, then took her brother's hand and brushed a kiss on his cheek. Even from the doorway, Rafe could see the tears streaming down her cheeks.

Rafe stepped away, feeling awkward and out of place. He found a chair down the hall and took a seat. The Gatos didn't need the presence of a stranger right now. They needed each other. He was an outsider who didn't belong, just like always.

But he had no intention to leave. He would stay and wait for her in case she needed him.

He had no idea how much time had passed before a shadow fell in front of his feet and he felt her presence.

"Hey," Eva said in a raspy and strained voice.

"Hey, yourself."

She plopped into the chair next to him, releasing a long sigh. "Thank you for staying."

He simply shrugged; he wasn't about to say aloud that he couldn't imagine leaving her during such a dark hour. "You're welcome. How is he?"

"Good news," Eva answered. "I was told he was awake for a while just before we arrived. The doctor said that means he's out of the woods."

A wave of relief washed over him. He didn't know Teo well, but the brief amount of time he'd spent with the man had shown him to be warm and genuine. And if Eva was right about the cause of his accident, Teo was a generous soul who'd just risked his life to help his sister.

He reached for her, interlacing his fingers with hers. "I'm so happy to hear that."

She leaned into his shoulder. "Teo's got a long road ahead of him. His leg took the brunt of the impact. There'll be a lot of rehabilitation before he has use of it again. And he might not ever get full use back."

"I'm sorry" was all he could think to say.

Eva nodded slowly against his upper arm. "We're just so grateful to have him awake again. To know he's going to be okay."

"We'll do everything we can to make sure he gets all the help he needs to recover as best as he can."

"Thank you, Rafe. That's if I can keep from throttling him for the scare he gave everyone."

Rafe chuckled. "Try to cut him some slack. He's been through a lot."

"I'll try." He heard her release a deep sigh. "I'm sorry we had to rush away from the resort before finalizing things," she began. "I know how much that deal meant to you."

He had to smile at that. "You really need to stop apologizing to me. Especially about something like this."

"Okay. Sorry," she said with a cheeky grin.

They sat that way for several moments, in comfortable silence. He couldn't bring himself to let go of her hand, and she made no effort to drop his.

Until he caught movement down the hall. She pulled her hand away then, placing it on her lap.

Eva's father stepped out of the room and approached them from the hallway. "Hola, Rafael," he greeted him.

"Hola, Señor Gato. I'm glad Teo will be all right."

"Thank you. It's a blessing from above." He addressed his daughter. "Why don't you two go get some rest, maybe something to eat? They're going to take Teo up for some more tests. By then visiting hours will be over and the hospital only allows two people in the patient's room after that. Nana and I will stay."

Eva didn't protest, a testament to how tired she was. "Okay, Papá."

Rafe stood to shake the man's hand. "I hope Teo has a restful night."

Señor Gato nodded with a tired smile.

"We'll be back first thing tomorrow morning," Eva told her father. "Please call with updates about how he's doing."

"I will, *mi hija*."

The two of them began walking down the hall. Eva slipped her hand back into his before they reached the elevator. Reflexively, Rafe brought it to his lips. She could cling to him for as long as she needed.

Eva waited in the lobby of a quaint one-floor hotel about three miles from the hospital. Rafe stood at the desk checking them in for the night. It had been his idea to stay close by, understanding without her having to tell him that she didn't want to be too far from her family and injured brother. The hacienda was about an hour away. Much too far.

She watched Rafe now as he spoke to the attendant. He'd really come through for her when she'd needed it the most, jetting them back home, supporting her through the panic and worry. And just listening.

Suddenly, it dawned on her just how much she needed him by her side at this moment. Yet another shock. Even though they'd only known each other a few short weeks, it had taken a near tragedy for her to realize that she wanted—no, *needed*—the strength and mental fortitude that Rafe somehow gave her. She couldn't imagine having taken that phone call from Papá without Rafe there to help her deal with the news.

That settled it. She didn't want to entertain any kind of pretense at this moment, not with everything happening. The thought of spending the night by herself alone, plagued with guilt and worry in an unfamiliar hotel room, suddenly both depressed and horrified her.

She strode to the desk before she could change her mind.

Touching Rafe on his arm, she waited until he excused himself to the attendant and turned to her.

"Everything all right, Eva? Did you change your mind and decide you'd prefer to go home?"

She shook her head. "No. If it's all right with you, I'd prefer if we shared one room." She sucked in a breath before continuing. "I'd rather not be alone tonight."

A myriad of emotions seemed to play behind his eyes. Eva couldn't guess what he might be thinking, just fervently hoped that he wouldn't turn her down. Without any further hesitation, he gave her a single nod. "Of course." He turned back to the attendant.

A few minutes later, they entered through the door of a cozy-looking and well-kept room. A flat-screen TV hung on the wall opposite the bed, while a colorful circular rug covered the hardwood floors. Cheery curtains with a colorful floral pattern hung parted on the sole window.

Rafe noticed it before she did. He swore quietly. "Sorry, Eva. I promise I asked for double beds. I'll go see about switching rooms."

Maybe it was the fact that she was just too tired to

cope with any further delays, or maybe her vulnerability was too close to the surface, but she didn't want him to bother. She stopped him with a hand on his arm before he reached the door. "Let's just try and get some rest. I can barely stay upright much longer."

He lifted an eyebrow. "I can sleep on the floor."

"It's okay, Rafe. We spent the night together in an abandoned cave. I think we can handle a soft bed."

Their gazes locked with the obvious left unspoken— the way things had turned out in said cave the next morning.

Eva didn't care. She just wanted a shower and to get some much-needed sleep.

Twenty minutes later, when she exited the bathroom, Rafe was already in bed scrolling through his phone. He'd shut his bedside lamp off.

"Good night, Rafe."

Eva crawled in next to him on the mattress. Surprisingly, the close proximity didn't make her self-conscious. In a way, it felt completely natural. She was reaching for her own lamp to turn it off when her phone dinged with a text.

She grabbed it immediately to check, heart pounding in her chest that it might be more bad news that her brother had taken a turn for the worse. Relief surged through her when she read the message.

"Anything new?" Rafe asked.

"No. No updates. Just my dad bidding us a good night."

Rafe shifted on the mattress. "I hope he and Nana manage to get some sleep. They both looked pretty spent."

"I hope so, too," Eva agreed with a sigh. "Though it's doubtful. Papá will fret all night and Nana won't leave Teo's side."

"You and Teo are lucky to have them."

Eva didn't miss the note of sorrow in Rafe's voice. She could imagine why discussing family might sadden him, given the way he'd had to grow up. He'd really had no one.

"Nana's been the only mother figure we had," Eva explained. "She's been a rock for all three of us since my mother left."

Rafe paused in the act of adjusting his pillow. "She left? I'm embarrassed to say that I just figured she was…"

Eva immediately knew what he meant. "No. She's fine. Just AWOL, so to speak. Has been for years."

He cleared his throat. "Do you want to tell me about it?"

She shrugged, then propped herself up on a pillow. "There's really nothing much to tell. Fairly common story, I guess. She left when I was about twelve. Teo was fourteen. She was born in Scotland and grew up in Switzerland. Spends her time traveling to various fashion events. She's a designer for a handbag company."

"Huh."

"She thought she could handle life on a Caribbean island after getting married, but decided after all those years that she didn't want to. She just left one day. Said she'd be in touch."

He let out a slow whistle. "Being abandoned by your mother couldn't have been easy at that age. I'm sorry, Eva."

No, it hadn't. Not in the least. For years Eva had

blamed herself, wondering what she might have done to keep her mother at home. She'd questioned all the reasons why it might have been her fault. Maybe if she'd helped out more around the house, been less sulky about doing her homework. If she'd just tried to be a better daughter… She shook a shaky breath before responding. "It wasn't at first. But eventually, the three of us adjusted. I learned to cook and helped dad out with the business. Luckily, Nana was nearby to help out." And thank God for that. Her grandmother had stepped into the maternal gap of her mother's absence without preamble or complaint.

"What about Teo? How did he take to being left behind by his mother?"

Rafe's question tore at her heart. No doubt he was thinking of his own experience as a child with a distant and uncaring mom. The truth was, Teo hadn't handled it well. The year Mama left had been the year he'd constantly been in and out of trouble—getting into fights, destroying property. He'd been angry and had lashed out at anything he could. But she couldn't begin to try and speak on her brother's behalf about how Mama's abandonment had affected him.

"I'll let him answer that in his own way," Eva told him. "You should ask him someday."

"Maybe I will," he answered.

"Papá has stayed in touch with her over the years," Eva told him. "Teo and I as well, to a much lesser extent."

"So you've had some contact, then."

She nodded slowly. "Minimally. Eventually, I just learned to accept that she wasn't going to come back and went about the business of growing up. Without her."

Despite the matter-of-fact delivery, Eva realized the conversation was churning up emotions she'd long thought dormant. She was trembling, her heart pounding in her chest. She refused to succumb to the temptation to give in to her anger. She'd long passed the angry phase and moved on to acceptance—right around the time she'd graduated high school and Mama's only response had been to send her a congratulatory card.

Rafe must have noticed her trembling. "Hey, come here," he said, gathering her in his arms. She didn't fight it, didn't even want to.

He still held her when she awoke the next morning.

What an eventful and harrowing twenty-four hours. Rafe couldn't remember the last time he'd felt so spent. Hard to even imagine how much more worn-down Eva must feel.

Last night had been…interesting. He'd simply held her in his arms until she'd fallen asleep. In the middle of the night, when he'd heard her sniffling and softly hiccupping in a clear sob, he'd simply pulled her closer, no words spoken. He'd just wanted her to know he was there.

He studied her profile as they were driven back to the hospital. Her features were set, her chin lifted in quiet strength.

Pity that she had no idea just how strong she was.

When they pulled up to the hospital entrance, a familiar figure bolted from the other end of the street toward the sliding doors. A smile spread across Eva's face and she hurriedly shoved her car door open before they'd even come to a full stop.

"Fran!" she shouted, jumping out of the vehicle.

So that's who that was. But Fran must not have heard her name being called because she rushed through the doors. They could see her in a near jog to the elevator.

"She really seems to be in a hurry," Rafe commented, joining Eva on the sidewalk.

Eva tilted her head. "Guess we'll see her upstairs."

When they got there Fran was alone in the room with Teo. Rafe was relieved to see the other man awake and alert, speaking to his guest. His complexion was much deeper than it had been yesterday. He looked good—healthy.

Fran on the other hand appeared something of a mess. Her face was streaked with tears. Purple blotches colored the area under her eyes. She'd clearly been crying for a good long time. Ironically, it looked like Teo was the one comforting her rather than the other way around. Interesting.

Eva rushed into the room, then gave her brother a big hug, squeezing him around the neck. "You're awake!"

"Hey, take it easy, sis," Teo immediately complained, though there was no real ire in his tone. "You really don't need to hug me in a viselike grip."

Eva tilted her head up in Rafe's and Fran's direction, not letting go of her brother even the slightest. "Could I have a moment alone with my muleheaded brother?" she asked them both.

Fran immediately stepped to the door, but not before giving Teo's hand another squeeze. Rafe followed her out of the room.

Rafe didn't mean to eavesdrop; he really didn't. But he couldn't help but hear the first snippet of their conversation as he was just outside the door.

"I know why you did this, Teo," Eva said. "I love you for it. But I really wish you hadn't."

Rafe heard Teo answer after a loud sigh. "I was the one who introduced you to him, Ev. I had to try and do something."

Out of respect, Rafe shut the door quietly behind him.

"You okay?" Rafe asked Fran when they were in the hallway alone together.

She nodded with a soft sniffle. "I was just so worried when I heard the news."

At least as worried as Teo's blood kin, it appeared.

Fran gave him a warm smile through trembling lips. "I'm really glad you were here for her through this."

"Me too," he simply responded.

CHAPTER FOURTEEN

Two Weeks Later

RAFE READ THE email in his inbox and couldn't help but pump a fist in the air in celebration. Paolo Bertrand had finally written to say they were anxious to sign on with Gato Rums as their sole distributor. Eva was copied in the message. Had she seen it yet?

Rising from his desk chair, he decided to find out. There was another email he'd received that he also was eager to tell her about. This one hadn't included her in the reply as he'd initiated the exchange without her knowledge. It was an exchange with one Bahamian Veterinary Center in Nassau. He couldn't wait to see her face when he told her about that one.

The sound of feminine voices echoed from the kitchen. He made his way in that direction to find her there with Nana. Both of them stood at the stove, their backs to the doorway. Nana was stirring something on the range and not for the first time, Rafe was struck by how comforting and homely it felt to share his residence with others. He'd lived alone most of his life, even as a child. His earliest memories involved sitting on the couch watching TV by himself while his mother went to work. He'd sit that way for hours, and when she finally came home, she'd often go straight to bed. By contrast, this was a completely new experience—one that made waking up in the morning just a bit brighter.

"My brother is too clueless to even suspect," Eva was saying to her grandmother in a rather mischievous tone. Neither had yet noticed his presence behind them.

"*Ay, Dios,*" Nana replied. "How can Teo not see how often she visits him? With all those trays of munchies she prepares and brings for him."

Some harmless gossip, then. Rafe knew they had to be speaking about Fran.

"Especially when she hears his pretty rehabilitation nurse has come by for the day," Eva added with a small giggle. They'd all agreed that it would be best for Teo to move into his old room on the first floor while his leg healed. A physiotherapist was to make biweekly house calls for his treatment. She'd started last week.

Rafe was about to announce his arrival when the door leading to the patio opened and Señor Gato wheeled his son into the kitchen in his wheelchair, his leg propped up on an extension. Without meaning to, Rafe stepped off to the side behind the wall. He wasn't even sure why, but he wasn't ready to be seen by the four of them just yet.

"What are you two so giddy about?" Teo asked the two women.

"*Nada,*" Nana answered. "Here, taste this." She held a wooden spoon covered in a thick burgundy sauce to his mouth.

Rafe's heart pounded in his chest at the scene.

Who was he kidding? It was laughable that for a minute back there he'd actually thought he could be part of such a cozy scenario. His name may be on the deed, but this wasn't his house. Nor his land. Nor his business.

He'd acquired it all by a sheer stroke of luck. And through the sheer misfortune of the people he stood watching right now—honest, decent people who loved each other and cared enough for one another that one had literally risked his life for another.

Rafe had no right.

It became so clear in that moment what he had to do. He wanted to kick himself for not seeing the truth sooner when it was so clear in front of his nose. Rafe had no part in the picture he was looking at. He didn't belong here.

There would be no need to tell Eva about that second email, after all.

"You wanted to see me?"

Eva stepped into his study about twenty minutes later, after he'd texted her. In a way, he wished she'd taken much longer to get here. But putting off this conversation wouldn't make it any easier.

He leaned back against his chair, then motioned for her to sit in the one across from the desk.

Eva's smile faltered as she did what he asked. Clearly, she'd picked up on the overall vibe of the situation. The air between them was thick with tension.

"What's the matter, Rafe? Did something go wrong with the wash? Raul hasn't said anything to me."

He held his hand up to stop her. "No. The wash is fine. There's something else I need to speak to you about."

She tilted her head. "All right. What is it? I can tell by your face that something's not right."

Rafe's mouth had gone dry. Telling her was going to

be even more difficult than he would have guessed. But he had no choice.

"I got a phone call about an investment opportunity back in the States the other day," he told her. That was the absolute truth. He got those calls fairly regularly. The next part would be where he stretched the truth.

"And?" she prompted.

"And I've decided that it's too good to pass up."

She blinked at him, her face scrunching in confusion. "I don't understand. What does that mean exactly?"

"It means I'm headed back to the West Coast to oversee it personally. You'll have to take over all my duties here."

Her eyebrows lifted, confusion flooding her face. "How long do you plan on being gone?"

"I wouldn't be able to say. Several months at least. Maybe longer."

Her mouth fell open. "What?"

"I'm sorry, Eva. But I know you can handle things on your own."

"You can't be serious about this." Her expression was so tormented, Rafe almost gave in to the urge to backtrack. But he couldn't, for either of their sakes.

"I am serious. My mind is made up. I'll be leaving immediately. I've already made arrangements for movers to pack and ship my things."

Her eyes grew wide. "You're not even staying long enough to pack yourself? I can't believe this is happening," she stammered, outrage dripping in her voice. "How could you have decided this all on your own, without so much as running it by me? What about the contracts with the resorts? What about purchasing new equipment? All that needs to be done to meet the new demand?"

"You'll have a consultant at your disposal to assist you going forward with all of that. I know just the firm. I've already called them."

"You've thought of everything, haven't you?" She cupped her hand over her mouth. Rafe itched to reach for her, to tell her was taking it all back—to just forget what he'd said. But that would simply be putting off the inevitable.

"What a fool I've been," she continued, her voice shaky. "I thought you cared. About the distillery. About this home." She gasped. "I thought you cared about me."

It took every ounce of will he had not to react to her statement. She would never know how much he cared—so much so that he'd fallen in love her. There was no denying it now.

It was why he had to leave.

She laughed in a way that held no mirth. "I can't believe it's happening again. This was just a game to you. My entire world, everything that meant anything to me, was just a business opportunity you took a chance on. And now you can just easily walk away. Like it means nothing to you."

Her words cut him like a razor blade. To make the pain stop, he cut her.

Rafe braced himself, preparing for what he was about to do. What he told her next would deliver the final blow.

He sucked in a much-needed breath before his last strike. "Eva, that's all this ever was. Just business. And it's time for me to move on."

She wondered if he would take the paintings with him— the one of the very scene she watched now, and the one with the rising phoenix.

Eva sat cross-legged on the sand and watched the slow, crashing waves of the ocean. She couldn't bring herself to stay in the house, hearing Rafe's footsteps upstairs as he packed the bags he would be bringing with him. She couldn't watch as he walked out the door with no indication of when he might be back—if ever. Hopefully, he would take the paintings eventually, or she would have to donate them. She wanted nothing in that house that reminded her of Rafael Malta.

She'd fallen for yet another man addicted to the game, one who found it so easy to walk away once that game was over.

But this felt different. The pain felt deeper, sharper. Because somewhere along the way, sometime between the walk they'd taken on this very beach and the day they'd left the Bahamas, Eva had fallen hopelessly head over heels in love with him. She hadn't even been paying attention, and couldn't even point out when exactly it had happened. More's the pity, for all she was left with now was a broken heart.

She was so entrenched in her thoughts, it took a moment for her to register that a shadow had fallen in front of her in the sand at her feet. She looked up to find Papá standing over her.

"Nana told me I could find you here," he told her, crouching to a sitting position by her side. "Not surprising," he added. "This is where you'd come as a little girl when you wanted to get away from the house. Or from any of us."

"I wasn't trying to get away, Papá. I just needed some time alone to think."

He nodded. "Rafe stopped by to see me," he told her. "Said he'd be gone for a while. Wasn't sure when he'd be back. Does your need for alone time have anything to do with that, maybe?"

"Is he gone?" she asked, unable to control the shaking in her voice.

"Left about an hour ago."

Eva hated herself for not being able to control the sob that escaped her mouth. How weak she must seem to this strong, proud man who'd always been a pillar of support for his children. How pathetic. "He was saying his goodbyes," she said, her voice breaking with both anguish and fury.

"You're in love with him."

Her silence was answer enough. They sat in wordless silence for several moments before her father broke the quiet.

"What did he say when you asked him to stay?" he asked.

His question unnerved her. "I didn't."

Papá turned to face her. "Until very recently, you always fought for what you wanted. What happened?"

She opened her mouth, then closed it again, unsure how to answer. Papá had to be able to guess the answer to his question. After her divorce, she didn't know what warranted a fight anymore. With Rafe, she'd thought maybe her ruinous marriage was finally something she might be able to put behind her…only to have Rafe turn his back on her as well.

"You let him leave without saying anything about how you feel," he supplied at her silence.

"I was too hurt to tell him anything," she said, her heart shattering in her chest. "What good would it have done? He wanted to leave. He didn't even want to stick around for the time it would take to do his own packing."

Her father wrapped an arm around her shoulders and pulled her tight up against his side. She leaned into him without a second thought.

"I'm sorry, *mi hija*. You should tell him when he comes back."

If he ever did. Eva had no faith that would happen. Chances were she'd never see him again, just his name on distillery business paperwork or assigned to various emails, moments she would have to lick her wounds at the reminders that came her way.

Her father continued, "In the meantime, you'll be plenty busy running a growing distillery on your own."

Eva blinked up at him in confusion. "What do you mean? Where will you be?"

"I was planning to do some traveling after the sale, remember? Now that Teo's on the mend, I think I'll resume that plan."

Eva didn't understand Papá's reasoning. Didn't he realize that everything had changed? They were back in charge. The buyer was gone. He'd left them to their own devices. "We have the distillery to run," she reminded him.

"Ah, that you will be running on your own with those consultants Rafe mentioned. You know the business like the back of your hand."

She was having trouble processing all the new information. But one thing was becoming increasingly clear to her as she listened to what her father was saying. "You really don't want to."

Papá released a deep sigh. "Did it ever occur to you that I would have fought harder to keep the distillery if I felt strongly about still running it?"

Eva could only blink at him in confusion. "I was

ready to give it up a while ago," he continued to explain. "I was tired, Eva. So very tired." His chest rose and fell. "Even with Nana's help, raising two teenagers on my own drained me and wore me down. On top of the business, I was ready for a rest."

Eva's head hammered at the revelation. She'd been so selfish not to see how much of a load her father had been carrying all these years. No wonder the man was weary.

Her father continued, "So when the need to sell happened, I figured it was time. The decision was made on its own."

"Huh," was all she could muster.

"And I knew you would find your own way. You always did. You always will."

Eva absorbed the shock of her father's words as the truth fully dawned on her. While she thought he'd been devastated by the loss of the business, Papá had already made plans about moving on with his future. It was both a shocking and freeing discovery.

"So where will you go next?" she asked.

He shrugged. "Not entirely sure yet. I might start in France or Italy."

"You want to go to Europe?" She would have never guessed, figured he'd want to stick to the familiar and hop the islands of the Caribbean. How wrong she'd been.

Her father flashed her a smile. "Sure. Maybe I'll start with a winery tour. I've had enough rum for this lifetime."

The disdain in his tone made her chuckle. She swiped at the moisture on her face. Eva was going to miss him. So much was changing around her, and the changes were coming at her like missiles. "That's what you want, Papá?" she asked.

He nodded once. "It is, *mi hija*. Who knows? I might even meet somebody. I've been told that even someone as old as me can find love."

Eva gripped his hand in hers. How she admired this man. She may have his DNA building her cells, but she would never be as strong and courageous as he was.

She hadn't been brave enough to tell the man she loved that she wanted him to stay with her—had never told him how she felt.

Yet another regret. This one she may never get over.

After several silent moments, her father stood to leave, bidding her goodbye. Eva couldn't let him go just yet. She stood as well, then stopped him from turning with a hand on his forearm.

"Thank you," she told him.

He tapped her nose with his finger. "For what?"

"For having faith in me still. I know I don't deserve it. And I'm sorry." Now that she'd started, she couldn't seem to stop. The words poured out of her like a gush of water from a broken dam. "I'm sorry I let you down two years ago. I'm sorry you can't be proud of me like you used—"

Papá shushed her before she could finish. "But I *am* proud of you. I've always been proud of you. I never stopped."

Eva didn't have the words that would even come close to a fitting response. So she did the only thing she could think to do. She threw her arms around his neck and hugged him with all her strength.

There was still the matter of the cat to deal with.

Rafe bit out a curse and rested his forearms on the railing of the balcony overlooking the pool. His flight back to the States wasn't for two more days. Unwisely, he'd decided to check in to La Ola, the San Juan resort that had given them their first supply contract. Now the memories of the time he and Eva had spent here together taunted him at every turn. Had it really been only a few short weeks since they'd been here? It felt like he'd lived a lifetime since then.

A lifetime in which he'd found the woman he would foolishly fall in love with. Rafe clenched his hands into tight fists. He had to forget about her and leave Puerto Rico before he did something even more reckless. The sooner the better.

As for the cat, he still had to figure something out. Rafe pulled out his cell phone and called the only person he could think of who might be able to help him.

Patty, his former assistant in Seattle, answered on the third ring. "Hello? Rafe, is that you?" She sounded breathless and distracted.

"Hi, Patty, is this a good time?"

He heard her laugh through the tiny speaker. "As good a time as any. I was just chasing my granddaughter around the yard playing tag. For a little four-year-old tyke, she can move quite fast."

He chuckled at the picture that created in his mind. "I can imagine."

"I'm so glad you called," Patty said. "It's nice to hear from you finally." She was probably wondering exactly why he had after all this time. He'd get right to it, then.

"I was wondering if you might be interested in adopting a stray cat?" he asked her, just blurting it out as if it made any kind of sense with no context whatsoever. "Maybe for one of your grandkids?"

Patty chuckled into the phone. "A cat? How in the world did you become responsible for a pet?"

"You wouldn't believe me if I told you."

Patty laughed harder this time. "Let me run it by Frank. The kids are always asking for pets, but I don't know... It's a big responsibility when one is already babysitting a brood of little ones."

That was progress at least; he would take it. "Thank you," he told her.

"You're welcome. So tell me. How's life on the tropical paradise of Puerto Rico?" Patty asked. "Are you at the distillery right now?"

"I'm actually in San Juan at the moment. At a luxury resort."

Patty squealed. "Oh, that sounds lovely. What are you doing there?"

"Waiting for a flight back to the States. So I can look for a new home."

Patty reaction was immediate. "What? You're coming back already? But why?"

Rafe wasn't sure what came over him at her simple questions. Before he knew it, he was pouring out the entire story, leaving nothing out—from the first day he'd arrived at the hacienda, to the night in the cave, to Teo's accident and everything before, in between and after.

Afterward, he felt spent and drained—also more than a little relieved at the unexpected purge. What had come over him?

Patty remained silent for several beats, so long that Rafe wondered if he'd gone too far and shocked the poor woman speechless. Finally, she spoke. "Will you accept some motherly advice from an old woman?"

"I could use advice of any kind right now, Patty," he admitted.

"Do you remember when you first hired me all those years ago?"

"Of course," Rafe replied, though he was perplexed as to where she might be going with this. What did her employment with him have to do with the current scenario?

"I would invite you to our family picnics and barbecues."

"I remember. That was very kind of you."

"You came to a few at first. And then you stopped. Turned down every invitation politely but firmly. Kept saying you had scheduling conflicts, even for Sunday dinners."

Rafe began to suspect where she might be headed. He'd begun getting antsy all those years ago when he'd started growing too familiar with Patty's family—and they with him. So he'd begun to avoid them. It was easier that way. He'd pulled away before he could form any kind of bond with her husband or adult sons.

Had he just done the same with Eva?

"I think I know the point you're trying to make, Patty."

"Good," Patty said gently. "I'm glad to hear it. And there's another thing you should know."

"What's that?"

"I've never heard you speak about anyone or anything with as much emotion as you just did about this Eva."

"Thank you, Patty," he said with genuine gratitude.

"You're welcome, son." Rafe stilled; she'd never called him that before. Rafe thought of all the years of affection he might have had in his life if he'd continued to accept those invites. Such a wasted chance at some small amount of happiness in his life.

He'd simply thrown it away.

The penalty fees the airline charged him each time he changed his flight were beginning to add up, but Rafe couldn't seem to bring himself to take a car to the airport and finally fly back the West Coast.

He felt unsettled and disoriented, unable to decide which direction to move in. He was stuck. The predicament marked the first time in his life he'd ever felt indecisive about anything. It was an uncomfortable and unfamiliar feeling.

He'd been at La Ola for ten days now, getting tired of staring at the same balcony view and listening to the same sounds. It all brought back memories of the day he and Eva had spent here together.

Yet he couldn't bring himself to leave. To be more accurate, he couldn't bring himself to leave Puerto Rico. And he had nowhere else on the island to go.

Biting out a curse, her strode off the balcony, through the suite and took the elevator to the ground floor. Only one stool at the poolside bar remained empty. Rafe sat and ordered the day's lunch special.

The couple next to him were draped all over each other. Rafe had to look away, unable to watch the intimacy they shared. The shiny gold bands on their fingers looked brand-new. Finally, the woman pulled away and told her husband she'd be waiting for him upstairs.

The man reached for his bill on the counter but Rafe took it first. "It's on me."

The gentleman turned to him in surprise. "You don't have to do that, man."

"Consider it a wedding gift."

"Wow. Very nice of you." A sheepish grin spread over the man's lips. "Is it that obvious?"

He had no idea. "Very. Congratulations."

"Thanks. We're on our honeymoon."

Rafe guessed as much.

"Got married last week," he added.

"Congratulations," Rafe repeated, unable to come up with anything else to say.

"Thanks, man." He reached out and shook Rafe's hand. "And thanks for lunch. I'm Manny."

"Rafe."

"It almost didn't happen," Manny announced with zero context, though Rafe figured he could guess what he meant.

"I got cold feet," Manny explained. "I almost backed out—called off the wedding a month before the big day."

Now his interest was piqued. Manny and his wife had looked so completely in love; it was hard to believe they'd almost not gotten married at all.

"It was the most miserable time of my life," Manny said, shaking his head sadly.

"What happened?"

"I came to my senses. Realized I was just scared and anxious. But I was more scared to be without her."

"Huh."

"Luckily, she still wanted me." Manny blew out a large sigh. "To think, I almost messed it all up."

With that, the other man stood and made his way across the pool deck.

Rafe watched him walk away and felt a loosening

of the tightness in his chest he hadn't even been aware had been there.

More scared to be without her.

Rafe swore out loud, earning a quizzical look from the bartender. He'd been such a fool. A stubborn and clueless fool, too afraid to take an emotional risk in case it all ended up going up in flames—like so many other times in his life.

But Eva was worth the risk.

Rafe pinched the bridge of his nose. He'd been so blind to what was so clear in front of his face. He loved Eva Gato. He needed to tell her so.

Ignoring his lunch, he pushed off the stool to gather his things from upstairs and check out of this hotel once and for all.

His phone vibrated in his pocket with an incoming call when he reached the elevator. Rafe answered when he saw the contact name on the screen. "Hi, Patty."

"Hey, Rafe. Wanted to get back to you about the cat."

It took a moment for Rafe to process what she'd said. His mind was racing. Now that he knew what he wanted to do, he couldn't wait to set the plan in motion.

Then he remembered he'd asked Patty if she might be interested in adopting the stray feline still being housed at the veterinary center. "Yes?" he answered.

"I talked to Frank and he thinks our grandkids might be too young for a pet right now, to be honest."

"That's okay. Finding an adopter won't be necessary after all," he told her. "I think I just figured out what to do with her."

"What's that?" Patty wanted to know.

"What I should have done all along before I foolishly

chickened out," he replied. "I'm going to bring her where she belongs."

It was where he belonged as well. If he was still welcome.

Eva had to read the text twice.

Her pulse had jumped when she'd first gotten the alert to see Rafe's contact icon pop up as the sender. He was texting her, a full two weeks after he'd left. A bloom of hope blossomed in her chest before she clicked to read the message.

Then her heart shattered to discover he was only sending her on a business errand. Eva tossed the cell phone onto the desk with such force it popped out of its protective case. She was an idiot to think Rafe might contact her about anything but the distillery. He was gone, probably texting her from Seattle or California—wherever his latest business venture had taken him.

He hadn't even bothered to tell her the specifics.

She took a fortifying breath and read his message once more. Apparently, a signature was needed on some document at the San Juan hotel before they could begin the exclusive distribution.

Funny, she'd thought they'd crossed every *t* and dotted every *i* that day before they'd left.

Not so, according to Rafe's text. The manager needed her there that afternoon to take care of it.

As much as she wanted to ignore the directive, Rafe was still technically her boss. She would have to go. Best to just get it over with. With a resigned sigh, Eva pulled a casual business suit of her closet. This would be the first face-to-face business meeting she'd be attending on her own, without her father or Rafe.

Another milestone for both her and the distillery, which had won yet another deal without so much as a visit to the latest resort to sign Gato as sole distributor. But she had no desire to celebrate. She felt nothing but hollow inside. The emptiness felt even worse than what she'd experienced after her divorce. Back then, she'd had the intensity of her anger at Victor to hold on to. With Rafe's absence, she had nothing.

Just a gnawing gap in the pit of her soul she didn't think would ever fill.

A little over an hour later, she walked through the lobby of the resort and made her way to the room number she'd been given. She'd had to give up her whole afternoon to sign a lousy piece of paper. What had Rafe been thinking?

That was just it. She couldn't guess the answer to that question. She'd never really known Rafe at all, it appeared.

Walking farther down the hall, she blinked in confusion. Something was wrong. The room number she'd been given didn't lead to any kind of office or conference room. Instead, she found herself in front of a glass door that led to an outdoor patio. She walked onto the brick walkway, the scent of roses and tropical flowers pleasantly hanging in the air. This couldn't be where she was supposed to be to sign a document. On top of everything else, Rafe seemed to have sent her on a wild-goose chase.

A voice called out her name—a voice she recognized. Eva gave her head a brisk shake. She had to stop thinking about him. Now she was hearing his voice in her head.

But she heard her name again just as a familiar figure stepped out from behind a tall Flamboyant tree.

Eva's heart stopped. Was she seeing *and* hearing things?

"Rafe?"

"Hello, sweetheart."

It wasn't her imagination. He was really here. Something black-and-white and furry wiggled in his arms.

Her feet somehow worked enough to move over to where he stood. "Oh, my… Is that…?"

He held the furball up to her. "It is. I flew to get her yesterday."

"Oh, Rafe."

"I've given her a name," he said. "But we can change it if you don't like it."

Her mind was still trying to process exactly what was happening. For now, she decided to focus on the small animal she'd grown so attached to all those days ago. "What name?" she asked.

"Coqui."

Eva laughed, his answer catapulting her back in time to the day they'd visited the rain forest.

He held the cat out and Eva gingerly took her, then snuggled her face into the soft fur on its back. "I've missed her so much. I love the name you've given her."

Rafe remained silent for several moments. Then he said the words that had her pulse skittering. "And I love you," he told her. Eva's breath caught in her throat. She felt dizzy. Was this really happening?

"You do?"

Rafe nodded. "With every bit of my heart and my soul."

This had to be some kind of dream. She couldn't really be here. Rafe wasn't really saying such words to her.

"I'm so sorry, sweetheart," he told her above her head. "For being a blind fool. I should have never left."

If this was indeed a dream, Eva wanted to remain immersed in it forever. But a cry of caution echoed in her head. There were questions that still needed to be answered, with zero doubt on Rafe's part.

"Why *did* you leave?" she asked. "And how can I be sure it won't happen again?" Eva choked back a sob as she asked the question. The thought of this happiness being yanked out of her hands yet again was enough to crush her soul. She didn't think she would survive the blow twice in one lifetime.

"Because I was skittish and scared and—" He stopped abruptly, then rubbed his forehead. "Because I didn't think I deserved you. But I vow to spend my days striving to be the kind of man who does."

Eva could only stare at him, breathless for several pauses. Finally, she found her voice. "There's nothing you need to strive for, Rafe Malta. You're the man I love. That's all I need."

His eyes darkened with emotion at her words. "Does that mean you forgive me?"

"Yes. I forgive you," she replied, with no hesitation and no qualms whatsoever.

His shoulders sagged with relief at her answer. "It's more than I deserve."

She stepped closer into his length, close enough to

feel his heartbeat against her chest. "Then you'll just have to make it up to me."

Rafe pulled her in for a deep, hungry kiss that had her weak in the knees. "I know just how to start," he said against her lips.

EPILOGUE

EVA HAD TO laugh at the scene before her when she entered the kitchen. How could he still be having so much trouble operating the coffee machine after all this time? A full year and Rafe couldn't seem to master exactly which buttons to push to get the beverage exactly the way he wanted it.

Eva bumped him aside to do it herself. Before she got a chance, he grabbed her by the waist and turned her to face him for a good-morning kiss. Heaven help her—even after all this time, the man's lips against hers still melted her heart.

And the things he did to her at night had her melting all over.

She was tempted to pull him back upstairs at that thought, but they had work to do. "Good morning."

"It is now," Rafe answered with a mischievous smile.

She rubbed her gloss off his lips with her fingertips. "Go take your usual spot on the patio. I'll brew us both some coffee."

"You're an angel sent straight from heaven," he told her before turning to do as she'd said.

The statement catapulted her back in time to a little over twelve months ago, when he'd said those exact same words to her. Little had she known then just how much her life was about to change with Rafe Malta's arrival on the island. Some days she still felt the need to pinch herself to make sure all of it was real.

When she reached the table outside and sat across from him, Rafe was thumbing through his tablet. Coqui sat wrapped around his ankles, her gentle purr ringing softly through the air.

"We'll have to make a trip to the Paradiso Resort together," he informed her. "Check your calendar when you get a chance."

The statement was rather out of the blue and alarmed her. They'd been supplying the Paradiso resort exclusively since shortly after their eventful visit—when they'd been stranded on an iguana-laden island. "Is there a problem?" she asked. "Are they thinking of not re-signing us for distribution this year?"

Rafe shook his head. "No problem. I thought we might visit to celebrate. I know it's a lovely spot for a honeymoon."

Eva stilled in the act of bringing her coffee cup to her lips. Surely, she had to be hearing things. It was then she noticed the object attached to Coqui's collar—a small box with a bright red satin ribbon.

"What's that?" she asked, pointing a trembling finger at the cat.

Rafe put his tablet down and leaned over to pick up the cat, but not before she caught a sly, sneaky expression flash over his face. He held Coqui toward her.

"Open it," Rafe prompted. "It's for you."

Eva reached for the box and opened it with shaky hands, gasping when she saw what sat inside on a bed of folded satin.

A sparkling emerald cut diamond on a woven gold band. The world started to spin. Then his arms were around her, lifting her out of her seat and taking her into his embrace. She inhaled his scent deeply, reveling in the feel of him against her.

"If you don't want to go back to the Paradiso, we can go anywhere else you like. Just say yes."

Eva worked her mouth, but no words seemed to be coming forth through her lips. Like the old saying went, it appeared the cat really had gotten her tongue.

Rafe removed the ring from its box, then took her hand in his. With a steady, firm grasp he slipped it onto the finger of her left hand. Eva stared at the treasure sparkling in the sunlight, catching the myriad colors that surrounded them.

Rafe leaned in to speak into her ear. "Evalyn Gato, will you do me the honor of becoming my wife?"

Eva thought her heart might swell until it burst in her chest. She answered Rafe's question by pulling his head down to hers and kissing him with all the passion and love for him rushing through her veins.

They were both gasping for air by the time they pulled apart.

"Is that a yes?" Rafe asked, flashing her a teasing smile.

"It is, my love," she answered, unable to resist planting another kiss on his lips. "It's a yes!"

From the corner of her eye, Eva could have sworn she saw the bright green feathers of a rare parrot fly from atop a tree toward the bright blue sky.

* * * * *

CINDERELLA'S FORBIDDEN PRINCE

RUBY BASU

MILLS & BOON

For Dev and El who are my world

CHAPTER ONE

PRIYA SEN REVIEWED her file with the notes detailing the preservation and restoration project for the fourth time that morning. She'd already read them ten times a day since finding out, a week ago, she would be taking over the role of leader of the conservation team working on the murals in the royal palace on Adysara, a little-known island country off the coast of India.

It was safe to say she already had the information committed to memory. But one last look over wouldn't hurt.

It was barely seven o'clock, but Priya had already been up for two hours. She'd woken to the sounds of unfamiliar bird calls.

It had been late evening when she'd arrived on Adysara the previous day. She'd been exhausted after the fourteen-hour flight from England, followed by a two-hour ferry ride from India. Once she'd finally arrived at the building her co-workers were living in for the duration of the project, she barely had the energy to say hello to the others before flopping onto her bed and falling into a deep sleep.

She woke up refreshed, rejuvenated and earlier than anyone else. She'd got ready, then rushed outside to breathe the island air. She immediately felt the sense of homecoming she always experienced whenever she was in India. Technically, Adysara wasn't India and, technically, she was a foreigner, having been born and brought up in England, but something about this place claimed her. She felt like she belonged—something she'd never felt growing up.

Now, after a quick breakfast of luchi and eggs, she was desperate to get to the palace and have her first look at the murals she'd pored over in photos.

Her group's quarters were in a wooded area about a mile's walk from the palace, no doubt to make sure they were hidden from the view of the royal family. Although the team had a minivan, Priya was too excited to wait an hour until it would depart. Clutching the folder with nervous fingers, she walked towards the palace.

It was only when the path took her out of the woods she saw the palace up close and personal for the first time. Four storeys of carved granite with large arched windows at every level. It was magnificent—and this was only the side view where the staff entered. She'd seen the front in pictures with its large central marble dome covering an indoor courtyard. The eighteenth-century architecture in the front and rear with its archways and turrets could rival Mysore Palace.

She held her breath as she walked through the door, half expecting the security guards to apprehend her immediately and remove her from the premises.

Once inside the palace, Priya could see a wide stone staircase on her right. She knew this would lead up to the back of the ballrooms and reception areas which were usually open to the public. Her team would be in some of those rooms since they wanted to protect the integrity of the murals and were working in situ.

In front of her, there was a rabbit warren of corridors with several doors, and more corridors, leading off them. These must lead to rooms used by the palace workers and somewhere, down one of the passageways would be a room for preparing the chemicals her team would be using, and there would be another room, which would be climate-controlled, where the art restoration was being performed.

She'd done conservation projects in stately homes before but nothing as grand as this. Only in her wildest dreams would she have imagined someone like her working there.

Doubts assailed her. She had no right to be there. She was a fraud. She was only there because her colleague had to return to England for a family emergency.

'Ah, Priya. There you are.' Her boss and head conservator, Toby 'Mac' MacFarlane came up behind her. 'I knew you'd want to get here early. Are you ready?'

Priya swallowed. Was she ready? This was the biggest job her company, Courtham Conservation Services, had ever undertaken. If they completed it successfully, they would probably be able to pick and choose what they worked on in future. And where.

If she could stay as team leader or be considered as a lead on future projects around India or the rest of the world, her professional aspirations would be fulfilled.

The role she was replacing was crucial to the project's success. She may not have been the first choice for it, but she was more than qualified to take over. She knew the details of the project. She could do this.

Couldn't she?

There was no time for self-doubt to creep in. She had to prove she was capable.

Priya breathed in deeply, straightening her shoulders. 'I'm ready,' she said. 'Lead the way.'

As they walked through the rooms of the palace, Mac pointed out where other teams were working. Members of her company had been working in the palace for months already and had concentrated first on the areas and rooms that would be used extensively for events for a gala taking place in two months. Initially the whole group had worked on the art restoration to ensure the areas were completed in time. Now, although there were still some pieces to finish off, the group had been split into separate project teams and she would be leading the conservation work on the palace murals and stone carved sculptures while other teams dealt with the painting restorations.

Finally, Mac led her to the mural she would be preserving for the next few weeks.

Priya might be an expert in conservation, but the first time she saw a piece of art in person she could never view it with a technical eye. She could only stand and marvel at it.

And the wall painting in front of her, depicting a royal family picnicking in a forest watched by various animals, was more magnificent than any photo or video could do justice with its vibrant colours and detailed brushwork.

But she couldn't just stand around admiring the piece—there wasn't any time to waste if her team wanted to get this area completed before the gala.

Priya had a quick meeting with her team, making sure she knew everyone's activities for the day. She already knew the majority of her colleagues since they were employed directly by her company, but there were four people who had been seconded from different organisations to build on the interdisciplinary nature of the job.

Her predecessor had taken an approach which divided the mural into sections at various stages of preservation. Priya decided to float between the sections during the day so she could observe the flow of work generally, but she could move easily if one section needed her to assist where time was of the essence for the process.

As she worked, she mentally braced herself for signs of upset or hostility. After all, who was she to come in as lead when they'd been doing the work for months already? If her co-workers did feel that way, they gave no outwards signs; all were welcoming and helped her settle into a groove.

After a few hours, the whole group stopped for a long break. They went downstairs back through the maze of corridors where drinks and food had been laid out in a room for them. Since they weren't permitted to have any liquids, not even water, where they were working, having this room for their comfort was an unexpected perk.

Mac came over to ask her how her morning had been. Although he was in overall charge of the palace conservation and restoration project, during the day he worked as a team leader on painting restoration—available to the other leaders whenever needed but letting them get on with the work at other times.

Priya appreciated his management style. Hopefully, it would give her an opportunity to show what she was capable of—she'd never been leader of such a large team before.

'If your team can spare you for a few minutes, why

don't you take a look around the palace and some of the areas we'll be working on next,' he suggested. 'Leo only started outlining the next wall painting so let me have your thoughts on how you think we should proceed with it as soon as you can.'

Priya nodded. 'Of course. Can I wander round on my own or should I find someone from the palace to guide me?'

Mac grinned. 'There are so many people working in the palace at the moment, with everyone getting ready for the gala, we've been allowed to come and go as we need. Believe me, if you stray too close to the royal family's private wing, you'll know.'

'They're not worried we're going to steal their crown jewels then,' Priya joked.

'Most of these rooms are open to the public anyway so anything of worth has been safely stored away. More so now the gala preparations and our restoration work is going on. Just walk around on your own, get a feel of the place. Look at the scope of the work we have ahead. You have the site plan, don't you?'

'I do. I may as well go now. I'll just let my team know.'

Priya spoke to her team then left the room to start exploring the palace. She wandered along corridors with walls covered in huge paintings, showing the island and the palace in different seasons and time periods. It was obvious which paintings had already been restored and she took a vicarious pride in the quality of work her company did. She only hoped she would meet the same thresholds of excellence.

She entered one ballroom where a large wall mosaic of a blue-grey elephant carrying a gold-and-purple howdah glinted in the sunlight coming from the floor-to-ceiling-length arched windows.

Her mother would have loved this. She'd passed away when Priya was eleven, but before then Priya had often gone to visit art galleries and stately homes in Britain with her when she was younger. Her mother had handed down her love of art and architecture. They'd already planned a trip to see the Taj Mahal, Red Fort and the Golden City of Jaisalmer in the summer before Priya started secondary school, which was when her father would be in England for a brief stint before his next posting.

But her mother got sick in Priya's last year of primary school.

Instead of spending time with her vibrant, loving mother, Priya had been sent to boarding school where her father seemed to forget about her existence. She barely saw him after her mother died; she begged to go abroad with him on his postings, but he had always refused. Her only bright moments were holidays she spent with her maternal grandparents who travelled from India to look after her and took her to the places her mum had wanted to show her.

But after a few years, her dadu and didima stopped coming over, so apart from the occasional week with her paternal grandparents who lived in England, she spent holidays at her boarding school.

She never knew why her dadu and didima stopped visiting her. They never replied to her letters or emails or answered her phone calls. After a couple of years she stopped trying. When she lived in India doing fieldwork as part of her master's degree course, she had tried to get in touch again but without success. She briefly considered trying to get in contact now again. Her didima grew up in Adysara; Priya thought she might want to know her granddaughter was working in the palace she used to tell stories about.

Priya grimaced. What was the point of trying to make contact? She would just be inviting further rejection.

Suddenly, the walls of the palace were closing in on her. She was no longer experiencing the awe and joy of exploring. She needed fresh air. She was some distance from the palace exits but she'd passed a ballroom which had open balcony windows.

She retraced her footsteps back to the room.

She walked onto the balcony and breathed in the scent of Adysara, so evocative of India. She tried to find somewhere safe to stand as people were bustling round tidying and decorating. She almost bumped into a platform which was supporting a ladder balanced against a pillar. Luckily she managed to avoid it since someone was perched on the top rung, holding a string of lights.

She lifted her gaze from the man to the top of the pillar. The sun was bright, but she was certain she could see shadows around the edge. Was that…?

'Stop!' she called out. The man tottered slightly on the ladder. Priya held her breath until he regained his balance.

A lady strode up. 'Can I help you? I'm Zivah Chetty, I'm part of the event organiser team at the palace. What is the problem? Who are you?'

Priya introduced herself then explained she'd noticed a hollow relief on the external pillars which hadn't been mentioned in the files.

'Why is it an issue?' Zivah asked.

'It hasn't been assessed yet. We don't know what materials were used. And importantly in this situation, what effect the heat from the lights could have on it. Have these external pillars been assessed for the effects of stringing the lights? I don't see them referenced in my notes.'

'They're pillars.' Her tone was condescending, suggesting Priya was making a fuss over nothing.

'Which are hundreds of years old,' Priya replied.

'If there was a problem your boss and Mr Blake would have pointed it out.'

Priya bit her lip. Zivah Chetty was right. They should have pointed it out. Why wasn't it in the report? Regardless of whether there were actual issues related to the pillars, the hollow relief should have been noted. Perhaps it was a clerical error and the information hadn't been transposed from Leo Blake's notes but she didn't have time to look into it right now. She needed to do an assessment before they went further with the illuminations.

Priya straightened her shoulders, she didn't enjoy arguing with people, but stone art was also an area she specialised in. She did know what she was talking about. As team leader, these were the exact situations she was expected to handle. She had to stand her ground. The potential to damage historical art was too important for her to doubt her abilities.

She needed to get up the ladder.

'Are my parents in their quarters?' Rohan Varma asked as he strode through the halls of the palace to his suite of rooms.

'The Maharaja is in meetings and the Maharani is visiting the children's hospital with Rajkumari Varasi,' his assistant replied.

'Varasi is here?' he asked, surprised his sister had already arrived on Adysara. 'I presume she and my mother will be out for lunch then?' His assistant nodded. His father wouldn't be stopping for lunch then. Rohan would meet his family for the evening meal, but they had a rule not to discuss business or politics at the dining table. 'Please find me ten minutes to speak to my father this afternoon.'

When he was younger, as soon as he returned home for the holidays from his boarding school, Rohan used to rush to greet his parents wherever they were. His father always stopped what he was doing to spend a few minutes catching up. His father might be the monarch and constitutional head of Adysara, but even when he was in important meetings, he had always made time for Rohan.

When Rohan had children, hopefully within the next five years, he wanted to be the same kind of father—making sure he had time to spend with his family. But before he could become a father, he would need to find a wife. Someone to be the future queen of Adysara. And that was the reason he'd come back from abroad. One of the reasons.

He was thirty-five years old, and fully aware of his duty as the crown prince. Although Adysara hosted a gala week every five years, this year's event would introduce him to eligible woman. Everyone expected him to choose a potential bride.

Rohan had always known this was coming. It was the reason all his previous relationships had necessarily been short-term, and he'd been upfront about it.

Now he was back home, he was ready to do his duty. He was ready to get married.

He went to his rooms for a quick wash and change from his travel clothes into a cotton shirt with a band collar and lightweight wool suit, his usual attire when he was staying in the palace and not having meetings.

Once he felt refreshed, he went to his study. As soon as he sat down, his assistant placed financial reports and policy briefings on his desk. After he'd read through the papers and provided notes he handed the papers over to his assistant. Moments later he could hear the papers being shredded.

Rohan rolled his eyes. Although the palace and the island had fast, effective internet and the palace used its own secure intranet server, his father maintained the tradition of paper reports.

It wasn't the only tradition his father maintained. Rohan was strongly reminded of that fact when he was sitting in front of his father's desk later that afternoon.

They'd spent a pleasant half hour having a quick catch-up on life in general, but his father was in the middle of a busy workday and Rohan wanted to talk about his proposals for Adysara's regeneration.

Rohan loved the history and tradition of Adysara. It was an honour and a privilege to be a member of their royal family. He didn't want to turn his back on it. He wasn't coming back to Adysara with new ideas from his time abroad with the aim of shaking up centuries of tradition. He just wanted to find ways to build on what they were already doing. The country already had a good education and health system but they were constantly losing talented people to emigration because they didn't have the business and market infrastructure to sustain prosperity. But in order for him to create financial stability, he needed his father's formal approval to take his ideas before the government.

It was a slow process. His father was a great believer in the phrase 'if it's not broken, don't fix it.' The problem was his father didn't always admit when something was broken.

Their biggest disagreement was about increasing tourism to the island. Adysara had never been a tourist spot, but its location made it a potentially attractive destination. In Rohan's opinion it could be as popular as the Maldives which had only become a luxury holiday option within the last fifty years.

After a long discussion and using up every ounce of his persuasive ability, Rohan was relieved when his father finally said, 'Fine, son. Look into this regeneration scheme. I'll expect a report from you. I'll put it through the same scrutiny any direct proposal would get. No favours.' He gave Rohan his special smile.

'I would never ask for one. But I have your permission to ask Courthams to do some investigation work?'

'Yes. We can definitely fund the early-stage work from the family finances. But there is one condition.'

Rohan was taken aback. 'There is?'

'Yes. This gala is very important. Not only for Adysara, but for me and your mother personally. I know you will do your duty.'

'Of course.' It was, always had been and always would be duty above all. It normally went without being said. Surely that wasn't the condition?

No, apparently the condition was for Rohan to discuss the guest list, specifically the female guests, with his father *and* listen to his father's opinions on who could be a good fit for Rohan.

Rohan understood to be a *good fit*, his potential bride would need to offer something which would help with Adysara's growth. Decades ago, one of his ancestor's marriage to a wealthy heiress had enabled the Adysarian royal family to become self-funding—not taking a single coin from the people. Since then, the dynastic marriages had always improved the quality of life for the people of Adysara in some way. At least Rohan didn't have the added requirement to marry someone of royal or noble lineage, although that was an added benefit. Rohan's mother was descended from another Indian royal family, in name only of course, but she still had landed wealth which was used to improve public amenities on the island. Rohan's sister's husband came from a family of tech industrialists which had provided the island with an excellent communication and internet network. Rohan knew he didn't just need to get married—his duty was to make an *advantageous* marriage. Without it, his country could decline even further and even lose its independence. He would never allow that to happen.

'We all hope for a successful outcome from the occasion,' his father said, once they'd gone through the top names under consideration, 'but we would like you to enjoy yourself. It's a time for everyone to have fun. We're not forcing you to make any decisions. Your mother and I just hope you find happiness the way we did.'

At a similar gala forty years ago, his mother had been one of the guests. His father thought they could be compatible together so they'd spent a few months getting to know each other before they agreed to marry. His mother hoped at this gala Rohan would immediately see a woman and fall head first in love, the way she claimed she did with his father.

Although Rohan would never have the temerity to say it to his mother, he believed it was more likely to be lust, not love. Love wasn't something that developed in the space of a few weeks. It grew slowly over time, with shared interests and shared values. It was laughing together, dreaming together, making plans together.

But now, anyone could see the love his parents shared for each other, and their children. And the same was true for his sister and her husband.

Rohan wanted the same kind of relationship with his future wife. He wanted to find someone with mutual interests, someone he could respect, someone he could talk to. Affection or love or whatever they wanted to call it could grow after marriage once they spent time together. He'd seen it happen with his family and friends. It was enough for him.

He'd never been *in love*—he wasn't convinced love existed that way. He'd experienced lust, naturally. He'd had plenty of girlfriends over the years but he was never unhappy when the affair came to an end, as it inevitably did. He was glad of it each time he saw a friend shattered over losing someone they were convinced was the love of their life, only to go through the whole rigmarole again a few months down the line. That kind of *love* was a romantic myth and he wanted nothing to do with it.

Back in his suite of rooms, Rohan walked over to his windows. The view here, of the manicured grounds with topiary leading to the woods and then his private garden, was very different from his offices in Dubai or Los Angeles where he'd spent most of the past few years. But this place, Adysara, was home. He was happy to be back—for good this time.

One thing he and his father were absolutely on the

same page about was that no business, no improvements should spoil the natural beauty of the island. He didn't want to introduce any tourism if it would entail large parts of the natural habitat being destroyed in order to build a sprawling resort. He had ideas to make sure that wouldn't happen.

He made a note to check whether the hoteliers he'd included on his personal guest list for the gala would be able to attend. The companies he'd invited had a reputation for eco-friendly development and sustainability. He hoped the gala events would give him an opportunity to discuss business deals; when he wasn't charming and entertaining his potential brides.

While the guests were staying at the palace for the gala events, Rohan planned to take his potential investors on a tour of the islands which made up Adysara. As well as its location, and the fact there was a functioning monarchy, it was his firm belief the wall paintings and rock-cut sculptures on one of the islands, actually a peninsula off the main island, could be as big a tourist attraction as the caves at Ajanta and Ellora. If he could include those on the tour, it would be a big asset.

He buzzed his assistant. 'Could you arrange for Mr Blake to see me when it's convenient, please.'

A few minutes later, his assistant came through the door, surprising Rohan. That was never a good sign.

'Unfortunately, Mr Blake had to leave. A family emergency I understand,' his assistant explained. 'They organised a replacement immediately—she arrived yesterday.'

Rohan's eyebrows shot up. 'Why is this the first I'm hearing of this?'

'Mr Agrawal was handling it.'

Rohan pressed his lips together. Technically, there was no reason for him to be informed. Govinda Agrawal was the project coordinator after all, but everyone in the palace knew of Rohan's interest in the restoration project. He'd been instrumental in hiring Courtham Conservation Services.

'Who is Mr Blake's replacement?'

His assistant pulled something up on his tablet. 'Priya Sen.'

Rohan frowned. He didn't remember seeing Priya Sen's name on the company website, which meant she couldn't be a recognised expert. The murals and wall carvings were too important to leave in the hands of a junior member of staff.

This was not good.

'Where will I find this Priya Sen?' He was heading to the door as he spoke.

'I can call her to come here.'

Rohan waved away the suggestion. 'No need. I'll go to find her. This can't wait.'

CHAPTER TWO

'PRIYA SEN!'

'Yes,' Priya replied, looking down from her ladder for the person who shouted out to her. There were too many people around for her to pinpoint the speaker. She turned back to the columns.

'Come down here, please!' the voice called out again, the tone of command contradicting the polite words. Whoever this man was, he was used to giving orders.

'Hold on a sec,' Priya called turning back to the column, only to be distracted by the collective gasp from below. They were all looking in the direction of one person.

Even from the height she was at, she could tell the man towered above the people in the ballroom. She watched him stride across to her, making the balcony seem somehow much smaller than it was before. He approached the platform which was balancing her ladder, holding it in an obvious indication he was expecting her to come down. Every instinct screamed at Priya to stay where she was—that going down the ladder and meeting this man was going to have an irrevocable effect on her career—on her life.

She glanced at the other people in the room. All of

them had stopped what they were doing and were focused on the interaction between her and the man at the foot of the ladder.

Gulping, she slowly began to descend, taking extra care with each step she didn't miss her footing. With all eyes trained on her, the last thing she wanted was to fall in a heap.

She hated being the centre of attention.

Once she finally reached the ground, she patted down her overalls then looked up at the man waiting for her.

And time stopped.

He was a walking work of art; his hair was black, so black the sunlight cast a blue sheen across it, his cheekbones were sharp as if they'd been chiselled from marble, his jaw strong and stubborn, impatient. And his deep, dark brown eyes didn't hide his annoyance.

'Priya Sen,' the man said, his voice rippling over her body.

She blinked, still not quite believing the image of beauty before her was real.

'You are Priya Sen, are you not. I hear you've taken over from Leo Blake.'

'Priya. Yes, yes that's my name. Priya. And I've replaced Leo.' Priya hoped she'd managed a genuine-looking smile but the stretch in her cheeks suggested otherwise. 'Oh, are you the palace coordinator? I've been looking forward to meeting you, Mr Agrawal.' She held out her hand. The man simply stared at it. Priya grimaced. So much for making a good impression. She immediately drew her hand back, then put both her palms together, touching her forehead with her fingers.

The man inclined his head.

'I'm not Mr Agrawal,' he said. 'I'm Rohan Varma.'

'Varma?' Priya tilted her head. It was the surname of the royal family. It wasn't a unique surname so it probably wasn't that much of a coincidence he also had the same one. But the expectant look he was giving her, put together with the deferential silence of the other people nearby who were still watching their exchange, gave her pause for thought.

Of course she'd done an internet search of Adysara and its royal family. She'd seen pictures of them. But the truth was she didn't have a great memory for faces and her focus had been on the heritage of the place, not the people.

She had to admit it was possible she was standing in front of a member of the royal family of Adysara. She stood immobilised like a deer caught in the headlights. Would it be rude to ask him if he were royalty? Wasn't it something she should be expected to know?

'Yuvaraja-sahib,' Zivah Chetty said. 'How can I assist you?'

Priya gulped. Zivah had addressed him as the prince, no not just the prince, the crown prince. There was now no possible doubt the man in front of her was part of the royal family. Not Mr Agrawal, the project coordinator. Not even Mr Agrawal's manager. But the crown prince. And she'd told him to hold on.

Was it too late for her to dip into a curtsey—no, the etiquette guide, which the team had been given before they started working, said curtseying was only necessary if she was a citizen of Adysara.

She slowly became aware the prince and Zivah were looking at her expectantly. While her mind had been filtering thoughts about etiquette and royal families, she'd obviously missed the conversation.

She inwardly berated herself. Being singled out by the prince wasn't a good sign. If there was anyone she wanted to make a good impression on it would be Rohan Varma. She'd been told the crown prince took a personal interest in the conservation work. She could only hope she could salvage the situation. There was no way she would be able to convince Mac she was the right person to keep leading the project if she couldn't impress the prince.

She opened her mouth, but the only thing which came out was a choked sound. She took a calming breath. She couldn't let her nerves and doubts get the better of her. Not now. This was too important for her future.

'Perhaps we could talk, Ms Sen,' the prince said.

'Of course, Yuvaraja-sahib,' Priya replied, using the same form of address Zivah had, assuming she must know the correct designation. She walked behind him as he led her out of the ballroom.

All her colleagues had talked about how invested the prince was, but from what they said, she'd been under the impression he wasn't on this island.

If she thought about it, she supposed it made sense he would return well before the gala. In the few hours she'd been on the island, she'd already heard the rumour this particular event was for him to find a bride. She wasn't sure whether she really believed that—it sounded too much like a fairy tale—but she was aware the Adysara royal family only hosted the lavish gala festivities every five years.

The prince led her towards an empty reception room. Once inside he closed the door and turned to her. She didn't have to be an empath to recognise the restrained anger in the tight lines of his jaw.

She had no idea what she could have done to cause his reaction. But if he didn't want her as project lead her professional dreams were over before they'd even got started.

'What were you doing hanging lights on the pillars?' he bit out at her. 'I was told you've taken over from Leo Blake as team lead on the wall restorations. I don't think decorating for the party is an objective of the role. If you're going to stay here, I expect you to do your job.'

Priya's mouth fell open. She blinked trying to understand what he was talking about. Hanging lights?

'I—I wasn't,' was all she could say.

His mouth tightened, making Priya gulp. Her denial made him angrier.

'You weren't on the ladder just now.' He quirked an eyebrow.

'Yes, of course, but I—'

'You weren't hanging the lights?'

'No!' Priya closed her eyes trying to remember what had happened to the string of the lights the person had been about to attach to the pillar before she stopped him. She didn't recall him bringing them down with him. He must have left the lights at the top of the ladder, she just hadn't noticed.

She supposed from the ground, it could look like she was helping with decorations rather than working. She needed to set the story straight.

'I know it may have looked like I was attaching the lights, but I wasn't.' She held her hand up when he opened his mouth to speak. 'I stopped someone because I needed to examine the pillar.' It was only when she noticed the startled expression on his face that she realised by her hand gesture she'd effectively told the prince to shut up.

Mortification didn't begin to describe the sudden heat in her cheeks contrasting with the feeling of cold dread rushing through her body.

Waiting for him to chastise her for her impertinence, she raised her eyebrows when instead he asked, 'Why did you need to examine the pillar?'

'I thought I'd seen an intaglio in the pillar. I didn't see anything about them in the reports. I needed to do an examination before they could be damaged by the lights or heat.'

'An intaglio in the pillars?'

'Yes. A hollow relief. It's a—'

'I know what a relief is.'

She gave a brief nod of acknowledgement. 'I wasn't one hundred percent sure from the ground. And I couldn't see anything on other pillars. So I had to go up on the platform to investigate.'

'You thought there was a relief on one pillar of the balcony nobody has noticed before?'

Priya looked at her feet. He made it sound like she was being ridiculous. 'I was right. There was something. There was no mention of it before—probably because our restoration project was asked to concentrate on the internal rooms. We should have checked all the areas which are going to be decorated. The artwork in this palace is so amazing, it's not a surprise to find there are gems hidden in unexpected places.'

The prince was quiet for a few moments. Then he nodded his head. 'So you think there could be other places in the palace with similar reliefs or other artwork?'

Priya nodded. 'We should definitely check any areas

which are being decorated, whether or not a main event is taking place there. Particularly outside.'

There was a knock at the door. Someone Priya didn't recognise popped his head in.

'Yuvaraja-sahib,' the man said, 'it's time for your call.'

The prince glanced at his watch. 'We can discuss this later. Come to my study after dinner. Eight thirty.'

He walked away without giving her a backward glance.

Priya took a couple of deep breaths. At least she wasn't fired. It sounded like he accepted she had a genuine reason to be on the ladder. It was probably as close to an apology as she was going to get for being accused of decorating rather than doing her job.

So on the one hand, she'd shown competence in her field. On the other hand, she'd told the crown prince of Adysara to hold on and then stopped him when he tried to speak. Priya closed her eyes tightly. If her actions had caused her to lose this position, she would only have herself to blame. No wonder Mac hadn't picked her for the initial team.

Suddenly, the thought occurred to her she had no idea where the prince's study was. She mentally shrugged. She was sure someone in the group would be able to direct her. Speaking of which, she'd been away from the work much longer than she planned. She couldn't risk her team thinking she was unreliable and not pulling her weight, not after all her mistakes with the prince.

She headed back to join them.

Rohan tried to concentrate on the policy document in front of him. He glanced at his watch. Priya Sen was five minutes late. He couldn't remember the last time someone kept him waiting. Well, apart from this morning. But somehow he didn't think Priya was doing it intentionally.

Perhaps it was arrogance on his part but he was so used to being treated with respect, almost reverence, whenever he was at home, he hadn't anticipated Priya wouldn't know he was the crown prince. She'd been polite but in no way deferential.

It was a relief nobody could see his face as he watched Priya come down from the platform. He'd never thought overalls were a particularly alluring item of clothing until he'd been entranced by Priya's curvaceous figure descending towards him. He'd been eager to see her face, and when she finally did look at him, something intense flared in him.

She was stunning. There was no better word to describe her.

His physical reaction to her was natural. But inappropriate. He was the crown prince, with a duty to choose a bride within the next few months; he couldn't indulge in a brief sexual fling. And even if it wasn't the case, his interest in Priya had to remain professional.

There could only be business between them.

The intercom announced Priya was in the waiting area. Briefly tempted to keep her waiting for a while, he curtailed the immature impulse and signalled his assistant to let her in.

She was red-faced and panting. Had she taken a shower before this meeting or was her hair damp with sweat? Whichever it was, it didn't detract from her innate beauty.

Rohan pressed his lips together, reminding himself he had no business thinking of the way Priya looked.

'I'm so sorry,' she gasped out. 'I got lost and nobody would tell me how to get here for security reasons.'

Rohan frowned. 'Didn't Hoshik meet you?' he asked, referring to a member of his personal staff.

Priya gave a small self-deprecating laugh. 'In the end yes. But I didn't know you were sending someone to fetch me. I didn't want to be late for our meeting so I set off before Hoshik arrived at our building. In the end I decided to return to our quarters and there he was. I am so sorry.'

Rohan quashed a laugh. She looked nervous and frazzled—he doubted she'd see the humour in the situation. Did she really think she could wander around the palace and be directed to his suite simply by asking people? He only hoped her job portfolio was accurate and her expertise in stone-cut art was better than her common sense.

'Can I get you a drink?' he asked, waiting for her to get her breath.

'No!' She looked horrified at the suggestion. Then she closed her eyes, clearly embarrassed. 'Oh, you mean get someone to get me a drink. No, thank you.'

Rohan rolled his eyes. He couldn't really take offence at the implication he couldn't get his own drinks—he didn't have staff or workers when he lived in the States and he had the bare minimum staff in Dubai—but unfortunately, the reality was in the palace he rarely lifted a finger for himself and was in fact going to ask his assistant to fetch her drink, if she asked for anything other than spirits he had in his study.

She perched primly at the edge of her seat, trying to maintain eye contact with him, but often looking down at her lap, whether out of nerves or deference to his royal status he wasn't sure.

He glanced at the folder on his desk. From what he'd read, she had no need to be nervous about her qualifications and ability to take on the project lead role.

'I had a chance to look through your portfolio,' he began, 'it's impressive.'

'Thank you,' she replied, her voice rising at the end, as if she was surprised by his comment. Didn't she know how strong her professional background was?

'You have a specific qualification in wall conservation. Why weren't you part of the project to begin with?'

'I don't know. I wasn't part of the decision-making process.'

He narrowed his eyes. She was clearly uncomfortable by his question. He suspected she had hoped she would be part of the group as well.

'I'm very happy to be a member of the team now. And of course, my manager has said we'd be happy to take a look at any other projects you have in mind while we're here.' She reached into her bag for a notebook.

He gave a brief nod, pleased she'd brought the conversation directly to the business at hand.

When they had met earlier on the balcony, he'd got the impression she was unsure of her position and role. It made him worry she wasn't the right person to take over the project. But a lot of it was due to her soft features and her delicate round face, which made her look far too young to be leading a project.

He huffed. What Priya looked like was irrelevant. He was only interested in her talents at preservation.

'I don't know how much you know about Adysara.'

'A little.'

'We're actually an archipelago of ten islands, although only four are currently inhabited. Technically those four islands could be considered peninsulas, but access is tricky by land. Although a lot of people assume we're part of India, we're actually self-governing and self-financing.'

She nodded her head. So she had done her research.

'We have good trading relationships with South Asia and North Africa, but if we are to be sustainable in the long term, we need to look at bringing in other revenue streams.'

She furrowed her brow, wrinkling her nose in a manner he found delightful. He averted his gaze so he could concentrate properly.

'We have a summer palace, which we don't use any more on one of the islands. It could be turned into a luxury resort island, but I believe cultural heritage also attracts tourists. To that end, there are at least six murals on some of the smaller islands which I think could be worthy of displaying as tourist attractions. But the major thing is on what we call Adysarina Island which has rock-cut architecture in caves. I want to do an exploratory project on whether we can open those caves up to visitors and perhaps get some tourist revenue.'

'I'm not the team expert on restoration matters.'

'I know.' He waved her portfolio briefly. 'Obviously I would like the wall paintings and cave art to be restored. But before that can be done, the first priority—'

'The first priority is to do a survey to assess the condition and causes of any deterioration.' She flashed a bright, but brief, smile at him.

'Precisely.' He sensed she approved of his priorities.

'Fantastic.' She clapped her hands together. 'I can do

a visual inspection with the equipment I have on the island. When can I begin the evaluation?'

'I will arrange for you to tour the islands, beginning
with the murals. Once you've inspected those, you can
look at the caves. It probably isn't feasible to attract tourists with merely the caves to entice them.'

Priya gave a one-shoulder shrug. 'Apparently Ajanta
and Ellora do quite well.'

His lips quirked. 'Have you visited those caves?'

'No. I've been to the Elephanta Caves. Actually my
visit there started my interest in heritage conservation.'

'I noticed you were a science major at university.'

She smiled. 'That's what my bachelor's degree is in,
yes. But then I visited the Elephanta Caves, saw the
dvarapalas and the linga shrine and knew I needed to
work in this field. It was a big gamble to change direction from the science doctorate I was sure I would be
taking, particularly since I'm not artistic and had no real
knowledge of art.' She paused then cleared her throat,
as if suddenly aware she was sharing unnecessary personal information. 'Do you have any photographs or
schematics for the murals and caves? What's their current preservation situation?'

'We already had architects and engineers appraise the
areas. I'll make sure you have their reports.'

She was sitting forward now, showing her eagerness
to find out more about the project, her finger tapping
against her mouth drawing his gaze to the lush fullness
of her lips.

He needed to stop this. Rohan stood up and walked
towards a bureau which contained a drinks cabinet. He
poured himself a Scotch, belatedly turning to offer Priya
something, which she refused. He worked with many

beautiful women, all the time. He never let their attractiveness distract him.

Perhaps it was the circumstances, which was causing this unusual reaction rather than Priya Sen herself. He was back home to find a potential bride. Someone he could spend his life with. Perhaps he was inadvertently assessing people he met—women he met—as future spouses. Which immediately knocked Priya out of contention. She would never be a suitable bride for him.

He had to remain professional. He might not be her direct employer, but his family were, and if they worked on the cave project together he would certainly be thought of as a client.

CHAPTER THREE

TWO DAYS LATER, Priya waited at the front doors of the palace for a car to be brought round. It was only February, which she'd read was the coldest, driest month on the island, but the sun hadn't received the message and was already threatening a scorcher. It was going to be a long, hot day.

Luckily, a palace worker had already handed her a cool bag with bottled water for her day out.

When the Jeep came into view, a tall, well-built man came to stand next to her. She gave him a small smile, but his face remained impassive. She tried asking him who he was but he gave no indication he could understand her English. She didn't know Adsahi, the native language of Adysara, so she tried in Hindi, one of Adysara's national languages, but he still didn't reply.

She shrugged. Hindi wasn't her family's regional language, but she'd picked up some words and phrases growing up, and it had improved when she was doing fieldwork in India as part of her master's. Apparently not well enough to be understood by the man next to her though.

A worker ran out from a small side building holding a long pole with a mirror on the end, which he handed to the man. When the Jeep came to a halt, the silent man walked round the vehicle, using the mirror to look under it. He gave a small nod to someone in the doorway.

Priya widened her eyes. Was he some kind of palace security? There had been so much freedom in moving around the palace and its grounds, she almost forget it was actually the home of the royal family.

The man took Priya's bags of equipment to load in the boot. Then he held one of the doors open for Priya so she got in the car. It was still early, but the heat made the temperature in the car uncomfortable. She reached into her bag to pull out a bottle of water and a cloth to wipe her face.

As she was taking a sip, a shadow to her side indicated someone was getting in. She pasted a bright smile on her face, wishing the first impression she would be making on Mr Agrawal wasn't with sweat pouring down her face.

But that would have been better than making the same bad impression on Prince Rohan, who had actually got into the car.

She wasn't usually vain, so why should it bother her she was never looking her best when they met? Her concern must be she wasn't looking professional. Particularly when compared to the effortlessly cool and poised man sitting next to her.

After a brief nod of acknowledgement he started speaking to the two men in the front seats. She took the chance to examine him, unobserved.

A bold, straight nose. His full, surprisingly sensuous lips prominent despite the shadow of his beard. Again, she imagined his rigid profile immortalised in stone.

Maybe it already had been. Was there a bust, or a full-length statue of him somewhere in the palace grounds? She would love to see it.

'Everything all right?' his voice interrupted her musings.

'Yes. Fine.' She smiled as brightly, but professionally as she could.

'Shall we go then?'

'Aren't we waiting for Mr Agrawal?'

'He's busy in the palace. I can show you the relevant murals.'

Wasn't the prince busy? He was heir to the throne. Surely he shouldn't be spending his time showing her around the island. From their conversation a couple of evenings ago, she could understand how important the regeneration project was to him, but she didn't want to be a burden—she could inspect the murals on her own.

'Yuvaraja-sahib—'

'You can call me Rohan.'

'Oh, I don't think I could,' she replied without thinking. 'I'm not sure it's appropriate.'

He took a slow breath, the kind she knew people took when they were gathering their patience.

'We're going to be working together for a while over the next few days.' He spoke slowly. 'I don't want to always be addressed as the prince. It's not necessary. It's also not safe to draw attention to my royal status when we're out in public. I don't want everyone to know I'm outside the palace. And luckily, when people don't expect to see me they can't be sure I am the prince, as I have no doubt you can understand.'

She knew he was making a dig about her failure to recognise him at their first meeting, but his tone didn't sound irritated—it sounded humorous.

'I also have this baseball cap,' he added, pulling one out of his pocket and placing it on his head. 'No one expects the prince to wear this.'

Priya laughed. She reached out and adjusted the cap to sit better. The cap did nothing to disguise his handsome features, but it made him look more down to earth—not so out of reach. She blinked then hastily withdrew her hand before turning her head to look out of the window.

Why had she done that? He *was* out of reach, she reminded herself. He was royalty. She didn't understand why she was having such an unusual reaction to him. He was an attractive man. Maybe she was experiencing what her friends felt about their celebrity crushes. That must be it—her shallow breath and accelerated heartbeat must be because she was in the presence of someone famous.

Nothing to worry about—her career was the only thing important to her and it didn't allow her room for distractions. Finding the crown prince attractive was safe in a way, because he was so far out of her league he would never be interested in someone like her and nothing could come from this harmless crush.

But if he wanted to be treated as a client, she could treat him as one. And she was often asked to call her clients by their first names.

She turned back to him. 'Very well. If you insist, Rohan,' she replied, emphasising his name.

'I do. Now we're going to be travelling down some very rocky and uneven paths, which is why we're taking the Jeep. If we do open this area as a tourist attraction, naturally we will improve the infrastructure, but I thought I should warn you. It could be bumpy.'

'I'm sure I'll be fine,' she replied. 'I'm made of hardy stock.'

He made a choking sound but didn't say anything. After a minute, he picked up the electronic tablet which was on his lap. 'Do you mind if I do some work?' he asked, but without waiting for a reply he started scrolling on it.

Priya turned to look out the window again. This was her first chance to get a good look at the island.

The road wound through a hill, and the altitude allowed Priya a view of the forests, rows of houses of different sizes constructed from stone or red bricks with flat rooves giving views over the beaches edging the seemingly endless ocean waters. She sighed, completely at peace.

As the Jeep continued to ascend, she began to experience the roughness of the terrain. Only a few bumps, but she braced one hand against the side of the car and checked the security of her seat belt with the other. More jostling, faster and harder now. She struggled to remain seated until they went over a large hump which flung her off her seat and across the car. She would have landed on the floor at Rohan's feet but strong arms caught her before she fell.

Without missing a beat, he helped her sit upright and reached round her to put her seat belt back on.

He gave an instruction to the driver, who slowed down significantly before coming to a stop at a safe part of the road.

The bodyguard came round to hold the door open for her. After she exited, he bent inside and she could see him fiddle with the seat belt. Rohan, the bodyguard and the driver had a quick discussion—plenty of hand gestures and shaking heads but Priya had no idea what they were talking about.

Rohan came over to her. 'We can't find anything wrong with the seat belt. It doesn't look like sabotage, but we will get our mechanics to look at the car when we return to the palace. Would you like to return now? You should be safe if you move to the middle seat. Alternatively you can swap places with Taj,' he said, referring to his bodyguard.

Priya was still trying to process the implication behind Rohan's use of the word *sabotage*.

'Priya,' Rohan's voice penetrated her thoughts. 'Do you want to return to the palace?'

'No, please. We've come all this way. There's no reason to delay this.'

'Are you sure?'

'Yes. I told you. Hardy—'

'Hardy stock. I remember.' The briefest hint of a smiled played on Rohan's lips, but it was enough to send Priya's pulse soaring.

She might be suffering a small celebrity crush, but Priya wasn't sure she really needed the added temptation of sitting next to Rohan for the rest of the journey. She glanced at Taj, standing where he could survey the land and protect Rohan at a moment's notice. There must have been a safety and security reason for the bodyguard to be sitting in the front seat to begin with. She wasn't going to do anything which would jeopardise the prince's safety.

She took the seat in the middle. Taj double-checked her seat belt and they continued the journey. Priya hyperfocused on the report on the murals Rohan had sent her, trying desperately to ignore the warmth from the body next to her and the shivers which ran up her spine at every unintentional contact.

She didn't think she'd ever been as relieved for a journey to be over when Rohan finally said, 'We're here.'

Priya got out of the car and walked round to join Rohan as he led her to an old, crumbling, stone building which was probably used as a hunting lodge or dowager's home in the past.

The lodge had been built into the side of a hill so when she entered through a large arch, it was onto a first-floor walkway which overlooked a courtyard, which once had a large pond. She slowly followed Rohan's gaze to one side.

'Oh, my,' was all she could manage as she began taking in the centuries-old wall painting depicting a group of women in dance poses although only their hands and faces were visible since the mural was the length of the two floors.

'How do we get down there?' She turned to ask Rohan. She started going round the walkway looking for steps that would take them downstairs, then came back to where they entered. 'Oh, I should get my equipment out of the car first.' She craned her neck to glimpse the top of the mural. 'This is simply breathtaking in person, Rohan. I can't believe something like this exists,' she said turning her gaze to his.

He gave her a warm, genuine smile. And for a moment she wasn't sure the mural was actually the most breathtaking thing she'd seen that morning.

'Come on, let's go,' Rohan said, so Priya hurried to collect her things.

Rohan stood at a distance from the wall. He never stopped marvelling at the artistry that went into this mural in front of him. There were no records detailing when the work was created—it wasn't unusual, written records had been rare on the island until the nineteenth century. It wasn't clear whether someone, possibly the royal family at the time, had commissioned the work or whether this was someone's labour of love. But the land it was on belonged to the royal family now and he was its willing caretaker.

'The problem with these murals is they weren't created with longevity in mind,' Priya said as she took moisture measurements and light readings. 'A lot of them were simply ostentatious ways to show how wealthy the person who commissioned the work was. And of course, they didn't have the chemicals and equipment we have today. But why am I telling you things you already know.'

'It's incredible how they created the colours at the time.'

Priya shrugged. 'Well over time the colours became easier to mix. You can see the difference as we come down the painting.'

Rohan frowned. 'What do you mean?'

'This mural isn't one cohesive body of work. You can see the slight changes where different artists took over.' She indicated some areas.

He wasn't an artist and hadn't studied art. To his untrained eye, everything looked the same.

'The bottom has been surprisingly well preserved, which is unusual since I would estimate this was the oldest part. I would say fourteen hundreds, but you would need Mac to test and verify. You'll also need an architectural and engineering report on the structural integrity of the building itself before any tourists come. It would help to have their analysis before we begin working here.' She went back to the mural, happily answering his questions as she worked.

'This is incredible. There are signs of early preservation attempts to some areas. None of our modern methods, but they are definitely using techniques from this century. Who has been maintaining this area?' Priya asked. 'Can I speak to them?'

'All the murals and the stonework you'll see later have been maintained by Mr Agrawal's team. We haven't had experts in, before now. Once these murals were discovered, a couple of hundred years ago, the family closed off public access as a way of conserving them. The palace records show they are open to the public for limited times of the year. But there isn't much interest. Once the islanders have seen the mural, not many come on return visits.'

'I can understand the desire to show this to the world. I saw in the reports you gave me these works are not considered to be within the areas of the Archaeological Society of India, but did you ask them to send someone to inspect it?'

'No.' He grimaced. 'My father and grandfather have never had much interest in opening this area to tourists so there was no need to consider conservation and preservation from such a perspective.'

'I don't need to tell you about all the extra considerations that need to be taken into account when exposing this kind of work to hundreds of people. At the same time it would be so sad to keep something like this hidden from the world.'

'It's not just because of the art, my father doesn't want

to encourage tourism.' Now why had he admitted that to her? It was a personal issue.

She paused what she was doing and tilted her head, waiting for him to say more.

He supposed it wasn't really personal—she already knew about his regeneration plans and the majority of the administration knew he wanted to actively explore increasing tourism to the island. He needed to be honest with Priya and let her know all the work she would be putting into the murals could never come to fruition. But how much detail was it necessary to tell her?

He briefly outlined the issues. As he spoke, he felt a deep sorrow he was at odds with his father. There was so much potential in this plan. But his family was more important.

He sometimes considered giving up on his proposal for regeneration in order to keep the peace despite being convinced it would reap benefits for Adysara's economic growth in the long run. He'd always gone along with what his family wanted in the past—and had been happy to. It was a privilege to be part of the royal family so he willingly carried out his responsibilities. He never wanted to disappoint his parents or have them worry he wasn't doing his duty.

'I understand,' she replied, breaking into his thoughts. 'I think it's important to look at conserving these murals, and if the stone-cut artwork in the caves is anything like this, it will be vitally important. I can prepare a couple of proposals since obviously if you don't have tourists you won't have the same concerns about footfall, lighting, et cetera.'

'Sounds good.'

She turned back to the mural. 'It sounds like being in a royal family is like working in a family business.'

'It's very much like that, yes.'

The horrified expression on her face as she looked over her shoulder at him made it clear she hadn't meant to make her comment out loud. He liked the way she spoke to him as any other client. Not even a client, a friend?

After spending so much time living in different countries where nobody knew about his royal status it took him some time to get used to the deferential, unearned respect people who knew he was a prince tended to treat him with.

'I did run a couple of businesses in Los Angeles and Dubai. I've spent most of my time travelling between the three places. It was good to create something without family expectations, although I can't pretend I wasn't hugely advantaged by the financial situation. From what you mentioned at our meeting the other night, it sounds like you aren't following in the family footsteps by doing this line of work.'

Her lips thinned. That was unusual. Why would the mention of her family cause her reaction?

'No. My father is in the diplomatic service. He has postings around the world.'

'What a great opportunity for you to explore different countries.'

She gave a toneless laugh. 'Hardly. I never get to see him.'

Her voice was so quiet at her last sentence, he almost missed it.

'You don't see your father?' Rohan couldn't imagine

not having a close relationship with his parents. They may have been busy with their royal duties, or away in different countries, but they always made time to chat, by video if necessary.

Priya shrugged. 'Like I said, he works away.'

'But you said postings. Doesn't he spend time with you in England?'

'No. He goes from one foreign posting to another. When I was younger, before my mum died, we used to travel with him, but afterwards I went to boarding school. He's deputy head of mission now. I think he would love to be an ambassador one day, but it hasn't happened yet.'

He could tell she was trying to speak in a matter-of-fact tone, but was he sensing some underlying sadness? No, he didn't know her well enough to understand the nuances of her conversations.

'Was your boarding school in England? Which one? I went to boarding school in England when I was fifteen to study for my GCSEs.'

She told him which one. He knew it well. His family had considered it an option for him.

'How come you went to England for your GCSEs?' she asked.

'I went to different boarding schools around the world. Until the age of eleven I went to a school in North India. Afterwards I spent a few years in the States, Europe and Africa.'

'Oh, God, that's awful. I know how miserable it can be.'

'What? No?' He'd loved being at boarding school. It had been the perfect environment for him. He made

friendships easily so moving to a new school was never
a problem for him. It sounded like Priya had a very different experience. Perhaps because, despite being in a
different country, he was constantly in touch with his
family and home. They were a strong presence in his life
even when they weren't physically with him.

There was something about Priya that prevented him
from feeling pity. Compassion, definitely. But Priya
wasn't giving the impression she felt sorry for herself.

'You mentioned you discovered your love of conservation after you visited the Elephanta Caves. Who took
you?' he asked.

'My grandparents. My mum's parents. It was the last
time I saw them.'

This time he definitely heard an underlying sadness.

'I'm sorry for your loss.'

'Oh, I don't know if they're dead. They just...' She
broke off and then shook her head. 'It doesn't matter.' She walked over to a corner of the wall. 'Look at
this. There's some damage here but I think the tabla
player and the flautist have their eyes covered. I think
this fresco is showing palace dancers. Do you know
whether this building was used for a king's courte-
sans?'

It was a good thing Priya had refocused their attention on the mural. On the project. He had started out
making polite conversation, trying to put her at ease.
But her background piqued his interest.

Not to mention the strong urge he had to take her into
his arms and comfort her for her unhappiness at boarding school; for the loss of her mum, and her maternal
grandparents; and her father though it sounded like he
was still alive.

There was still a lot he wanted to unpack but, despite some of the openness in her sharing some of her childhood experiences, she had immediately erected a barrier between them.

And that was a good thing.

CHAPTER FOUR

PRIYA RUSHED THROUGH her lunch then had a quick meeting with her team, making sure everyone was happy with what they were doing that afternoon, before heading outside to the waiting car ready to visit the next mural. After seeing the first mural three days before, she had been impatient to see Adysara's other hidden treasures but had determined, since she was still new to the team, it would be best if she spent at least two days working on the palace murals between each site visit.

The car set off as soon as Priya had settled in. She sank back into the seat—Rohan wasn't coming with her. What had she expected? A prince would be her tour guide every day? But he was so excited when he showed her the mural the previous time, she'd secretly been hoping he'd accompany her again.

Perhaps it was for the best. She still couldn't believe she'd told him about her father. She never talked about him with anyone.

After their rather rocky start, Rohan had made her feel at ease to the extent she kept forgetting he was a prince. In fact she sometimes forgot he was a potential client, speaking to him as a colleague who shared her love of the artistry they were viewing. He didn't seem to mind. Even encouraged her to share her stories.

It had been nice to talk to someone about the work. She regularly worked as part of a team, but she found it hard to make small talk as most of the other team members did. They usually did scoping work in a small group, but since this wasn't something previously scheduled and the team had deadlines to meet for the conservation and restoration work in the palace, Mac suggested she could complete the scoping on her own. He sounded pleased with the potential of the future project and was happy for her to take whatever time she needed to prepare the report so their company would, hopefully, get the contract.

If they did get the job, it would be big. And she would honestly achieve one of her biggest goals if she could persuade Mac she should lead the project—not just one of the teams but the entire project. She couldn't imagine anything more incredible or rewarding than to be responsible for not only preserving the glory of the island's murals and sculptures, but also doing it in a way that would potentially allow the glory to be seen by others, rather than hidden from sight for their protection. She had the qualifications and experience. Would that be enough? Perhaps she should broach the topic with Mac.

Not yet—she needed to prove her value to the team before she could expect anyone to think of her as capable of fulfilling the role. She also didn't want to step out of place. If Leo Blake returned and wanted to lead the work, then she probably wouldn't be considered. What would be the point of submitting an expression of interest if Leo wanted it? When the palace contract had originally come up she'd wanted to express her interest, but then Leo told her he was applying for the stone conservation lead so she'd dropped the idea. Why risk being turned down?

The car came to a halt outside a small woodland area. The driver helped her out of the car and then led her down a path until they came to a clearing where a mural depicting the trees and bushes they had just passed had been painted onto the stone side of a small cliff. Unfortunately, the birds, brightly painted in blues and golds, didn't have real life counterparts she could see.

She sighed at the beauty in front of her, sending up a wish even if she wasn't good enough to lead it, she would still get the chance to be part of this work.

She'd been conducting her examination for a while, when she heard someone clear their throat behind her. She glanced at the time and realised she'd become so absorbed in what she was doing, a few hours had passed. Turning around she expected to see the driver telling her it was time to return. Her heart skipped a beat when she saw who it actually was.

'Rohan,' she exclaimed in delight. 'I didn't know you were coming.'

He gave her a puzzled look. Had she been too informal? She was always getting this protocol wrong. She didn't know what the protocol was. The previous time he'd invited her to call him Rohan, but today he looked surprised by her use of his first name. Was she expected to wait for his permission to use his name each time?

He was a client and a prince. A prince and a client. Not a friend.

'It's another masterpiece,' she said, turning to the mural after he still hadn't said anything.

'Incredible. Can you imagine having this much talent.

I couldn't stop thinking about the craftsmanship after I first saw them when I was still young. I knew they were special even though I haven't studied art.'

'Well neither have I,' Priya replied, with a slight laugh.

'Oh, yes. I remember. You did a science bachelor's.'

'That's right. Natural sciences.'

'Your boarding school has a reputation for being a science school. Was that why you studied science rather than art or art history?'

She giggled. 'No. I didn't study art because I can't draw. It's part of the reason I went into the conservation and preservation side, not restoration.'

'No family expectation you'd be a doctor then?' he asked. She recognised the stereotype immediately.

'No. No doctors in my family. How about you? No pressure to be a doctor for you?'

His lips quirked and she didn't understand why he was looking at her like she'd just said the funniest thing he'd ever heard.

'What?' she asked.

'No. No doctor for me.' He cleared his throat. 'Actually the family expectation is I will be…um…king.'

Priya didn't know how it was possible for her body to run hot with embarrassment and at the same time freeze with mortification.

She held her hands to her mouth. 'Of course. Of course you're going to be king. You're the prince.' She covered her mouth with her fingertips then fluttered them against her lips as she said, 'But of course you know that.' She closed her eyes as if not being able to see meant she was the one who would disappear. Could she say anything more ridiculous?

'Priya.' Rohan's voice was gentle. 'Priya, it's all right. There's nothing wrong with forgetting I'm a prince. I try to do it all the time.'

She opened her eyes quickly. 'What? Why?'

'My parents wanted us, my sister and me, to live as normal a life as we could for as long as we could. My mother wasn't brought up as royalty, despite being descended from one of the royal families in India, and she didn't want our position to shape us negatively. Whenever I'm outside this country, I live as Rohan Varma. Ordinary citizen. It's an adjustment to be back on the island, back in the palace where I'm Rohan Varma, Yuvaraja, and I have a bodyguard and people to make my food and tidy my clothes away.'

'But you don't mind it.' She could hear in his voice he wasn't complaining.

'Not at all. It's my duty. It's what I was born to do. The first time I returned after living on my own and fending for myself, I thought I didn't need all the staff and asked to make a reduction. But the palace is a large employer for the island. If I didn't have those people carry out tasks they've been doing for years, even though I can do them myself, then they become unemployed and I wasn't going to be responsible for that. So if I have someone hang my clothes then it's a privilege. Although I did draw the line at someone spreading toothpaste on my brush.'

Priya's celebrity crush just got a whole lot bigger. What a considerate person he was.

'Anyway,' he continued, 'I'm grateful my parents gave me the opportunity. I appreciate I got the chance to get to make friends as me, as the person I am.'

It would be hard not to want to be friends with

Rohan—but he was her client not her friend. She had to drill it into her brain somehow and get her body to pay attention.

'I can see how it would be special,' she said, trying to adopt a measured tone. 'Will your friends be coming to your gala?'

'I'm expecting some close friends. Friends I was close enough to reveal my royal status to. I hope some friends I had at boarding school will be able to come too. We've kept in touch over the years although we haven't had the chance to meet up as much as we wanted to.'

Priya gave a tight smile and then turned back to the mural. She hadn't made any close friends when she was at boarding school. She didn't blame her fellow classmates. She didn't accept the few invitations she did receive, knowing she could never return the hospitality. After a while people stopped asking her. She'd been utterly miserable and probably didn't give anyone the impression she wanted friends.

It was strange how she and Rohan had similar backgrounds, but from what she could gather, he'd been extremely happy growing up—even loving his boarding school experience.

For her, boarding school had been a constant reminder of how her dad didn't want her with him. He'd definitely kept her out of sight and out of mind.

She tried to imagine how her father would react if he knew she was working in the palace, on first name terms with a crown prince. She sighed. The truth was she didn't know her father at all and had no idea whether he would be proud of her. She never received a response to her message telling him she'd completed her master's with distinction or when she told him she'd got the job with the world-renowned Courtham Conservation Services. And her attempts to keep in contact since then had been brief to say the least.

There was no point thinking about her father or her family. Her priority was to get the murals in the palace completed, and hopefully do a good enough job she would be considered for the preservation work on these murals.

'Have you seen this?' Rohan said, beckoning her over to something painted on the ground.

'I've never been able to work out what this is,' he said. She grinned as he ran through all the ideas he'd had—his excitement clear. She made a feeble joke suggestion for what the damaged area showed, but his laugh was hearty, the sound sending tingles along her spine.

Rohan was probably taught how to be charming and entertaining at the same time he had learned his alphabet but Priya recognised these few hours in his company were some of the happiest she'd felt in a long time.

She had to keep her attraction under control.

It was a good job she knew she wasn't good at being in a relationship—her previous boyfriends always found her lacking. She had promised to save herself the hurt of rejection and the disappointment of failing at something again by never having a romantic relationship again.

Not that a relationship was on offer from Rohan. Just because Rohan was standing next to her physically didn't mean he wasn't miles away from her. Developing a crush on Rohan was as pointless as fancying Michelangelo or his *David*.

It would be easier to deal with her unwanted crush if she wasn't in Rohan's company so much. But she couldn't exactly tell him to stay away. He was the crown prince; he didn't take orders from her.

CHAPTER FIVE

ROHAN SPENT THE morning attending government reporting sessions with his father. He then met his mother and sister for lunch. They hadn't been able to spend as much time together as he would have wanted. His mother was notionally overseeing the gala preparations which made her busier than usual.

She tried to get Rohan involved by insisting he have a say in the arrangements. Usually he tried to give his mother his full attention when she told him what had been organised because the gala was as important for him as it was to the rest of the family, but a large party was the furthest thing from his mind.

He was thinking about the regeneration project. And Priya. He thought about Priya a lot more than he should. According to her proposed scoping timetable, she would be visiting another mural today, the third. He missed having a chance to witness her reaction when she saw a mural for the first time. It was exactly the kind of reaction he hoped thousands of tourists would have one day.

'Is something wrong, Rohan,' his mother asked, clearly noticing his lack of concentration.

'I'm sorry, Ma. I was thinking about the summer palace. I hope there'll be time for me to take some of the guests round the sites.'

His mother didn't say anything. She pressed her lips together, but he wasn't sure whether it was because he'd annoyed her or whether she had something else on her mind.

'Do you know when you'll be able to present your proposal?' his sister asked.

'Not yet, there's still a lot of work to do before I get to that stage.' He frowned. His true desire was to convince his family to fund this regeneration project through investments and family finances, or at least the conservation work. At the moment, his father's opinion was if it went ahead, it would be a government-funded scheme. Which meant once Priya submitted her condition report, he would be assigned policy clerks who would then work with him to develop and cost the proposal fully. Only once that was complete would he be able to get an item on the annual agenda for further discussion. It could be years before the regeneration could start. Of course if his family financed the restoration work he wouldn't be able to use government clerks so he would have to work closely with Priya to develop the proposal.

It wouldn't be any hardship for him. She was intelligent, interesting and was as enthusiastic about the murals she'd seen so far as he was. He enjoyed the time he spent with her.

And she was easy on the eye.

He sat bolt upright. That was an inappropriate thought. She was here to perform a job. What she looked like was irrelevant and had no bearing on her ability to complete the work. How many times did he have to remind himself?

'Are you sure everything is okay, Rohan,' his mother asked again. 'You are acting quite strange.'

'Stranger than usual,' his sister added.

'I'm fine. Tell me about the Melwanis,' he said, naming a family of wealthy industrialists. He was interested in their work pioneering alternative fuel sources which could be valuable for Adysara's future sustainability. For his parents, the attraction was the Melwanis had two single daughters. Rohan knew what was expected from him at this gala and afterwards. His duty was to make a good marriage—getting his regeneration tourism proposal didn't alter the fact.

But since there was nothing he could do about his marriage prospects until the guests started arriving for the festivities, he could focus his attention on attracting investment into the island. And having cultural attractions for visitors would make the investment more likely.

After his meeting with his mother finished, Rohan returned to his rooms where he immediately asked a member of staff to bring him a light jacket and for his car to be brought round. He knew exactly which site Priya was supposed to be scoping.

Within half an hour, Rohan was standing behind Priya, watching as she was engrossed in conducting her condition survey. He stood as silently as he could, admiring how efficiently she carried out her examination.

She was so absorbed it was a good ten minutes before she noticed his presence. He liked how her instinctive reaction was to greet him as a good friend, before she remembered he was technically her client and royalty.

'How's it going?' he asked her, gesturing towards the mural.

'Good. This one probably won't take too long. I should be done in an hour.'

'Great. Will that be too much for you today or are you up to seeing the next one.'

She glanced at her watch, then put her hands on her hips. He was sure she hadn't intentionally drawn his attention to their shapely contour and the narrowness of her waist, but he had to force himself to drag his gaze away.

'If we can fit a small mural in today it would really help. I want to complete this part as soon as I can.'

'Bored of it already?' he teased her.

'Never,' she said with a grin which transformed her somewhat stern resting face to a vision of soft loveliness.

Suddenly he became aware she was looking at him. Was she waiting for a response? He'd missed what she said because he was admiring her features. He couldn't pretend he hadn't noticed she was beautiful. He'd worked with attractive people before and never let it distract him from the task at hand.

'I'm sorry, I shouldn't have expected you to know the exact size of the mural we'd go to next,' she said. 'The papers you gave me didn't have complete information so why should you know? And you're the prince so if you did have the data there's no reason for you to have it at instant recall.'

His lips quirked. He liked it when she began wittering, almost talking to herself, each time she remembered he was royalty.

He reached out to put his hand on her arm, his intention was to reassure her his silence wasn't due to anything she said. But the moment he touched her skin, heat seared through him, like an electric jolt.

He took a step back. Her breath was shallow, she gave him a quick look of alarm then turned to her tools. Had she felt something too?

She was quiet, polite and reserved as she finished her work. But by the time they arrived at the next mural, she'd turned back to her natural self, excited to see what was in store.

He turned to look directly at her so he could take in her initial reaction. Instead of the open-mouthed awe he anticipated, she was looking…puzzled.

'Is everything all right, Priya?'

'Hmm.' She glanced at him briefly before returning her full attention on the mural so he repeated his question.

'Yes,' she replied, 'it's just this mural seems so familiar.'

Rohan looked at the wall painting. The central feature was a peacock displaying its train. In its glory days the colours would have been vibrant blues, greens and golds. But it was probably the simplest arrangement out of all of them.

'Peacocks are common in Indian art,' he offered.

She shook her head. 'It's the filigree plates on the corners, with the initials in them.' She pointed at them as she spoke. Slowly she began to smile. 'I think my didima told me about these. She must have visited them when she was a girl.'

'Your didima?' he asked, raising his eyebrows. She'd mentioned her grandmother on their first site visit. Perhaps the love of art had passed from grandmother to mother to daughter. 'Did she come to Adysara on holiday?'

Priya stared him, the wonder and delight of her realisation still shining from her expression. 'No, she was born on Adysara. Didn't I tell you that? I guess it makes me a quarter Adysarian. Fancy.'

He rarely met people who'd heard of Adysara; it seemed strangely fitting Priya would have a tie to his home country. Perhaps it explained why he felt so connected to her.

'Do you still have family on the island?' he asked.

'No, unfortunately. My didima's father emigrated to India for work and the family didn't come back.'

'You said you lost contact with your grandparents. That's a shame.'

'I know. But it's partly my fault because I didn't realise when their visits ended at first. My father remarried three years after mum passed away. I was hoping I could travel with my father and stepmother, the way I had while mum was alive. Or I was expecting to visit them during school holidays. That's why I thought my dadu and didima weren't visiting.' She grimaced. 'But I didn't see my father in the holidays and by the time I asked about my grandparents I couldn't contact them.'

'Your grandparents visits stopped around the same time as your father remarried?' he asked. At her nod, he furrowed his brow. It sounded like there was more going on behind the scenes than Priya knew. He made a note to ask his assistant to look into her didima—as an Adysarian. If her grandparents had no interest in meeting Priya then she wouldn't have to know. And it would be their loss.

'We've had a real problem with emigration over the years,' he said, as if they hadn't just had a personal conversation. 'Part of the reason I want this regeneration is to improve job prospects and make Adysara a great place to live and raise families, perhaps try to encourage immigration.'

'Oh, I think it would be wonderful,' she said before starting her examination of the mural.

As she worked, he heard her quietly humming a song from an animated film about lions.

He couldn't help chuckling. 'On the contrary, I'm in no rush to be king.'

Joy bubbled when, instead of being embarrassed she grinned back. 'Well of course not. Not when it means your father... Well you know.'

'My father's thinking of abdicating within five years. I could be king a lot sooner than I expected.' Now why had he told her when no one outside his family knew. He wasn't worried she would gossip about it to anyone in the palace. He trusted her implicitly.

Later that evening in his study he looked through some reports which had come through about the hotel companies he wanted as investors. Inevitably his thoughts turned to Priya again.

It was odd how he shared so much of his hopes and dreams with her. At first he thought it was because she was a stranger who understood his desire to show the world what his island had to offer while, at the same time, wanting to protect it and hide it so its glories would never diminish.

Was it his imagination or was there was another moment at the peacock mural when she'd asked him to pass her some equipment and their fingers had touched, their eyes locked, neither wanting to break the connection? The atmosphere was charged. Had she noticed? Could it be why she'd started avoiding looking at him directly when they talked? What would he do if she was attracted to him?

Nothing. She was technically an employee, despite not directly working for him. He had to ignore how stunning she was.

The problem was, this was something a little more than looks. He liked her. He enjoyed spending time in her company. She was beautiful. It wasn't surprising he was attracted to her. He had no intention of acting on it.

He wasn't in a position to offer her a relationship. All his previous relationships had inevitably been time limited. He made that clear to his girlfriends from the start, even though he hadn't always been completely honest it was his duty that prevented him from anything else.

But in this situation even a time-limited affair wasn't on the cards. In less than two months guests would be descending on his island, and among those guests was hopefully someone who would one day be his future wife. She might be a nameless, faceless person at the moment, but didn't he owe it to her, to himself, to his family, to only think about his guests. Increasing tourism and getting external investment didn't change anything for him in terms of the expectations people had of him.

Unless he made an advantageous marriage, Adysara's growth and prosperity would stagnate. Talented young people would continue to leave the island for better opportunities and slowly the population would decrease leading to further stagnation. He had a duty and he wasn't going to let anything get in the way of it. But to be on the safe side, he wouldn't go on any more visits with Priya.

CHAPTER SIX

IT HAD BEEN nine days since Priya had visited the final mural. Each one had been magnificent in its own right, but as a collection they were priceless. She could fully understand why Rohan believed Adysara could become a huge tourist destination with its glorious weather, golden beaches, crystal-clear warm waters. Its cultural heritage was the exquisite icing on top.

She was desperate to scope the caves. Rohan had said they would make the murals pale into insignificance—which she did find hard to believe. She was hoping to go later that day, depending on how far she got with her actual work. Sometimes it was difficult to concentrate on the palace murals when she knew what was outside, but she had to do her best, not only to hopefully demonstrate to Mac she was capable of working on the regeneration project—perhaps even leading it, but for the simple satisfaction of a job well done.

So far everything was progressing well, despite the disruptions being caused by the gala preparations, and her regular absences. Her team had already completed the restorations in the areas that were going to be used for the gala events and were now working on different areas, which, although still accessible by guests, weren't being used directly for any events. Mac was hoping they would be ready to begin the restoration to the artwork in the royal family's quarters. Since there weren't any murals in the royal wing she, personally, wouldn't be needed.

If the regeneration project didn't proceed, or she wasn't selected for it, there was a chance she would be returning to England in a matter of months.

She couldn't bear thinking about it. Because she would be missing out on a major work opportunity, there was no other reason.

She wondered whether Rohan…whether the prince would be accompanying her when they visited the caves. She'd enjoyed her time at the murals more when he was there, chatting with him and exchanging stories of their childhoods. He had seemed to be taking a personal interest in the work but hadn't accompanied her to the last few murals. She knew he was a busy man, but that hadn't stopped her disappointment.

As her mind started to relive her time with Rohan, Priya stretched and stood up. She took a step back to survey the work the team had accomplished that day.

She'd made some changes to the process they used, which took slightly longer but would make their effort more effective. So far it hadn't caused a substantial delay in their progress. Now, at least, when they left the palace, she could be reassured the preservation work would last more than the twenty years possible with the previous process.

She was packing away the tools and chemicals when a man, one of the palace workers came up to them.

'Madam,' he said, 'can you come with me, please?'

'Me?' Priya pointed to herself.

'Yes. Mr Agrawal has asked if he could speak to you if you've finished for the day?'

'Of course.' Priya turned to her colleagues. 'I guess I'll see you back at our quarters.'

'Would you like me to wait for you?' one of them asked with a worried expression.

She smiled. What did he think was going to happen to her? 'No, it's okay. I don't know how long I'm going to be and I'm sure you're eager to get back and wash and eat. Can you let Mac know I've been called to see Mr Agrawal, please?'

She followed the worker through long corridors, heading behind the large drawing rooms and lavish halls, now set up for the gala, careful to avoid disturbing anything. As they progressed, it was obvious how the decor was becoming less ostentatious as they moved towards the staff offices.

Still more extravagant than anything she'd experienced in her normal life, but there was definitely a difference.

She hoped the meeting with Mr Agrawal was to let her know when she would get a chance to see the caves. For a moment, her steps faltered. What if it wasn't the reason?

What if Mr Agrawal was unhappy with her changed process? She'd got Mac's approval but Leo Blake would have run everything by Mr Agrawal first. Regardless of the fact her team's project was going to have a more successful outcome because of her changes, she could have jeopardised any chance of remaining as team lead, and definitely any hope of taking on the role of project lead of the larger island work because she hadn't liaised with the palace's coordinator directly. It was such as foolish omission.

Or what if Mr Agrawal had become annoyed she was absent so often on the scoping visits. She'd been brought to Adysara specifically to take over from Leo Blake, not spend her time outside the palace. Or what if Rohan... the prince...complained about her informality and lack of professionalism?

She interlaced and unlaced her hands several times as she waited outside Mr Agrawal's room waiting for a response to her knock. The man who'd accompanied her nodded and left.

'Enter,' she heard.

The voice sounded familiar but it still startled her when she saw Rohan—no she had to start thinking of him as the crown prince again—standing by the desk. There was no one else in the room.

'Yuvaraja-sahib, I was expecting to see Mr Agrawal.'

He looked stern. 'Didn't I tell you to call me Rohan?'

She grimaced. 'I don't feel right calling you by your first name in the palace, Yuvaraja.' He pressed his lips together. 'In case someone hears me or I forget and use your first name in front of others and they think I'm being over-familiar. I'm quite new as team lead, I don't want to single myself out.'

'Fine. But don't call me yuvaraja or sahib, please. If you don't want to call me Rohan you can call me Mr Varma. I would ask anyone in your team to call me the same if we spoke directly.'

Priya gave a brief nod of acknowledgement, pleased he accepted her feelings above his own request—it wasn't something she was used to.

'How has your work on the murals gone?' he asked.

'Good.' She gave him a brief rundown of her initial findings and thoughts. 'I should be able to let you have my report within a couple of weeks.'

'That's quick,' he remarked.

Priya bit her lip and smiled self-consciously. 'It's such a thrilling project, I'm too enthusiastic to waste any time. I've been working on my report every evening.'

He grinned at her. Her heart seemed to skip a beat at the warmth of his smile. Her reaction was wholly inappropriate for the situation and she had to ignore how attractive the man was. He was her client. Not to mention a prince.

'I felt the same way when I first saw the caves. Come round here, please,' he said, indicating his side of the table where schematics were laid out in front of him. 'This shows where the caves are on Adysarina Island. There's one main stretch of four caves around this range. Then a few other areas around the other islands. Eight in total I think are worth scoping. My favourite sculpture is in this cave.' He indicated with his finger. 'Cave six. It's a little bit off the beaten path so if we did open it to the public we would have to create a new roadway. I think it will be worth it. We could start with it, but I think I'll build up your anticipation before I take you there.'

'Oh, will you be coming with me?'

Her heart started to race again at the thought of getting to talk with him, hear his ideas and stories about the island, laugh with him, be close to him. She sighed. She was doing it again.

It's a crush. You don't do relationships and definitely not with royalty. Be sensible. Don't spoil the chance to work on this project because there happens to be an attractive man in the vicinity. Behave!

'I asked Agrawal to pull out all the historical docu-
ments we have about the caves,' he said, indicating some
papers. 'Will you be able to go out tomorrow, or do you
need some time to organise things with your team?'

Priya mentally ran through the work she had scheduled for the following day. With a small amount of re-
jigging she should be able to be away without having
too great an impact on the work.

She explained that to him, adding, 'But I do need to
confirm with Mac.' She didn't want to risk any possibility Mac would think she was shirking her job as team
leader. Mac had told her, when she first discussed the
prince's project with him, he was happy for her to spend
time scoping out the work—particularly if it meant their
company would be considered for the job. But she always remembered she wasn't first choice as the team
leader, and when Leo Blake's emergency was over she
could be sent back to England just as easily as she was
brought over.

'Of course.' His eyebrows lifted and a brief smile
played on his mouth.

Priya blushed. It probably was a safe assumption her
boss wouldn't refuse a request from the prince, but she
wasn't going to take anything for granted. It was too
important.

'How should I let you know?' she asked. 'Shall I send
a message via one of the workers?'

He furrowed his brow. 'Come with me, back to my
study.'

Curious she followed him out of the room. She
quickly realised there had to be back corridors for the
staff since the path he took to his study was much more
direct than the way she'd been brought that first evening,

and more richly decorated. Another stark reminder, if she needed it, despite the things they had in common, their lives were light years apart.

Once in Rohan's quarters, he asked her to remain in his waiting room while he went into his study. Priya took the time to look around the room, something she'd been too nervous to do the last time she was there.

The modern, bright furniture should have looked incongruous against the old architecture but it blended together seamlessly. Rohan's study was designed in a similar style but his desk was old, reminding her of the Resolute desk.

'Sorry about that,' Rohan said, popping his head through the interconnecting door. 'Come through. It will be a few minutes. Take a seat.' He indicated the comfortable sofa arrangement at the side of his study, rather than the seat opposite his desk. 'I'm sorry, I realised I must have kept you from your evening meal. I've asked for some food to be brought.'

Priya was overwhelmed by his thoughtfulness. 'You didn't have to do that. There's always food around and they keep a fully stocked fridge for us so I could make myself something if I need to.'

'There's always plenty of food around,' he said, waving his hand in a gesture of dismissal. 'I've also asked for someone to bring you a new mobile phone, specifically to contact me directly. You're going to have to complete some paperwork about non-disclosures and confidentially on threat of death which you'll have to sign with a blood print.'

His expression and tone were so sincere, Priya couldn't do anything but stare at him until he finally broke into a huge grin, laughing at her alarm. She joined in, giggling at her own gullibility.

'Anyway,' Rohan said, leaning back in his armchair, 'tell me what you thought of the last few murals. Not their condition. I can wait for the report. Tell me how they made you feel.'

She hoped her conversation made sense because all she could focus on was the idea she would have direct access to Rohan, she could phone him or send him messages. It was a special link between them.

And she was being ridiculous again, letting her attraction rule her common sense. She had to maintain distance and professionalism at all costs.

'You don't need to accompany me to the caves,' she said, hesitantly. 'I know you must have a lot to do. I'm sure the papers you've given me will be enough.'

She held her breath, dreading his response, but not entirely sure which option she dreaded.

CHAPTER SEVEN

ROHAN HAD BEEN stuck indoors for days finalising the sale of his business and divesting himself of all investments which could impact his role as maharajah in the future. Sooner than he planned, if his father kept to his stated intention of retiring, or abdicating, in five years.

Not to mention, with the gala a little over a month away, his involvement in the preparations was increasing with more frequent fittings for his suits, going over the arrangements for the events with his mother and with the different coordinators for the various activities. On top of which he continued to have regular discussions with his family about the lineage and advantages of the female guests.

He knew his duty, and he would perform it willingly and happily, but sometimes he just wished the gala could happen without all this disruption in the run-up to the event.

And if that wasn't enough to interrupt his plans, the art restorers were getting ready to work on his family's quarters. One of his favourite paintings had been removed from the wall and taken down to the studios. It was a shame the royal rooms didn't have any murals. He wouldn't accidentally bump into Priya.

He wondered how her scoping visits were going. He hadn't accompanied her since they went to the first cave. A clear image came to mind of her face when she first saw the stone cuttings. Entranced—her full lips forming a perfect O.

He'd been training his lamp on her instead of the wall and when she'd reached out to direct his hand to the spots she wanted to illuminate, his skin had felt hot under her fingers, his mouth going dry and his lungs forgetting how to breathe.

All from a simple touch, which she'd done without thinking; she'd dropped her hand quickly enough when she'd realised.

He sensed she was keeping her distance from him. She'd been politely professional on the visit, something he wouldn't usually mind, but he'd missed her openness, her unguarded chattiness when they were together before.

Since then he'd been so caught up in palace affairs he'd had no choice but to stay away. But it had been a week. He could do with a day away from the busyness of the palace and going to the caves always helped his mood. Priya being at the caves was simply a chance to kill two birds with one stone.

But since they would be together, it would be pleasant to share a meal again. If they took a picnic they could stay at the site longer. Rohan called his staff to make the necessary arrangements.

The following day, Rohan paced around the mouth of the cave. At first he'd been inside with Priya while she was examining the stone-cut architecture, but she explained his presence could affect the humidity and she needed a baseline reading. He left her to it, trusting her when she said it helped with the preservation.

It was a shame, because he'd enjoyed observing her as she worked, fully focussed on the task at hand. He suspected she wouldn't notice if a herd of elephants trampled across the cave, his presence was completely ignored.

He waited for her impatiently until she finally surfaced, a bright smile on her face.

'I know I sound like a broken record, but what you have on this island is beyond anything I've seen before. It's a privilege to be able to work on this,' she said.

Without waiting for his response, she went to sit on a rock and began to write some notations.

He went to the car to collect the picnic lunch and water cooler. He'd sent the driver and his bodyguard to wait in the shade, lower down the road, but they both started to move towards him when he reached the car so he put his hand up to stop them.

He could imagine Priya's reaction if he couldn't carry his own lunch and water. And part of him didn't want the others around while they ate. He wanted to chat with Priya and try to close the distance between them.

She was still writing when he came back, her tongue poking out the corner of her mouth. He wished it was his tongue tracing the contours of her full, shapely lips. Alarmed at the direction of his thoughts, he put down the picnic basket and hurried inside the cave.

There he took a few deep breaths as he tried to concentrate on the stone carving of a tiger in front of him but all he could think about was the image of Priya, sitting on a rock like a modern-day goddess.

Was that why he was spending this time with her?

Because he was attracted to her, desired her? She was a beautiful woman. He'd noticed how stunning the first time he saw her but on an objective level, as he'd appreciate a fine painting. He hadn't thought there was anything more to it.

She was right when she'd told him he didn't need to come with her. He tried telling himself he was concerned about the project, it was too important not to deal with it personally, but it wasn't true. Certainly not to the extent he was letting other things build up on his desk and leaving the palace when gala arrangements were moving at an accelerated pace.

If she was similarly attracted to him was irrelevant—he couldn't do anything about it. His priority should be concentrating on the hundreds of single women who would soon be arriving on Adysara—any one of which would make a suitable wife and queen. The last thing he should be doing right now was going out of his way to spend time with Priya Sen. After this visit he would turn the project over to someone else or ask for government permission to let Mr Agrawal lead on it.

Rohan paused, his eyes roving over the carvings. He really wanted to show Priya his favourite cave. Number six. He wanted to watch her expressions as she took in the stone cuttings in the cave for the first time. He wanted to hear her initial, unfiltered reaction. And when he took her through to see what he considered would be the showpiece of the whole island…

'Rohan,' Priya's voice called from the cave entrance. 'Are you okay down there? Aren't you coming to eat?'

'Yes, I'll be right out,' he called back. Whatever he was feeling, he couldn't let Priya suspect he wanted her.

Unless she already did, and that was the reason she was distancing herself.

He joined her by the rock where she was helping his bodyguard lay out plates and cutlery on a small trestle table. There were also two folding chairs open next to the table. Once they were done, his bodyguard left them.

As Rohan sat down, he caught Priya's amused glance. 'What is it?' he asked.

'Oh, I don't think I should say,' she replied, shaking her head with exaggerated fake apprehension.

'Well, now you have to say.'

'When you mentioned you'd organise a picnic lunch for today I was imagining sandwiches on a rug. Not this.' She gesticulated at the table and glass containers with meat and vegetable curries, luchis, naans and salads. Even though she was mumbling under her breath as she opened one of the containers, he heard her say, 'I guess the royal bottom can't sit on the ground.'

He let out a deep chuckle. 'I'll have you know this royal bottom can endure some discomfort.'

Her eyes widened and colour flooded her cheeks as she realised he'd heard her, but she gave him a shy, embarrassed smile. She was enchanting.

'Of course, we have to take extra precautions here,' he continued, 'because the insurance won't pay out if the royal bottom is injured through careless action.'

He struggled to maintain his serious expression when her mouth fell open. 'You've insured your...' she said, waving her hand in his direction.

He threw his head back and gave a hearty laugh. 'You're so easy to tease.'

She closed her eyes and shook her head slowly, but her smiled proved she wasn't upset. 'You know you're lucky there aren't bread rolls here or I'd have lobbed one at you.'

He shrugged. 'That would be treason.'

'It would be worth it.' She finished opening the last container. 'Is the royal personage capable of serving himself or would you like me to wait on you?'

He titled his head pretending to consider her question. 'Hmm, I'll be able to manage. In fact, to prove it I'll serve you.' Before she could protest, he stood and began holding out dishes for her inspection, enjoying playing the role of butler, hamming it up as if he was performing in a British historical drama.

They chatted as they ate, their conversation flowing easily.

It had been a long time since he felt so relaxed with someone, as if he'd known them for a lifetime instead of days.

She was intelligent, interesting, curious, passionate, beautiful. He liked her. But it wasn't as simple as it sounded.

During their conversation they often referred to his royal status—he didn't usually bring it up outside the family. He never liked to distinguish himself from the people he was with. But with Priya, it was almost a form of protection. A reminder because of who he was he had a duty to marry someone who could help the island improve and grow, he wasn't free to choose who he liked.

If it had been any other time he might have asked Priya out for a meal. Perhaps they would have dated for a while. But inevitably it would end, because all his relationships had to. This time there was no point entertaining the thought of a brief relationship. In a few short weeks, guests would be arriving at the palace for

a gala event and he would be expected to charm potential brides.

If he hadn't been Rohan Varma, Yuvaraja of Adysara,
duty-bound to marry someone who could improve the
prosperity of the island and improve the quality of life
of its people, but just plain Rohan Varma, maybe things
could have been different. He suspected the end would
always be the same though. He didn't see any reason to
get married apart from carrying out his duty. He wasn't
going to fall in love. It was something he didn't believe
was real or lasting. Sooner or later, just being together
wouldn't be enough and the woman could start to want
something he couldn't give.

It was a moot point. He wasn't plain Rohan Varma.
His romantic future wasn't in his control.

CHAPTER EIGHT

SITTING NEXT TO Rohan in the back of the Jeep, she could feel the anticipation and excitement emanating from him. Cave six was the one he was most excited about, the one he considered to be particularly special. Since all the caves she'd already inspected had been sensational, she couldn't wait to see how magnificent this one would be.

She glanced at Rohan and caught him looking directly at her. She gave him a shy smile, but his face was severe. What had changed from only seconds before?

After today, she didn't know when or if she would see him again. A huge, painful knot twisted inside her at the thought.

She would miss spending time with him. If he wasn't Rohan Varma, Crown Prince of Adysara, she may have tried to keep in touch, found a way of holding on to the phone he'd given her. She wanted to get to know him better still.

No. She shook the possibility from her mind. It didn't matter who he was. She wasn't looking for a relationship. She was wary of them.

She was only interested in doing her job. Exceeding expectations so she was even in the running for better career opportunities. It's what she needed to concentrate on now.

Her attraction to Rohan was an inconvenience she had to ignore.

But sometimes, with the way Rohan looked at her and the way he spoke to her, she couldn't help sensing he felt something for her too. Although it was probably wishful thinking.

Experience, in the form of her last couple of boyfriends, taught her she was difficult to love. Her own father didn't care enough about her.

A member of royalty wasn't going to suddenly develop feelings for her.

'Are we almost there?' she asked, like a child who'd got bored of a journey.

'Hmm?' Rohan was obviously miles away from her in his thoughts. 'Sorry. I missed what you asked?'

'I was wondering whether we were close by.' She gestured outside the window. 'I noticed the topography has changed. We're moving into a more elevated terrain.'

Rohan looked out the window. 'Yes, we're almost here.' He sat forward in his seat—the excitement and anticipation was back.

The car stopped. Once again, Rohan gave the driver and bodyguard permission to wander round so they didn't have to stay with the car.

They were at a hillside with a number of man-formed entrances carved into the side.

Rohan reached for her hand. He led her down a narrow gap that didn't appear to be a cave mouth at first but widened as they went further.

'The main cave is through here,' he explained. 'There are a number of interconnected chambers and passageways. Access might be a problem but believe me it will be worth it. We'll probably need to have restricted guided tours down here.'

While Rohan spoke about the issues concerning opening the caves to the public, Priya was only conscious of the warmth emanating from her hand, sending sparks along her arms. The sensual thrill should have alarmed her and made her remove her hand, but it felt so safe, and secure; perfectly enveloped by his.

The stone cuttings she'd examined so far were in excellent condition considering their environment. But the darkness had probably helped delay any deterioration. Once light and heat, caused by a number of visitors, impacted the cave then decay could be rapid if they didn't get the preservation process right.

'Close your eyes,' Rohan said, turning to her just before they reached the end of the tunnel.

'What?' Priya asked. 'It's dark enough, isn't it?'

'Please.' He looked like a child trying to cajole more chocolate from his parent.

She giggled. 'Fine.' She made an exaggerated showing of closing her eyes, jutting her face out for his inspection. A warm hand covered her eyes. 'Rohan. Is it necessary? Don't you trust me?'

'Always.'

His succinct response touched her. She felt him move so he was behind her, one hand still over her eyes. He put his other hand on her shoulder and gently guided her forward.

Her skinned burned where his fingers made contact, his body so close she could feel his breath whisper against her with every exhale. Her steps faltered as she tried to control the explosive currents coursing through her.

'Almost there,' Rohan said after they'd taken a few paces. He carefully moved her and turned her to her right. 'Keep your eyes closed,' he instructed as he removed his hand from over her eyes and stepped away.

Priya felt air begin to circulate around her. She wasn't sure whether it was because the space around her was larger or because she was no longer in such close proximity to Rohan. She instinctively moved as if searching for him.

'Wait,' he admonished. 'Be still. You're in the perfect spot. Ready?'

She nodded.

'Okay. Open your eyes now,' he said.

Slowly, Priya raised her lids. She was staring at an intricately carved tableau of multiple figures of different shapes and sizes forming a circle around a centrepiece. The carved figures were in rows, with one row standing on the shoulders of the figures below. Each was carrying something—a musical instrument, parchment, baskets containing grass, probably rice, stones, or classical weapons. The centrepiece consisted of a larger bovine creature, not a cow or a buffalo, maybe a mithun. The animal was carrying a small child whose hands were raised up, holding a globe-shaped structure splitting to reveal a tiny plant shoot. The whole piece depicted the variety of people which made up Adysara; which made up a country. It was a celebration of life and death and rebirth.

There were small, discrete carvings around the rest of the cave which complemented the tableau of the main wall.

It would be a crime to risk letting this craftsmanship

be damaged by the footfall of tourists. But it would also be a crime to keep this hidden from the world. Photos would never do it justice.

Her hands itched to trace the detailed contours along the carvings, but her professional instincts overrode inclination, knowing the barest trace of oil from her fingers could degrade the work.

She turned her head to see Rohan, who was watching her expectantly.

'I can see why this is your favourite,' she whispered, reverently.

He shook his head, surprising her. 'That's not all of it. Come on, I want to show you. You need to close your eyes again but we're going through another passageway first.'

Priya's anticipation mounted. If the crowning glory of the cave wasn't the tableau in front of her, she couldn't imagine what lay in store.

Again she followed Rohan through a dark man-constructed corridor until he told her to stop and close her eyes, at which point he guided her forwards.

'Almost there,' he said.

She sensed, from the change of air, they had come through to an open area. And she was certain she could feel the sun on her. Had they walked out of the cave? Was what he wanted to show her outside?

This time, after he had positioned her where he wanted, he came to stand next to her.

'Open your eyes,' he whispered in her ear.

The sensations rushing through her body at the heated breath from his voice rendered her momentarily incapable of movement.

She quickly opened her eyes to dispel those feelings.

Trying to get her bearings, she almost couldn't take in what was in front of her.

'Priya?' Rohan said in an uncertain tone.

She forced herself to focus on the shape in front of her.

'Oh, my!' she said, as soon as her mind was able to process she was actually standing next to a megalith, carved from the cliff face, of a palace guarded by tigers and lions at each of its corners. She instinctively reached for Rohan's hand, as if he could somehow ground her.

She'd had no idea this existed. It was much smaller than the Kailasha temple in the Ellora caves, of course, but it could rival its artistry.

It felt completely natural to walk around the megalith with her hand in Rohan's. Occasionally, whenever she squealed because her eye landed on a particularly intricate or unexpected carving, Rohan would squeeze her hand, grinning at her obvious enthusiasm.

It was almost as if they were just a couple of ordinary tourists, viewing one of the most impressive stone-cut megaliths in the world and she wasn't Priya Sen, conservator, walking with her kind of client who also happened to be the crown prince of the island.

With that reminder, she almost flung his hand away. He blinked, but she didn't miss the brief flash of hurt in his eyes. She stepped towards the structure and pretended to examine the ground for signs of deterioration.

Why did it have to be Rohan who caused these feelings in her? She'd already decided to focus on her career. She wanted to be project lead on this work. She was trying to prove she was capable.

She wasn't looking for romance. And if she was, Rohan would be the last person who would be suitable.

Even if he was interested in her, and she couldn't believe it was a remote possibility, he was so far out of her orbit. He could never be hers.

Everybody knew he was searching for his future wife—the next Maharani of Adysara. He wasn't going to give it up to have a quick affair with Priya.

And she couldn't let her attraction to him distract her from her goal. Her work was everything to her. It had to be.

Forcing herself to concentrate on carrying out her investigations she took out some equipment and worked diligently for a while. She came across a section which she could use Rohan's assistance for, so she turned around to ask him to help.

He had moved back to stand in the shadow of the surrounding rocks. The powerful set of his shoulders and his broad chest cast a long shadow over the rocks which, though imposing, made her feel protected and safe.

She wished she had the artistic skills to commit this gorgeous specimen of a man to posterity.

Something above him caught her attention.

Without thinking, she leapt in his direction, throwing her arms around him and pushing them both out of the way. She heard a small thud behind her from where the object she'd glimpsed falling towards Rohan had landed. She slowly became aware she had her arms around him and he had, at some point, thrown his arms around her.

She was in Rohan's arms. And she felt like she belonged there. She never wanted to leave.

She was in Rohan's arms because he had been in danger—the implication of that renewed her alarm.

She pushed herself out of his arms and began pacing. 'This is dangerous. You shouldn't be here. If something happened to you…' Her voice trailed off as her imagination played out the frightening possibilities.

'Nothing happened. I'm all right.' He reached for her but she kept out of his grasp.

'All right? What if I hadn't reached you in time. We shouldn't have come. *You* shouldn't have come.'

Rohan walked over to the stone on the ground. 'Come over here. Look at it.'

Priya walked to stand next to him. In the scheme of things, the stone was small and wouldn't have done any major harm if it had hit Rohan, but that could be luck. There could be larger rocks on the brink of tumbling towards them.

'You should get out of here,' she said, pushing him in the direction of the exit. 'There's no need for you to join me. I can work on my own. It's too big a risk.'

'It was a small, displaced stone. The cave walls aren't coming down.'

Priya shook her head. 'This could have been so bad.'

'But it wasn't.'

'If something had happened it would have been my fault.'

'It would have been an accident.'

'I would have been blamed. What if they didn't believe it was an accident? What if they thought I was trying to assassinate you?'

Rohan made a choking sound.

'Could I be tried for treason?'

'Priya, nothing happened.'

'You shouldn't be here. You need to leave.'

'It's okay. Calm down.' He pulled her back into his arms until they were standing so close together no light could be seen between them.

She inhaled deeply a couple of times, her heart rate gradually returning to normal.

Home.

The word resounded in her mind. Followed closely by alarm bells.

Her rational mind told her she had to move. She had to get away from him. This wasn't her place and Rohan wasn't her home.

But he could have been injured. Concern tore through her heart. And it wasn't because he was a client. And it wasn't even because he was the crown prince.

It was because she cared about him.

She began to tremble. As he stroked her back to calm her, the sensations flooding through her body soon switched from concern to desire.

'Are you okay?' he asked in a low voice.

'I think so.' She took a deep breath but a picture of Rohan lying on the ground knocked out by a rock filled her imagination. She tightened her arms around him.

She felt the lightest touch against her hair. She slowly lifted her head. He was gazing tenderly at her.

Her lips parted as his head descended, inviting his kiss.

The spark between them ignited as their mouths met. They leaned into each other, their bodies pressed tight.

Soon, their kisses became greedy as if they were taking life-sustaining oxygen from each other.

It was powerful, dynamic, sensual, imbued with feelings.

And it shouldn't have happened.

Later that evening in his study, Rohan relived their kiss. He didn't know what would have happened if his bodyguard hadn't called out to them from inside the cave, asking if they were ready for lunch.

He hadn't expected the conflagration that flared between them, but Rohan hoped he would have had the decency to stop the kiss before it went too far—he wouldn't have actually given in to the temptation to lay her on the ground and make love to her in front of his favourite rock sculpture. And now he would never know.

Because it could never happen again.

He had nothing to offer her. He wasn't free to enter into a relationship with her. In a few weeks he would be meeting lots of woman, any one of whom could be his future wife. He couldn't suggest a brief fling—that would be unconscionable behaviour.

After his bodyguard's interruption, they'd returned to the car. Priya had claimed she was feeling faint from heat and asked to return to the palace. During the journey home, she refused to meet his gaze.

He hadn't attempted to engage her in conversation then, but he needed to make sure she was all right so he'd asked a member of staff to request she join him after dinner and was now pacing his study waiting for her.

It felt like hours before he heard a knock at the door. He rushed to it, pulling it open with unnecessary force.

Priya took a startled step back. He drank in her beauty, hoping to read her thoughts in her deep eyes, but she still refused to meet his gaze.

'Come in,' he said, as he nodded his dismissal to her escort.

She went to stand in front of his desk, her head bowed as if she'd been summoned before the headmaster.

He went to his seating area and called her over. He knew how important her job was to her and he had to reassure her that her rejection of their kiss would have no impact on her work for the palace.

'Priya,' he began once they were both seated.

'I'm so sorry, Rohan,' she said, giving him a quick glance before looking down at the hands she was wringing. 'I should never have done it. Please excuse me. Chalk it up to the circumstances. It was relief when I thought you could be injured.'

Rohan crossed his legs as he leaned back against the couch. 'You're apologising to me?'

'Yes. I'm sorry.'

'About kissing me?'

'Of course. It was completely inappropriate of me to have done that, I should—'

'But I kissed you.'

She did look at him then. 'No, you didn't. I started it.'

'I did,' he replied.

'No! It was me,' she argued back.

He grinned. Only with Priya would he be arguing about who was responsible for initiating the most incredible kiss he'd ever experienced. His smile faltered. Their kiss may have been incredible, but he had to make sure she knew it could never happen again.

'Priya, let's just agree it was mutual,' he said, putting up his hand when it looked like she was going to continue arguing. She gave him a tight nod. 'But it was wrong. It shouldn't have happened. I'm sorry.'

She bent her head, not saying anything.

'I'm sorry,' he repeated. He didn't know what else to say. He couldn't tell her he was attracted to her. Couldn't let her know he liked her, he admired her, he loved spending time with her. It was all true but he couldn't act on it. He needed to stay away from her. Otherwise he could be accused of leading her on.

Her stomach growled. He chuckled at her embarrassed expression. She covered her midsection with her hands as if doing so would stop the noise, but all it did was draw his attention to the apex of her thighs.

He blinked to clear the direction of his thought. 'Haven't you had dinner?' he asked. 'I didn't expect you to miss it to come here.'

'I didn't. I wasn't hungry. I haven't had much of an appetite since...' She trailed off.

He didn't have to be a mind-reader to understand what she meant.

'Come on,' he said, getting to his feet. Instinctively he put his hand out to help her but pulled it back. Reducing physical contact between them was essential.

Rohan led Priya out of the study into his private living quarters and down the corridor to the kitchenette. He rarely used it, but it was always kept fully stocked with ingredients to make a simple meal.

Priya glanced around. 'What are we doing in here?'

'Getting you something to eat.'

'Oh, that's okay. I can get something when I get back to my rooms.'

'No, I insist.'

She looked uncomfortable.

'What's the problem?' he asked.

'I don't want to bother any of your staff. I'd rather make something when I get back.'

'I'm not going to call someone.'

She released a breath of relief. 'Of course, if you don't mind me cooking something here, I'll see what there is.

Have you eaten or shall I make something for you too?'
she asked, walking towards the fridge.

'Sit,' Rohan said, pointing to the small table in the
corner of the room. 'I'll make you something?'

'You can't do that!'

'I can cook. I did live independently when I was
abroad you know. And I didn't resort to takeout every
evening.'

'I'm sure you're very capable,' Priya replied, with a
slight roll of her eyes. 'But I can't let you cook for me.
It's not right.'

He didn't know why it was so important to him Priya
didn't think he was someone who spent his days being
waited on hand and foot. Rationally, it would make more
sense if he did emphasise the difference in their status.

But he valued her good opinion of him.

'Let's compromise,' he suggested. 'We can make
something together. Eggs is probably the fastest. What
about with sausages or some omelette.'

'Omelette.'

He pulled out some eggs, onions and chillies and
spices while Priya looked for the pan and cooking uten-
sils.

'Is this okay or would you prefer something different
in your omelette?' he checked.

Priya looked at his ingredients. His forehead furrowed when he saw her lips tremble.

'Priya?' he asked, with concern.

She gave him a tremulous smile. 'My mum used to
make omelettes like this. I haven't had them for years.
Thank you. It brings her back to me.'

He puffed his chest out, as if he'd accomplished something monumental, rather than being lucky in his choice of fillings.

'I'll chop, you whisk,' Priya said. When he would have reached for the knife she swatted his hand away. 'I'm not going to risk you getting a knife injury now. Not after this morning.'

He swallowed, his mind instantly reliving their kiss. From the faint blush in her cheeks, he hoped she was also remembering. He turned away. Cooking together in such intimate circumstances wasn't the wisest decision when part of the reason he'd asked her to come to his study was to reinforce why any relationship between them was impossible.

Rohan sighed. He still hadn't broached the subject fully. He looked over at Priya standing at the hob, turning their omelettes. Foolish though he knew it was, he didn't want to ruin the small scene of domesticity. But he had to.

'Priya,' he said. 'We need to talk.'

Priya straightened her shoulders. What could this be about? She'd already apologised for kissing him. What more could she do? Should she apologise again?

She still had trouble believing they'd kissed. She'd claimed her action was a result of thinking he was in danger. That heightens the emotions. Makes people react out of character. That's all it was. But the truth was, she'd been dreaming of kissing him, oh, for days now.

But what happened was so different from her dreams. She could still feel the pressure of his lips on hers, the warmth of his breath. The strength of his arms around her.

She closed her eyes savouring the moment again.

When she lifted her lids, she met his penetrating gaze. It took her an immense effort to tear her eyes away. They needed to talk, he'd said. And he was right.

'What did you want to say?' she asked.

'About what happened today...'

'I've already said sorry. I promise it won't happen again.'

'I don't know if that's true.'

She jerked back. That was a concern. As much as she was attracted to Rohan, she knew there was no prospect of a relationship. Now there was a risk her behaviour had affected his inclination to work with her. Although the scoping work could be completed on her own, if she got the chance to lead the project, which was still a big *if* she knew, then she would probably have to report to Rohan on a regular basis.

'I know it was unprofessional,' she began.

'That's not what I mean.'

'Then?'

'In my opinion it's always best to be open and honest in these situations. Prevarication doesn't help anything.'

'Okay.'

'We kissed. We both know it can never happen again.'

Priya nodded. Hadn't they already agreed this?

'I like you. I think you're beautiful. In any other situation I would be interested in exploring a short relationship.'

Priya's jaw dropped. She wasn't expecting that. His wide eyes told her the words came as a surprise to him too.

'But I'm not in a position to do anything.'

Not in a position? What a strange way to phrase things. It sounded like it was outside his control.

'I can't start anything with you because it wouldn't be fair, to you, or to my future wife. You've probably heard rumours this year's gala is a particularly special event for me as Yuvaraja of Adysara because I'm expected to get married soon and hopefully someone suitable will be at the gala.'

She nodded.

'It wouldn't be fair to start anything with you because the most I could offer was a fling for a couple of weeks.'

What he was saying was reasonable. She understood his position, but she couldn't help being curious. 'Is that what you want or are you just doing your duty?'

Rohan pursed his lips. 'Doing my duty is what I want. I'm not being forced to marry anyone in particular. I get a choice. And I hope true affection with my wife will come with time.'

'Affection, not love?' she asked, before biting her lip. Why was she bringing up love?

'I don't believe romantic love exists. It's a hormonal myth. A lie people say to excuse some of their behaviour. I do believe a companiable love can arise after time together, which is just as easily done after marriage as before.'

Again he sounded completely reasonable. And she had certainly been fooled when she thought she'd loved her previous boyfriends. She thought she'd never get over them at the time but in reality, those feelings passed fairly quickly.

'So you understand, Priya. There are expectations and responsibility that come with my position. I have a duty to make a suitable marriage. I cannot start anything with you.'

She bent her head. She didn't need to be a genius

to work out he was telling her she wasn't suitable for a prince. She just wanted to curl up into a ball and hide. She didn't need another reminder she wasn't good enough.

CHAPTER NINE

PRIYA TOOK A step out of the final cave. That was it. She was finished with the scoping exercise. Now all she had to do was write up the report and submit it to Rohan.

Her heart felt heavy at the thought of Rohan. He hadn't accompanied her for any more visits. She hadn't expected it, not after their conversation, when he'd categorically told her she wasn't good enough to be in a relationship with him. If she hadn't kissed him, if she hadn't made it so obvious how attractive she found him, perhaps he would still be coming to the sites with her. She packed up her belongings and got into the car.

She couldn't regret their kiss. It felt like it was the first time, like she'd never been kissed before. Automatically, her hand went to her mouth trying to recapture the memory of his lips. No, she couldn't regret it. Even if her wholly inappropriate reaction meant she was on her own.

She sighed. It didn't matter. She was used to being alone. The stone sculptures were all the company she needed. Her work was all she wanted.

Her dream job had come true when she was asked to take over from Leo as team leader on the palace preservation work. But now she had a new aspiration, which was to work on the preservation of these stone cuttings.

It was exactly what attracted her to conservation work in the first place. If she could lead on the work…it would be the pinnacle of her career.

She needed to pull herself together. She had to quash all thoughts of Rohan and get over these feelings she didn't completely understand. Instead she needed to focus her attention on showing she was capable. She hoped Mac and Mr Agrawal would notice. She wasn't ready yet to put herself out there and risk rejection by broaching the idea of staying on herself.

Rohan had to stay out of the picture. It was rare for her to meet someone she felt in sync with and how totally natural and completely herself she was in his company. It wasn't that she sometimes forgot about the difference in their status—it was she sometimes forgot she hadn't known him for years.

She expelled a deep, lonely breath. If only he had been anyone but the crown prince of Adysara—someone who actually lived in her world.

But it was probably better this way. Any relationship would have inevitably fizzled out. They always did. It didn't matter who the guy was. She just didn't have what it took to sustain a relationship.

She had decided long ago, after her last boyfriend broke up with her, she wasn't the kind of person who would have a husband and children; she wasn't the kind of person who deserved to be loved.

She was determined her career would be her whole focus. And she loved what she did with a passion she hadn't expected. She loved the impact what she did had on the world's heritage.

One day, if she kept trying she would be the lead on one of these conservation projects. Perhaps it wouldn't be the one on the island; despite every effort she would make, she wasn't sure she would be picked over some-one like Leo. But one day, with hard work and determi-nation, she might be considered for another major lead position. That was her future. She couldn't let anything derail that. It was all she had.

Back at her quarters, she received a message asking her to go to Mr Agrawal's office. Her heart leapt. Was it really a request from Rohan? Did he want to speak to her? Had he missed her as much as she missed him?

She was slightly surprised to see Mac waiting for her outside their quarters. Disappointment flooded over her when she found out he was also going to see Mr Agrawal. As they walked over, she quickly gave him an update on the scoping work, expecting it was the reason she was invited to the meeting.

Before they got to Mr Agrawal's office, Mac halted her.

'You've been here over a month now, haven't you?' he asked.

'That's right.'

'Are you enjoying it?'

'Very much,' she replied, her expression brightening up thinking about the work. Was this the right moment to bring up her desire to continue as team leader? She took a deep breath, then let it out and shrank back a lit-tle. No, she shouldn't put herself forward in such a way.

'With the work in the palace and the site visits you've worked through the weekends and haven't taken any time off. You must need some time to relax.'

'Oh, I haven't felt that way,' she hastened to reassure him. 'We've got the public holidays with the gala coming up. And with the site visits, I've been touring round the island so it's like time off.'

'But it isn't, Priya. You should take this weekend off. In fact take Friday and Monday too—have a long weekend. Tomorrow, after you've finished for the day give me a status update and then you can start your leave. Rest and relax, ready to get back refreshed on Tuesday.'

'It's not necessary. The team have had to deal with my absence when I was on the site visits already. I shouldn't take more time away.'

'I insist. Priya, I'm responsible for your well-being while we're here. You wouldn't let any of your team work continuously without taking any time off would you?'

'Certainly not,' she replied. Although the work in the palace didn't stop over the weekends, she always checked the roster to make sure people were taking time off.

His look was enough to show there was no arguing with him. Like it or not she was going to have an enforced long break.

She didn't know what she was going to do with the free time. Perhaps visit the megalith again if she was allowed. At the very least, she could get most of the report written up.

During their meeting with Mr Agrawal they gave a general update on the work in the palace. There were three separate teams, with Mac in overall charge, so Priya presumed her presence was required, while the other team leaders weren't, because they would discuss the scoping work. Instead, when Mr Agrawal asked for the initial assessment now they'd completed the site visits he directed his question at Mac.

Mac answered, in a way which suggested he'd been supervising her scoping work much closer than he had in reality. She didn't mind. It was better than being the centre of attention where she was most likely to slip up and make a bad impression.

They were briefly interrupted when Mr Agrawal took a phone call. He spoke in Adsahi but from his tone he was excited and she could understand him saying 'of course' and 'definitely'.

After the call, Mr Agrawal looked expectantly at the door. Moments later, Rohan strode in.

Priya's heart began to pound. She hadn't seen him since their conversation over omelettes. He was dressed casually in a cotton shirt with the sleeves rolled up. She remembered being in the embrace of those sinewy forearms. She cleared her throat and turned her attention to Mr Agrawal. That was safer for her thoughts.

'Sorry I interrupted,' Rohan said.

'Not at all, Yuvaraja-sahib. Mr MacFarlane was finishing an update on the scoping exercise.'

'Mr MacFarlane was?' Rohan raised, his eyebrows looking between Mr Agrawal, Mac and her. 'Ms Sen has been doing the site visits. Wouldn't it be better to get the update directly from her?'

Priya threw a worried glance at Mac. He knew Rohan had accompanied her on some of the site visits, but Mac might not like Rohan going round his authority to her for a report.

She waited a moment in case Mac was going to reply. When he made no sign he intended to speak, she spoke looking down at her lap. 'Oh, I update Mac regularly. He knows everything I do, Ro… Yuvaraja-sahib. His report to Mr Agrawal is comprehensive.' She quickly looked at Mac again, hoping she'd said the right thing, but he was looking at Rohan.

'Then please go on, Mac,' Rohan said.

While Mac repeated his report, Priya took a chance to surreptitiously peek from under her eyelashes at Rohan, expecting his attention to be on Mac. But Rohan was looking directly at her. His expression was contemplative.

She hastily dropped her eyes. Why was Rohan looking at her like that? She replayed the scene since he came into the office quickly in her mind. Rohan had, probably unknowingly, given her the opportunity to showcase her expertise and passion for the project. And she'd blown it. Self-doubt had overridden her desire, her dream, to lead this work and she let her manager speak for her instead.

After hearing the report and asking questions, which Mac was able to answer because of the comprehensive briefings she gave him every day, Rohan left the room. Mr Agrawal and Mac wanted to discuss another potential scheme on restoring the paintings in some government buildings. Since restoration wasn't Priya's area of expertise, she took her leave of them.

She had barely walked a few steps when Rohan called her name. She turned and saw him coming out of the shadows. Although he'd left through the door leading to the royal corridor he was now in a staff corridor.

Did it mean he purposely waited to see her?

Her heart began to race. But she forced herself to think rationally. They had shared a kiss. An out-of-this-world, never-to-be-forgotten kiss, but Rohan had made it clear it was a one-off.

She waited patiently for him to speak. After the silence stretched out she said, 'Can I help you with something, Yuvaraja-sahib?'

'Um…how is everything with the site visits?' he asked.

Priya furrowed her brow. He'd just received an extensive update on the subject. 'I may be able to have the report with you earlier than I expected.'

He nodded. 'Excellent. Is the work on the palace murals progressing faster than expected then?'

'Yes, but I've been given a few days leave over the weekend. I'm going to work on the report then.'

'If you're on leave, shouldn't you rest and relax?'

'I'll do some relaxing—maybe tour the island. I would love to see cave six again. If it would be all right, even if it's not for a site visit.'

'I have no problem with it. But why don't you go to mainland India? Lots more to see there. I can ask my assistant to help you with any arrangements.'

'Thank you, sir. That isn't necessary. I'm happy to stay around here.'

'It's going to be chaos around here from now on,' Rohan said with a grin. 'If you think the preparations have been hectic so far, they're about to enter warp speed with the gala so close. Not only in the palace but over the whole of Adysara too. Believe me, you don't want to be here if you don't have to be. Take my advice and escape while you can. You'll thank me.'

They laughed. 'I'll think about it.'

Laughter fled as they continued to gaze into each other's eyes. Desire clear in them.

'Priya,' he whispered, coming to stand closer to her. 'I… I…'

Priya waited for him to close the gap between them, for him to take her in his arms and cover his mouth with hers.

'Yes,' she breathed back.

'I have to go.' He stepped away, squeezed her shoulder then turned towards the royal quarters.

She stared after him. What an impossible situation. Why did she have to fall for a prince?

CHAPTER TEN

OVER BREAKFAST THE next morning, Rohan listened to his mother as she updated the family on the final arrangements for the gala. He could feel the tension as she spoke, since, although this wasn't the first gala she'd overseen since becoming the Maharani, it was going to be a landmark one. If she'd constructed the perfect guest list, Rohan would meet the woman he would one day marry.

Although his mind accepted the factual reality, his heart rebelled against it.

He'd always accepted his role, his duty was to this island and the people on it; he was usually happy and eager to do what was expected of him. Adysara needed economic growth; without it his country would decline and the way to avoid that was by marrying someone who could help bring investment to the island, directly or indirectly. He knew he didn't have the freedom to choose his life partner in the way some others did. It had never been a problem. His parents had grown to love each other and Rohan always believed he would grow to love the woman he married, in so much as love existed at all. But over the last few weeks, for the first time in his life, he wished it could be different and the idea of marrying someone he didn't know became less appealing.

Not that his parents were expecting him to marry a stranger. The intention was to invite a few select guests to stay at the palace for a few days after the gala. It was an unspoken tradition that many families with marriage-able females would be hoping for an invitation for after the festivities. He would get to know the women better, without hundreds of people watching their every move.

At her request, he accompanied his mother as they inspected the rooms which had already been prepared. There was an aura of excitement among the palace work-ers, over and above the usual excitement for a gala. Ev-eryone knew this particular gala was a prelude to a greater occasion—his wedding.

Suddenly the bustle around him felt oppressive. As soon as he could, without drawing unnecessary atten-tion, he excused himself and went straight to his suite of rooms. But the walls seemed to close in on him there too. Needing fresh air, he walked onto the balcony.

He needed to get away. Out of the palace. Off the island.

He'd suggested Priya go to the mainland for a few days. Perhaps he should follow his own advice. Since Priya also had some time off, it would make sense if they travelled together. Taking his plane would be more convenient for her than her taking the ferry across to the mainland. He could act as her tour guide.

Was it a bad idea to spend more time with Priya when, despite his best intentions, his mind involun-tarily replayed their kiss on a regular loop? They had already discussed their mutual attraction and agreed they wouldn't act on it again. Priya knew he couldn't offer her a brief relationship, she understood there was no future for them.

Did it mean he had to stay away from her? He'd already done that over the past few days, not going on the site visits with her. He hadn't expected to see her in Govinda Agrawal's office yesterday evening.

They way her face had lit up when she first saw him before she pulled herself back and gave him a polite smile. The polite smile meant she wasn't comfortable in the situation. The polite smile meant she wasn't thinking of him as Rohan but as Mr Varma, or worse Yuvaraja.

He disliked that polite smile intensely.

Before they'd given in to their attraction and shared their explosive kiss, she was relaxed in his company. Could they go back to an easy-going friendship if they spent more time together rather than less?

Could he honestly ignore his attraction to her?

It would be difficult. Last night, when it was the two of them alone in the shadows, he'd almost given in to temptation and kissed her again.

But he hadn't. He'd overridden his impulse and stepped away. That was a good sign. He'd rather have Priya as a friend than avoid her because he desired her.

The only problem with his decision to go to the mainland was Priya hadn't sounded eager to take the time off, so would she come away? Rohan replayed some of their previous conversations, trying to come up with an incentive.

Moments later, an idea came to him. He sent her a message and asked her to meet him in his private gardens after she'd finished work. It would be the perfect place to talk. It was a short distance from the palace so it wasn't overlooked. And it was walled with a single door which was kept locked so nobody else had access to it unless he wanted them to.

It used to be his grandmother's place. She wanted an area which she could tend herself—planting her own flowers and vegetables. A small oasis where she could throw off the trappings of royalty. After she passed away, his father gave the garden to him.

And he wanted Priya to see it.

Walking to his desk, he clapped his hands together ready to put his plans into action. Once seated he paused. He wasn't going to demand Priya accompany him. And she might, she probably would, have some ideas for how to spend her weekend. He would put his plane on standby for the following morning but otherwise he wasn't going to assume she'd automatically fall in with his plans just because he wanted her too.

But he couldn't wait to tell her what he had in mind.

Hours later he was in his garden. He'd rushed through his work with an eagerness which had been missing since he arrived back at the palace. All because of his desire to have a clear plate to go away for the weekend. He would be going regardless of whether Priya wanted to come with him.

His parents had been understanding when he told them his intention. Almost sympathetic. His father had already gone through the same experience so he probably had an idea of how Rohan was feeling.

Rohan glanced at his watch. He'd been waiting in his private garden for ten minutes—he hoped Priya was going to turn up. He'd sent her directions, but what if they weren't clear enough and she was wandering through the vast grounds of the palace looking for him. He would need to organise a search party unless someone in her team was able to track her.

He should have asked her to share her location with him. He laughed as the thought crossed his mind. That was too close to stalker behaviour.

Priya was probably fine. She was simply running a little late. His wasn't so high and mighty as a royal he couldn't wait a few minutes for someone.

'Sorry, sorry,' Priya called as she rushed through the door. 'It took longer to finish things because Mac is still insisting I take the long weekend.' She smiled, then slowly did a three-hundred-and-sixty-degree turn. 'This place is beautiful. I haven't seen some of the trees anywhere before.'

'It's become a little wild,' Rohan admitted. 'The trees come from different parts of the island, but they were cultivated to grow in this garden. There's a bench over here. Why don't we sit down so we can talk?'

'Of course,' she replied, following him. But he could see her eyes dart around the garden trying to take everything in.

'Do you like gardening?' he asked.

She shrugged. 'Don't know. Never had a garden.'

'Never?'

'Well, we had a small garden when my mum was alive. But I was too young to have much to do with it at the time. Then it was boarding school. And mine didn't have a gardening club or anything. Now I live on the third floor of a block of flats. But one day, I'm going to buy a house with a garden.'

It was such a simple goal. One he could help her achieve with the click of his fingers—there were plenty of lovely homes with gardens on Adysara. What other goals and dreams did she have? He wanted to make every dream of hers come true.

'I think we should go away together this weekend,' he blurted out.

She whipped round to face him. 'Pardon?'

'I want to get away from the palace for a few days. I thought it would be a good opportunity to visit Ajanta and Ellora—tour the caves, examine how the sites have been preserved and generate some ideas which we can implement here. Since you've got a few days off too, I thought you might want to come along.'

He held his breath, waiting for her response. Would the caves at Ajanta and Ellora be enough of an inducement? He thought it was perfect. He hadn't visited them in years and he knew Priya had never visited them.

'Ajanta and Ellora?' she repeated. 'You're going to see them this weekend?'

'Yes.'

'And I can come too?'

'If you want.'

'What about transport and accommodation? Won't it be too short notice to arrange those?'

'No,' he answered emphatically. He liked that she forgot he was royalty most of the time. He could go about almost incognito when he was off the island, but his status had its advantages—such as having a private plane at his disposal and hotel suites whenever he needed them.

'Are you sure it's a good idea for us to go together?' she asked, unable to maintain eye contact.

'Why not?'

'I thought you were avoiding me.'

He laughed to cover his guilt. 'No, I've just been busy.'

'Of course. Of course, you've been busy. You're the

prince. I was silly thinking you were avoiding me because I kissed you.'

'We'll have to agree to disagree on who kissed whom since you insist on taking the blame. But there's no reason for us to avoid each other is there? We already discussed this. I can't offer you a real relationship. A real romantic relationship. But we can be friends, can't we?'

She swallowed—he could tell her mind was whirring a mile a minute. 'I'd like that,' she said.

He hadn't realised he was holding his breath for her response until he felt an overwhelming sense of relief.

An alarm went off.

'I'm going to have to go back soon,' he said. 'They've organised a dance tutor to show me some of the formal dances. Nightmare. But it'll be worth it if you save a dance for me so I can show you what I've learned.'

'A dance?' her tone making her astonishment obvious.

'At the gala ball.'

'The gala?' She snorted. 'I'm not going to be at the gala, Rohan. I work here. I'm not a guest.'

He paused, the thought she wasn't going to the dance never occurring to him before. She was right. She wasn't a dignitary. She didn't have a wealthy family. She wasn't invited to the event that was consuming every waking moment of the people around him.

Instead she'd be going to the celebrations in town. And he would be whisking some stranger round the dance floor.

He didn't know what to say, but if the reminder of the difference in their situation was bothering her, she didn't show it.

Instead she grinned and bit her bottom lip. He groaned wishing he could run his tongue across the impressions her teeth had left. He worked hard to concentrate on what she was saying.

'I can't believe I'm going to see Ajanta and Ellora. It's like all my dreams are coming true.'

She carried on telling him everything she knew about the caves and in what ways they were similar to the caves on Adysara—her face animated and flushed with the passion for her subject.

He also had a dream, one which he'd been having since he got to know Priya. But it was one which none of the advantages of being a prince could ever make come true. In fact his royal status meant the opposite.

CHAPTER ELEVEN

PRIYA WOKE UP with the dawn on Saturday morning. She still couldn't believe she would be seeing the caves at Ajanta today. They were planning an early start since it was still a three-hour drive from the hotel.

After a quick shower and freshening up, Priya got changed into a lightweight pink cotton T-shirt and beige linen trousers and put a headscarf into her bag. From everything she'd read, it could be very hot walking between the caves although the interior of the caves would be cool.

Once she was ready, she walked out of her room into the living area of the suite she was sharing with Rohan. A breakfast of cut fruit, poori bhaji, stuffed paratha, lassi, fruit juice and coffees and teas had already been laid out for them. She would never get used to this level of opulence. She was still recovering from flying in a private plane, which as a luxury in itself, meant they could fly directly to the airport at Aurangabad.

On the flight, Rohan told her his assistant had booked a two-bedroom suite, with the assumption it would be more practical for meals and discussing work. But Rohan offered to arrange a separate hotel room for her if she preferred.

She'd told him it wasn't necessary. His assistant was correct that sharing a suite would be practical. It had been an easy decision to make.

They'd already had a frank discussion about their attraction, a couple of times now. There was something special about knowing he wanted her as much as she wanted him—she'd never experienced that before—even if they couldn't be together. And she accepted that, with his bride-finding gala coming up, he couldn't even offer her a brief relationship. She wasn't naive enough to think it would be easy, her attraction to him wasn't going away all of a sudden. It was something she could keep in check. And she wasn't going to turn down the opportunity of spending time in his company.

The previous evening, they'd checked into their rooms by early afternoon so they decided to take a visit to Panchakki, the water mill complex which offered scenic views of Aurangabad. It had gone well—they were relaxed and at ease with each other.

'Morning,' Rohan said as he walked into the room. Priya couldn't help noticing how wide his chest was as he stretched. 'Did you sleep well?'

'Very well thanks. I think all the walking and fresh air helped. How about you?'

'Good, thanks. Hopefully you'll have a similar sleep tonight after walking around the caves.'

She nodded. Hopefully not. It was partially the truth she'd slept well. She'd fallen asleep quickly but her dreams featured Rohan heavily and she woke during the night massively aroused and aching for him.

Over breakfast they discussed which of the thirty caves they definitely wanted to see on their tour. Rohan had arranged a private guide to meet them at Ajanta to show them around.

A few minutes later, the hotel phone buzzed. Rohan answered it.

'The car's waiting for us,' he said.

The journey to the caves went by quickly. The car dropped them at a viewing point, before they reached the caves' entrance, then went to park.

From where they stood, Priya and Rohan were able to get a panoramic view of the basalt rock-cut caves carved out of a vertical cliff.

'Wow!' Priya expelled a reverent breath. 'Can you believe we're standing in front of structures crafted in first century BCE? How in the world did they have the tools to create something so perfect?'

She took out her camera to capture the vista before her. Then she turned and walked up to Rohan. 'Thank you. Thank you for bringing me here.' It was such a thoughtful, caring gesture from Rohan to invite her. He could have gone anywhere for his weekend away but he'd picked a place which he knew she'd dreamed of visiting. A cautionary voice in her head was telling her to stop, but she ignored it, giving in to the impulse to throw her arms around Rohan.

'You are most welcome,' he replied, returning her hug and resting his cheek on the top of her head. She felt the whisper of a kiss on her hair before he pulled away. 'The guide will be waiting for us.'

For the next few hours, they wandered around the vihara and worship halls, examining the painting which narrated the Jataka tales.

Outside cave sixteen, she grabbed Rohan's hand to point out the palace scene fresco, very similar to ones in the caves on Adysara. When they moved on to the next relief, neither had let go.

Priya reassured herself she was a sensible woman. They admitted they fancied each other. But she hadn't admitted her feelings or touched on the emotional connection she felt with Rohan. She wasn't ready to explore those feelings too deeply, her protective instincts kicking in. It had been safer to focus on the physical.

She always tried to ground herself in reality but standing in the Ajanta caves she'd always wanted to visit, her hand safe in the strong hand of the handsome, intelligent, thoughtful man next to her, for a moment she indulged in a flight of fancy where she could make believe they were simply a couple, enjoying a tour round a place with a beautiful history. For a moment she could make believe she wasn't plain Priya Sen of nowhere from nobody; and he wasn't Rohan Varma, Yuvaraja of Adysara. For a moment she could make believe he could be hers.

But reality, in the form of their tour guide, called her back. She pulled her hand from Rohan's, noticing how he tried to hold on a little longer. She flexed her hand—now empty and cold.

Was it a mistake coming away with him if she couldn't control herself in his company? She stared at the statue in front of her. If she couldn't pull herself together, she was going to waste the opportunity of a lifetime having a guided tour of Ajanta's wonders.

She took a few moments to compose herself and adopt her professional persona. No more thinking about Rohan. No more thinking about things that couldn't be.

Priya was exhausted when they finally left Ajanta, falling asleep in the car back to the hotel. After a quick stop in their room to freshen up, they decided to take a taxi into the town to look for somewhere to eat.

After their dinner, they went to Bibi Ka Maqbara.

As she stood next to a pillar, viewing the mausoleum with its resemblance to the Taj Mahal, she thought about the story of Shah Jahan's monument to his lost love.

She would never regret this weekend and being with someone who made it clear he liked her and enjoyed her company. He would never know how rare that was for her. So if the mistake wasn't coming away with Rohan, what if the mistake would be not acting on their attraction? If only for the weekend.

She glanced at Rohan through the corner of her eyes. He was looking at the same view, but occasionally he looked in her direction with an enigmatic smile.

Priya had never been the kind of person who put herself forward. She tried not to stick her head over the precipice. And sometimes it meant she waited for things to happen. She was always hoping people would notice her—previous boyfriends, employers, her father. But waiting never got her anywhere.

She was with Rohan; a man she liked and wanted, who didn't hide that he liked and wanted her too. She wasn't naive. He had a duty to his family and his country and his people. She understood duty better than many people.

So what if they couldn't have for ever? So what if they couldn't have weeks or months?

What if a few hours was enough?

This was one of the scariest things she would ever do, but she was going to do it. She was going to claim a brief moment for something she desperately wanted.

She stepped away from the pillar, walked over to Rohan, and slipped her hand into his.

It was the biggest, loudest gesture she'd ever made.

Priya's hand fit perfectly in his own. He'd almost stopped breathing when he'd felt the first warm touch of her palm, before her fingers entwined with his.

What did their clasped hands mean?

He'd been clear he couldn't offer her a relationship of any kind. She'd accepted that and, knowing her as he did, she wasn't the kind of person to try persuading him to change his mind. But something was different.

He wanted to know what she was thinking, but it wasn't a conversation they should have in public. The temptation to hurry Priya through Bibi Ka Maqbara was strong. She laughed and chatted as easily as the other times on their site visits, before they'd kissed. But there was something more between them now. Although the surface level of their conversation was about their visits, there was also a subtext in the looks she gave him from under lowered eyelids, in the light caresses on his arm as she walked past him, in the slow, seductive smiles she gave him when he glanced her way.

Was it his imagination or was she moving faster than before?

He hailed a taxi and they were soon on the way back to the hotel. The tension in the car was electric, both of them staring straight ahead, not looking at each other, as if they knew they couldn't control themselves if they did.

He had no expectations. Yes, of course, he hoped the looks and gestures meant Priya wanted something to happen between them that evening. But if holding hands and secret smiles were all they would share, it would be enough for him. He would take whatever she offered.

He turned to look out of the car window. And if she did want to make love with him, would one weekend really be enough? Did it matter? It had to be enough. He wasn't free to love someone totally of his own choosing. He'd always known his duty was to improve the quality of life for the people of Adysara by any means possible, including his choice of wife. And he wouldn't change that. Even if he knew how.

As they got closer to the hotel, Priya looked in his direction, her lips parting as she ran her tongue across them. He groaned. This was torture.

As soon as the car stopped, he rushed out, not waiting for the hotel doorman to open the door for them. Holding hands, they entered the hotel, walking straight through the foyer to the private lift that would take them to the suite. The moment the lift doors closed, he turned to her. They both took a step forward.

'Priya,' he groaned.

She stretched her arms around his neck, pulling his head closer to hers, as his arm enveloped her waist, drawing her to his body until there wasn't a centimetre between them. His mouth covered hers, devouring all the sweetness she had to offer.

He lifted her so her feet were off the floor and carried her to the door of the suite, never breaking contact with her lips. He fumbled with the key card like a teenager on the night of the prom, desperate to get inside. Priya wasn't making it any easier, meeting kiss after kiss, barely taking a breath, wrapping her legs around his waist.

He swore as he still couldn't get the door open. Priya

giggled and shimmied out of his arms, back onto the floor, taking the card out of his hands. The door opened on her first attempt.

The lamps in the room were casting a low light. The curtains were still open but the view wasn't of interest right then.

The door had barely closed behind them when they were reaching for each other, as if the only place they could imagine being in this moment was in each other's arms. He couldn't believe how lucky he was to have this woman he'd desired from the first moment he'd seen her returning the passion of his kisses with equal ferocity.

He inhaled sharply when he felt her hands creep under his shirt, tracing the outline of his abdominal muscles. Before he threw all caution to the wind he had to make sure they knew exactly where they stood. With a Herculean effort, he removed his mouth from hers.

Her lips were swollen, her cheeks flushed, her hair mussed from where he'd run his fingers through.

'Priya, Priya,' he whispered, dotting kisses over every inch of her face. 'You are so beautiful. Perfect. Are you sure this is what you want?'

'Yes.' Her answer was simple. Sincere.

'You know this is all I can offer, this short fling. I can't offer you a future.' He punctuated each word with a kiss.

'I know. I understand. I'm not asking for more. But we can have this weekend. That will be enough.'

Rohan swept a curl behind Priya's ear, resting his forehead against hers, trying to calm the maelstrom within him. Would it be enough, he thought again. He wasn't sure it would be for him. But it was all he could offer, and it was what she was willing to accept. He was too selfish to do the, probably, honourable thing and walk away.

His hand moved under her top and eased a bra cup to the side. A moan of pleasure escaped Priya's lips as he lightly skimmed his fingers over her curves. Hastily she undid his shirt buttons, splaying her hand across his chest, before moving lower.

Trousers and pants caught at his feet. He hadn't stopped to take his shoes off. He kicked them behind him with a clumsy haste, not wanting to break contact with Priya in case this turned out to be another one of his sensual dreams.

'I have condoms in my bathroom,' he said as he unbuttoned Priya's trousers. He couldn't wait until he had her under him on his bed.

'I have some in my bag,' she said twisting round to look for it.

She bent over to pick up her bag and take out a pouch. He groaned. They weren't going to make it to the bed.

Priya woke up before the alarm the next morning. She snuggled back under the blanket, reluctant to leave the warmth. Her eyelids refused to lift—she felt like she'd barely slept. Which was true.

As if they didn't want to waste a single second of their time together, they talked and made love until finally succumbing to sleep just before dawn.

'Good morning,' a voiced rasped in her ear before Rohan's lips moved to nuzzle into her neck, tightening his arm around her waist.

'Morning.' She turned onto her back, reaching round his neck to pull him in for a kiss. 'We should get up soon. We want to get to Ellora as soon as it opens.'

Rohan murmured, bending to press light kisses from her mouth down her neck to her breasts. 'Do we?' he asked, looking into her eyes as his hands captured the places his mouth had just been.

Heat flared. Did they have to visit Ellora? Wouldn't the caves be the same as Ajanta's?

Amused by how tempted she was to blow off a visit to a heritage site she'd wanted to visit since she first heard about it, she made a big effort to throw the covers off them. The air conditioning in the room was not quite as effective as a cold shower, but it was enough for Rohan to roll off her with a groan of protest.

'Fine. I promised you a trip to the caves and I will deliver. Why don't you get ready while I'll arrange for breakfast? Or I could you join you in the shower?' he suggested with a lift of his eyebrows.

'You know if you do that we won't leave for hours,' Priya replied, forcing herself to get out of bed.

He shrugged. 'Spoil-sport.'

Priya laughed, throwing the first thing that came to hand at him. Unfortunately it was her panties.

'Not helping,' Rohan said, holding them up, as if taunting her to take them from him, which would involve her climbing onto him.

She shook her head. She wasn't risking that. 'Come on, no dawdling. Have patience. We have tonight.'

Rohan's face froze. She'd meant to tease him with the promise of later. Instead she could only think how the night would be the last time they could be together like this. Once they got back to Adysara, life would go on as before.

As Priya got ready for the day she considered her options. She could waste their precious little time together, whining and complaining about how just how little that time was. And why do that when there was no guarantee this attraction, this desire they felt for each other would last beyond a few days anyway.

Or she could make the most of every second she had, touring round the beautiful caves of Ellora with a gorgeous man by her side, then spending the night back in this hotel making love to him until dawn.

CHAPTER TWELVE

'HEY PRIYA,' Mac greeted her. 'I didn't see you at breakfast this morning. I wasn't sure whether you were back. I was hoping perhaps you'd taken my advice and extended your break.' He was referring to a message he'd sent her while she was away.

Priya tried to smile, but her lips barely moved upwards. 'I came back last night, it was later than planned, so I went straight to sleep. I skipped breakfast because I wanted to check everything was ready for our work today.'

She hadn't been able to sleep anyway. She needed to keep busy. Her weekend with Rohan had been sublime but on Monday evening, as she and Rohan had approached the airstrip on Adysara, the space between them had increased, literally and figuratively. Priya wouldn't regret, couldn't regret spending the weekend with Rohan; it had been the most magical time she had ever experienced. But it was never real. Reality had been nipping at her heels for too long and she couldn't ignore it any more.

She'd spent two perfect nights in his arms. Now, whatever it had been, it was over.

She needed to concentrate on her job. She couldn't

expect Rohan to offer her a future—he'd been very clear on that. And who was she to ask him to change his mind?

Priya and Mac had a quick chat about her trip—swapping their impressions of the different sculptures and wall paintings at Ajanta and Ellora. She still needed to finish her report and then Mac would probably want to visits the caves and murals before they submitted the report to the palace, but they had some enforced time away from work coming up where they could fit it in.

In the four days she and Rohan had been gone, the preparations for the gala had advanced at a hectic pace. Most of the rooms, which would be used for the events, were decorated and cleared of all evidence of the hordes of people who had passed through getting them ready.

There was still two and a half weeks until the first event, and her team wasn't expected to finish all the mural restorations before the gala, since they were working in an area that would be closed off to the guests. But they would be expected to cordon off the mural and leave the area cleared of their tools by then. None of the restoration team would be doing anyway work in the palace for the duration of the gala.

Six days without any work to do. She didn't need the time off since she has just taken the long weekend, but she wasn't going to be given any choice in the matter. Again. While the gala was on, she would be spending time with her co-workers, touring the island and taking part in the festivities organised for the islanders.

For the next few hours, Priya was able to throw herself into her work. Her team was excellent. She would love to continue working with them on this project but she had overheard someone saying Leo Blake's family situation was under control and he was available to return.

Mac hadn't mentioned anything to her. Perhaps if she kept her head down, buried in the sand, she could stay on Adysara. She would go wherever the company sent her, but she couldn't imagine any other project offering anything like the artwork on Adysara.

Her job was all she had left. She had no family to speak of, no partner—her fling with Rohan was a moment out of time.

For the next few days, before the gala hiatus, she would try to show how capable and indispensable she was. They didn't need to go to the trouble of asking Leo Blake to return. Would it be enough? Would she be able to show Mac, Mr Agrawal and Rohan she was good enough to carry on leading this project, and perhaps the larger project that was potentially her company's for the asking?

It was only when her team members started packing away their tools that she realised it was the end of the working day. She stretched and eased out the kinks in her back and neck. Tempted as she was to continue, Priya knew the light would soon fade until its quality wasn't suitable to do the detailed technical work.

She hadn't joined the others for a lunch break and now her stomach was rumbling. It was still a couple of hours before dinner would be served. She went to the break room hoping there would be some fruit or snacks left out. Unfortunately, there wasn't.

Instead she headed back to her quarters to cook something for herself. All she could find in the kitchen was some bread, eggs and onions.

Immediately, her mind went back to the day Rohan

had cooked an omelette for her. She grunted out of frustration. Why was it the second she didn't have physical tasks to occupy her, her thoughts went straight to Rohan? It was the reason she'd avoided taking a lunch break.

She was physically attracted to him and now she had slept with him. It should have been enough to scratch that itch. It wasn't and she knew it wouldn't be. It didn't alter the fact it was all she could have. The sooner she accepted it and didn't hope or wish for the impossible she would be able to move on.

Love, marriage, children weren't in her future. And if she didn't know this already, it would never be—could never be—with Rohan.

Not for the first time, she wished her mother was there to confide in. There was no point wishing she could talk to her father or stepmother. She already knew they weren't interested in anything she did.

How could someone who wasn't loved by her family, the people who were supposed to love her most, ever expect a prince to care about her?

After dinner, instead of joining the rest of the team in the lounge, she would spend her evening working on her report. The sooner she finished it, the sooner she could hand it over. From now until the end of the project she needed to reduce the chance of meeting with Rohan again.

She opened her laptop and was pulling up her report when her phone pinged. Not her personal phone, the phone Rohan gave her, with a message asking her to meet him in his private garden in half an hour.

She'd just given herself a lecture on getting used to being alone, on the necessity, for the sake of her heart, to avoid coming into contact with Rohan. All he'd had to do was send her a text and those sensible decisions evaporated faster than a snowflake would in Adysara's heat. He was still the royal family member with the interest in the preservation and conservation work, she rationalised. Maybe he wanted to speak to her about their project and the ideas they'd had when they toured Ajanta and Ellora. And maybe he wanted to meet in the garden because he needed the fresh air.

Whatever the reason, she couldn't give up the chance to see him again.

Half an hour later, she was on her way to Rohan's private garden despite her instincts screaming it was a bad idea. Whenever she was in Rohan's company, her libido threatened to override her common sense.

She'd already replied to his message saying she would meet him; she couldn't really change her mind. But it was time to behave sensibly again.

Now they were back on the island, the same rules from before their weekend applied. She was part of a project team and he was the crown prince. They weren't going to have clandestine meetings in the garden.

In fact, the best option would be if they kept their meetings to a minimum—only about work and, preferably, never alone. Priya didn't know why Rohan asked to see her but she hoped he was thinking along the same lines. She would make her view clear if it wasn't the reason he wanted to meet.

He was already in the garden, pacing back and forth by the bench. She stood at the entrance, watching his powerful strides. He glanced at his watch then looked towards the entrance.

Her heart flipped at the way his face lit up. He never

tried to hide how happy he was to see her. Despite her determination, only seconds earlier, when Rohan ran over to her and swept her off her feet, she met his kiss passionately.

'Hey,' he said, when they finally broke apart.

'Hey.'

'How was your day?' His mouth moved over her hairline.

'Good. Busy. Making good progress. How was yours?'

'Busy. I spent all day in meetings going through protocols for our guests and running through where I have to stand and when,' he said, punctuating his words with kisses to her cheeks, her eyelids, her brows and finally her lips again.

Caught up in the haze of desire, it took a while for his reminder that the gala was more than a big party for him to penetrate her consciousness. It should have been enough to stop their embrace but Priya didn't want to let go.

'No regrets about the weekend?' Rohan asked, when they finally stopped kissing.

'None. What about you?'

'Only that it couldn't have been for longer.'

A warm glow flowed through her at his admission. If only they'd met months or even years before so they could have spent real time together before his responsibilities inevitably pulled them apart. It didn't seem fair that the weekend was all they could have.

'But it can't be,' she said, taking a few steps away. 'We knew that.'

He walked up to her, taking her hand to lead her to a

bench where he pulled her onto his lap. 'Let's not talk about it now. I've been waiting to see you all day.'

The next minutes were spent with little talking and lots of long, drugging kisses and caresses until they were panting and dishevelled. Priya got off Rohan's lap and sat next to him to put herself back in order.

'Will you meet me tomorrow, same time?' he asked.

She almost laughed from pure delight at the realisation he couldn't bear to say goodbye. After so many years, and bad relationships where she'd felt unloved and uncared for, it was a heady feeling to be wanted by such a caring, thoughtful, gorgeous man.

'Is that possible?' she asked, eagerly. 'Isn't your time going to be spent getting ready for the gala, greeting your guests. I heard some of them have started to arrive already.'

'Some guests from the States,' he admitted. 'I haven't met them yet, but I'll meet them over dinner. But it doesn't mean I can't spend time with you.'

Priya hesitated. Was continuing to meet Rohan wise when he would be meeting potential brides in a few days?'

'Priya, I'm not promised to anyone yet. We aren't doing anything wrong by meeting here. We're not hurting anyone.'

Priya wasn't sure it was entirely true. She suspected the way she was feeling was going to lead to a whole load of hurt for her soon.

But she could deal with that afterwards. She'd have the rest of her life to deal with it. For now, she was going to grab on to a small sliver of happiness with Rohan while she could.

CHAPTER THIRTEEN

ROHAN STOOD ERECT, dressed in his official regalia, behind his father's throne. He was at the first official event for the gala celebration—the formal receiving of the guests.

Each family would walk up the long, carpeted aisle, make their pranam or bow, receive a nod from his father and a smile from his mother before moving off to the side to watch the next family enter.

It was old-fashioned. It was pomp and circumstance. It was slightly ridiculous but it was tradition.

He'd already met most of the guests, informally, as they arrived over the past week. There were several eligible women present, but he'd been careful about how much time he spent in their company.

Everybody knew this year's gala was also where he would be looking for his future wife. If he gave one particular woman more attention than any of the others, he could risk gossip and speculation. Since he had no intention of carefully calculating how long he spent with someone and making sure he spent the same amount of time with everyone else, it was easier if he restricted himself to only meeting when everyone was together.

At least that's what he told himself. If he was being completely honest, there was only one woman who he wanted to spend time with. And she wasn't even allowed in the palace at the moment.

Since they'd returned from Aurungabad, they'd met every evening after work in his garden. He wanted to cover her with kisses, with his body and make love to her over and over. But he knew he had to maintain some distance so he restricted himself to holding her in his arms. And they talked. And it had to be enough.

As soon as he was finished with the reception line, he went to his room to change out of his uniform. He tried to be patient as his staff helped him remove the regalia and handle it careful when he really wanted to fling it off him and get to the garden as soon as possible. From tomorrow, the festivities would begin in earnest and he wouldn't have the time to leave the palace. Who knew when he would get the chance to see Priya alone again?

He was sure his family knew where he was going in the evenings, and he had to tell his assistant where he would be for security purposes—but once they were in the garden and closed the door, the walls provided a sanctuary. As if the walls were keeping the secret of his relationship with Priya.

She smiled when she saw him, walking over to greet him with a hug. Although he knew he shouldn't, the re-alisation this could be the last time he was holding her made him hold on tighter, lowering his head and lifting her mouth to his.

She didn't push him away, meeting his kisses with a reciprocal passion.

He held her away from him slightly, drinking her in, committing her form to his memory. She looked so beautiful and serene in the moonlight. She would make an incredible queen. It wasn't fair he wasn't free to choose her.

CHAPTER FOURTEEN

TWO DAYS LATER, it was the night of the gala ball and Priya was in the town centre with the rest of her company, watching the dance performance which was part of the celebrations which had been put on for the islanders and other people who weren't attending the ball itself.

They'd already had a long and lavish meal which had been arranged on behalf of the royal family. She could understand how all the islanders looked forward to this gala week, and this evening in particular. The atmosphere was relaxed, fun, informal. She wondered whether the people at the palace were having as much fun. Ever since Rohan had mentioned his dance tutor, in her imagination, the ball was like a scene from a Regency film with groups of dancers moving in formation to set pieces.

What would Rohan be doing? He must have been spending time with all his guests, with the large number of women who had come to Adysara knowing Rohan was looking for a queen. Perhaps at that moment he was dancing with the woman who would be his future bride.

'This is amazing,' one of her co-workers said. 'They really know how to throw a party.'

'Think what the actual gala is like if this is the non-official one,' another co-worker replied. 'Think about what the wedding festivities will be like. I hope I'm still working here when it happens.'

'We probably will be here,' the first speaker said. 'I heard the wedding usually happens within eighteen months of this event. Priya, do you think we'll still be working here?'

Priya forced her mouth to smile. 'It's a long project,' she replied, although a hollow pit had formed in her stomach.

How had she failed to realise the next big celebration on the island would be Rohan's wedding. If she continued working on the preservation and conservation of the stonework on Adysara then she could still be on the island when he got married. She would have to watch it happen.

The idea was devastating.

She'd always understood Rohan couldn't offer her a future. He'd been clear about that and she'd been under no illusions. It wasn't something she could protest against, even if she was the kind of person who kicked up a fuss. It was simply a fact. It was what it was.

But it was one thing to know on an intellectual level Rohan couldn't be hers and another to actually see him married to someone else, out of her reach for ever.

She stumbled back as if she'd been punched in the gut.

This reaction wasn't the kind she would have if this was simply a short-lived love affair coming to an end. The pain she was reeling from was worse than when any of her former boyfriends, men she believed she was in love with, ended things with her.

She needed time and space, and quiet, to process what

her reaction meant. She should head back to her room. There was too much activity here, too much noise, it was too full of life. She needed to be alone.

Her phone vibrated—the phone Rohan had given her. She wished she had the strength to ignore it, but she took it out of her handbag and read the message from Rohan asking him to meet her in the garden.

She frowned. The last time they'd met, he'd told her he wouldn't be able to come to the garden while the gala festivities were taking place. Although he hadn't specifically said so, she assumed from that point on the only times she would see him would be on a professional basis because he would have surely met and narrowed down his choice of potential brides and would be expected to entertain them.

Why, then, was he asking her to meet him? Was something wrong?

But a rational part of her knew by now this behaviour was par for the course for them. So many times they'd made agreements they weren't able to stick to—first they'd agreed there could be no relationship between them, then they'd agreed it would be a short weekend fling and everything would be back to normal when they were back in Adysara, afterward they'd agreed they would only meet until the gala festivities began, but they hadn't kept to that agreement either.

Rohan constantly showed her how much he liked spending time with her. It was almost as if he wasn't ready to say it was over.

Priya felt a heaviness in her chest. Soon what they wanted wouldn't matter. Rohan didn't have a choice in his future. He would have to marry for the good of Adysara. Soon he would forget about her completely while she would always cling on to her memories of their time together.

'Enjoying yourself, Priya?' Mac asked, coming over to her, an almost welcome interruption to her introspections.

'Yes. It's been brilliant.'

'I hear the dancers are going to invite us to join them in the centre soon. You should prepare yourself.'

'To be honest, Mac, I'm getting a bit of a headache. The incense probably. I may go back to my room and take a quick nap. I'll join you all later. It's going to be a long night.'

He nodded but didn't say anything. She was sure her absences most evenings had been noticed by her co-workers. She still tried to spend as much time with them as she could, wanting to get to know them properly in case she worked with them in the future. But she couldn't give up the brief moments of time she got to spend with Rohan.

She was also sure many people suspected she had a lover, although she doubted anyone would guess it was Rohan. She wasn't the only team member who'd found romance on the island. But as long as they were safe, and it wasn't interfering with their work, as far as Priya was concerned it was none of her business. She hoped they gave her the same courtesy.

As she started walking back to the palace grounds, her thoughts about Rohan, and the conservation project, and his wedding, and his queen came flooding back. Why it did it matter so much to her? When she'd heard a previous boyfriend of hers had married, she hadn't batted an eyelid. Their relationship was over—she'd done her crying at the time. But Rohan made her feel cherished and adored in a way she'd never experienced before. Was that the reason why it felt different this time even though she'd gone into this relationship with open eyes? She wasn't the kind of person who expected weddings and doting husbands and children to be in her future.

She'd accepted the reality of becoming involved with a prince and she knew she wasn't good enough to be his queen. There was no future for them. So why was she having so much trouble with the idea Rohan was getting married soon?

She slowed her pace as she approached the garden, taking some breaths to calm herself. She didn't want Rohan to guess at any of her turbulent thoughts. He was already far too perceptive.

Inside the garden, there were a few lanterns dotted around the wall but most of the area was in shadow. When she met Rohan there previously, it had heightened the romantic ambience. Now it felt lonely. For the first time ever she was a little scared of the garden.

'Hello,' she called out nervously.

'Hi,' a deep rumble came from the trees. Warmth flooded through her when she heard Rohan's voice. All of a sudden, her concerns and fears dissolved away, comforted by his presence.

As Rohan stepped into the light, she sighed with relief. A small part of her had worried Rohan's message was because something bad had happened. But she could see he looked all right. He looked more than all right. He looked rakishly handsome in his cream prince's jacket with gold-and-red kalka pattern on his sleeves and his rich red epaulettes with gold brocade.

He took one of her hands in each of his and gave them a light squeeze. 'Hi,' he said again with an irresistible grin.

'Hi,' she replied with a light laugh. 'What are you doing here? Shouldn't you be waltzing around a dance floor somewhere?'

'There's a refreshment break.' His fingers gently stroked her palms causing her body to heat. She made an effort to be sensible.

'Then aren't you expected to chat with your potential brides? Won't they be looking for you?' She tried hard to keep the bitterness from her tone but his questioning look showed she hadn't succeeded.

'I told my family I would be in my rooms for twenty minutes.'

'Okay.' So why was he in the garden with her instead? He didn't seem in any hurry to tell her his reason.

'How is your party?' he asked.

'It's good. Probably not as dignified as yours, but a lot of fun.'

'I wish I could go to your party instead.'

'You're the prince. I'm sure you could go anywhere you want.'

'I have much less freedom than you would imagine.'

She sighed. She couldn't argue with that. Beyond their one weekend away, Rohan didn't have the freedom to be with her the way she wanted them to be.

And she would never ask him to risk his family and his island to take a chance the tentative relationship between them could develop into something real and lasting. Not that Rohan had indicated he wanted anything more than the fling. As far as she could tell, it was only her who was thinking about love and marriage.

But it was so hard to even think about saying goodbye for good.

Rohan stood in the dusk of the garden, away from the music and crowds in the palace, enjoying the peace and Priya. She was wearing a peach lehenga choli with silver embroidery. He'd never seen her in traditional South Asian outfits before. She looked like one of the figures from his murals come to life.

He'd always found cholis flattering. But seeing Priya's, cropped below her ribs displaying her taut stomach; he wanted nothing more than to run his tongue from the edge of her blouse across her skin, past her navel and lower.

He groaned.

'Rohan, are you feeling all right.' Priya came close to him, putting her hand on his arm, concern clear on her face.

'I'm fine. How is your party?'

'Good,' she replied slowly, with a puzzled look.

Of course, he'd just asked her that. He'd spent hours politely escorting different women, selected by his parents, to the dance floor. They were all beautiful, intelligent and accomplished, but he didn't want to be with them. The only woman who could remotely hold his interest wasn't in the room.

His parents were beginning to look concerned that despite him spending the previous day sailing, games in the garden that morning and many lavish meals getting to know his female guests better, there weren't any he was inclined to invite to stay longer.

He certainly hadn't laid his eyes on any of the women and known instinctively she was the one he was going to marry the way his parents claimed they had—he'd never understood why his parents felt the need to make up a story about it. It was clear to anyone who saw them together there was deep affection between them, stronger because it grew as they got more comfortable with each other.

It was what he had wished for in his marriage. *Had* wished for? He still wished for that kind of marriage, didn't he?

'How have the events gone so far? Is everything going to plan?' Priya asked.

He frowned. She was doing that thing where she made polite small talk to cover deeper thoughts. He would indulge her for a short while, but then he was digging into what was bothering her.

'Yes, all going to plan,' he replied. 'No mishaps. Not that any would be allowed. Every eventuality and contingency has been accounted for.' Every eventuality except him not choosing his future queen.

'What are you doing tomorrow? I heard there's six or seven events going on during the day. But surely you can't be doing all of them. Or is there a secret agenda for the royal family and specially chosen guests?'

Why was she trying so hard to make conversation? They never usually had this difficulty. Normally when they were together, they talked about anything and everything—how their day had gone, about the island. The only topic they stayed away from was the future they weren't going to share. With the ball, the future was intruding where it wasn't welcome. No wonder Priya was subdued. He couldn't deny he was also feeling low. Defeated.

He sighed. He knew what he was supposed to be doing with his life. And it wasn't standing in his garden with a beautiful woman he could never marry.

Perhaps ordinary conversation would have to do. 'My family usually have a lie-in the day after the ball. I've never known the gala to end until the early hours and I'll be expected to stay until the last guest leaves or the band stops playing from sheer exhaustion. My parents will probably retire in a few hours or so though.'

She was silent, walking through the garden, softly humming to herself. 'And your guests? Have you met anyone interesting?'

He furrowed his brow. Was she asking about women? Her tone was so matter of fact, as if she didn't care he may have been talking to the woman he was going to marry.

'Plenty of interesting guests. I've been spending a lot of time with potential investors—a couple of hotel chains. They like the sound of the summer palace. I'm going to show them round before they leave.'

She tilted her head and gave him a look of amused exasperation. 'Now, Rohan. I don't think that's the kind of merger your family have in mind.'

He'd never thought of his name as particularly pretty before. But on Priya's lips, in the darkness, it sounded lyrical, sensual.

'You haven't been to the summer palace yet,' he said. 'You should come with me when I give them the tour.'

She straightened suddenly. 'Does it have murals you want me to inspect?' she asked, with a stiffness to her tone.

'No.'

'Then that's hardly going to be appropriate, is it? I'm sure there'll be other guests who would love to see it though.'

He blinked against her harsh words. 'I suppose you're right,' he replied.

'Why did you ask me to meet you here?' she asked, meeting his eyes directly.

He could hear the orchestra start to play their next set. He didn't have much longer before he had to choose his next dance partner. Although he knew exactly who that person would be if he had the freedom of true choice.

He wanted to dance with Priya in the grand ballroom. To whisk her round the room and hear her laugh from sheer exuberance. Since it wasn't an option, he would settle for the only thing he could.

'Would you honour me with this dance?' he asked, bowing as he held out her hand.

Priya stared at him, scrutinising him with her dark, round eyes, as if making a momentous decision. He held his breath. Finally she smiled, dipped into a curtsey and replied, 'I would be delighted, kind sir.'

He gathered her to him, her body fitting perfectly against his. Sparks flew where his hand rested on the bare skin above her waist. He didn't think this feeling would ever dissipate.

He led her round the garden, in an old-fashioned waltz, making the moves up since those weren't in the lessons from his tutor.

By the time the music came to an end, they were breathless and laughing. Instead of releasing her, he gathered her closer to him, letting go of her hand so he could cradle her neck. Her lips parted as he lowered his head towards her.

An alarm went off.

'My break's over,' Rohan said. 'I'll have to go back in a few minutes.'

Priya extracted herself from Rohan's arms, and

walked over to the bench. His alarm was the sobering bucket of cold water she needed to bring her back to the stark reality there was a gulf between them. He was leaving her this evening, but ultimately he would walk away from her for good. There was no compromise solution for them. There was no *them*.

Rohan sat next to her. He looked worried. 'Is everything all right, Priya?'

'Well, I shouldn't keep you from your guests,' she replied, getting ready to stand. Rohan placed a restraining hand on her arm.

'What's wrong, Priya?'

'Nothing's wrong. You need to go back.'

'I wish I didn't have to. I wish I could stay here with you all night.'

Her body was a mass of contradictions, buzzing with exhilaration at the certain knowledge of how much he wanted her while at the same time heavy with despair because it didn't matter what they both wished. He couldn't stay with her.

'But you have to return. You have no choice,' she said.

'And it annoys you?'

'Annoys me?' Her voice rose an octave. 'No. It doesn't annoy me. You have a duty to perform. We both know that.' Suddenly her confused emotions bubbled to the surface. 'But what are we doing here tonight, Rohan? What have we been doing for the past couple of weeks? It's madness. You said yourself you aren't in a position to offer me a relationship. And I know you're expected to find your wife from these events. What do you want from me?'

Rohan opened his mouth but nothing came out.

Priya stood, steeling herself for what she needed to

say. 'We should have gone back to the way things were when we came back from our weekend. Our affair was a moment out of time and it's all it should have been. It was a mistake trying to prolong it. I was living in a fantasy and now it's over.' She tried to keep the bitterness from her voice as she said, 'This isn't a fairy tale. Not for me. It's time for you to go back to being Rohan Varma, Yuvaraja, and I'll go back to being…me.'

'I see,' he said in a clipped tone.

She waited, hoping, daring to believe he could tell her she was wrong and there was a way they could get a happily ever after. He didn't.

'I'd better go.' She took a few steps, then turned back and kissed him on the cheek. 'Goodbye, Rohan. I hope you meet someone who'll make you a wonderful wife. You deserve all the happiness in the world.'

CHAPTER FIFTEEN

A WEEK LATER, the gala was over, the decorations were being taken down, the palace was being returned to its usual state and Priya was back at work on preserving the murals.

Although it was unlikely she would bump into Rohan accidentally, she was on tenterhooks. The last time she'd seen him was when they danced in his garden.

It had felt like she was caught in a whirlwind, transported into a magical place—Cinderella at the ball. It almost came as a shock to find the fireworks she'd seen as they waltzed round the garden were only figments of her imagination.

Walking away from him after his alarm went off, actually she ran away, was the hardest thing she'd ever done. She still didn't know where her resolve had come from. She'd gone straight to her room and let the tears fall freely.

She cried for the young teenager who grew up unwanted and unloved. And she cried for the young woman who had started to open her heart to a man who left her in no doubt that she was very much wanted, desired and cared for. But someone she could never have.

Since that night, even though she told herself she

didn't expect to hear from him, she was still disappointed when she hadn't received any messages.

Seven days. It was the longest they'd ever gone without seeing each other since their first meeting on the balcony.

She'd held on to this false hope that, despite her parting words, he'd ask to meet her again in the garden. And despite any words of common sense telling her it was futile and would bring nothing but heartache, she knew she would run to him.

But she heard nothing.

The palace was still abuzz with speculation on whether any of the guests who were staying on had captured Rohan's interest. Had he found someone he could see himself spending the rest of his life with? Was that why he hadn't got in touch. Did she really want to know? Why was she torturing herself?

Priya took a deep breath and stepped back from the mural she was working on. The paintwork was too delicate for her to continue unless she could give the task her full concentration. She cleared away her tools and told her team she was taking a quick break to get some fresh air; it wasn't unusual for her team to do that since they were working with harsh chemicals.

Once outside she wandered into the woods, purposely walking away from the direction of Rohan's garden.

What was going on with her?

This wasn't the first time one of her relationships had ended. In the past, work had been her solace. She had always been able to distract herself from anything in her life by concentrating on the detailed preservations she was doing. Why was she finding it so hard this time?

The answer was simple. This was the first time her heart was truly broken.

She'd heard broken hearts can heal over time. She'd assumed it was true because she'd got over her previous boyfriends. But what she felt for them hadn't been a fraction of the strength and depth of her feelings for Rohan.

She loved him.

The realisation didn't come as a shock once she'd admitted it. It had been creeping on her for weeks, surfacing on the night of the ball but remaining unacknowledged, unnamed. It wasn't only a physical attraction but an attraction of minds and souls.

She could try telling herself she was being fanciful, or she was confusing lust and love, as she had before. But it would be doing a disservice to her heart.

How could she not love someone as wonderful as Rohan? He made her feel loved, valued and protected every moment they spent together. He showed her in his countless thoughtful gestures that he cared about her. Of course she loved him.

This wasn't a flame that would shine brightly then burn out, but a banyan tree that would only grow and strengthen with time.

As if on autopilot her feet were taking her back towards the path which led to Rohan's garden. She stopped and turned round. From now on, Rohan would go there with his family, which would one day soon include his wife and later on his children. It was closed to her.

But her heart didn't want to listen. She loved Rohan. She wanted to run and find him so she could tell him how she felt. Beg for more time with him.

To what end though? He could never be with her. He hadn't contacted her in seven days—he was already

staying away from her. He had a duty to his family and
to the island. What made her think she was worth him
turning his back on it?

Nothing.

She had nothing to offer. She'd been ignored and forgotten by her father. Dumped by a boyfriend for 'someone better' on more than one occasion. She was nobody.
A nothing.

She had no right to think Rohan could abandon his
duty or he would refuse to do what was expected of him
just because she loved him and wanted to be with him.

He wasn't meant for her. It didn't matter how she felt.
They weren't destined to be together.

And if she stayed on Adysara working on the sites
she'd visited with Rohan, she would never get the chance
to heal. Her heart would break even more as he forgot
about her and moved on with his life.

She gave a bitter laugh. Here she was with the possibility of the chance of a lifetime to work on a culturally
significant project and she didn't think she could do it.

It should have been a dream. Instead it was a nightmare.

For the first time since she had heard about the caves,
she wished she'd never seen them.

She headed back to the palace where Mac was waiting to tell her Mr Agrawal wanted to see her.

As soon as she approached Mr Agrawal's office she
noticed Rohan's assistant waiting outside. She licked her
lips unsure whether she was hoping Rohan wanted to
see her or hoping he didn't so she wouldn't have to face
him again so soon after her revelation.

The assistant escorted her to Rohan's study.

He was standing next to the window when she entered. The afternoon light should have been harsh, casting shadows across his nose and jaw. Instead it emphasised the perfection of his features.

She loved him. She could never be with him. She would laugh if it wasn't so poignant.

'Priya.' He smiled at her, gesturing for her to take a seat on the couch. 'Thank you for coming.'

He was polite but distant. That was good. That's what she needed. She noticed he looked at the door and give a small signal to his assistant who handed him a folder then left. She hadn't realised they weren't alone.

After sitting opposite her, Rohan stared at her, a strange smile playing on his face. He was so gorgeous. She wanted to reach across the gap and fling herself onto his lap.

She shifted in her seat. This wasn't going to help her situation. She had to go into protective mode.

'How have you been?' he asked.

'Good thanks,' she answered, deliberately using a tone of polite distance.

'I missed you.'

She stiffened. His words didn't help her resolve. 'You wanted to see me?'

He beamed. 'I have some wonderful news for you. About the island.'

'What is it?'

'The hotel companies I met with are interested in investing. With the money we can get from leasing the summer palace, my family can finance the preservation of the caves ourselves. We won't need government backing.'

'Wonderful.' His face was the happiest she'd ever seen it and she couldn't help responding to his unbridled joy. She wanted to hug him. Luckily, being seated would have made it awkward. 'What does it mean, your family's financing it?'

'Because we don't have to go through the government's policy approval and procurement process, we can start the work immediately and sign the contract with your company. I spoke to Toby MacFarlane and Govinda Agrawal already. They're ready to proceed. And we'd like you to lead.' He paused giving her an expectant smile.

This was it. The moment her dreams should have come true. Turning this down was one of the hardest things she would do. But it would be harder if she stayed on Adysara and had to watch while Rohan got engaged then married. She had to walk away from him, leave him before she was forced to watch him leave her for good.

'No!' she called out.

'What?' Rohan visibly started at her unexpected response.

'I don't want it this way.'

'What do you mean?'

She didn't want Rohan to know she loved him. It wouldn't help anyone. She tried to come up with a valid reason for her refusal. 'If I get the role I want to know... I need to know I got it on my own merits.' That sounded feasible. It also had the benefit of being true—she would want to know that.

'But you have got it on your merits. I've seen how skilled and proficient you are. You have the qualifications.'

'I know I'm qualified. But our relationship will always make me question whether it was a factor.'

'I can assure you I would not let my emotional attachment affect important decisions,' he replied, his posture and tone stiff. Her heart leapt at his causal reference to his feelings. But now she'd offended him.

'Rohan, I really appreciate your trust in my abilities. It means the world to me. But I can't stay on Adysara. I'll help Mac recruit someone suitable, but as soon as Leo Blake is able to come over, I'm returning to England.' She held her breath.

'No,' he replied. 'You can't do that. I won't allow it.'

'Please, Rohan. Can't you understand how hard this is going to be for me?'

'No. This work is too important to me. If you're worried about favouritism or nepotism or anything like that, I can assure you I didn't make this decision alone. You are the most qualified person to lead this work. If you don't accept then I'll need to scope different companies.'

Priya bent her head. She couldn't tell Rohan the real reason she wanted to leave. And she couldn't let her co-workers miss out on the opportunity to work on this massive conservation project just because she'd had the monumental stupidity to fall in love with a prince.

What she wanted was of no importance. She had no choice but to accept.

After Priya left, Rohan went out onto his balcony staring over the gardens. It had taken months to get the palace and grounds ready for the gala festivities and only days to dismantle it.

But time was surprising. It was really only two months since he'd met Priya, but he felt she knew him better than anyone, even his own family. And he'd thought he knew her too.

He was still reeling from her admission she didn't

want to take the lead on their project. And in his mind it had always been *their* project. She was the first person who could envisage the same possibilities he did, who shared his values on accessible art versus protection. He'd expected her to hug him from happiness. Instead she'd turned him down.

Not only that, she didn't want to work on the project at all. She wanted to return to England.

It had been her dream to work on the conservation of stone-cut sculptures. She'd admitted it to him.

He was right to refuse to accept her decision. She was being irrational, worried their relationship had clouded his judgement. As if he would let his feelings affect something so important to the prosperity of the island.

He'd already discussed the situation with Agrawal and Mac before mentioning the proposal to Priya. In fact it was Mac who suggested Priya with Agrawal supporting the suggestion. They had assured him his initial assessment of her abilities was correct and she was the perfect person to lead the project.

A buzz from his intercom brought Rohan back through to his study. His assistant entered to tell him one of the hoteliers who'd discussed potential investment was still on the island and wanted to meet him.

Rohan needed a distraction from thinking about Priya so he arranged to meet with the hotelier immediately.

After his meeting he went to his parents' rooms. There wouldn't be any government business for his father since they still had guests.

Rohan closed his eyes. Those guests were out during the day on excursions, but he would be expected to have dinner with them and entertain them over drinks afterwards. He inwardly cursed the tradition which prolonged the gala by inviting select people to continue their visit. It happened after every gala, but this year everyone knew the reasons behind the invitations.

'Rohan, I wasn't expecting to see you so early,' his mother greeted him. 'But I'm glad you came. I wanted to talk about our guests with you, since you didn't ask me to invite anyone specific.'

'Of course, Mother,' he said, taking a seat opposite her and his father. She looked frustrated with him. He grimaced. He hated that he'd upset her.

His parents had been, understandably, disappointed when he hadn't found any of the charming women who'd attended the gala charming enough to ask for an extended stay. Instead, he'd spent most of the gala chatting with the hotel magnates. His mother had to take matters into her own hands and had invited the families she thought would be most suitable.

How he hated the word *suitable*. What did it actually mean? An impeccable blood line. More wealth than more people could imagine. It didn't make a difference; it was his duty to meet these women and select one to marry.

He ran a finger around his collar, as if by doing so he could loosen the burden of his duty.

'But before we talk about our guests, I want to update you on further discussions I've had with one of the hoteliers,' Rohan said. 'They've updated their proposal.'

'This is the man who's prepared to increase his investment contingent on the tourist flow we can expect if the wall painting and caves are attractions?' his father asked.

'That's right. He thinks there's potential for making the summer palace and its surrounding area an island paradise. But if we can offer the historical artwork too, maybe gain World Heritage status…well you know what it would mean for our country's finances. And he's prepared to part finance the work as a grant.'

'A grant?' his father perked up at hearing his family wouldn't have to invest as much upfront.

'That's right. This is a great company. Very focused on eco-tourism. Whether or not they offer the best financial package, I would be inclined to go with them. And we'd be able to start almost immediately.'

'And the project team's ready?'

'Yes. On standby.' Rohan pressed his lips together as he recalled his conversation with Priya. 'I have to admit there was some uncertainty around the person I've chosen as lead. She was thinking about returning to England, but I've persuaded her to stay, I think.' He hoped.

'This woman,' his father said, 'Priya Sen isn't it? I hear you've been spending a lot of time with her.'

'Yes, she was doing the scoping investigation.'

'And you went with her to Aurangabad.'

'That's right. We wanted to examine Ajanta and Ellora for ideas on presenting the caves.'

'What's her background? Where are her family from?'

'I don't know all the details,' he lied. 'She doesn't come from royalty or wealth, if that's what you're interested in.' He noticed the look which passed between his parents. He shouldn't have spoken to them so sharply. 'You have no need to worry,' he told them. 'She only considers me a client. She's leading on the preservation work. That's all. I know my duty.'

'But…' his mother began.

'Please excuse me, I still have a lot to do. I'm going to return to my rooms. I'll see you at dinner.'

Once back in his study, Rohan sat at his desk and pulled up a paper about his regeneration proposal.

He should be happy. Everything was falling into place. His family were finally on board with his plans to increase tourism. Buildings which had remained empty would soon be useful again. And, slowly but surely the wall painting and the caves would be preserved then restored.

The project would take years. He knew the team members would change over time, and in the long term they hoped to bring in conservators from India or other neighbouring countries to share and develop expertise. But at least Priya would be with them for a few years. He would still get to see her and spend time with her.

He froze. No, he couldn't. He would be married. It was his duty.

The thought of her being on the island, of having meetings with her for status reports, but not being able to hold her again, or meet with her alone again, was unbearable. And once he was married, he couldn't spend any time with Priya. It would be wrong. It would be unfair to both her and his wife.

No wonder she said she couldn't stay on the island. He would want to get away too. He grimaced as he recalled his implicit threat he would consider putting out for tender if she didn't lead it.

She'd said it was too hard to stay. What if her initial refusal wasn't about favouritism, but because she couldn't bear the idea of working in proximity to him when he was married to someone else.

He ran his finger around his collar again. This was an impossible situation.

If Priya took on the role, then he would hand the project to his assistant to oversee or make it part of Summer Palace Island's regeneration project so it wasn't under the royal family any longer. If his father kept to his plan of abdicating in five years, the long length of the project meant Rohan wouldn't be able to have direct oversight anyway, since he would be king.

Stepping away from the project was the best option for all of them, even if Priya still wanted to return to England. He hoped she would lead the work—she really was the best person for the job. But he couldn't bear the idea of her being unhappy so he would also let her know she could return to England if she still wanted.

He couldn't risk meeting her, not when he knew one smile from her and he would blurt out how much he wanted to be with her. He took the coward's way out and sent her a text message.

CHAPTER SIXTEEN

PRIYA READ THE message for the fifth time. Rohan wrote that he would be stepping away from the project, but he'd changed his mind and she could return to England instead if she still preferred to leave. Very short, very succinct.

She understood the subtext—he was letting her go.

Not wanting to be alone with her thoughts, Priya left her room and forced herself to join the rest of her team in the recreation room. Fortunately, they were watching a film so she was able to zone out without anyone noticing.

Why had he let her go? Only hours before, he'd categorically refused to accept her decision to return to England. What had changed in that short time?

She should be happy. Ecstatic. Hadn't she got what she wanted?

For the first time in her life, someone had put her wishes above their own. Prioritised what she wanted.

She'd never felt more miserable.

Not wanting to waste time, Priya went to speak to Mac to let him know her decision. He looked stunned.

'Priya, are you sure about this?' he asked. 'I mean, you can take annual leave once the palace mural is finished. But I thought you'd be eager to work on the stone murals and sculptures. It's exactly in your sphere of expertise. I hoped to have my best person on the job.'

'Your best person?' Priya couldn't help repeating. Had he really said that about her?

'Yes. I had hoped you'd be part of the initial palace project. You sounded keen when I talked to you about it, but you didn't submit an expression of interest for the lead role.'

'Leo said he wanted to do it. I know he has more experience than me. I was hoping you'd select me to be part of the team though,' she admitted.

'Priya, let me be frank. When you didn't apply for the team lead position, I assumed you didn't want to work abroad for an extended period. Sorry for assuming, but I specifically spoke to you about applying and you chose not to. If you'd put yourself forward, the position would have been yours.'

Priya sat in shocked silence, absorbing what she'd been told. She had been devastated when she wasn't selected for the team. She had no idea he'd taken her failure to express her interest as a sign she didn't want to work abroad.

'Priya, you can be honest with me. Is your indecision because of your relationship with Yuvaraja?'

Priya had thought nothing could surprise her more than hearing she was first choice for the project. She was wrong. The expression on Mac's face was concern rather than anger.

'Perhaps I should have told you about it,' Priya began.

'Why? It wasn't any of my business. You weren't breaking any ethical or company guidelines. The only reason it was brought up was because Yuvaraja wanted to make sure we were aware he had a conflict of interest when Agrawal and I proposed you lead the work.'

'Rohan told you?'

'It was appropriate for him to do so.'

'Of course. I didn't think.'

'I don't understand all the ins and outs of your relationship. And I have no reason to. But don't let a love affair that ran its course affect the trajectory of what could be an amazing career. I see huge things in your future, Priya. Think about it.'

After Priya left Mac she went for a walk. Despite being distracted, she stopped to speak briefly to people as she passed them. As well as her co-workers, she'd got to know the palace staff who lived in the buildings near hers. If she stayed on Adysara and worked on the project she would get to know more people and her sense of belonging would grow. She still couldn't believe she could have been working here months ago if only she'd put herself forward.

How many times had she let an opportunity pass her by because she didn't think she was good enough, or worth it? Because of her own low expectations?

When had she learnt to expect nothing but rejection and disappointment? It was an easy question to answer. After her father left her at boarding school, always putting work and travel above her, she'd got used to never being a priority. But she hadn't recognised just how far she'd let her father's abandonment cloud her perception of herself.

A part of her still longed for some kind of relationship with her father and stepmother, but if that never happened she would be all right. Just because her dad didn't care about her didn't mean she was worthless.

But if she wanted others to see that, she needed to believe it herself first.

It was okay for her to stand up for what she wanted. Sometimes she would put herself forward and she would get knocked back. It was fine. It would be a disappointment, but she was strong enough to get back on her feet.

So what did she want now? She sighed. She wanted Rohan.

But it was one thing to put herself forward for a job. She couldn't apply the same philosophy to her love life and beg Rohan to be with her. Could she?

Priya rolled her eyes. Of course she couldn't. Rohan was Yuvaraja of Adysara. He had always been honest with her that he couldn't marry her—had admitted to her he needed to make a match which would bring some material advantage to his country. She certainly had nothing to offer in that regard.

Besides, he'd told her he didn't think people really fell in love. He believed true love was a 'hormonal myth'. He probably didn't care about her the same way.

Why invite that kind of rejection?

Priya stopped where she was. It was exactly the kind of thinking she'd been scolding herself for.

What would she have to lose in reality if she told Rohan how she felt? What was the worst that could happen? He could turn her down. She fully expected him to. He'd already told her he wasn't free to choose who he married. She'd told him she accepted it. And she did.

But since their first kiss next to the megalith, they'd agreed nothing more could happen between them and each time they kept going back to each other. It had to mean something.

Was she being naive thinking Rohan could have feelings for her? Could he feel more than sexual attraction? He'd never said anything about the way he felt.

But then she'd never told him she loved him either.

She'd never expected to fall in love. She hadn't asked for it. Rohan was probably the worst person she could have chosen. But love didn't give her a choice.

She loved Rohan and she wanted a real relationship with him. She wanted them to try.

And she was worth it. She was worth putting herself out there. She was strong enough to cope if things didn't work out the way she wanted.

Taking a deep breath, she sent Rohan a text asking if he would meet her in his garden. It felt like for ever but was probably no more than a few seconds before his reply came telling her he'd be there in ten minutes.

As she made her way to the garden, Priya cursed inwardly for not giving herself time to think through what she wanted to say.

The garden door was locked. Of course it would be. It was Rohan's private garden. Nobody could enter without his permission. And she was nobody. What had she been thinking, summoning him to meet her as if she was the member of royalty, not him?

This was a terrible idea. She turned to go but had only taken a few steps when her resolve returned. She had one chance to say her piece. She wasn't going to back out now. She went to stand against the door, as if it could provide some additional backbone for her.

The minutes passed by in a flash and at the same time seemed to go on for ever before Rohan was walking towards her.

'Priya.' His smile when he noticed her made her heart

soar. Hope blossomed that everything could work out the way she wanted. 'Is everything okay?'

She nodded, too overcome with emotion to risk speaking. Rohan unlocked the door, then waited for her to precede him.

She took a couple of steps inside then, without looking at him, she said, 'I love you, Rohan.'

'What?' She couldn't interpret his tone so she slowly walked towards him trying to read his expression. But it was blank.

'I said I love you. I know we barely know each other, and I know you don't think people fall in love quickly, but I feel like you're the person who knows me best in the world.'

'Why are you telling me this?'

She didn't know what kind of response she was expecting, only what she'd been hoping for. And that definitely wasn't it.

'I wanted to tell you the truth. I love you and I want us to be together.' She spoke in a rush, relieved to finally get the words out.

'I have a duty,' he said, helplessly.

'I know. I know you have a duty to your country and your family. But I think I could be your wife. I think I could be your queen.' She gave a bitter laugh, then held up her hand when he opened his mouth. 'But I know it's impossible. I'm not asking for that. I'm not asking for marriage. I'm not expecting for ever. I don't know what the future holds. All I know for certain is I love you. I am worthy of you. I'm asking you to have a real, honest, not secret relationship with me, for as long as it may last.'

'Priya.' He swallowed.

She formed her hands into fists, drumming up every

ounce of courage she had left. 'I'm here, Rohan, doing the scariest thing I've ever done in my life. I'm telling you how I feel. I'm telling you what I want. Because I love you. All I'm asking for is more time for us. With no expectations. I know you're supposed to be choosing your future bride now, but I'm asking for you, right now, to choose me instead. For as long as you can. Put me first. Choose me.'

Priya held her breath and hoped. And she hoped. Then she bent her head with dejection as she learnt how fragile hope could be.

CHAPTER SEVENTEEN

CHOOSE ME.

Priya's words repeated themselves in Rohan's head as he sat at his desk the following morning trying to absorb the figures on the spreadsheet in front of him.

Choose me.

She'd waited for him to respond, her expression nervous but hopeful. And he'd done nothing. Just stared at her. After a few minutes Priya had nodded her head, as if his silence was the answer she had expected, smiled sweetly and then left.

Even after she'd gone, he'd stood there like an idiot until his assistant messaged that he was expected for dinner. As he'd left the garden, he'd started in the direction of her quarters, tempted to go after her.

Like he wanted to go to look for her now. But what would be the point? There was nothing he could say that could change their situation. He wasn't free to choose her.

Rohan gave up on deciphering the report and went to stand out on his balcony. Usually standing there helped him relax and calm his thoughts. But not today.

Choose me.

What response had Priya expected him to give her?

Did she want him to disappoint his parents, his people, his country for a few more months with her?

How dare she put him in this position? He was Yuvaraja of Adysara. He prided himself on always being open at the beginning of any relationship, letting girlfriends know from the outset he couldn't offer them anything long-term. He never lied to anyone about it. He'd been upfront and honest with Priya that he had a duty to make an advantageous marriage. He loved his country, but his country needed proper investment and economic growth. Without it Adysara would decline and even lose its independence. He couldn't allow that to happen. He didn't have the freedom she did to choose who she married, or, with the expectation now on him to find a bride soon, even who he had a relationship with.

Just as quickly as it had risen, his anger left him. It wasn't a fair reaction. He'd let his frustration at the situation cloud his thinking.

All Priya had done was stand up for what she wanted. Put everything on the line to do that. He knew what it would have taken for her. He grinned, wishing he could tell her how proud he was—how he wanted to applaud her.

She was so brave telling him how she felt. Telling him she loved him. His heart had beaten so fast he thought it would explode from his chest when he heard her say those words.

Three little words. He never expected such a simple phrase could have so much power over him.

But love wasn't enough. People fell in and out of love so quickly—and he'd seen, in close friends, the hurt caused when a love affair ended. He'd always been grateful it was an emotion he hadn't experienced before.

He'd also seen how love and affection could come after marriage and be strong and lasting—he was a product of that kind of love—he'd convinced himself that kind of love was better because it came from companionship and shared values. Because of that belief, Rohan had never objected to carrying out his duty before. He thought by making his family and his people happy, he would be happy too.

The way he was feeling now wasn't remotely close to happy. Rohan released a slow, miserable sigh.

How could he feel happy when his lack of response, his inaction, had made Priya unhappy? She'd become so important to him his happiness depended on hers.

The previous evening, Priya hadn't told him whether she'd decided to take on the role or not. Or perhaps she had, he didn't remember much other than her saying she loved him and asking him to choose her.

He hoped she would take the role—he knew it would make her happy. Theoretically he would be happy too, simply knowing she was. But whether Priya took the role or not, he couldn't see her any more. And how could he be truly happy when he was letting the love of his life walk out of it.

Rohan clasped onto the balcony railings. The love of his life. Priya was the love of his life.

How was it, he was only able to admit to himself the true depth of his feelings now, when it was too late. But now he had admitted it he couldn't help repeating it—he loved her. He wanted to rush to her side, to gather her in his arms and to feel her heart beat in time with his as he told her how much he loved her.

If she really loved him too, if the way she felt was

one scintilla of how much he adored her then perhaps they could—

No, he didn't want to think about it. Couldn't let himself wish for that possibility. It would make things so much harder. He wasn't free to act on his feelings. He needed to bury them deep if he had any hope of doing his duty to make an advantageous marriage.

He laughed without humour. This suitable wife he was supposed to marry seemed more hypothetical every second. How could he promise forever to another woman when the only woman that pervaded his thoughts, who filled his heart and soul with joy, was Priya—someone who wasn't meant to be his.

Rohan wanted to yell. To rail against his fate. He accepted he lived a privileged life. He knew it came with responsibility. With duty. He had never shirked his duty.

But he'd never been in love before.

How could he ever contemplate marrying someone else when his heart belonged to Priya? How could he do his duty to his people and his country if he couldn't be true to himself?

Priya had asked him to choose her. What were his choices? He could do what was expected of him, marry someone of his parents' choosing. It wouldn't matter who. He could never love that woman, but he knew there were women who would accept a loveless marriage for the privilege of being queen.

Or he could follow his heart and risk everything for Priya.

The thought scared him. How he felt for Priya scared him. The feelings were new. They made him vulnerable. What if those feelings left as quickly as they came? Not for him. But he was worried Priya's feelings would fade or she'd realise she made a mistake.

What would happen if he gave up everything for her and she stopped loving him?

Not that she'd asked him to give up anything. She hadn't asked for ever. She'd only asked for a longer relationship. Perhaps it's all she wanted.

He discarded that notion. No, Priya had said she knew it was impossible for her to be his queen. She'd asked for what she thought she could get.

All Priya had asked was for him to delay choosing a potential bride until their relationship had run its course.

It was a foolish suggestion. If he and Priya started a real, out in the open relationship, the way he felt wasn't going to 'run its course'. His love was the never-ending, undying kind. And Priya wasn't the sort of woman who did things by half measures either. When she gave her heart for real, she would give it wholeheartedly.

He wanted to spend the rest of his life with Priya. He couldn't imagine any other woman being his wife. If Priya decided to return to England, he would go with her. Priya was his world. He had to be with her.

His choice was simple.

With the weight of making his decision removed, Rohan could breathe easily again. There was still a lot to do. He had to make plans for seeing Priya and telling her how he felt.

But first, he needed to speak to his parents. He went to their rooms. If they were surprised to see him so early in the day they didn't say anything. His mother's welcoming smile gave him the courage to begin.

'Father, Mother, I love you.' He swallowed when he saw the concerned expression on his parents' faces at his declaration. His parents had always supported him and encouraged him to strive to make his dreams come true. He never wanted to disappoint them, but he had to make them understand how he felt. He took a deep breath. 'I respect you as my parents and as my Maharaja and Maharani. I love the people of Adysara and my country. You know I have always tried to live up to your expectations. I've always done my duty when I could. Now I need to tell you something.'

'Of course, beta,' his father replied.

'You can tell us anything, darling,' his mother agreed.

'I've chosen the woman I want as my wife and yuvarani.'

'Well, that's wonderful news,' his mother said. 'You had me worried for a moment.'

He noticed his father reach out and cover his mother's hand, clearly sensing there was more to come. 'Carry on, Rohan,' he said. 'She's not one of our guests, is she?'

Rohan shook his head. 'No. It's Priya. Priya Sen.'

His mother furrowed her brow. 'Isn't that the art conservator?'

'Yes. She's amazingly talented at her work. You should hear her proposals for the caves. She's incredible.'

His parents exchanged glances.

'Beta, if you aren't ready to get married yet, if you need more time, then there's no hurry. You don't have to choose someone straightaway,' his father said. 'Spend some time with this Priya if you want to.'

Rohan straightened. Did his parents think he was indulging in a brief fling or having a small rebellion against his duty? He was all too aware of what his decision to marry Priya would mean for Adysara.

'I love Priya,' he said, with a quiet determination. 'I don't need more time. I love her. I want to marry her.'

His parents were silent. Looking at each other and him with concerned expressions.

He hated that he was worrying them; that he was disappointing them. He had to make them understand how difficult this was for him, but also how important Priya was to his happiness.

'Adysara means so much to me,' he said, 'I will do anything to improve life on the island for our people and help us remain independent. I know that would have been easier and faster if I married someone who could help with our country's growth. But I'm certain Adysara will prosper anyway—we have the basic infrastructure and we can find other ways to bring in investment. Maybe if I hadn't met Priya I would have married one of the lovely women you've introduced me to and I probably would have been happy. But I have met Priya and I can't be with anyone else now. I love her.'

He noticed the sheen of tears in his mother's eyes. He would always regret that his choice made her sad but he couldn't lose Priya.

His mother reached out her hand. 'We love you, beta. All we want is for you to be happy. Come,' she said.

'Yes, Rohan, come over here,' his father added, 'Tell us all about this wonderful woman. Our future daughter-in-law and yuvarani. When can we meet her?'

Rohan went over to embrace both his parents.

'I'll contact the wedding planner,' his mother said as they all broke apart. 'We have so much to organise.'

Rohan laughed. He shouldn't have doubted their love for him would support his decision. They would learn to love Priya too. But not nearly as much as he loved her.

CHAPTER EIGHTEEN

PRIYA STOOD IN front of the mural her team had been working on since the gala ended. It had been in better condition than the other ones they'd completed and would probably only take a few more days to finish.

'Mac wants to speak to you, Priya,' one of her team members said after returning from her break.

'Did he say it was urgent?' she asked.

'He said whenever you're free. But you know Mac. He probably means now.'

Priya grinned as she removed her gloves. Since she didn't know how long she'd be away, Priya left instructions for the other members to adjust for her absence, reminding them to take their breaks as necessary.

She still hadn't given Mac her decision on whether she wanted to leave Adysara. Perhaps that's why he asked to see her. She didn't have an answer for him. Working on the palace murals weren't a problem. They didn't have any association with Rohan for her.

But would Rohan's invisible presence be with her at the external murals and in the caves they visited together? Priya pursed her lips. Her work was all she had left. Rohan had promised her he would hand over the project so she wouldn't have to deal with him any more.

She knew what a big gesture it was for him to make, the preservation work was vital for his regeneration plans. He was making it as easy as he could for her to stay. She would be foolish to turn down the job of a lifetime simply because she'd been a bigger fool and fallen in love with someone so far out of her reach.

And when Rohan got married? Well, then she would take a very long vacation back in England.

She was ready to give Mac her decision.

'Ah, Priya,' Mac began when she found him, 'Mr Agrawal says he's heard there's been a development at cave six. Would you mind going to take a look?'

'Of course. What kind of development?'

Mac shook his head. 'No idea. Mr Agrawal didn't know much.'

'Okay. I'll head over first thing tomorrow.'

'A car's already been arranged for you today. It's probably already outside waiting.'

Priya furrowed her brow. If the development required her urgent attention it could be something serious had happened. Cave six was the one with the palace megalith. Her stomach churned at the idea it could have been damaged.

'Go now,' Mac said, ushering her towards the exit. 'I'll make sure your team's sorted.'

There was a strange twinkle in Mac's eye and she was sure he was trying to hide a smile. But it made no sense. Perhaps, because it was such a rare sight, she'd misinterpreted his humour.

Unfortunately, as soon as she was in the car, memories she'd rather not relive flooded her mind.

It had been two days since she'd laid her heart and

soul bare before Rohan. Two days. His silence, as the saying went, was deafening.

She'd allowed herself one evening to brood at the final sign her love for Rohan was going nowhere, then she'd thrown herself into her work, spending long hours on the palace murals until the light prevented her from making progress then, after work, she made sure she stayed in the common areas, never on her own.

She'd told Rohan she loved him. And he hadn't replied. He barely said three words their entire exchange.

It was surprising she hadn't cried. Yet. Perhaps she was too numb, too hollow, and the emotions hadn't had a chance to rise to the surface.

She couldn't regret the time she did have with Rohan. After her previous failed relationships, she was convinced she was done with romance. Instead, she'd been given a couple of wonderful weeks with an interesting, intelligent, thoughtful, not to mention unbelievably gorgeous man. And she would concentrate on those memories, rather than the ones that came recently.

Why should there be tears? She'd started her relationship with Rohan with her eyes open, knowing there wasn't a future. She hadn't asked for anything but the few days they would have together—a weekend away and stolen kisses in the moonlight. She had no expectations. She'd certainly hadn't expected to fall in love.

And she didn't regret asking him for longer. She was proud she'd been honest about her feelings and asked for what she wanted. She was never again going to measure her self-worth on the acceptance or rejection by other people. Not even Rohan.

Her body clenched as the car slowed down near the

cave entrance. She couldn't see any signs of damage from the outside.

Was her trepidation due to the possibility her megalith was damaged or was it because she was going to be entering cave six—the cave where she kissed Rohan for the first time? This would be the perfect test for her to find out whether the ghost of his presence would make working on the caves difficult.

She first examined the rock-cut structures inside the cave but couldn't see anything had changed from her last visit. She took measurements of the humidity and light but the readings were also within safe limits. That left the megalith.

She started walking down the passageway. It was so dark, Rohan probably hadn't needed to cover her eyes. She laughed at the memory although she felt a pang in her chest.

Once in front of the megalith she stood frozen in awe, as if seeing it for the first time. At least nothing was wrong with the stone sculpture. She slowly began to walk around the structure to check for changes, taking the opportunity to examine the cliff face in case there were any visibly loose rocks.

As she was finishing her examination of the final side, she heard movement coming from the tunnel. She peeked her head round the side expecting to see her driver.

Instead, her heart began to beat at a rapid pace, her breath became shallow as if the oxygen had been sucked out from round her and her mouth went dry. Her typical reaction every time she saw Rohan.

He looked at her, as if he was drinking her in; as if

it had been years rather than days since he'd seen her. The same way she was looking at him.

She was too frightened to move in case the action jolted her out of this hallucination she must be having. What was he doing here?

'Rohan,' she said, when she finally managed to find her voice. 'I didn't know you were coming. Did Mr Agrawal tell you there's been a development here too?' She gestured at the megalith. 'I can't find anything wrong. I don't think there's a problem.'

Rohan had been looking so serious, nervous almost, but when she mentioned Mr Agrawal his face broke into a wide grin.

Her heart jolted. Priya couldn't help feeling there was something more behind his smile than relief at hearing there were no problems with the megalith, which was confirmed when Rohan said, 'I know.'

'What do you mean, you know.'

'There's nothing wrong here. I asked Agrawal to get you to come here.'

She furrowed her brow. 'I don't understand.'

'I wanted to speak to you.'

'Why here? I could have come to your study.'

Rohan's cheeks turned rosy. He looked at the ground then swallowed before saying, 'I never gave you a response the other day.'

Priya shook her head. 'It's all right. I should never have asked you. You were always honest with me about your situation. I should never have tried to ask you for more than you could give. I'm sorry I put you in that position.'

He didn't reply immediately. Instead he walked over

to the front of the megalith next to one of the stone tigers guarding the palace.

'I was standing here when you hurled yourself at me to save me from the debris.'

As if she could forget.

'That was the start of everything,' he continued. The intensity of his gaze made Priya's mouth go dry. She started to shake—something she didn't understand was happening, but it was something big.

'I bet you sometimes wish I hadn't,' she said trying to diffuse the tension. 'Then we wouldn't be in this situation.'

'I think we would have ended up exactly where we are, somehow. It was fate.'

Priya couldn't suppress a slight anger towards a fate that let her fall in love with a man she could never be with.

'And I don't ever wish that moment didn't happen,' he continued. 'It was the moment I began falling in love with you.'

Hundreds of conflicting moods and emotions rushed through her. He loved her. She was ecstatic. He loved her and she loved him and it was the greatest gift.

He was still the crown prince. It didn't change anything in the long run. Despair overpowered her. Why did he have to tell her he loved her? It made everything worse.

Unless he was trying to say he was prepared to have a real relationship with her. That he was delaying his duty to find a bride for a few more months with her.

'You're choosing me?' she said, holding her breath as she waited for his response.

'Yes,' he replied with the cheeky smile she loved so much.

Letting out a yelp of joy she ran into his arms. He picked her up and twirled her around. Both of them laughing from giddy happiness. Lowering her back to the ground, he ran his fingers through her hair, moving to her nape and drawing her closer for a kiss.

'We should get back to the palace,' Rohan suggested.

Priya nodded. Their passion, as always, threatened to overwhelm them. She wanted to get somewhere private. Where they could talk. There was still a lot for them to discuss. Eager as she was to make love with Rohan soon, it was sensible to make sure everything was out in the open.

He'd chosen her. She couldn't believe it was real.

The journey back to the palace was torture. Rohan had sent her driver away so they both went in his limo. They had the privacy screen up but after a few minutes on Rohan's lap, the bumpy road dictated safety came first and he moved her off him and ensured her seat belt was fastened.

As if by unspoken agreement, once they reached the palace they walked round the grounds towards Rohan's garden.

She was vaguely aware of the curious glances from people they passed. She and Rohan weren't touching but she was sure the tension in her body from the anticipation of soon being in his arms was radiating from her.

They barely stepped into the garden before turning to each other.

'I've missed you so much,' Rohan said.

Conversation seemed impossible when the urgency to kiss was so strong.

She'd missed him too. She had been trying to reconcile herself to never being with Rohan like this again. He'd really chosen her.

'Are you sure you want to do this?' she asked, finally managing to break apart and putting an arm's length distance between them.

'Of course I'm sure,' he replied as he drew her to him again.

She pushed him away. 'No, I don't mean that! Are you sure about your decision? You've chosen to be with me?'

Rohan laughed as he adjusted his clothing and took a few minutes to compose himself. He stared directly in her eyes and said, 'Yes, Priya Sen, I choose you.'

Tear's pricked Priya's eyes. The simplicity of his words made their truth undeniable.

'And your family won't mind you're not getting married yet,' she asked.

'What?' Rohan raised his eyebrows. 'Of course, I'm getting married.'

His admission was like a knife to her heart.

The glow on Priya's face faded. Rohan inwardly cursed himself for making such a pig's ear of everything. When he'd planned this day out, it seemed so romantic—arranging to meet in the place they first kissed.

He hadn't counted on how good it would feel to have Priya back in his arms, back where she belonged. He hadn't factored in how interminable the car ride back to the palace would be.

He'd initially thought when they arrived at the palace he would take her to the ballroom balcony to stand next to the pillar where they first met, but the need to be alone with Priya, where they wouldn't be interrupted was paramount so they came to his garden.

Once there, a conversation should have been their priority, but having the chance to draw Priya to him was too irresistible and from the moment he held her, he needed to kiss her like a thirsty plant needs water. Which was why he was in this mess, blurting things out without thinking.

'I'm sorry, I can't do that, Rohan,' Priya said moving away from him and wrapping her arms around herself. 'I'm sorry. I love you but I won't be your other woman for a few months while you're courting your future wife.'

The blood ran from his face as he realised how she'd interpreted his comments about getting married.

'No, Priya, no,' he said quickly. 'It's not what I meant. I don't want a relationship with you for a few more months.'

He couldn't mistake her hurt expression. Why was everything he said coming out wrong? Perhaps actions were louder than words in this scenario. He reached into his pocket and pulled out a small box.

Priya took a step away when he presented it to her.

'Rohan?' she said, shakily.

He opened the box displaying a kundan ring in a floral design with diamond petals around a central emerald.

'This is a family heirloom,' he explained. 'Each man presents it to his chosen bride and she holds on to it until it's ready to be passed on to the next generation. I asked my mother for it.'

Priya blinked, looking confused. He still wasn't doing this right. Smiling nervously as he looked directly into her eyes, Rohan bent onto one knee.

'Rohan,' Priya said, clutching her hands to her heart.

'Priya Sen. You are the love of my life. You're the reason I wake up in the morning and my last thought before I go to sleep. Please do me the greatest honour and make me the happiest man in the world. Will you marry me?' It wasn't the most eloquent proposal, but it was heartfelt. He held his breath.

She stared at him, as if making sure he was serious.

'Please,' he added.

Her lips lifted in an uncertain smile, then straightened again. She made a small sound, like a laugh of disbelief. Then as he continued to look at her, trying to convince her of his sincerity and silently begging her to say yes, her smile grew stronger.

She bit her lip, then nodded slowly at first, then faster as tears started to pour. 'Yes, Rohan. I'll marry you.'

He almost tripped in his haste to stand and embrace her.

A long while later they sat on the bench, Priya on his lap, gentle touches and kisses replacing the frantic passion of earlier.

'You'll need to think about who you want to invite to the wedding,' Rohan said.

'It's a bit soon for that isn't it?'

'Are you kidding? My mother's going to summon the pandit and the wedding coordinator as soon as we tell her we're getting married.'

Priya tensed next to him.

'I haven't met your parents yet. I can't meet them for the first time and tell them I'm marrying their son.'

'There's nothing to worry about. They're going to love you. I haven't met your father either,' Rohan pointed out. 'I'm just as nervous to see him to ask for his blessing to marry his beautiful, amazing daughter.'

She shrugged. 'Hopefully one day you will.'

'Are you thinking of inviting him to the wedding?'

'Of course I'll invite him. He is my father. I don't know if he'll attend—it'll probably depend on how busy he is. I don't need his attention or his approval. If he doesn't come, it will be his loss.'

Rohan wanted to cheer. 'Exactly. And what about your dadu and didima?' he asked, slowly.

Her smile was sad. 'I told you I don't know where they are. I don't know if they're alive.'

He expelled a breath. 'I do. I found them. They want to get back in touch with you desperately. It sounds like a lot of things happened in the background which they should tell you about. But they never wanted to break contact with you. I can bring them here if you want to see them.'

Priya hid her face against his chest. He could feel the dampness in his shirt.

'Thank you,' she mumbled. 'I can't believe you did that for me.' She lifted her head. 'No I can. It's just who you are as a person. No wonder I love you.'

'And I love you,' he said, kissing the tip of her nose. 'And your grandparents love you, and my parents will love you too.'

Priya gave a scared laugh. 'Your parents are the Maharaja and Maharani of Adysara. Oh, my goodness. This is so much to take in.' She bent forward holding her head in her hands. He could hear her trying to regulate her breathing.

'Everything okay?' he asked, gently moving her hair so he could see her profile. 'You're not thinking of changing your mind are you?'

'Maybe. No.' She sat up and stared intently at him.

'How are you going to tell your parents you want to marry me. A nobody. I don't bring anything with me.'

'You are enough.'

Priya convulsed with emotion. All her life she'd wanted to hear those words, never truly believing they would be true. But sitting on the bench, sitting in Rohan's embrace, she knew for Rohan it was true—she was enough.

'I already told my parents,' Rohan continued. 'They know I was planning to propose.'

'And they didn't try to talk you out of it?' She was still trying to wrap her head around the idea of marrying into the royal family of Adysara. 'Oh, Rohan. What about your duty and your family's expectations? I can't ask you to sacrifice everything you are for me.'

'There's no sacrifice. I have a duty to my people, but I also have a duty to myself. If I carried on searching for an advantageous match I would have been acting dishonourably because you're the only one I want as my wife. If I had to give up being yuvaraja I would because it would mean more to me to be your husband.'

He was turning her into a leaky tap.

'You're not being asked to give up your position?' Priya asked anxiously.

'I'm not. I'm still Yuvaraja, in line to become the next Maharaja of Adysara which I will reign over with my maharani.' He paused. 'Unless you want me to give it up. We can live a quiet life in England if that's what you prefer.'

Priya shook her head, staggered by the lengths Rohan was prepared to go to put what she wanted first. He'd contacted her grandparents—she never thought she'd see them again. But he made it happen because he thought about what would make her happy.

But her happiness was entwined with his.

She smiled. 'There's still a lot of the islands I haven't seen yet. And there's the murals and caves to preserve.'

Rohan laced his fingers through hers. 'My father said it's what you'll bring to the country—your skills in conservation which will help the regeneration and bring greater prosperity to us.'

Priya's laughter pealed out. It wasn't close to what the royal family must consider a real advantageous marriage, but it warmed her to know Rohan's parents were prepared to accept her as part of his life.

She bit her lip. 'Would it be appropriate for me to lead the work though, if I'm part of the royal family. It could be awkward for my team members to treat me the same as before.'

Rohan chuckled. 'You know we can sort through this kind of thing later. The only thing that matters is you love me and I love you and we're getting married. The rest can wait.'

She was about to relax back into Rohan's arms, but she said, 'Are you sure this is what you want?'

'I have never been more certain of anything.'

Priya didn't know when, if ever, she had felt so at peace, completely enveloped in love.

They sat in each other's arms in blissful peace until Rohan said, 'We should make some decisions before we tell my parents. Would you like to get married in England or here?' he asked. 'It's probably the first thing they'll need to know.'

It still sounded surreal to think about wedding details.

'We can get married in a register office, it it's what you want,' he continued.

'Oh, you're embarrassed to be seen with me, then,' she replied with a twinkle.

'What? Of course not. But I thought you wouldn't want the pomp and circumstance of an Adysarian royal wedding.'

'Well, it wouldn't be my first choice. If it was up to me we would elope tomorrow.'

He laughed. 'I'm open to that idea.'

Priya had no doubt Rohan would begin to arrange an elopement immediately if he thought it was what she really wanted.

'I love you. You are Yuvaraja of Adysara. Your people have been waiting for your wedding since you were born. As soon as the gala was over, it was all they talked about. The circumstances of our wedding wouldn't normally be important to me, but they're important to your people, which makes it important to you, which makes it important to me after all.' She grinned. 'I'm happy to get married here, with all the traditions and spectacle that involves. All that matters is I get to be your wife.'

'I love you for offering, but I know how you don't like being the centre of attention.'

She swallowed. 'I never felt I was worth being the centre of attention. I worried having the limelight on me would show everyone how underserving I really was. You helped me see that I have worth. You've given me the confidence to take my day in the sun. I would be proud to stand next to you in front of all your people and become your wife.'

He kissed her deeply, making any further conversation difficult and unnecessary.

EPILOGUE

Five years later

'AND THIS SECTION here required a special paste, which we had to mix ourselves, to stabilise the area before the conservation team could start work on it,' Priya said, indicating part of a recently restored mural in the grand dining room. 'Do you want to know what we used in the paste?'

'A little young to be your apprentice, isn't he?' Rohan's voice came from the doorway.

'Dada!' From her arms, her two-year-old stretched towards his father.

'Never too early to start an appreciation of the arts,' Priya said, lifting her face to Rohan's for his kiss as she transferred their son over to him.

'We should head back. Your dadu and didima are in our quarters waiting for this little man,' Rohan said as he nuzzled his son.

Priya's heart warmed, as it always did at the mention of her grandparents, not just because they were part of her life now, but their reappearance was a constant reminder of Rohan's love for her. Because he knew how much they meant to her, he'd gone to huge efforts to find them and then brought them to the island. Amidst many hugs and tears, they'd become reacquainted and Priya now completely understood why they'd fallen out of touch, but instead of dwelling on the past she wanted to concentrate on spending more time with them in the future. And shortly after their reunion, her dadu and didima had moved to Adysara permanently. Even though Priya's father had attended her wedding to Rohan four years ago, it was her grandparents who'd accompanied her down the aisle.

As they made their way back to their quarters, she watched Rohan and their son blow raspberries on each other's cheeks as they recited nursery rhymes. They looked like any happy father and child. But in two days they would be the Maharaja and Yuvaraja of Adysara.

'How did your meetings go?' she asked, once they'd left their son with her grandparents and were making their way to their private garden.

'Everything's going according to plan,' he replied. He'd spent the day going through the final arrangements for the handover of power from his father.

She'd already had many practice sessions in the palace's great chamber, being directed on where she needed to stand and what actions to do on the day her husband was crowned. The day she would become the Maharani of Adysara. Sometimes it still felt like a dream.

They reached their garden and made their way to the bench where she took her usual place on Rohan's lap. Even though they no longer needed to meet in secret, they still escaped to the garden whenever they could. Or to cave six. Both places were special to them, but cave six was the first cave the conservation team had worked on and restored and it was a huge draw for tourists.

Adysara's tourism industry was booming since Summer Palace Island had opened for business three years before and the island had already become one of the go-to luxury holiday destinations bringing wealth and investment to the country. Just as Rohan had predicted.

'I heard all hotels are at full capacity for the gala and coronation,' Priya said.

Rohan's smile was pure joy. 'It's worked out well,' he said in a true understatement.

'Perhaps we missed a trick having the gala and your coronation in the same year—separate events would have optimised the number of tourists.'

Rohan laughed then was silent a moment. 'My coronation. In a way I've been preparing for this since I was child, but now it's only days away I don't think I'm ready.'

She wrapped her arms around him in a comforting hug. 'Of course you are. You always have been. But if you'd like I can have a quiet word with your dad, persuade him not to abdicate,' she said with a cheeky grin.

'Well, if anyone can, you can. You have both my parents wrapped around your little finger, the same as you have me. And not just us. The whole country too.'

Priya bit her lip. It wasn't the first time Rohan had pointed out how the people of Adysara felt about her, but after growing up not feeling loved or wanted, she was only slowly coming round to the idea it was true. It had been through Rohan's love that she had begun to believe that it was possible that she was cared for by so many people. He made no secret of how much he adored her—making it obvious to the world he never regretted his decision to choose her as his wife.

'I love you so much, Rohan.' Her words were simple but heartfelt.

'And I love you,' Rohan replied, lifting her mouth to his.

Even now, five years after she'd first come to the island and fallen in love with its prince, she sometimes had to remind herself she wasn't going to wake up from this fairy-tale life. But Rohan's love for her was real, deep and everlasting—the same as her love for him. And they would live a long, happy life together, full of love.

* * * * *

COMING SOON!

We really hope you enjoyed reading this book. If you're looking for more romance, be sure to head to the shops when new books are available on

Thursday 2nd February

To see which titles are coming soon, please visit
millsandboon.co.uk/nextmonth

MILLS & BOON®

Coming next month

TEMPTED BY HER FAKE FIANCÉ
Kate Hardy

So what did you want to run by me?' Charlie asked.

'The wedding stuff.' She looked awkward. 'I know this is a big ask, so I didn't want to bring it up in front of Mum and Dad—but you said you'd be the face of the farm.'

'Ye-es.' He'd already agreed that. Why was she repeating herself?

She took a deep breath. 'Could you be our groom, too, until we get a real one?'

'A fake bridegroom?' That was a horrible idea.

His distaste must've shown in his face, because she said hastily, 'Fake's probably the wrong word. What I mean is, would you act as the groom in our narrative?'

His head was spinning. 'I...'

'Don't worry. I thought it was an ask too far,' she said. 'I was hoping we would save on the budget. If you'd do it, we wouldn't have to pay models or agency fees, but maybe I can call in a favour from someone.'

Her expression said it was pretty unlikely. And he'd rather the money for the marketing campaign was spent on something more urgent, like building the booking system and shopping cart. 'What would it involve?'

'We'd be cross-selling everything, showing that the farm's the background to every bit of a romance.

The story is that a couple stay on the farm in the accommodation, and watch the sunset together or the sunrise.' She spread her hands. 'Maybe both. A romantic dinner, a stroll in the woods or through the wildflower meadow, an afternoon cuddling newborn lambs. Then a proposal—I was thinking at the beach, to give people an idea of the wonderful bits of the countryside nearby. And we can have the barn all dressed up for a small intimate wedding.'

'And who would be the bride?'

'Me,' she said.

Elle, acting as his girlfriend and then his bride. His heart started to thud. Maybe this would put an extra barrier between them, making her safe to be around. And maybe it was what he needed: pretending to date, as the next step to actually dating. Finally moving on.

It wouldn't be putting his past in a box—he'd always love Jess—but maybe it might be the catalyst he needed. 'Who's going to take the photographs?' he asked.

'Of us? We are. Selfies,' she explained. 'I want to keep an intimate feel.'

Intimate. Now there was a word that made him feel completely flustered.

Continue reading
TEMPTED BY HER FAKE FIANCÉ
Kate Hardy

Available next month
www.millsandboon.co.uk

JOIN US ON SOCIAL MEDIA!

Stay up to date with our latest releases, author news and gossip, special offers and discounts, and all the behind-the-scenes action from Mills & Boon...

 @millsandboon

 @millsandboonuk

 facebook.com/millsandboon

 @millsandboonuk

It might just be true love...